THE NATION BY THE RIVER

A Novel

by

Gabe Galambos

A small town New England Mystery . . .

because good as it is to find something,
it's even better to find out something.

Published by Garnet Star Publishing
Boston

ISBN: 978-0-9882579-1-7 (sc)
ISBN: 978-0-9882579-2-4 (e)

Library of Congress Control Number: 2012949639

 Registered Trademark

Garnet Star Publishing, Boston, Massachusetts

Printed in the United States of America

Publisher's Note:
This is a work of fiction. Names, characters, places and incidents either
are the product of the author's imagination or are used fictitiously, and
any resemblance to actual persons, living or dead, business establishments,
events, or locales are entirely coincidental.

"There comes a time in every rightly-constructed boy's life when he has a raging desire to go somewhere and dig for hidden treasure."
— Mark Twain,
The Adventures of Tom Sawyer

"'Though there are no Auto-da-Fe's in Lima now,' said one of the company to another; 'I fear our sailor friend runs risk of the archiepiscopacy.* Let us withdraw more out of the moonlight. I see no need of this.'"
— Herman Melville, *Moby Dick*

* the power of the archbishop

Acknowledgments

The endeavor to write a book is hard work. It calls on the author to search the far recesses of imagination even while demanding complete focus on the page, or screen, but inches away. The book—the book, the BOOK, THE BOOK—it never leaves an author alone, and yet writing is as isolating as isolating can be.

Every author requires help, and I am not the exception. Inspiration and encouragement came by way of friends and family. Advice and critique came by way of friends and family too. And all kinds of computer help was needed all along the way. I in particular want to thank my good friend, Linda Stone, who helped in the above ways, and also Joyce Graff for her technical and industry related assistance.

Much gratitude to my publisher, Garnet Star; to Professor Francisco Maduro Dias, the Director of Culture and History of the Azorean island of Terceira, for meeting to share his insights; and to Dr. Manuel Luciano da Silva, the force behind all things Dighton Rock. And on a final note, a shout out to my local Starbucks, my writing home.

—Gabe Galambos, 2013

THE NATION
BY THE RIVER

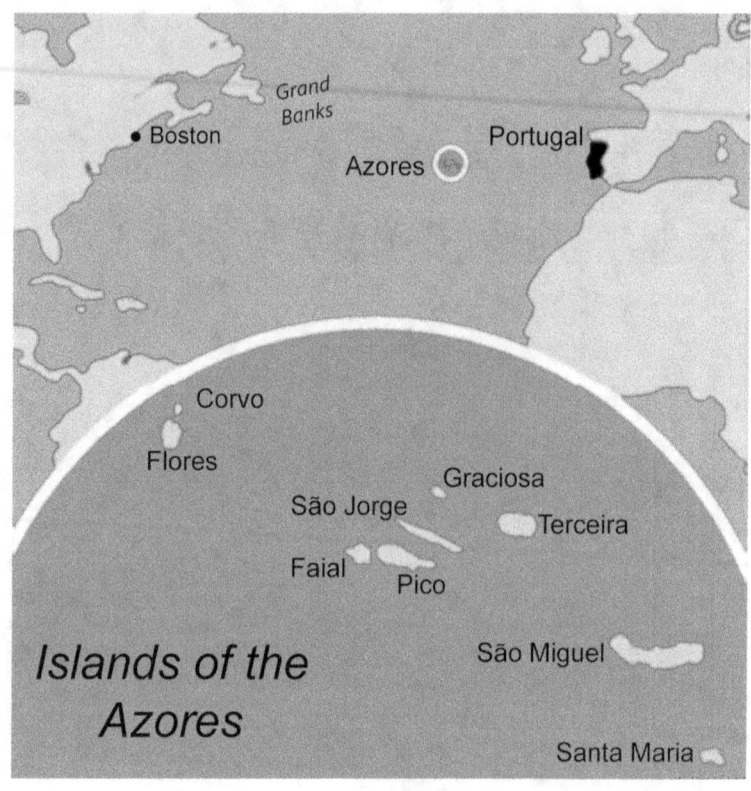

The Archipelago of the Azores (or Açores in Portuguese) is composed of nine volcanic islands in the North Atlantic Ocean, located about 930 miles (1500 km) west of Lisbon and about 1200 miles (1900 km) southeast of Newfoundland.

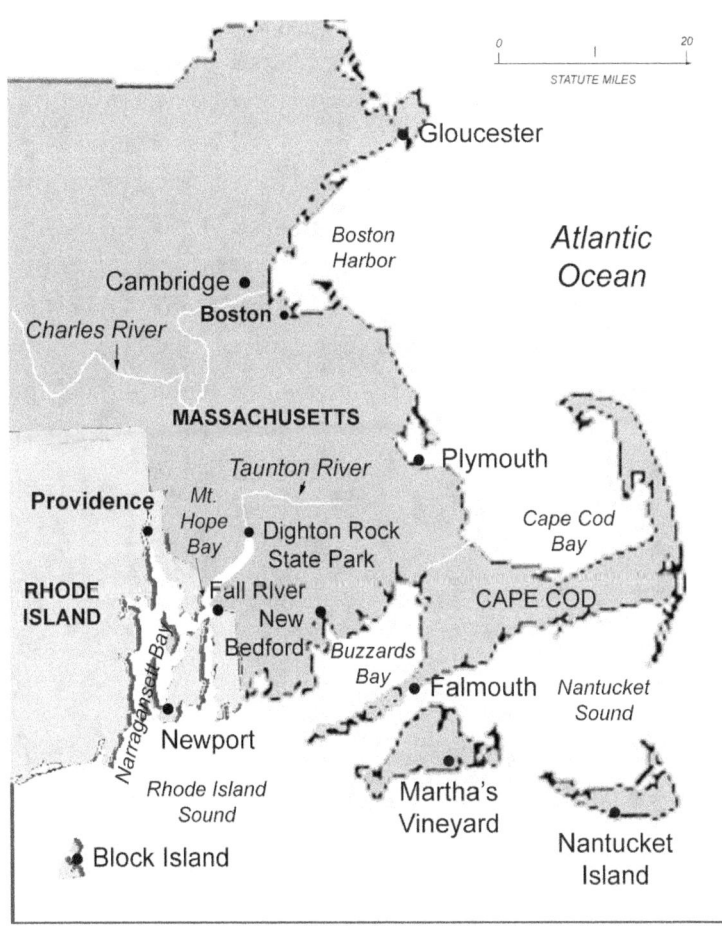

The fictional town of Best Harbor, Massachusetts, is located north of the city of Fall River, Massachusetts, along the Taunton River, near Dighton Rock State Park.

PROLOGUE

Here I am standing watch.

I'm standing watch here over a hole in the ground, me just standing, me faithfully watching, my stand just and—not by coincidence—deep in the deepest of living night; my watch faithful and—as so often happens—calling on me to be sentry of blackest black of the black forest.

Like, what the Hell? I mean—*just what the Hell?*

The thing really is though ... I always look. It's what I do, look, always look, always—but always.

Like look at our river. Just look at her!

She's tidal, for crying out loud, she's like tidal, she is, her waters all rising with the rising of the sea, and all falling with the falling of the sea, all that rising, and falling, and rising quiet, just oh so quiet, night to day to night quiet—that quiet. And waters—like sure, her waters they ebb a little, and okay, her waters, they flow a little, but the little is really little, like so really little as to be unmeasurable—virtually unmeasurable—as if not happening, not even at all.

And what's more, her waters they tug, I mean they tug on in hints of sea salt, and tug 'em out too, the hints though somehow always lingering in my nose, lingering there long after vanishing from the very air, I mean ... *the very air.*

All of this rising and ebbing and tugging stuff though, it's normal, just normal life here in Best Harbor, Massachusetts. And noticing all this comes natural too, 'least it comes natural enough for a kid like me growing up here.

But here's the thing, okay. Here it is. There's something else I do, something more I do.

As I look in on the river, and look as well at all that's by the river, I also look out. Something off, something not quite right, I look out for it. I watch for it, my every watch a lookout.

See, normal ain't always necessarily normal. And natural, well, sometimes that goes unnatural. Spitters from the Spit section of town—perched on a spit of land barging out to the ocean—we Spitters have a kind of a sixth sense for it. And being one myself—a Spitter, that is—the smallest of breaks in the rhythm, or the littlest of turns in the flow, or the slightest of shifts in the air—I spot it. And like how do I spot it! This doesn't, however, necessarily mean that I understand it.

Take for instance the hole, the hole in the ground, the one we'd dug, the one somebody saw fit to secretly fill—now that's a case in point if ever I saw one. I mean it's perfectly normal for me and L.T. to have dug that hole, but it ain't at all natural for somebody to go then and fill it. In fact it's so unnatural it's weird, so really weird it left us with no choice but to go and then re-dig the damn thing back and down all over again.

So, seeing as how like now the next move really is the hole-filler-upper's, here I am at this whole hole watching thing, this standing in the deepest deep of night thing.

Like, I mean—what an idiot! A hole? I'm standing watch over a hole in the ground, the kind of hole in the ground that's got nothing in it? Who does something like this? Who? No, really—who ?

Who? An idiot, an idiot does something like this.

Who? The idiot, that's who, the idiot.

Who? Who but me, who but little old stupid idiot me. I do something like this. I always do something like this.

Inching my feet the slightest bit nearer for a better look, I stretched my neck out and over the hole for a closer one. I mean like I stuck it, my neck, just stuck it so far out there it might just as soon have been on a chopping block—a damn executioner's block!

Not too close now, Michael. Don't you get too close.

Quickly backing myself up, already I could all but see my head go flying from off my neck, flying till and finally it just rolled to a stop—and a thud—inside the hole.

Careful. Careful now, Michael.

Like who's to say this crazy hole-filler-upper wouldn't just as soon push me in, push me and my lopped-off head in, go shovel dirt on top of us both?

Of course I could just sit with my hands over my neck so as to protect it, make the hole-filler-upper's life just oh so hard—his life a living hell should ever it come to toppling me, a genuine hell on earth should ever it come to decapitating me. But in so doing—the sitting, the neck protecting, the hell on earthing—would I in the process just be making myself just an ever easier target? For that matter, would I in the process just be making myself just an ever more idiotic target to boot?

I wrapped my fingers tight around the cool slick of my flashlight, looked at it, sighed. Turning it on to see better would only make me be seen better, and as for using it as a club to bludgeon the hole-filler-upper to death with, in my puny hands the flashlight was nothing more than a security blanket of aluminum casing and alkaline D batteries.

God, but it's dark. God, it's so, so very dark.

The darkness of the woods around me felt like a movie theatre, an eerie black movie theatre with all eyes no doubt trained on me. And right there among all those eyes naturally there would be those of the hole-filler-upper—all eight of them—as well as all of those other night-time eyes, those of the fox, and the weasel, and the owl—especially the owl. Why even now I practically could see those eyes of his, all round and yellow and non-blinking—watching me, watching me, watching me. And no matter whether perched high or low, or near or far, or facing me or with its back to me, the owl with just a simple swivel of its feathered head forever watched me, just as I forever watched it.

What was he thinking, that owl: a hole, a kid, a hole and a kid, in the dark, in the woods? If an owl truly were wise, eventually he'd figure it out. But would I?

Of course I knew the reasons why we went and dug the hole in the first place. I mean seeing the *H.M.S. Bounty* back in the days before superstorm Sandy took her, seeing her back in the good old days when she was docked in Fall River's Battleship Cove, seeing her on the DVD in movies like *Treasure Island* and *Mutiny on the Bounty* and *Pirates of the Caribbean*—I mean like how could our heads not but be filled with crazy notions of buried pirate treasure? And I do mean pirates—real pirates—really here, here in southern New England just searching the shores of Connecticut and the bays of Rhode Island and Massachusetts for places to hide their booty. From Captain Kidd to Blackbeard, from Gardiner's Island to Grassy Isle in the Taunton River, this area once was crawling with 'em, those pirates.

What's more, how could we not but be digging what with a mystery like Dighton Rock just lying there—lying right there just across the Taunton?

Dighton Rock! Dighton Rock! Low down and dirty Dighton Rock!

Seems everyone ever passing this way felt somehow compelled to go leave graffiti on it. From Indians to Vikings to the great 16th century Portuguese explorer, Miguel Cortereal, all of 'em left strange inscriptions on it. So what I want to know is: just what exactly was it that Cortereal thought he was doing here anyway? I mean after sailing across the great wild Atlantic, like why would he ever enter Narragansett Bay, only to then enter smaller Mt. Hope Bay, only to then sail both himself and his crew up a river like the Taunton?

The Taunton? I mean, *the Taunton?* Like what did Cortereal want to do, fall off the end of the world? Like I can sort of see how Spitters fell off the end of the world, let ourselves fall there. After all, we keep our profiles low; we keep 'em that way. Our day-to-day lives day-by-day; we unfurl 'em just that way. Our selves to ourselves, we guard our selves, they, after all, Ours, and God's.

But Miguel "Michael" Cortereal, he wasn't us, and for that matter, no way in the world should he ever be like us. Swashbuckler, adventurer, explorer—like I mean he was everything I wanted to be ... and wasn't.

It gets weirder still: Miguel Cortereal, Miguel Cortereal ... he actually and for some unknown reason stayed here. I mean like what was he, crazy or something? I mean why settle in a strange land, on the banks of a rocky river, in the middle of nowhere? To me the whole thing didn't make sense. Then again, it didn't make much sense either for somebody to go running around all night filling holes.

Thing is though, really—since when did things ever have to make much sense 'round here anyway? I mean wasn't it just three miles from here, in Fall River, where crazy Lizzie Borden "took an ax, and gave her mother forty whacks?" Wasn't it just three miles from here where, "having seen what she had done, she gave her father forty-one?"

I looked down at the hole, looked away, looked again. All in all, I had to admit, it was a pretty good hole—for a hole. More or less round, maybe four to five feet across, it also was close to being about four to five feet deep, not that I could actually see the bottom in the darkness.

But was it deep enough, that hole? Was it deep enough to uncover the secrets of pirates, the secrets of Cortereal, or any of those other secrets, big or small, that might just be lurking in the ground below our feet?

When looking at it just right, with head cocked back and eyes all squinty, the hole seemed like a mirror, a mirror draped in black, a mirror that if only undraped might just reflect back secrets, secrets of the past.

Then, when stepping closer, when stepping with head straight and eyes as open as they were wide, the hole morphed into something else, into a sort of closed door, a closed black door that if only opened might just reveal secrets, secrets to the future.

"Hoo, Hoo, Hoo?" the sudden hoots of a great horned owl made my head spin off the hole, made my feet jump off the ground.

"Hoo, Hoo, Hoo?" it hooted again, this time the Hooing sounding more like Whoing—Who? Who? Who?—woodsy replies coming back at me from every which way.

From off somewhere I heard a screech owl screech. From off somewhere else I heard a barred owl bark, yip, just yip-yap and bark itself silly.

As for me, I dared not make a sound. Not that I had much of an answer to the *Who? Who? Who?* anyway. To be honest about it, I didn't understand the question. 'Least I didn't understand it without there at least being some *Why? Why? Whying?* going on in that mix too.

I mean like why was our digging such a problem for the hole-filler-upper anyway? I mean, really, what else were we supposed to be doing this summer before the start of our first year of high school?

Holes? Hell, holes—they're likely to get dug any old time.

And as for the ones that get dug in the ground, they're pretty much just what happens when obsessing over Blackbeard, fixating on Cortereal. Hole-digging? Like give me a break! Hole-digging's natural, almost even normal, for boys like us.

And so there it is. There it is and here I am, joined at the hip with some hole-filler-upper who obviously doesn't think normally, doesn't for that matter act none too naturally either. I mean that hole-filler-upper—*he's sick!* He just has to be. Like how else could he have figured out that my treasure hunting and my Cortereal-solving weren't what they seemed to be? How else could he have figured out that my motivations weren't innocent—not at all innocent? It all left me wondering whether the hole-filler-upper hadn't somehow figured me out before I'd even had the chance to figure myself out.

I looked again to the hole. It was L.T.'s fault! I mean if not for him this whole hole-digging thing wouldn't have happened, 'least it wouldn't have happened the way it just now was happening. L.T.'s problem—now my problem—is that when first moving to Best Harbor, all L.T. saw was a simple town in need of some complication. And when first meeting Spitters, all L.T. saw were a simple-looking people who, while not exactly goobers, needed some complexity brought into their lives. And when first getting his first good load of me, all L.T. saw was a tall, gangly goof of a kid, one pretty much begging to get his life muddled up, screwed up, turned upside down, and made not only miserable, but horribly, hideously miserable.

But to L.T.'s credit, I think just about from the moment he turned over his very first rock he realized that on all accounts he'd judged us wrong. Not that that of course stopped him from turning over more rocks. If anything, all it did was go and make him turn 'em so much the faster.

L.T. Haymaker and his mother, Mrs. Haymaker, they

moved from Boston to Best just a year ago under pretty suspicious circumstances, though, truth be told, just moving to Best is cause enough to usually go raise suspicion. And it certainly didn't help L.T. none either for people to go about believing his real name to be "Dutch," or to go about believing he was Jewish, which of course in L.T.'s own mind he considered himself as being. And while I personally didn't at that particular go-about-believing time agree that L.T. was what others made him out to be—"a little gangstah"—I do now have to admit he sure has got the "instigatah" in him, okay, a lot of the "instigatah" in him, he instigates, all right, he's just backed up and packed full of "instigatah."

But Jewish, as for being Jewish, L.T.'s as much Jewish as I'm a Swedish Martian. I mean for crying out loud, L.T.'s a Viking—a short Viking—but a Viking nevertheless. Like I mean, L.T.—he pillages! L.T.—he plunders! And not that I know for sure, but from everything I've ever seen 'bout Jews they don't much pillage, don't much plunder. And more, what's more, L.T.'s mother, Mrs. Haymaker, she once personally told me that she herself personally nicknamed "Dutch"—or whatever his real name was—to be L.T. because if he was even half as Jewish as he claimed to be he'd have to be a Lost Tribe kind of Jew, an L.T. kind of Jew.

The thing was, if I could tell L.T. wasn't actually "a little gangstah" terrorizing quaint New England villages, or actually a "little Jew" in a sea of Portuguese Catholics, then others should have been able to tell as well, (most in Best's sea Good Portuguese Catholics; virtually all in Spit's not all that good, not even all that Catholic). And yet, from the moment the Family Haymaker—consisting only of L.T. and his mother, Mrs. Haymaker—moved here, a weird unease somehow had seeped its way into our community of Spit, a level of unease, and a type of unease, that was weird even by our standards of unease and weirdness.

I looked again to the hole, stared at it. What was it? Like what the Hell was it? All the reasons in the world for digging it weren't explanation enough to explain why we went and dug it. Yeah, maybe L.T. had his explanation; Ollie and Richie maybe they had theirs too, though somehow I doubted they could coherently explain theirs. I mean, for crying out loud, I couldn't even explain mine! I couldn't! How could I explain mine when I didn't know what I was digging for—that is, what I truly was digging for?

I drew nearer again to the hole—not too near—but still plenty near enough. Empty now of the dirt that once had been in it, what exactly was it? As best I could tell it was nothing— nothing but man-made nothing. I mean it made no sense; it didn't fit. Could that also be what the hole-filler-upper saw? Did he see the hole, see the emptiness, see emptiness and only emptiness where before there had been no emptiness? Did he see the hole, see the nothingness, see where before the nothingness there at least had been somethingness, even if the somethingness was only dirt? I mean was it wrong of us to make emptiness? Was it wrong of us to make nothingness? For that matter, did we even make anything at all? I mean like we didn't add anything, or mix anything, or join together anything, did we? At best all we did was take, take away, take away and show what always was there, what always was underneath, what always was inside. Was that what the hole-filler-upper didn't like about our holes? Was that what the hole-filler-upper didn't like about us?

Or could it just be that the hole-filler-upper saw something else, saw something different, saw something different altogether? Could it be that he saw our digging up of dirt as just some take-away, just some keep-away, just some play? Could it be that he saw our digging up of dirt to reveal only more dirt as just some shuffling of cards, just some hocus-pocus, just some shell game? Could it be that he saw our holes as a game, a game he decided to play? And what if he saw our holes as a dare? Could it really be he saw our holes as a dare, a dare that he decided to accept?

A sliver of moonbeam stabbed through the trees, catching me with the hole, catching me and the hole. I could sense the moonbeam's silvery light encircling us like a spotlight, showing us to all the eyes of the night. As far as the hole-filler-upper was concerned, me and the hole were as good as one now. The hole wouldn't exist without me, and I wouldn't be here without it. And the hole-filler-upper, already mad that I went and re-dug the hole he'd so carefully filled, he'd know that. He'd know I was the one who wronged the right, made nothing where before there at least had been something. He'd know I was the one who played the thing like a game, one-upped the dare.

What was I thinking? What on earth was I doing?

Turning to get away from the hole, suddenly I felt the ground slipping on out from under me. I was sliding … sliding … sliding into the hole as if sliding into a bad dream, and there was nothing I could do to stop the slide, stop myself.

Reaching for the ground, I got fistfuls of air. Looking for what to grab, I got nothing—just eyeful after eyeful of the nothing. And bracing myself for what I knew was happening—happening to me—I shut my eyes, clenched my teeth.

The fall took forever. I somehow felt suspended in midair, in a sort of limbo, pulled from both below and above—pretty much on the line, on the verge, on the rack.

What were they doing to me—these pullers? Why?

Then, free fall, free fall, free fall … then, slam, splash, splat … then, crash, crunch, crack … then, and of course … concussion, concussion, concussion … and a real, real, real good one too.

I'm in a torture chamber, a torture chamber of some sort, medieval,

musty and dark, the pullings from below and above so bad I can actually
hear my cartilage pop, feel my ligaments snap, hear and feel my bones
break—the popping, snapping, and breaking very loud, very clear.

Clear too now is the purpose for this pulling, about as clear as the
aim behind it is unclear.

"Is it not true," I am asked, "that your digging is sinful?

"And is it not also true that your digging is in pursuit of the unholy
way?

"And is it not also true that your digging is after that which has been
deemed forgotten?"

I look to my interrogator, really can't see him past the white hot fires
burning away inside my body, the red hot denials that are firing away
inside my mind.

"Is it not true that your digging is deep, your digging is wide?

"And is it not true that you are digging where you shouldn't—digging
where you can't?

"And is it not also true that that for which you are digging has been
deemed ungodly—that it, and indeed your very digging itself, insults us?
That it spits on us?"

"I only dig," I softly say, "I dig only for that which is mine."

"Silence! Silence, damn you! You are digging for your soul! Cursed
are you and cursed be you—you are digging for that which is ours! Ours!"

"Get out!" at once my mind screamed, "Get out!" I could
actually hear it scream. "Get out, get out, get out!"

I scrambled up to my feet. And though petrified to look
and maybe see the hole-filler-upper above me and about to
bury me alive, I looked anyway. But instead of seeing him, what
I saw, and all I saw, were stars. Stars brilliant, stars twinkling,
the stars lit up the night sky like an airport runway, starlight
pulsating toward me as if to reach me.

With my eye-level now at just over the rim of the hole, the
woods all around seemed a horizon, the kind of sea horizon
I'd've expected to see from the bow of a ship. Full of floating

obstacles and submerged mines, it was however something else I now saw making me duck—duck back down inside the hole.

The eyes of the night!

Not just round and yellow and non-blinking, the eyes now were slits, blood-shot red slits, and they weren't just watching me, but glaring at me.

Who? Who? Who?

And so—so, of course, and because—putting my one hand to one side of the rim and my other hand to the other side, digging my one foot into one side of the hole and my other foot into the other side, I climbed out that hole, that dirty stinkin' dungeon—climbed only to find that now it was me doing the glaring, and I was doing it—glaring—doing it right back into the eyes of the night.

Everything, I knew, would be different from here on out. Everything would have to be. For now I had a foe, had made myself an enemy. Watches would be high alert, it no longer enough simply to spot unnatural turns in flow, shifts in air, breaks in rhythm. Rather, I'd have to expect them—the turns, the shifts, the breaks—and be ready for them. For now they weren't simply unnatural, they were dangerous. And those blood-shot red eyes of the night, they weren't now simply glaring ... but glaring evil.

And what's more, I'd made them that way. I made them—and maybe even made myself—glare that way, be that way.

1

Me and L.T. pushed off from the boatyard early, so early that the clang-clanging of its flag-draped pole sounded like a ship's bell being rung not just by an old sailor getting woken for his turn at the watch, but by an especially old sailor especially cranky over having to stir his old bones for his turn at the watch. I mean, the flag-draped clang-clanging pole—it wouldn't shut up! Ringing out something nautical, something sounding like eight bells after eight bells after eight bells, it was as if the especially old and cranky sailor had just had it with all the watches, all the lookouts, all the duty shifts.

'Best watch out,' he seemed to say. 'Best be careful,' he seemed to warn. 'Sailors at sea are always on watch. Ain't no need to be wakin' us sailors, specially wakin' us sailors for some goddamn watch so early in the goddamn mornin'.'

The flag-draped pole, swaying in the wind first this way, and then swaying in the wind the other way, for the most part really did look like the mast of the tall ship it was supposed to look like. In that way, it was just one more reminder of our once could've-been, and forever should've-been, glorious seafaring past. Though the pole had no sails, it did have rungs, and having climbed them before, I knew that from the topmost one it was possible to look out over the river, the bay, and even the horizon. I also knew that from that particular vantage point and distance, Best Harbor too looked like it was supposed to—kind of still, kind-of asleep.

The boatyard night watchman, a fat guy under an awning and a fishing hat, he too kind-of looked like he was supposed to, kind-of still, kind-of asleep. Kind-of watching too as we pushed ourselves off, he picked a cold beer from out the bucket of ice at his feet, gave himself a good swig and gave his beer belly a good pat, his stinkin' bare feet just a dangling there right 'top the bucket.

Eyes to the river, Michael! Keep your damn eyes to the damn river.

So keeping them there just as they were meant to be kept, it was only once we at last paddled our kayaks a distance distant enough away that my eyes at last un-kept looked back the night watchman's way. Fishing hat down by his eyes, the night watchman looked asleep—leastwise he looked to be asleep—the only signs of life the swarm of flies just now feasting there at his bare and stinkin' feet.

Had we drifted too far? Had we simply just drifted too far away? Is that why the night watchman stopped watching? Or did he stop because he knew us, leastwise thought he did?

Whatever! For all I cared that night watchman could watch us, stare at us—even spy on us. Really, what did it matter? Like, what was he going to do, the fat asshole watchman—kill us, kill us or something?

Is that what you'd do, you fat asshole watchman? Is that what you'd do to us, you good-for-nothing fat asshole watchman? Well, then—bring it!

Yet, and still, and despite myself, I just could not help but feel shivers run down my back while watching him, watching him and that black cat at his fly-infested feet, the cat just lying there motionless as if dead, and if not dead, surely wishing that it indeed were.

On up ahead I could see L.T.'s orange Pamlico skim past a couple of mastheads, a dinghy, a cabin cruiser too. "Hey Michael! Hey Michael," he hollered back at me. "Know what? My kayak—it's bigger than yours. It's bigger than yours."

"So?"

"What so?"

"You heard me. So? So what does that matter?"

"Michael, you mean to tell me you don't know? You mean to tell me you don't know 'bout the ratios? You mean you don't know the bigger the kayak the bigger the dick? Like who doesn't know that?"

"Up yours, L.T.! I like my Pungo. I like it just fine. Size don't matter none."

"Well, so long as you think so." L.T. laughed, splashing me just as my kayak pulled on even with his.

On stormy days the stretch of river 'round Best gets gusty, its currents tricky. But on this particular morning the Taunton was almost flat-water smooth, just a bit choppy on account of the wind. With a hint of Atlantic salt already in the air, the sun was already finding the back of my neck. It was surely gonna be a killer of a hot day.

Using my paddle, I pushed myself clear of the old stone wharf to my right, let my paddle bump along it some so as to not go by it too quick. Mostly underwater, the wharf in its heyday had been a dock for boats carrying sea cargo to inland river towns, and a way-station too for inland river town goods and rubbish to head on out to sea. Now just bunches of weather-beaten stone blocks and green lichen-covered metal moorings, old-timers said the old stone wharf was a shame, said it was a dirty rotten shame, said everything and all of it was just a dirty rotten crying shame. What those old-timers called it was "a relic." A relic.

On up ahead by the riverbank I could see a brown cottontail scurry into tall marsh grass, could see a couple of great blue herons lift suddenly from out a beech grove. And nearby a white-ringed pheasant ruffled its red and purple feathers, pretty much gave itself away. I pointed it out with my paddle.

"I see it," L.T. said.

Some of my very best thinking is done at the river, better even than when I'm fishing on Mt. Hope Bay. I mean the Bay is big, big as an ocean, and when I'm on it I feel like just a speck that bobs up, and bobs down, and doesn't get much of anywhere. The coast seems far away, seems out of focus, and as for the horizon, well, that's something I think I'll never reach. But on the river, no matter whether fishing for striped bass or just paddling along, most everything fits. I flow with the river, the trees along its banks drift by like markers, and things more or less make sense. Leastwise anyway, they used to more or less make sense.

I mean after all, how much sense was anything going to really make what with L.T. here? Looking his way, why even now I could see him just like that go stand in his kayak, and then for no possible reason—maybe for even a bad reason—go rock his kayak, I mean just rock the hell out of his kayak. Then, and for no good reason—maybe even for a really low-down reason—I could see him take that apple he'd been munching on, take it and chuck it at that poor hollowed-out maple there by the water.

"Raccoons. Raccoons," he said.

"You are such an idiot, L.T. Like you are such an idiot, you know that? Why do you have to go and make the stupid raccoons go and run for their stupid lives?"

"Just wanted to shake 'em up, let 'em know, you know, that there could be a hawk or something up 'top their tree, you know, like just waiting in ambush."

"But there was no hawk or something up `top their tree just waiting in ambush, was there? Right, right L.T., no hawk? No hawk, no falcon, no eagle—I mean, not even a sparrow. Fact is nothin's there, nothin', that is, till you put it in your head that there was."

"Well, you never really know, Michael, you never know. Who knows just what could've been there? Ain't no need to be getting so all and pissed 'bout it though. Here," he said, taking a bag of chips from out his kayak's hutch, tossing it my way. "Breakfast."

Not feeling much like eating, I let the bag land in the river, wound up thinking, thinking what I do sometimes when not eating. And when thinking, there's almost nothing that I think about more than Dighton Rock.

We were gliding past it, or at any rate gliding past the little white museum the Rock nowadays is housed in. L.T.'s mother, Mrs. Haymaker, she researches the Rock for her thesis. She is what L.T. calls a "Rock Buff," which is short for an anthropologist, or an archaeologist, I always forget which. Whatever, Mrs. Haymaker is Buff—period!

On hot July days I see her by the riverbank, and no matter whether rising up from clumps of marsh grass or stepping out from a snare of cattails, river mud melts off her like ice cream off a sugar cone. In cut-off shorts, a white tank top and flip-flops too, I see her backpack fall over her shoulder, see her blond hair fall over her face, one fall with a little bend of her back, another fall with a little sweep of her hand, the falls just falling as she toes about there in the shallow waters that may just be hiding bits and pieces and clues. Then, with a rise to fix her hair, and then with a rise to straighten her backpack too, I see her arch her back, arch it just to make sure that Best's best get a better look—a real good look.

But on this particular morning I just could not find Mrs.

Haymaker. Still, in my mind's eye I could see her by this stretch of riverbank, bending a little here among the marsh grass, sweeping a little there among the cattails—she herself looking too.

I've heard it said that before Dighton Rock was moved to the museum it lay in the river like some damn sandstone dory. In warm months seen for four hours a day, ocean tides would rise up to cover it in four feet of water. In cold months it was seen with a cap of ice. The cap proved vital in preserving all those strange inscriptions that've puzzled everybody for what is now well over four hundred years. And it seems just about everybody left those inscriptions, too—for sure Indians, but early settlers as well. Some theories have Chinese and Irish explorers as making them, while really crazy ones pin them on the ancient Romans, Phoenicians, and Vikings. One really out-there theory even has the inscriptions as being made by visitors from Atlantis, while a still more out-there theory has the Lost Tribes of Israel as etching them. Nowadays though it's all but accepted that it was the great Portuguese explorer, Miguel Cortereal, who made the most notable inscriptions. One has even been deciphered to read, 'Miguel Cortereal, by will of God,' along with the date 1511 and a Portuguese coat of arms. Some claim to have even seen the words 'Chief of the Indians' there beside Cortereal's name.

"So what did Miguel Cortereal come here for anyway?" I asked L.T., though I'd heard all kinds of answers before.

"My mother says that in 1502 he went looking for his brother, Gaspar. Gaspar had disappeared a year earlier."

"So did Miguel ever find his brother?"

"Don't know. Gaspar was never heard from again, though I suppose you almost could say the same 'bout Miguel. Two of Miguel's ships, however, did wind up making it all the way back to Portugal."

I stopped paddling; looked around. We'd left behind the meadows by the boatyard, were now in the woods, swamp oaks to both sides of us. It was precisely this sort of spot that always bothered me about the Cortereal story. If I had it right, Miguel Cortereal sailed down the coast, sailed from Newfoundland to New England, sailed to of all places wind up here—on the Taunton? This is where Miguel thought his brother got lost? Why would Gaspar ever have even come here? There had to be something else going on, something I was missing.

I sometimes wonder whether Miguel actually did go looking for Gaspar. I mean what if instead he just went looking for the same sorts of things that his brother looked for? Could that possibly help explain why he didn't sail back to Portugal with either one of his two ships that did go back? Could that possibly help explain why he didn't just settle in one of the great harbors he would have come across when sailing down the coast? Could that possibly help explain why, once in New England, he didn't just settle down on good old Cape Cod? Could that possibly help explain why he didn't just settle along the wide Sakonnet River of Sakonnet Peninsula just southeast of here? Could that possibly help explain why he instead went middle-of-the-road, chose to take what the mariners later would call "The Middle Passage," the narrow pass between Aquidneck Island and East Bay? Could that possibly help even explain why after sailing through the pass and arriving at a bay as beautiful as Mt. Hope, he then would leave it for the Taunton River, leave it for this stretch of overgrown swamp riverbank that at times got to being 'bout as dark as the dark night itself?

What was Miguel Cortereal doing? Was it possible that maybe what he looked for in a home wasn't what other people looked for in a home? Was it possible—was it just possible— that maybe what he wanted in a home was for it to not be open, not be welcoming?

"How did the Wampanoags feel about Miguel?"

"At first the Wampanoags weren't all that crazy about him," L.T. said, his kayak coming back 'round so that he faced Dighton Rock, faced me too. "According to my mother their legends talk about his ships being wooden houses, describe how the houses swam up the river to fight them. But Miguel and his men must have eventually learned to live with the Wampanoags. After all, the Rock says he was Chief of the Indians, and years later settlers meeting the Wampanoags were surprised at how many Portuguese words they had in their vocabulary. They also were surprised by the light color of their skin, and you know what that means, don't you, Michael? You know, like with the squaws and everything?"

I grimaced, let L.T.'s remark go. "The inscription has the date 1511 on it. That means that Miguel probably didn't get here till then. What that also means is that once he left Portugal in 1502, he sailed his wooden houses for years, sailed 'em all over the place."

"So?"

"So that means no matter whether or not Miguel actually did find Gaspar, all along he obviously had the ships to go back to Portugal. But he didn't go back. He didn't go back."

"Maybe he wound up wrecking his ship here. Maybe he couldn't go back."

"Yeah, but wooden houses is plural, L.T. Even if Miguel's own ship wound up getting wrecked once he got here, still he had more than one. And remember, we already know two of his ships made it back to Portugal. They were seaworthy enough to make the trip. Geez, L.T., don't you think it's weird Miguel sailed to the ends of the world, sailed to a land of strange Indians, and didn't go back home when he had the chance to go back home?"

"Maybe Miguel didn't go back 'cause here he could be Chief of the Indians? Maybe that's why he didn't go back."

"I don't buy it. I don't buy that Miguel would leave everything behind in Portugal and settle here just 'cause he could be Chief of the Indians. Notice, L.T., notice he didn't call himself King of the Indians? I mean—*Chief?* Like what's a Chief? A Chief ain't no King. And even if he was a King, just what kind of a King could he have been anyway? There ain't no gold 'round here, no diamonds either. Nothin's here to have made him want to stay here."

"So what's your point?"

"My point?" I said.

My point?—I asked myself, the murkiness of the river water suddenly becoming about sharp as sharp could be. "Know what? Know what, L.T.? I don't think Miguel wanted to go back. I don't think he ever wanted to go back. Seems to me that what he wanted was to get the heck away from Portugal, just get as far away as he possibly could."

We paddled on, the stroke of our paddles something like bug legs flailing in water. I knew we weren't the first to be digging holes by the river. Even before the Revolutionary War people knocked themselves out digging in the belief that the inscriptions on the Rock were directions to the buried treasure of Captain Kidd or Blackbeard. Another thing I knew, if Captain Kidd or Blackbeard had indeed buried treasure, we'd find it. We'd find it, quit school; find it, become rich; find it, become famous—and to boot, pirate style, get any girl and every girl we damn well wanted!

But as exciting a daydream as that was, especially for the others of our digging crew, buried pirate treasure and all that went with it wasn't so much what me and L.T. were going after—that is, really going after. Not that I, of course, knew what we really were going after. That only L.T. knew, or didn't know. But even if L.T. did know what we really were going after, who's to say that what he considered we were going after was what I'd consider I was going after, if of course I knew what I was really going after? For that matter who's to say it even was what I really should be going after? I mean, L.T.—no way could he, and no way should he, know me better than I knew me. For damn sure no way could he, or no way should he, know what was best for me.

As far as I could tell, for this to end well, either my 'after' would have to turn out to be one and the same as L.T.'s 'after', or my 'go' would have to turn out to be as on target for me as his 'go' for him. And even then, even if my 'go' somehow were to turn out as on the mark for me as his for him, who's to say my 'go' would go as far as his? Who's to say it could? Who's to say it even should?

Bottom line though—all the 'goings' and all the 'afterings'—while they for me and L.T. may well have differed over details, overall they were much the same. What this was about was much the same; and what me and L.T. were about, that too was much the same. For what me and L.T. knew— beyond even a sliver of a doubt—was that as good as it was to find something—and it was good—it even was better to find out something, better by far.

Deep in thought over just what it was what it was L.T. was going after, and—most importantly—just what it was I was going after, I didn't even notice Grassy Isle till it was just off to the side of us. Most times easy to miss anyway, the ebb and flow of the tide sneaking up to submerge it, both sneak and submerge happening every day, twice a day, on the day-in, and on the day-out.

Sometimes, sometimes it seemed to me that I too was under the influence of some tide, some tide so sneaky, so subtle, and so regular that I barely could even sense it there. Washing over me the tide rose then fell, rose then fell so predictably it made me feel safe—but safe from what? Washing over me the tide rose then fell, rose then fell so consistently surely it had to be shaping me—but shaping me for what?

I mean always flowing under me, or over me, or around me, like just when would this tide finally be done with me? When it also flowed within me? I mean God only knew when that was going to happen. One thing I knew though, one thing for sure, dangers were out there, dangers to all of this washing and flowing. And if I knew it then others knew it. And Spitters? Spitters they especially knew it, sure as shit they knew it too.

See, I mean—interruptions, surprises, obstacles—they ain't welcome, they ain't welcome 'round here. L.T.—so close, so clever. L.T.—too close, too clever. Why even now 'the little gangstah' in his kayak probably was thinking—likelier than not, scheming. Smiling, just now I saw him pucker up his lips, pucker 'em good as if now to whistle, or worse, sing.

"No. Oh no, L.T.! Don't!"

Overall, L.T.'s a good whistler. But when it comes to singing, he can't. I mean he can't sing at all. Puberty's set up shop in his throat, made his singing like a bullfrog croaking its last croaks. And yet despite that, and despite my plea—maybe even to spite it—I could tell L.T. was gonna go croak, was gonna go just croak away at that old song we'd learned at the scout overnight.

"Michael, row the boat ashore, Hallelujah.
Michael, row the boat ashore, Hallelujah.
Sister, help to trim the sails, Hallelujah.
Sister, help to trim the sails, Hallelujah."

Truth is, though I kind of like having my name in the song, I hate hearing it there. I mean what if someone actually were to hear L.T. singing that song, actually think it actually me doing that stuff, that stuff that, from the sound of it, sounded sort of heroic, sort of good? I mean that heroic? That good? It's embarrassing.

"For the love of God, cut it," I pleaded. "Cut it out," I

pleaded some more, my eyes searching riverbank to see if someone were there. I mean if someone were there, I'd just kill myself, pretty much would have to.

"The river Jordan is chilly and cold, Hallelujah.
Chills the body, but not the soul, Hallelujah.
The river is deep; the river is wide, Hallelujah.
Milk and honey on the other side, Hallelujah."

L.T. pointed with his paddle, the blade leveled at me, cast on me. Then, falling back in his kayak with sounds sounding something like a humpback's blow-hole grunting and a sperm's sonic squeaking, the nose of his kayak lifted from out the water like a turned-on, jacked-up, twittering beluga baby.

"Hallelooojah, Hallelooojah, Hallelooojah!" he laughed. Just like that—rapid-fire and all hyena-like. "Halleloojah, Halleloojah, Halleloojah!"

Nuts, like I mean he was going nuts, I guess whatever it was he found funny starting not only with me, but ending with me. "Hey, Michael," he snorted, "if you sing, if you sing I'll stop."

By now I was ready to hold my head underwater just not to hear his laughing, more so his croaking, and more so still all his snorting. Let's see, sing or hold my head underwater? I mean what kind of choice was that? L.T.'s offer was so easy, and my decision so obvious, that for a moment I actually thought he wanted me to sing, that he genuinely wanted to hear my voice.

Thing is, the thing is I sing a lot anyway. I sing walking a path at night. I sing sitting alone in the woods. And I sing for myself, nobody—'least I think nobody—knowing a thing about it but me, and, well, the voice doing the singing.

It's complicated—me, the voice, me and the voice. My voice but not me, inside me but not the inside me—the voice is my inside friend, but really, I don't know it, I don't know it at all. Whispering, talking, singing—the voice reminds me that I'm not alone, that there's more to me than bunches of idiotic thoughts, more than the occasional serious thoughts not thought through, more even than the rare serious thoughts I convince myself I'm thinking through.

Sometimes too the voice reminds me that I won't make a shot till I shoot. And when it comes to that—shooting—truth is the voice yells a whole lot more than it sings.

I think my mother and father, I think they know about the voice, or at any rate that I have one. And they probably wish that it were me doing more of the singing—the yelling too—and not the voice. If you asked them I think they would say that they want me pushing the voice more, and pushing myself more, all the pushing I guess somehow raising the voice, bettering me.

I think Father Sousa at St. Peter's also knows about my inside friend—what he would call my soul. And he also wants me pushing him. But if I won't, or if I can't, then he's more than ready to do it himself—do what it takes to save him, my inside friend. I'm not really sure, but Father Sousa probably wants my friend, my soul—wants him not only to get pushed, he wants him, and me, getting good and pushed. I guess Father Sousa doesn't want my soul to be neither here nor there, just kind of hanging forever and ever in limbo. And I think he doesn't want me being just a little here or a little there, just kind of going about things half-assed.

"Michael, row the boat ashore." It seemed the song was calling on me to do something, do something important, but what? Like what boat? Which shore?

"The river Jordan is chilly and cold." Whatever it was that I was supposed to be doing sounded hard.

"Milk and honey on the other"—I shut up, my kayak at once grinding up on the muddy, muddy banks of Chippascutt Point. L.T., up already on the bank, he'd clearly shut himself up well before me. Tethering his kayak to the big maple, he stared at me, and he stared hard.

"What? What, L.T.?"

"Nothing."

"Then why are you looking at me like you're looking at me?"

"'Cause, Michael, when you get lost, lost in song, like you really get lost."

Of course the kayak way to Chippascutt Point wasn't our usual way to Chippascutt Point. Our usual way was the night watch way: a winding dirt path and then a cut into the woods at the break. And the break was perfect: a mere crack in a group of trees just narrow enough to let us in, just wide enough, too, to let us back out. As for the kayak way though, it truly was a river road: sprawling and open, people on it or near it, people going upstream or down.

So people, I knew, might very well just now be watching me and L.T. take our shovels from out our kayaks, take out our pick-axes too. For that matter they might very well have been watching us the whole damn time we were on the river, watching all along.

And this, of course, this was L.T.'s plan. It certainly wasn't mine.

"If we show ourselves," he said, "then they'll show themselves."

Now to someone not from here I can see how thinking like that makes sense, how it may even be kind of logical. Thing is that kind of thinking, that kind of logic, it just doesn't work, not around here it doesn't. Besterners don't want to show. For that matter they don't really want to see much either. Spitters we're much the same, same but different. We too don't want to show, though somehow we always manage showing just enough—showing just what we want to show. And as for seeing, we really don't want that either, though somehow we always manage making ourselves see—our sights sharp as an owl, one in the woods, in the night.

"So tell me, L.T., tell me again why we're going to the hole by the kayak way?"

"You know why, Michael."

"I do?"

"Sure you do. 'Cause you want to."

"I do?"

"Yeah, Michael. You do. Deep down you know that if you don't play with everything you got, you won't get everything they got, everything they got on you."

I let it go, his knowing what I got and what they got. It was already way too hot to be arguing with the likes of him at any rate. And it already truly was way too hot to be lugging around any shovels and pick-axes on any winding dirt path anyway.

Up 'top a crest, I found myself glancing on back towards the river even as some of my thoughts raced on up ahead to the hole. Was it there? I mean was the hole still there? What if somebody already had filled it? What if somebody managed to somehow move it? I mean moved, switched—what if it was moved or switched so well it now was by any river, any old river? And filled in, covered up—what if it was filled in or covered up so well it now was any spot, any old spot in the ground? Moved, switched—would it be possible to tell once it had been by this river? Filled in, covered up—would it be possible to tell once it had been a hole, this hole, this particular hole by this particular river?

Just beyond the topmost part of crest I collided with L.T., him having come to a stop, me having not paid attention. His head down, his eyes down, he leaned on his shovel, and he leaned hard.

What? What happened? Was something wrong?

Gone. The hole—gone. Not that the hole's going was that

much of a surprise. The surprise was that in filling the hole, the hole-filler-upper hadn't tried at all covering the spot. Rather, it seemed, the hole-filler-upper went out of his way to actually not cover up, not disguise, not conceal what had been the hole, make it look just like any old spot in the ground. Rather, what he did, what that hole-filler-upper did, was leave a message.

Clear, and yet unclear; stupid, and yet cunning; the message was oh so careful, and yet oh so careless.

Hitting home—hitting my home—the message was sent to me, was meant for me. I knew it wasn't meant for L.T. because, unlike him, somehow I understood it, understood it even as I at the same time could not understand such a thing.

At the very spot where the hole once had been, there now was ash and cinder, gray ash and black cinder, and the burned lumped remains of some poor tortured animal, his life … his little life … his little life snuffed out.

2

Me and Ollie sat in a booth at Captain Jack's Diner, he across from me and trying as best he could to touch the tip of his curled tongue to his eyebrows, me trying as best I could not to look. Ollie—like, Ollie—well, Ollie's a train wreck, okay? He just is. And despite my trying as best I could to twist myself into the most knotted up pretzel there ever was, still I saw more than I needed—for sure saw more than I wanted. With his eyes crossed inward to better follow just how close he was to pulling off this tongue-to-eyebrow thing of his, the strain made Ollie's stubby fingers spread out wide on the table, turned his stubby fingers bloodless white.

As the story goes, Ollie's mother and father, they're kissing cousins, kissing cousins that I guess one day just up and decided to go for it, consequences be damned. Scary as that is—and it really, really is scary—Ollie's my cousin, and I don't mean the type that's once, twice or three times removed. Fact is there ain't no removal—I mean, ain't no removal of any kind! There ain't no ten-foot pole, there ain't no buffer, there ain't no nothin'! He's first degree. His kind of blood races around with my kind of blood each day, every day! God only knows what will become of me. I mean the very idea of my Aunt Lolly and my Uncle Jiggy *doin' it*—well, it just makes me want to jump in the Taunton.

The miracle of the thing is that the pairing of my Aunt Lolly and my Uncle Jiggy also brought about Rookie, Ollie's twin sister. Rookie's ravishing, has a talent for tight sweaters. What with her long brown hair shining, and her brown eyes sparkling, and her smile glowing, her heart's gold—pure gold. Yup, Rook's got it alright, got all of it, and I love her, I absolutely love her.

And therein lies a problem, leastwise one of my bigger ones. I mean like I don't want me and her to one day be known as Uncle Mookie and Aunt Rookie, the proud kissing cousin parents of any Ollie II. Don't get me wrong, Ollie's a good kid—at times actually downright ingenious—why even now discovering brand new ways of drinking his iced coffee with that straw that for some reason or other happens to just be up his nose.

In other places I don't think first cousins marry first cousins, 'least they don't do it very often. And in other places I'm pretty sure a visual of a cousin drinking iced coffee through his nose would go scar a kid for life. But seeing as how this is Best, and seeing as how this sort of stuff's all I've ever known, over the years I've managed building a pretty big immunity to it, leastwise to most of it.

Isaiah Best was the one who founded our town in 1642, and the town's been doing little more than a doggy paddle ever since. While the whaling boom went splashing its way on New Bedford and Nantucket two plus centuries ago, here we only got some lousy ripples. And that, that's our fault. We let ourselves become river-benders—let ourselves drift ever further and further from the sea. And the shame of it all is that Mt. Hope and Narragansett Bays lie just two miles down river, and just beyond lies the mighty Atlantic, just teasing us over what great sailors we were once upon a time upon it.

It was my great-great-great-great-grandfather who

happened to hop a whaling ship that docked in the Azorean Islands to take on crew. And three years later, after enough sperm oil blubber had been boiled down to satisfy even a Captain Ahab, both the ship's voyage and my great-great's great ocean adventure ended in New Bedford. Family followed, of course, once there was money enough to bring them, and here they worked—I mean worked themselves near to death in Fall River mills that long ago either got boarded up, got mysteriously burned to the ground, or both.

So, here I am in Best. And though I'm still a month short of fourteen, and though Boston is the farthest I've ever been in my entire life, even I know by now there's nothing truly best about Best Harbor.

But I am proud to be a Spitter.

Our Spit neighborhood runs along a spit of land, runs several blocks back from the river, runs from the boatyard to the little cove just beyond the river's bend. The cove is pulverized cobble, pressed gravel. But owing to the last ice age, the riverbank's strewn with rocks of all shapes and sizes, rocks all up the bank, and all down it. While in time most rocks do wind their way ever closer to the sea, some rocks, other rocks, always somehow manage ending up in our little catch basin of a cove. Like, I mean, they always do. And they always will. Some rocks—other rocks—are just meant to be pulverized cobble, pressed gravel. Some rocks—other rocks—are just destined to have their home be a little cove, one just beyond the river's bend.

The long and the short of it is, basically—basically we're a bit of a mess. Aside from the cobbles and gravel, river plant roots trap silt and sand to make us part marsh, and seawater running into river water makes us also a good part estuary. And sometimes, sometimes the seawater doesn't even so much run in as crash in, no more so than when a full-blown Nor'easter storm churns on up the coast.

Truth is though, truth be told too, sometimes just a high tide and a full moon, just a high tide and a full moon are plenty Nor'easter 'nough for us.

I like to think all this survival among rock and sand makes us Spitters pretty tough. I like also to think that it makes us Spitters kind of special. But for sure and for certain, I know it makes us peculiar.

"Hi girls," L.T. said. He slid into the booth seat next to Ollie, in no time went about the business of giving him the business, his knuckles rubbing Ollie's Patriots cap so hard it fell from his head onto his iced coffee.

"Hey, what did I do?" Ollie complained, his own lunge for L.T.'s cap missing badly, and truly badly at that, obviously his cap-grabbing skills not as yet up to par with those of his nose-drinking.

"Know what?" L.T. grinned, his beady eyes flashing out from under his GO TRIBAL cap. "Know what, Ollie? It happened. It happened again."

I kind of hoped L.T. would spare Ollie details of what we found at the hole—I mean he being my cousin and everything. But L.T. being L.T., I just knew that not only would he not spare him details of our gruesome discovery, he'd actually drag out the telling of those details, drag 'em out just as long as humanly or L.T. possible just to get max effect out of the thing.

Finally, when the last detail of the blackened limb had at last been thoroughly described, when the animal's seared mouth had all but been painted and then some, as one last and truly ugly gasp, poor Ollie, overcome by the build-up, and the beadiness, and the grin, cracked.

"Hey, it wasn't on my watch! It didn't happen on my watch! You believe me, right? You believe me, don't you?"

"I don't know, Ollie. I just don't know. I just don't if you're reliable enough."

"I am too 'liable 'nough. If I'm not 'liable 'nough then how was I able to stay 'wake long enough to wake Richie for his watch, you know, with the pebbles I threw at his window?"

"Yeah, but did you wait around to actually see him go outside? Did you wait around long enough for that?"

Ollie brought his fist to his head, shook them both. "That good-for-nothin' Richie. He must've gone back to sleep. I'm gonna kill him."

"Michael?" L.T. said, looking for my take.

"Well, I don't know if we have to like actually, you know, kill him. Wouldn't just cutting Richie out of the loop be enough?"

"So what else happened last night?" Ollie said, his fat ass rocking all over those stubby fingers of his. "Something's wrong. There's something you're not telling me."

I suddenly heard a pot clang, saw a swinging door swing, saw an Ol' Cuss a-comin', heard that Ol' Cuss a cussin' too. Drying his hands on a dishtowel, he—Ol' Cuss—joined us in our booth.

"Michael. Michael Costa. Don't you and your posse have anything better to do than hang in my diner?"

"No, Captain Jack. Actually, we don't."

Truth was we were taking our air conditioning wherever we could get it, this July in particular only about as hot as all hell. Like it was so hot that even by Best standards people walked slow, sat long. And no matter whether reminiscing hard when alone to themselves, or just talking softly when among themselves, old people sat on front porch rocking chairs, and shopkeepers sat on outdoor stools, all of them watching and watching, just watching time go by—good-bye. I mean funk— major FUNK! Why even my idiot kid brother, Billy, like even he just lies there in puddles of his own sweat, his eyes open— for the life of me it just impossible to tell if he's actually awake, or simply asleep, or just plain out.

Yup, *saudade* days were here alright. They were back.

People like L.T. can't understand saudade. Even Portuguese have a tough time with it. In the air if not in the lungs, in a whisper if not spoken aloud, saudade seems never to get explained 'cause it can't be explained. Eventually, I think, Portuguese wind up knowing what it means, 'least what the notion of it means. And they probably wind up knowing too when they have it, but honestly, I don't think they ever understand it.

When saudade nostalgia hits me I have a kind of feeling that something is missing from my life, but what that something is I'm not sure. Whatever it is, I have this strange feeling that I'm cut off from what's missing, and that what's missing—it never again will be part of my life.

It's sad, sad to feel a thing like that. It even can be painful. Saudade is in the blood; it gets passed along from generation to generation to generation. And whenever I have it I try to remember what's missing, and really it isn't such a bad thing to try and latch onto a memory. I just wish whatever it is I'm trying to remember, I just wish it wasn't so fuzzy—wasn't so damn frustrating.

Adjusting the kerchief-style bandanna on his head, Ol' Cuss swatted at his nose with his apron, hitched up his pants. "So, so Master Haymaker, so what's your pleasure?"

"My pleasure?"

"What do you want?"

"He wants hot and black," I said. "Hot and black is what he wants."

"Damn it, boys! Damn it already!! Hoist the sails! Hoist 'em! For Christ's sake, shake things up and do different than you're doin' 'em."

"We're trying, Captain Jack, really we are. I mean just yesterday didn't we want black and hot, right guys, black and hot and not hot and black? Besides, Captain Jack, you know the accepted drinking age in Best is fifteen. We're stuck with coffee, stuck with coffee and that's that."

Ol' Cuss got himself up, made as if to spit. "Fish out of water stink!"

"Ollie stinks," L.T. said.

"Y'all stink! Every last one of you stinks! Never seen such a thing—boys wastin' their every day talkin' 'bout holes, and dirt in holes, and dirt out of holes. I keep my ear to the ground, you know, Indian style. Think I don't hear that diggin' around of yours? Think you're foolin' me? Think you're foolin' anybody? You know, when you raise three sheets to the wind you're liable to quickly go somewhere you ought really not go." With that, Ol' Cuss swung his dishcloth over his shoulder, headed for the kitchen, muttered as he went something or other about having fish to fry, better fish to fry.

Ol' Cuss—Cuss to his friends, and Captain Jack to anyone my age—is a living legend in Best. Having sailed the Grand Banks as a young man, he actually has lived the life most Besterners only dream of. Ol' Cuss' saudades—'cause he has them too—have to do with the sea, always the sea. And when he has them he tells me to belly to the bar, belly right up against it. And then after pouring some brandy for himself, and then after considering a while too, he pours a little for me—pours a little for me too. Then, then that Ol' Cuss, then that Ol' Cuss he tells me stories.

He tells me stories of the sea, tells me stories about himself, tells me of how alone in a dory, and having paid out a mile-long line of hooks, he'd wait for the big catch of cod that surely would come his way. He tells me stories of how his oiled lugsail would carry him away from the other dories, away from the mother schooner too. He tells me stories of how he'd shiver in the cold, how he'd right near die in it. He tells me stories of how he and the other dory men, unable to see each other in a fog so thick you neither could spit nor pee, would fortify themselves with brandy. He tells me stories of how dory men sang, and the way they sang, and how they'd sing out songs about sweethearts back home, sweethearts lost, and sweethearts that never were.

Stories, stories, stories—stories and more stories—Ol' Cuss waves his arms when he tells them, and he tells them loudly. But long ago I learned that it was best to listen to Ol' Cuss those times when he spoke softly, spoke with his hands. That was when stories came with decisions, ended in conclusions. That was when Ol' Cuss told me his regrets, be they over having made wrong decisions, be they over having made right ones too.

"He's a spy," L.T. whispered. "Ol' Cuss is a spy."

"What?"

"He's a spy, Michael. You heard him, all that ear to the ground stuff. He's listening, listening in on everything."

"He ain't no spy. And he ain't the problem. If anything, L.T., you're the problem. If you didn't talk so loud he wouldn't hear."

"Sure he would. Don't you understand? He wants to hear. He wants to hear 'cause he wants to know everything that we're doing. He wants to know everything going on in this place. He's got built-ins, Michael, built-in antennas same as everybody here. They all got 'em. Even you got 'em."

Ollie stuck his fingers antenna-style out from 'top his head, to me looking not so much a Martian Ollie as much as an in-bred, whacked-out Ollie Martian. It bugged me, bugged me somehow to see him like this after what L.T. had said. I wasn't sure why exactly, but something about L.T.'s linking me with the "we," something about his linking me with the "they," and something about his linking my place with "this place" made me so anxious I could feel my heart flip-flop, feel my muscles tense.

"Captain Jack!" I called. "Captain Jack!"

"What, Michael?" Ol' Cuss said, running from out the

kitchen. "What? What is it? Is somethin' the matter?"

"I don't know, I'm not sure. It's probably nothing, really nothing, but can you tell that story again, Captain Jack, the one about the guy in the dory? You know, the one with the guy who kept talking and talking?"

"That one? Sure, Michael, sure I can do that." He nudged my coffee away from me, slid in beside me in the booth. Then with a good stare into space, and then with a clearing of his throat—a really good one—he was about ready, both good stare and good voice essential for any real good storytelling. At last I saw him let his eyes lock, saw him let his mind go.

"Well, boys, we was out there, way out there alright, each man and his dory."

"Out where?" Ollie asked.

"Why, the Grand Banks of course. Surely you heard of it, Ollie? Ah, the Grand Banks, the Grand Banks. Such a place, such a wonderful place, such a far off place. Why, the Grand Banks, would you believe once it had so many fish it was just impossible to count 'em all? Then again, thinkin' back, everythin' and everythin' 'bout the Banks was impossible. From the closeness of the twinklin' stars above, to the deep black of the swells below, to the ache of the broken heart inside—impossible, just impossible."

"Yeah, yeah, I heard of the place," Ollie said.

"Well, anyway, like I was sayin', we each was in our own little dory, each man and dory an island in the cold night fog, each island with saudades all its very own. Then, suddenly and all at once, somebody, somebody he starts a-singin'. And when he finishes, somebody else he starts a-singin'. And round and round and round it went. But this one fella, Italian I think, maybe Greek, he starts a-talkin' when his turn come 'round, starts a-talkin' 'stead of singin'."

"Captain Jack," Ollie said, "sorry to interrupt, but what was this guy doing way out there, you know, way out there with us?"

"Don't know. I suppose there must have been a dory or somethin' that wasn't manned and needed to be. Anyway, the thing is, this fella he wasn't Portogeez. And this fella, he wasn't Nation—certainly wasn't Nation—that much I can tell you too. So he talks, this fella, and as you know when you're talkin' you're likely as not to 'least be doin' some thinkin', and if you're doin' some thinkin' you're likely as not to be askin' some questions, both the thinkin' and the askin' not always necessarily good, for sure not always necessarily right.

"'Why aren't we more than one in a boat?' the fella asks. 'What if we tether our boats together?' he keeps askin'. 'How come you sing? What are you singin' about?' he asks, and asks some more. 'How come we don't do that, and how come we don't do this?' he winds on and on.

"Now boys, could be all this talkin' was just this fella's way of dealin' with the fog, dealin' with the swells, dealin' with the dark and the cold too. Really, I don't know. But the thing is, talkin', this sort of talkin'—it ain't our way. Christ, all this talkin' of his was doin' was makin' us crazy. It was makin' us sadder than we needed to be, makin' us sadder than we had any right to be. See, all we want, boys, is to be left alone. We don't want to be watched, we don't want to be analyzed, and for damn sure we don't want some outsider tellin' us what's best. I mean, an outsider, how does he know our swells? An outsider, how can he see our dark, understand our saudades? He can't. He doesn't. He can't understand what a sweet thing it is to remember those things we can. He doesn't understand how wonderful a thing it is to try and remember those things we can't."

"So what did you do?" Ollie asked. "I mean about him, the fella."

"What could we do? We shut ourselves up, stopped singin'. And we kept our eyes on this fella, let me tell you, kept our eyes on him till we got all the way home. We figured if we watched him he couldn't watch us, 'least he couldn't watch us very well. We figured, hey, why go and give this fella anythin' that's at all temptin'? Temptin', boys, temptin's dangerous, and nobody wants dangerous. You have to understand. Wrong people, wrong people watchin' are likelier than not to do wrong with what they watch, do wrong if not do the despicable and the cruel, the ugly and the evil. See, only we—we Best Harbor Portogeez—only we watch. Only we watch because only we can be trusted to do what's right by us—right by the Nation."

"And the Nation? The Nation watches too?"

"Watches and then some. But for the Nation it's different. The Nation watches not 'cause it should; the Nation watches 'cause it has to. It has to. Well, anyway boys, I ought be gettin' back to the kitchen, you know—fish to fry there too. Michael, Ollie, warmest saudades to your folks."

I felt better, hoped L.T. would realize what he said about Ol' Cuss being a spy was wrong, that what he hinted at about me and we, and me and they, and my place and this place couldn't possibly be right. But instead, all L.T. did instead was go back to telling Ollie of the hole creature's seared mouth. And he went into and over every last detail of its charcoaled tail too.

"No way," Ollie said. "Like no way. Charcoal? No shit, charcoal?"

"No shit," L.T. said. "Charcoal. That's how come we need somebody more reliable than Richie to help us watch these holes. We got to make sure there won't be any more charcoalin' goin' on."

"How 'bout my sister? Rook, she's 'liable. Bring her in. Right, Mook, ain't she 'liable?"

"Yeah," I said, quickly running through in my mind a checklist of her many talents. "Sure, Rookie, Rook's good."

That at last settled, L.T. turned around his Go TRIBAL cap,

a sure signal that our meeting was over. "Just one thing," he said. "So how come, how come Captain Jack didn't go wishing my mother a warm saudade?"

"He doesn't like you, L.T."

"Oh."

"Nobody likes you," Ollie added.

"Oh yeah? Yeah, Ollie? Well, know that animal we found at the hole? There's one thing more I didn't tell you. What I didn't tell you is that it'd been tied down, tied to a pole, tied down to a pole with chicken wire, and not a little amount of chicken wire, it took lots of chicken wire."

"But the animal's already dead—it's already burned. Why would the hole-filler-upper go and then tie it down?"

"I don't think you understand, Ollie. The hole-filler-upper wouldn't go and tie down the animal if it were already dead. The hole-filler-upper tied down the animal, and only then tor—"

I kicked L.T., kicked him hard, the table between us jumping so that the coffee in our mugs spilled out all over the place.

Tormented? Torched? Tortured? Whatever. Whatever it was L.T. was about to say, the hole-filler-upper, I knew, had done it all.

"Only then what?" Ollie asked. "What do you mean?"

"Nothin'. I didn't mean nothin'," L. T. said, rubbing his shin. "So anyway," he went on, "like what exactly is this saudade thing anyhow? And Nation, like what's up with that?"

Nation, I knew, while different from saudade, was kind of like it too—it too a notion never explained, and yet somehow understood. But not wanting to even try and explain either of the notions to someone the likes of L.T.—let alone have someone the likes of him in particular—possibly understand Nation, I shut up and kicked Ollie—kicked him just to make sure he too knew to shut himself up. Ollie, though, Ollie was cool, and I was glad to see he was. As for L.T. though, he eyed me, and he eyed Ollie, eyed the both of us as if we not only were in cahoots, but were cahoots.

Coffee like mud at the bottom of my cup, coffee stains along its sides like dirt, I worried I was out of control, feared I was, feared I was getting way too dangerous. I mean I was kicking everybody—kicking everybody in sight—and for the life of me I just did not know who it was I kicked the hardest: L.T., Ollie, or myself.

3

When we left Captain Jack's, Ollie took off to do whatever it was he did—that naturally and of course leaving L.T. to do what he did, namely hang with me like a puppy dog that just doesn't quite know what to do with itself. I had some ideas what L.T. could do with himself. But for now, at least, I just hinted at them, tried being semi-polite though certainly not nice.

Then with L.T. in tow, we bounced our way all up, and all down, and all over Best's Main Street. I mean from Best Sporting Goods, to Benny Booksmith, to Iced Iggy's Ice Cream, I ran L.T. into all of them—and just as quickly ran myself out of them—and still nothing worked. I just couldn't shake him.

"Go home," I said. "Go home, L.T."

Kneeling as if to tie his sneakers, L.T. lagged a while, but soon enough was again on my trail. "My Mom's in Fall River," he at last said. "Shopping for the weekend," he went and explained.

Despite L.T. being just about the coolest kid I know, there's something kind of off there, something kind of pathetic there too. I mean, like L.T., he bounces funny, careens around and around like a pockmarked, off-kilter pinball in search of a groove. Without brothers, without even any sisters, he's alone—is that way more than he wants to be, is that way more than he should be. As for his father—as for him, the best I can tell he's in California, in California out surfing.

Me? As for me, I don't much mind being alone. Actually, sometimes I even kind of like it. The way I see it is—if I'm not doing much of anything, then I'd just as soon not do much of anything by myself. Like I've got stuff to sort, other people just getting in the way. And though there's always more still that I've yet to sort, that stuff I have sorted has left me with a hunch—one I think I might even just like. Then again, I just might not like it—what the Hell do I know?

L.T.? Him? Yeah, he's got stuff to sort too, the difference being he's barely even begun making a dent in his. His hunches are pretty much just stuff he throws up in the air, all he really just doing is just stabbing at air. Not that L.T. doesn't have at least some faith in his hunches, but he's smart enough to know that they in all likelihood aren't very real, are a little too impossible to be possible. That must be hard, I think, to believe in something and yet know different at the same time. It might even just be harder than to believe in something and yet act different at the same time.

But back to L.T., back to him, I think he figures the stuff he needs to sort is just so hard it'd be better—better and more devious—simply to stir through other people's stuff, mine especially. That—that at least is what I think.

Main Street makes up just one side of the triangle that's Best Harbor's Village Green, Saint Peter's Church making up the better part of another side, and a couple of fancy old houses making up the last side. All tidy enough, I guess, but once away from the Village Green, Best Harbor's streets get all messed up. I mean crooked streets branch off to even more crooked lanes, each crooked route falling apart, every crooked route turning to nothing. In the end all the crooked routes wind up as only rotting apple orchards, as just drying pumpkin patches, only orchards, just patches.

Though the river way is the surest and simplest way of going home, I naturally and of course took L.T. the apple-and-pumpkin way—took him that way in hopes it would shake him, would maybe make him give in, would maybe make him give up. But I should have known: L.T. doesn't give up. He doesn't. He just doesn't. He doesn't give in, he doesn't give up, he doesn't give a shit. And for my troubles, all my crooked ways did was just leave me there teetering on the brink of dehydration, the verge of sunstroke, the outermost edge of heat stroke—like, my God, heat stroke!

I sat myself down on an old stone fence and, head in hands, stared at the bleak landscape around me, and at the brown dirt below me, and back again at the bleakness, it wavering now—undulating too—the whole damn thing enough to push me right from the brink, the verge, the edge, and straight to a Hellish seasickness—one knowing no bottom, knowing no end.

L.T., he meanwhile kept himself busy by removing stones from the stone fence right under my ass, and then checking their underbellies for like God-only-knew what. Basically, as best I could tell, basically what he was doing, and all he was doing, was undoing all the handiwork of some nut who two hundred years ago painstakingly built this fence to separate corn field from corn field, cow pasture from cow pasture.

Carefully tracing each stone's edge with his finger, he squatted to study how each stone came precisely to rest upon the other, why each stone exactly came to be where it be. Then, upon finishing with a stone, he tossed it—like that he just tossed it—tossed it aside so as to simply go on to the next.

I had to stop it!

Springing off the fence, I got right in his face. "What are

you doing? Like what the hell do you think you're doing, L.T.? Leave the fence, leave it alone!"

I'm bigger than L.T. and, dehydration or not, I think I'm stronger. And I think he thinks I'm stronger too. So carefully fitting the stone in his hands back into its place in the fence, L.T. backed up, held his now empty hands up in the air.

"But, Michael, don't you want to know?"

"Don't I want to know what?"

"Secrets."

"Secrets?"

"Yeah, secrets. You know, the secrets of the stones, the mystery of the fence."

"There is no mystery of the fence, you idiot. Besides, just figuring out who's filling up the holes you got us digging is mystery 'nough."

"Okay, okay then. So long as you think it is."

I gave him a push, he gave me a smile, and despite myself, I found myself smiling too.

The nearer we got to Spit the more and more L.T. ran ahead, each time waiting for me to catch up before again bolting— Hell-bent, of course—to get himself there, and get me there, just get the both of us there just as quickly as possible.

"That's it. That's it," I at last had to say, my shaky hands on my shaky knees. "I'm not running any more." I was gasping, white sunstroke spots and black heatstroke spots popping up before my eyes, popping up pretty much all over the place. For all I knew, or could now care, I truly was going to Hell, L.T. dragging me there, and me all too ready to let myself go and get dragged there.

Resting behind a tree, we took stock of our situation, 'least took stock of it as we saw it. And without so much as really a spoken word, me and L.T. understood just where we were, just what was happening, and just what it was we now were about to do.

Looking down on Spit, seeing the people, seeing them where they lived, seeing them there on the inside; seeing ourselves, seeing ourselves here, seeing ourselves here on the outside—to us, Spit was a fortress, its inhabitants dug-in troops, while we, meanwhile, were the advance scouts, ready to scout, ready, too, to infiltrate.

Flanking Old Willow Mill with a classic backdoor maneuver, we pretty much were in before we knew it, in deepest darkest Spit before we even gave a thought to thinking about it. Split rail fences and grass-green lawns, tall leafy bushes and sharp thorny flowers, front door flags and gray-shingled houses, the flags they hung very red, quite white, and truly true blue. And with brown welcome mats spread out before brown maple doors, and shiny brass knockers centered above bright brass doorknobs, it all certainly seemed at first glance to be welcoming enough.

But upon a second look, and a third take, was it truly welcoming? Peepholes, I knew them for the looking out, certainly and by no means for the looking in. And as for the closed screen doors, they not only were closed, but the front doors themselves, they were closed. What's more, I knew them not only to be closed, I knew them to be locked.

"It's a trap," L.T. whispered.

"Yeah, camouflage," I said.

We dropped to the ground, crawled under a fence railing, slithered our way around a hedge. Though the neighborhood itself by and large seemed tranquil enough, it was anything but inside the house we targeted for surveillance. Clanging metal utensils, the buzzing hum of activity, the barking of orders here and the issuing of commands there, the house truly was a fortress. And it was a pretty familiar one at that, the fortress, after all, not just being a house, but being my home.

Now about to look at the family on the inside from the outside—and at the same time knowing the family on the inside from the inside—I suddenly felt queasier than I already was feeling. These people, who are they? I mean these people, who are these people, my family? Like what do they do when no one is watching? Who are they when no one is watching? Who are they when by themselves?

Finding that out at long last was about to maybe be real, maybe too real. This moment, I'd long dreaded it, and I'd long anticipated it too.

Just as I was about to tell L.T. that maybe this particular house wasn't such a good idea, and that maybe this whole thing really wasn't all that bright of an idea, he said, "Cover me! Cover me, Cover Boy!" And with that, he took off. With a sprint across the lawn and a headfirst dive right into a clump of tall bushes, his hand emerged moments later to signal that he was okay, wave me in.

I sprang from my crouch, picked up speed, and just a few mere feet away from the bushes—I tripped, the culprit my very own shoelace.

Flat on my face, eyeball to eyeball with dirt, I could just hear L.T. laughing, and laughing much too giddily at that. Then, with a crawl from out the bushes, he dragged me to their cover, his laugh by now a chuckle—still an all too giddy chuckle.

"Leave me. Leave me be, L.T. Save yourself."

"You okay?"

"I think so," I said, checking my knees for blood, checking my elbows too. "But you—you're an asshole. Know that? Like, you are such an asshole."

"Me? Hey, what did I do, other, that is, than just save your life?"

"Oh, yeah? Yeah, L.T.? Well, like, who asked you to? I was fine. And my life, like that was just fine too."

"Sure, sure—flat on your face like that. Do you even know

how out of it you were, how out of it you are? Like, do you, Michael? I mean I bet you can't even tell your up from your down."

"Like look who's talking. You're the one who's lost, L.T. And everyone knows it, everyone that is but you."

I regretted it, regretted saying it the moment I said it; wished I could somehow take it back. Seeing L.T.'s eyes quiver, I saw them go down. Then, then I saw them go away.

'I'm sorry,' I wanted to say. 'You're not lost,' I also wanted to say. But saying any such thing only would have let L.T. know I knew; would only have let him understand I understood.

"Screw these sons-of-bitches laces," I said instead. "So now, like what now, Sarge?"

L.T.'s answer was a stomach crawl on knees and elbows from the bushes to the basement window, followed then by a sticking of face right up to glass. Peering in from just over his shoulder, I could see my mother, could see my grandmother and my Aunt Lolly too, in the basement kitchen cooking. Their sleeveless arms glistening in sweat, the kerchiefs on their heads were soaked through and through. A fire blazed in the fireplace, and in the nearby dining room I could see my big sister, Patty, place white napkins onto white tablecloth, place white napkins onto white tablecloth. Dishes, my mother's best, were set for what looked to be about twenty people, and when Patty finished placing the very last napkin by the very last dish, she went over to the kitchen to kneel with a dustpan in hand and collect whatever Grandma swept together.

Suddenly a dough ball whizzed by Patty's head, whizzed and then exploded like a fireball in the fireplace. But a second round, and a second dough ball, caught Patty, caught her square in the back.

"Patty's been hit!" L.T. said. "She's under attack! We got to do something. What are we gonna do, Michael?" he said, shaking me by the shoulders. "What, what we gonna do?"

"Nothing, you idiot, we do nothing. Patty should've known better. She should've known that the only thing more dangerous than Aunt Lolly's baking is her aim. It's Patty's fault. She should've gotten herself out the line of fire."

"But Lolly, she's glaring! She's like glaring, Michael! I mean, look at her. Look at the size of her. She'll squash Patty. She'll squash her like a bug!"

"Yeah, Aunt Lolly is big alright. My father says Aunt Lolly's strong—'strong like boooll.'"

With a wave of Patty away from the fireplace, Aunt Lolly again went to lobbing dough balls, lobbing them right at the fireplace, into the fireplace. Patty, meanwhile, poor Patty, she sulked her way over to Mom, helped her crack eggs on the lip of a bowl. And after the cracking of one particular egg, I saw Mom shake her head, show something in the yolk to Patty, and toss that particular egg straight to the garbage.

Usually I stay clear of Costa women when they're in the kitchen, the commotion really something I'd rather not see. But looking in on them from the vantage point of the basement window, I saw stuff I'd never before bothered to see, saw stuff that now bothered me. Why was the dustpan emptied into the fire? Why were dough balls thrown into the fire? Just what was wrong with the egg that was tossed to the garbage?

"What's up with the fire, anyway?" L.T. whispered. "It's a hundred degrees or something here. And your kitchen, what's it doing in the basement, you know, hidden in by bushes? And that, that there?" he said pointing to the backyard, "what's that?"

"That? That's a shed."

"I can see that. I mean, what's with the clucking?"

"Chickens."

"Chickens? Chickens for what, eggs?"

"Yeah, that too."

"Well, I'm going in for a look. Cover me again, Cover Boy."

Dashing from the cover of the bushes, L.T. disappeared behind the shed's far wall when suddenly, and all at once, he again was in view, back in view again and bouncing—I mean actually bouncing—just bouncing, bouncing, bouncing all along the ground, just all over it. "I'm hit," he groaned, rising to his knees, about to pass out, and pass out but good.

With a blowing of my cover, I rushed over to help. Easing him to the ground, I slapped him lightly across the face to see if it'd revive him, slapped him again just for calling me 'Cover Boy', and for good measure slapped him some more—and harder—for no real particular reason I could think of. Suddenly something—a humongous shadow or something—hovered over the backyard, just about blocked out 'least half of it. Turning, I squinted into the sun, and there, there and looming over us—'least sideways over us—stood my Uncle Jiggy.

At about five foot four, Uncle Jiggy's a Portuguese muffin short of two-fifty, All-county as a high school nose tackle. Grandpa calls Uncle Jiggy a 'five by five,' I think he actually likes calling him a 'five by five.' My bet—my bet is he can still take my Aunt Lolly.

"Hello, Mookie."

"Hello, Uncle Jiggy. What are you doing here?"

What with me and L.T. sprawled out as we were all over the backyard, even to my ears my question sounded pretty ridiculous. Ridiculous too in its own way was the shimmering slimy something or other getting reflected off of Uncle Jiggy's white apron, a sort of butcher's apron. Shading my eyes to better see the shimmering slimy something or other—God, please let it be only chicken slimy something or other—I leaned on back into the shade cast by Uncle Jiggy's shadow, his humongous shadow of a shadow.

Blood, like real blood—and not just a little of it but a lot of it—covered Uncle Jiggy, covered him from head to toe. I mean there was so much blood that the apron itself was bleeding. Red sticky polka dots obliterated Uncle Jiggy's face, obliterated his hands too.

"You know," L.T. said, "normal people apologize when running over someone half their size. Then again, normal people, they don't even go running over other people in the first place."

I looked at L.T., could see his own blood from his getting bounced all along the ground just oozing and mingling with the blood Uncle Jiggy had just smeared him with. I think I then said something to L.T. about how a bit later on I was gonna kill him, how it wasn't bright to antagonize a 'five by five', especially antagonize that 'five by five' when he happens just to be standing right over him. It was less bright still—and a whole lot scary—to then see Uncle Jiggy carefully take out a knife from under his apron, the knife very long, and very sharp, and very, very bloody.

"You're family, Mookie. Too bad for your friend he isn't."

"He's sorry, Uncle Jiggy. Really he is, he's sorry. Right, L.T.? You're sorry? Aren't you real sorry?"

"No, I ain't sorry."

"Yes, you are. Sure you are."

"No. No I'm not."

"Yes, you are."

"No I'm not."

"Yes, you are."

"No, I'm not."

"Yes, you are; yes, you are; yes, you are! L.T., you're really, really, really sorry!"

With that, L.T. shut up—a good thing, too, because I didn't know how much longer I could keep on insisting just how really sorry he really was.

"And you, Mookie?" Uncle Jiggy asked. "You, what's your story?"

"Me? My story?" I wasn't sure what Uncle Jiggy was asking, didn't know what he wanted to hear. "Heatstroke?"

"What?"

"Nothin', nothin', Uncle Jiggy. Me, yeah, I'm sorry too. My story, it's also real sorry. Me, L.T.—all of us are sorry, just sorry, sorry, sorry." I bowed my head, scratched at the ground like some miserable caged chicken, a pretty pathetic chicken at that.

"So what is it that you're sorry about, Mookie?"

"You know . . ." Most of all I was sorry we got caught, not that I could very well go telling that to Uncle Jiggy. I also couldn't tell him I was sorry for what it was that we'd been doing. I mean how could I tell him I was sorry I spied on my family, watched when they didn't know I watched? Worse still, how could I tell him I was sorry for watching with someone who not only wasn't a Spitter, but was someone the likes of L.T.? No, saying anything, saying anything at all just now, it'd be an admission of guilt, would pretty much be a confession.

A truck rolled on up the drive—Dad now home from his shift at the plant. Holding a bag of dry-cleaned clothes in one hand, and holding a bouquet of flowers for Mom in the other, he looked especially tired. The very last thing he needed seeing was this, this fiasco: a wounded L.T., bloody and bleeding all over the yard; a pissed-off Uncle Jiggy, blood-soaked and wielding a knife as if it were a fly-swatter; and me, idiot me, his eldest son guilty and looking like sin, just pathetically standing there and kicking up his newly-seeded lawn.

"Go inside," Dad told L.T. "We'll clean you up. You too, Michael, into the house."

I trudged up the backyard stairs right behind L.T., Dad staying behind awhile to talk to Uncle Jiggy. And by the time the screen door even had time to shut behind us, already Mom, Aunt Lolly, Grandma—even Patty—were up from the basement to see what all the commotion was about. Horror-stricken faces, hands pressed onto those horror-stricken faces—the scene was as bad as it got, and then some.

"Michael, are you alright?"

Seeing as I was—or at least seeing I was about as all right as I ever got—Mom grabbed her first aid box to tend to L.T., Aunt Lolly meanwhile steering me to the sofa to tend to me. The casualties all the while, they kept coming: first Uncle Jiggy, as red as the blood he was covered in, and then Dad, looking just about as steamed as the heat outside. I mean so much, so fast, and so wrong, was going down, I worried L.T. would get the impression that we were dysfunctional or something.

What with my wounds turning out to be nothing more than run-of-the-mill shock, and Dad's wounds turning out to be nothing more than run-of-the-mill disappointment in me, Aunt Lolly left me to check on Uncle Jiggy while Mom left L.T. to consult with Dad. Hushed whispers, sidelong glances—it didn't take much to see that the whispers and the glances had everything to do with me, that's to say, what me and L.T. had been up to.

With the base of his hand, Dad dabbed sweat from his face, suddenly and quickly got up to come my way. Putting his hands on his knees, he got his face in mine. "What are we, Michael? I mean what are we to you? The enemy? Is that it? Is that who we are?"

It was a real question, a real question asked with all sincerity. And I answered it with silence, anything else likely to bring a slap to the face. Beyond that, though—much more than that—I said nothing because Dad's question hurt. How could he think I thought such a thing? Didn't he know that our snooping was goofing, 'least for the most part just goofing? Did he really think I would betray them? Betray them how? Betray them over what?

I must have looked like I was about to cry because the

next thing I knew Mom was at my side, at my side using her hands to wipe my face. She looked me in the eye, gave me a hug anyway.

Having by now ditched the bloody apron, Uncle Jiggy came out of the bathroom with his face washed clean of any bad blood. Giving me a belt on the shoulder, he gave me a wink, L.T. all the while just sitting in a corner, just sitting there nibbling on some cookies and sipping on some milk, just taking it in, taking it all in.

"Mrs. Costa," he said. "Can I stay for supper? My mother's in Fall River and she wouldn't mind. I can give you her cell number if you want."

Mom looked at Dad, and he at her. He shook his head. "You need to go. I'll take you home, L.T."

Glad as I was to see L.T. go, I kind of wasn't glad to see him go. Mom and Dad were now free to dump all their anger on me, all their disappointment too. But I had some of that stuff going too—in fact I had lots of it—and I was oh so close to using it too. I mean would it have killed them to let L.T. stay for supper? Was it such a big deal to let L.T. stay, stay if only for a while?

I closed my eyes, got myself away, got myself way the hell away. Here to there. Now to then. Down the river and over to the Bay ... I knew the way.

Creaking, creaking, creaking—the caravel's timbers creaked as if crying. Twitching, twitching, twitching—the caravel's sails twitched as if sobbing. Dark clouds chasing from behind, white fog looming up on ahead, lightning in the horizon and thunder down below—just where to go ... where to go ... where to go? Mouths open without sound, eyes crying without tears, those on board were too accustomed to clouds, were just all too familiar with fog. And familiar too were they, the damned to me, and yet not one single face could I recognize.

Sails filling at once, they filled as if one. And wildly pitching sternward, and wilder still pitching portside, surely the ship it would soon capsize. Howling wind and raging sea, sounds exploding from mouths and tears gushing from eyes, the ship was on the move now, really clipping. Heading for a bay, it entered and stalled, so unsure as to the where, just so unsure as to the here. So on it sailed, on and on into yet one more bay, one smaller even than the first. There slipping into a river, it slipped in deep, but not too deep; put in with sails down, but oars out; tucked in with hopes high, but certainly not pie in the sky. For it had been in other seas before, and other bays as well, and other rivers and other waters, and it knew—knew only too well—that where it went and wherever it went, others also would go, go for so long and so far as they could go. But this river, this particular and peculiar river, this river was different. This one had a cove, one around the bend, and it not only was hidden, it was made of cobble, made of gravel.

Ordering his men to camouflage the ship in vegetation, the ship's captain then directed them in the unloading of provisions. But not all went unloaded; some provisions remaining on board, and out of view, and in reserve should anchor one day have to quickly be lifted. For even now, even as the sun shone on their faces, and their mouths smiled, and their eyes gleamed, still their heads turned ever so subtly, reluctantly, fearfully to the sea. And yet, strangely, there was also something else in their turn, something that for lack of an explanation seemed somehow to be as if purposeful, longing, almost hopeful, actually hopeful.

I opened my eyes, felt air escaping from the sofa cushion as Aunt Lolly sat herself down beside me. Though I'd been to there and then many a time before, the caravel had only been an impression, the people on board a glimpse, the dark clouds above a feeling. But this time the caravel, the people, the clouds, they really rattled me, to me were as real as the monster saudade rising inside me.

Provisions, they should have been unloaded—never were. Essentials, they long ago went missing—and yet still were missed.

But what provisions? What essentials? I didn't know. The only thing I knew was I missed them. But if I somehow were ever to know what essentials went missing, did I miss them enough to go get them, actually go and get them? For that matter, could I even go and get them? I mean if I got them, what kind of Portogeez would I then be without a saudade? And if I somehow actually did manage to get them, what kind of Nation could I be without my saudade, my very own personal one, that particular one?

I was sure other kids got themselves the hell away better than this, had to. Last second shots, ninth inning homers, Hail-Mary touchdown passes, their daydreams were about scoring on the field, and off it too. So next time, I told myself, it'd just be football on the beach for me, me and Rook, just touch and sand, just us getting it on, just us getting it done.

"A young boy like you shouldn't look so sad."

"Aunt Lolly, quit tickling me," I said, squirming, trying—but not trying too hard—to get myself away.

"You know, nobody knows better than me that this family's not easy. But this one is the one you got."

"Not easy I could understand. Really I could. But Aunt Lolly—Aunt Lolly, we're insane."

"So," she said, with another tickle, "so what do you want for dinner?"

"Yes, Michael, what would you like to eat?" Grandma, sitting to my other side, said. What with her beefy arms pinning me as they were, and what with Aunt Lolly's even beefier hips squeezing me as they were, the vice felt good, felt safe.

"You're too skinny, my poor Michael, much too skinny," she went on. "You need *malassadas*. They're warm and sugary, Michael, just made."

"Sure, Grandma," I said, her hand on my belly reminding me how hungry I was. "Some soda too, please. I'm thirsty.

Actually I'm real thirsty."

As Grandma got herself up, Aunt Lolly leaned on in. "The Pereiras and the Oliveiras are coming for dinner, Mookie. And you know who else is going to be here?"

"Who?"

"Rookie."

I figured that. But just the same I felt better simply hearing her name.

"Ollie, he'll be here too, of course."

Of course.

When Grandma returned with malassadas, she went to my other side again, she leaning in too. "You really like her, don't you, Michael?"

"'Cause, Rookie, she sure likes you," Aunt Lolly said.

I gulped the iced soda, picked at a malassada, grateful that L.T. wasn't now here to see this particular blow-by-blow round of in-family matchmaking.

"Rookie, she's going to be the princess at the Holy Ghost Feast."

"I know, Aunt Lolly. Like she's only mentioned that to me about a hundred times."

"She's a wonderful girl, Michael, just wonderful."

"You know what," I said. "I think I can hear Billy out back. I'm gonna go and play catch with him, okay?" I said, rocking myself free and feeling the air rush back into my lungs.

"Half an hour, Billy," I heard Mom yell from the window. "Then in you go for a bath."

"An hour."

"Half an hour, Billy. And for dinner I want you to wear your new shirt."

"Okay, half an hour, and the new shirt, but no bath."

"Listen, Billy. I'll give you forty-five minutes to play, but that's with the bath and the shirt."

Noticing me standing out on the deck, Mom said, "Michael,

you too. You too," she said pulling me into this thing without so much as even missing a beat. "Clean yourself up. And dress normally for a change, okay?"

Billy gave me a look, but seeing as how I only was watching, and only would watch, he went to playing with a tennis ball, bouncing it up and against the garage. Of course the outcome of his negotiations with Mom hadn't in the least surprised me. Sure, while she had size going for her—power, too—Billy had stubbornness and cuteness. They made a sure-fire winning combo nine times out of every ten.

In some ways it would've been great being Billy's age again, but seeing as I was thirteen, almost fourteen, I no longer had his advantages. At my age stubbornness wasn't cool. And cuteness, that was going, going, gone with every pimple on my face and every hair on my body.

Sooner and not later, they'd have a sit-down with me about this spying thing. And they'd tell me it was stupid, tell me it was wrong, tell me it was so much worse than wrong that it violated everything, most especially violated everything like family trust—stuff like that. But would they actually talk to me? Like would anything get actually explained? I mean if things were explained maybe next time I wouldn't go spying, 'least maybe I wouldn't go spying with L.T.

Anyway, now that I had spied—spied on them—what was it that I saw anyway? Whatever it was, it must have been important, that much for sure, what with everybody freakin' the way they were. As for L.T., as for him, now for sure and for certain he knew that not only were we weird, we were really, really weird. And as for me, now I knew beyond any doubt at all that not only were we peculiar, we were really, really peculiar.

My parents, I'm guessing, probably they'll go calling this spying thing something like 'our little incident,' or 'our little mistake,' go calling it that if for no other reason than calling it 'your colossal fuck-up,' just would be too cruel. However Father

Sousa in his sermons says there is no little—says incidents are incidents, says mistakes are mistakes, says wrong is wrong, says those doing the wrong have sinned and are screwed, leastwise they're screwed if no penance is done. Not that Father Sousa says any of this kind of stuff to me, mind you. I mean he doesn't even look my way when sermonizing, doesn't even look anywhere near my way.

Maybe that's 'cause we Spitters, near as I can tell, don't believe in the same kind of Hell Father Sousa believes in. Maybe that's 'cause we Spitters, near as I can tell, don't see incidents involving us as being mistakes, leastwise mistakes for us. Maybe that's 'cause we Spitters, near as I can tell, don't see things we do as wrong, leastwise wrong for us. Lastly, maybe Father Sousa doesn't look my way 'cause we Spitters, near as I can tell, don't do penance, leastwise we don't do the same kind of penance expected of others.

Penance? We simply don't seek advice from a priest in a confessional on how to repent. We simply don't want any middlemen handing over absolutions to us. I mean if ever I actually was ever to do something so sinful I risked approaching even any kind of Hell, my family, knowing for themselves just what to do, would first go raise holy Hell with me, and then, if I still was to somehow wind up there, go storm right on in for to get me. Penance? Penance is a rite we simply do not do, 'least not if we can help it.

Penance? We pray. We only pray, and we pray only directly to God. And forgiveness, if there is to be any, that's only for Him to decide. I mean there's no how-to, there's no middlemen, and for that matter no guaranteed forgiveness. And the praying that we do do—I'm pretty sure that in any sort of real crisis that only would come some time after the raising of holy Hell, or the storming of it.

I went on inside and went down to the kitchen, Patty there

checking on the food and double-checking the place settings. Upon seeing me she just rolled her eyes—sighed too—just her little way of showing me just how much I'd screwed things up this time.

Grandpa, he too was in the kitchen, his rocking chair several feet from the fireplace and rocking. I sat down cross-legged on the floor beside him, watched a long time as the fire in the fireplace turned to tinder, turned to sparks. Reflected in Grandpa's eyes—there too I saw sparks, sparks shiny and bright, the still remaining sparks brighter and shinier than any fire's afterglow really had any right of being. Leaning my elbows down onto the insides of my knees, and putting my chin firmly in my hands, I went back to watching the fireplace, sparks turning now to embers, embers only all too soon to turn to dust.

Back and forth, back and forth, every forward rock of Grandpa's chair squeaked, and every backward rock squealed. Right hand finding the back of my neck, his strong fingers rubbed my neck, kneaded it as would a trainer in a fighter's corner. And all the while his rocking chair rocked fast, and then rocked faster still.

My watch a stare—the last sparks and embers kicked off a flurry of smoke, and I could just feel my head become light. Spellbound, engrossed, I was going in … going in … going in. I was going back.

White candles set back deep in the hearth, white candles set deep inside silver candlesticks, white candles set deep, and just waiting to be lit.

Fridays! Of course, Fridays.

4

What with our kayaks tethered to the big maple at Chaippascutt Point, me and L.T. took a step back, the both of us, I think, pretty much reaching the same conclusion at the same time: though our kayaks now were secure, we now were anything but. My Pungo, L.T.'s Pamlico, they were neon lights, for crying out loud—big yellow and orange neon lights that might just as well have been broadcasting public service announcements—L.T.'s going something like, 'Hey everyone, come see us stick it up the Hole-filler-upper's ass,' mine going something like, 'Hey everyone, come see the idiots do their idiot show.'

"Yeah, L.T., this'll sure get the hole-filler-upper's attention alright. But it'll probably get everyone's, including that of my parents. And just so you know, while they're good and pissed at me, they're really, really pissed at you, think you're no good, just no good at all. You're the devil to them. You're the devil, L.T. I think I heard them say something about an anti-Christ."

L.T. had no comeback, 'the incident' at the house I think shaking him, showing him just how crazy we Costas were, and Uncle Jiggy showing him just how psycho we Costas could get.

Having dragged our kayaks to the woodsy area beyond the big maple, we were just about done camouflaging them when who shows up but Richie Silva—he of course riding his bike over, the bike's wheels kicking up a cloudburst of dust, the cloudburst probably seen all the way from 'top Mt. Washington.

"I thought we were cutting Richie out of the loop," I mumbled.

"I couldn't let him go," L.T. mumbled back. "He's promising not to screw up his shift again. Besides, do you have any idea just how few kids there are willing to watch a hole in the middle of the night?"

"A dearth?"

"Huh?"

"Not many."

"You got that right. And once Richie's up, like actually out of bed, he's really up. The boy's a coffee drinkin' fiend!"

"He's a what?"

"He drinks a lot of coffee."

Richie, Richie he's sensitive; takes too much to heart. So when he let his fucking bike drop right in the middle of the fucking path, I tried to be nice, really I did.

"Hey, Richie, you nincompoop. Get your friggin' bike off the friggin' path. Can you do that? Please. Okay?"

And still Richie blushed, his reddish hair red as if on fire. It was just what me and L.T. had worried about when first recruiting Richie, that he'd one day just up and spontaneously combust, give away the location of our hard-dug holes, sabotage the whole operation.

"Stop it, Richie. Just stop it! For Pete's sake, you're lighting up the sky, like—the daytime sky! Can you stop long enough to at least just let us know where Rookie's at? Can you do that?"

"Rook? Rook's on the way. She doesn't ride fast like me."

"And Ollie?"

"Ollie? Ollie's walking. You know, lollygagging."

"He's what?"

"He's on Ollie-time."

As Richie went to go help himself to a shovel, L.T. went to go help himself to a pose. Sticking a big wet-willie in Richie's ear, he held the finger up to the air. "That's interesting," he said, looking to his compass.

"What's interesting," Richie asked, sitting down on a dead pine. He was by now concentrating so hard on L.T.'s now begun dog-and-pony show that I fully expected seeing a red bulb light up his face, half expected seeing red question marks follow in line behind the red bulb.

As for me, I lay down on my side, sucked on a blade of grass, marveled at L.T.'s abilities to absolutely hocus-pocus all those willing to get themselves hocused-pocused. L.T., he calls this little hocus-pocus thing of his 'Dead Reckoning.' Me, I call it 'Baloney.'

"You see, Richie, in olden days great explorers like Columbus and great sailors like Miguel Cortereal didn't only use celestial navigation, they also used Dead Reckoning. By studying their compasses and seeing the direction in which they were headed, and by also tracking distances they knew they could cover in a given amount of time, they more or less could figure out on their maps where they were—that is if they had any maps."

"Yeah? Really, L.T.? Really?"

"Yeah, Richie, really. Their records are right there in their Captain's Logs."

"Dead Reckoning," Richie said. "Dead Reckoning," he repeated, more so for himself. "Sounds piratey, L.T."

"Does at that, Richie. You know, Captain Kidd and Blackbeard, they even had a funny saying about it. 'Dead Reckon right and live right. Dead Reckon wrong and die wrong!'"

"Funny, those pirates," I said. "Funny guys. The sad thing,

Richie, is most people live their entire lives never truly knowing just how really funny those pirates were."

L.T. picked out a pinecone, whipped it at me.

"Okay," Richie said, "I sort of understand how Dead Reckoning helped pirates know where they were. But how's that gonna help us find their treasure?"

I rolled another blade of grass in my mouth, rolled myself down onto my back. "This, this Richie, this is where it starts to get really interesting."

"I've devised a brand new way of using Dead Reckoning," L.T. said. "See, Richie, because pirates used it to figure out where they were, we can use it to figure out where they were. And once we do that we then can figure out where their treasure is. It's just a question of Dead Reckoning the way they Dead Reckoned."

"Which is how?" I asked, just so as to help Richie out.

L.T. took a stick, began drawing on the ground. "Pirates had to hide their treasure. So what they would do is sail themselves away from open-ocean, head for Narragansett Bay and then Mt. Hope Bay. But because even Mt. Hope wasn't safe enough from people after their treasure, they rowed small boats up the Taunton. Naturally though, they made sure never to go too far up. If they went too far up, if they went too far in, it'd make it all the tougher to get at the treasure should the coast clear."

I scrunched my eyebrows, admired the way L.T. could make anything sound almost reasonable, almost possible, almost doable. Hearing L.T. say it, pirate treasure hiding sounded a little like Miguel Cortereal treasure hiding, actually a lot like it. "Richie. Are you paying attention?"

"Yeah, Mookie. The pirates stopped rowing 'cause their arms got tired."

This time around L.T. threw a rock at me, a look too, the rock just missing, the look not missing. "Richie," L.T. said, "sure pirates didn't want to row any further than about a day upriver 'cause their arms got tired, but the main reason they didn't row further was 'cause that way it'd be easier to re-find their treasure. Instructions to re-find the treasure would simply say to do a day's worth of rowing. That way instructions weren't long, directions weren't complicated."

"Instructions? Instructions for who? Directions for who?"

"Instructions and directions for those coming later. See, Richie, not everybody made it, not everybody made it back. Instructions and directions were to help those coming later re-find their treasure. They were to help those coming later re-treasure their treasure. After all finding treasure is one thing, but treasure can only really be treasure if it's treasured."

"Oh, give me a break," I said. "Directions? You mean like row a day upriver then hang a left at the Burger King?"

"Richie," L.T. said, this time hitting me on the foot with a rock, "if you do a day's rowing upriver from Mt. Hope, you know where you wind up?"

"Here?"

"Here at this very spot," I said. "All makes perfect sense to me."

"Richie, don't pay any attention to Michael. Michael's an idiot. Dead Reckoning works. There is this one problem though I need to tell you about, something capable of gumming the whole thing up."

"What's that?"

"Drift."

"Drift?"

"That's right, Drift."

"The dreaded D word," I said.

Drift is something that weighs heavy on L.T.'s mind. His Drift theory goes like this: over time there are forces that change the direction of everything. And it happens slowly, happens slowly this change, this Drift, happens so slowly that it's not noticed, is not seen. L.T.'s theory is a belief, a belief in

Drift being everywhere, affecting all things. From the best of best-laid plans to the best of best-navigated ships, Drift steers both off course.

"Corrections for Drift have to be made, Richie, adjustments have to be made. Usually tweaks are enough, but there are times when even just the littlest of tweaks cause big problems for Dead Reckoning."

"How's that, L.T.?"

"Well, as hard as it is to know in what direction to tweak, it's even harder to know how much. Too much is not a good thing. Too much and you knock everything off-kilter. Too much and you might even knock it all in the opposite direction, the wrong one."

Richie nodded, the full ramifications of Drift Theory sinking in, turning a once simple and carefree Richie into what would no doubt now be a tormented Richie, a Richie incapable of sleep, a Richie whose nights would be spent agonizing over every little problem of Drift, and every big consequence of it.

"Drift sucks," he said.

Now having chalked up another victim to the destructive abilities of Drift, L.T. let himself roll onto his back, let his eyes go skyward. "I don't know, Richie. Drift ain't all bad. Sure, it leads to mistakes, but it also leads to discoveries. We'll find something in these holes. And if it's not what we expect, then fine. It'll just have to be the unexpected."

Ring, Ring, Ring.

Rookie!

Riding in on her shiny red bike, Rookie rode in just in the nick of time. I mean Richie and L.T. talking Drift was like a moron and a snake oil salesman talking over all the ways grass grows right under their very feet.

I sat up just as Rookie blew by, her bike's streamers stretching out horizontal in the wind and kissing my face. With a release of the handlebars, she held her hair out and away from her perspiring neck, and gave a wave—the homecoming queen at last home to greet her adoring subjects.

"Hi guys," she said, standing on her tiptoes, straddling her bike, her white T crisp and her white smile wide. Laying a checkerboard tablecloth down to the ground, she opened a package of cheese, opened a packet of crackers, put out bunches of purple grapes and clusters of red cherries.

"You know, Rook, it's not like we're here for a picnic."

"I know that, Richie. I know why we're here. You want to check me, see if I've got the right stuff."

"We know you're cool," I said. "But you know how it is, Rook. I mean you're a Spitter. You know how it works."

"Hey, like even I went through it," L.T. said, "'least I think I went through something."

"That's right, Rook. And just look at our L.T. now. Spit just loves him. It just loves him to death."

I crouched under a barrage of cherry pits, let Rook's fingers pick them off from my shirt and shorts one by one by one.

"And here comes Ollie," Richie announced, standing to give him a round of applause.

Knock-kneeing his chunkiness on over to us, Ollie smiled his sheepish smile. "Bathroom. I had to go."

"For an hour? That's how late you are."

Ollie, he wears his shorts baggy, wears the legs way down below his knees. And by the look of it he could have been hiding a week's worth of hour-long craps in there, nobody knowing but for the stink.

"Drop it," L.T. said. "Okay, let's drop it, get the show on the road."

Moving himself to the center of the checkerboard tablecloth, he turned to Rookie. "For two weeks now a group of intrepid fortune seekers have been unearthing the buried past, the belief being that men who went so far as to bury something must be burying something important. You follow,

Rook?"

"I think so. You're digging. You're digging to find what it is Miguel Cortereal's hiding."

L.T. looked to me, his eyes open—wide, too.

"No, Rook," sighed Richie. "No, it's Captain Kidd's booty—his booty we be after."

"And Blackbeard's," Ollie added. "His too."

Rook gave her head a shake, sent wisps of hair flying from her eyes. Then, putting her hands behind her back, she looked down, and she looked up … just looked open and pure and ready. "Go."

"Rookie, are you from these parts? Have you always lived here?"

"Yes, Michael. I was born in Best Harbor, Massachusetts, in Spit to be exact. And here is where I've lived my whole life. Here too is where I've learned, though next year I'll be at Taunton Regional, same as you."

"What's your real name?" Ollie asked.

"Rachel Rose Carvahal. I was named after my great grandmother on my father's side."

"Rookie," Richie said, "I don't know exactly how to put it, but like how were you brought up? What I mean is I'm sure you're from a good family and everything, but what kind of family? Do you know what I mean?"

Rookie smiled. "I think I do. All I can tell you is that I go to Sunday school and I go to church. And even though the right road sometimes is hard, I try staying on it."

Rookie, I knew, was performing brilliantly; her answers right on, her words perfect.

"One last question from me," Ollie said. "Do you like it here? Do you like being a part of Spit Nation?"

Rookie started to answer, paused to find just the right way to put it, just the right way to do it. "The river is a big part of my life. And I'll always live near it. And if I don't actually live near it, I'll always live by it. The river flows inside of me. It always will. What I'm saying is, I love it here. And if someday I do leave Spit, still I'll be Nation, always Nation."

L.T. listened quietly, stood to the side to better see Rookie, better see us. Similar questions were raised of him and his mother when they moved to Best, the difference being that the questions posed of them had only been hinted at, never actually asked. In fact, they were hinted at so well that L.T. and his mother possibly never even appreciated that the questions had even been posed, for sure did not understand just which questions had been posed. And for sure too they did not understand the nature of the questions—just did not realize they themselves were in question. And while questions were important, answers were critical, not so much for them being asked, but for us doing the asking. By comparison though, this, this little Q and A with Rook, this basically was child's play. She already knew us; we already knew her.

While I'm pretty sure L.T. understood that this was just play, still he never stood a chance, not with questions like these, certainly not with the kinds of answers that Rook gave. He looked helpless, just so helpless I just had to smile.

I gave a thumbs-up. "She's good—knows her stuff."

"Congrats," L.T. said. "Seems you passed, Rook. Welcome to the club."

"Thanks, but is this a good thing?"

"Depends on whether you like digging," Richie said. "Depends on whether you like watching a hole in the middle of the night."

"Wait there just one minute," Rookie said. "I knew about the digging, but what's this about hole watching?"

"Well, the last couple of holes we dug got filled up, " L.T. said. "And we want to know what sort of weirdo is doing the filling. So we've been taking shifts watching the holes that we dig. And you know what, Rook? This is your lucky day—we're just about to go and dig a brand new hole."

"You are, huh? Well, lucky, lucky me."

We walked away from the dirt path, made sure to keep it to our left, keep the river to our right, and yet still somehow deal with the unending running commentary coming from L.T. up ahead. His gibberish played like background music—a little here, a little there—unfortunately never quite ignorable.

"Treasure would be buried upriver," he said. "But it'd never be buried right by the river on account of it being too easy to find. And it'd never be buried too far from the river on account of it being too much to haul. What we're doing here is following the natural breaks in the woods, the same breaks that the buriers would likely have taken. We're heading"—L.T. stopped, his gibberish stopping too as a ruffled grouse exploded to a run at his feet. Jumping, he gave out a yelp, 'least something sounding like a yelp.

"Geez, L.T., if a little grouse scares you, what are you gonna do when crazy Uncle Jiggy gets anywhere at all near you again?"

Rook and Ollie stopped in their tracks, looked to me for an explanation.

"Sorry, guys. Sorry, no offense intended."

"None taken," Rookie said. "Dad can be pretty scary. But what's this all about? Does he have it in for you or something, L.T.?"

"Who knows? I mean there I am one minute just running around minding my own business, and the next minute there he is body-slamming me. And that's after he's gone and sliced up the throats of some chickens. What's more, he threatens to do the same to me."

Just this morning, L.T. went to calling Uncle Jiggy 'the Butcher of Best'—went so far too as call him 'Attila, the Scourge of God'. And there was no doubt that if even given just half the chance he'd keep up the tirade, tirading being something he loved doing—keeping up with tyrants in history, something else he loved doing.

"That's not exactly what happened," I said. "But the hole? The hole, L.T.? Can we get back to that?"

L.T. looked around for another rock to throw at me, settled instead for flicking me the finger. "Our route's north by northwest," he said, taking the lead again, "slightly more north, and somewhat less west. You may have noticed that we're heading to higher ground, same as the buriers would've. They wanted their treasure to be well away from any tidal waters that'd rise during a storm."

Coming to a large outcrop of rock, L.T. knelt down to study it. Rubbing his hand over its white surface, he brought his hand to his nose. "Pee-yew! Double pee-yew!"

"You smell something?" Ollie asked. "You saying that rock smells? You saying that rock stinks?"

"Stinks and how! Like every animal in the woods has pissed on this thing."

"Why do you think they would do that, L.T.?"

"I don't know, maybe it's a landmark or something, you know, an animal landmark. Thing is, if it's an animal landmark it might just also be a people landmark. This rock, it probably hasn't been covered with dirt for three hundred years, maybe four hundred or five hundred. This rock, it's exactly the kind of rock that treasure buriers would've spotted."

"Like how do you know?" Richie said. "I mean like why it and not that big tree over there?"

"There are lots of trees, Richie, too many for buriers to single out for identification. Besides, the buriers knew it might be years till they or those after them could come back for the treasure, and that's plenty of time for trees to die. But a rock doesn't die. It's pretty much forever."

"Okay, so now what?"

L.T. looked around, shaded his eyes with his hand, stuck his nose up to the air. And we, we all looked too. But me, all I could see were trees, and ordinary trees at that, certainly nothing that at all could be mistaken for yet another landmark.

Checking his compass, L.T. walked over to a cluster of pines, disappeared behind them. A minute passed, two, three— it was as if L.T. had up and vanished!

"L.T.?" Ollie called.

"Hey, L.T.?" Richie yelled out. "Hey, L.T.?"

"Boo!"—a voice at once screamed. "Boo!"—it bellowed, the bellow as blood-lusting as it was blood-curdling, coming from somewhere off behind us. The scream knocked Richie into Ollie, knocked Ollie into me, knocked me into Rook.

"L.T.! L.T., you asshole!"

"Scared you, huh? Well, you wanna see real scary? Observe this—Dead Reckoning in action, Dead Reckoning come to life."

Pacing from the rock back to the cluster of pines, L.T. counted and counted out. "Three, four, five, six, seven, eight, nine, ten," he said, keeping a tally, pausing to catch a breath. "Eleven, twelve," he went on, we, all the while like ducks in a row behind him. "Thirteen, fourteen, fifteen, sixteen, seventeen," he said, pausing to just emphasize the number. Then turning his pause to a stop—both complete and final— he pushed branches out of the way, pointed to the ground, pointed to a spot just one pace ahead.

"Eighteen," he whispered. "Eighteen," he repeated, the number said as if it were some damn victory declaration.

I looked at the spot, to me the spot nothing but a patch of dirt, ordinary dirt dried dull brown by the few rays of sun managing to reach it. And that truly was what it was too, the spot, ordinary brown dirt, that and nothing more, that and nothing less. Leaning on over it, Richie looked skeptical, while Ollie, he looked confused.

"Eighteen is one of the lucky numbers," L.T. said.

"It is?"

"It is. See, you've just got to read the lay of the land. Notice how the slope runs past here? See how the ridge winds past here? And there, the gully," he said, tracing his finger along the little gully in which we stood, "see how it all intersects? See how it forms an X? See how it makes a star, an asterisk, one right at this very spot?"

I tried seeing it, this magic star, but to me the slope was simply a molehill, the ridge simply a wrinkle, the gully simply a latrine ditch, the kind we dug on camping trips.

"I don't know," Rookie said. "You'd think the buriers would want to pick a spot they could see from the rock. But from there we couldn't see this spot at all. You'd need really good instructions to know how to pace here. You'd need really good directions to find this star."

"It's Drift," Richie said. "The young pines—Drift."

L.T. congratulated Richie; slapped him on the back. "The buriers didn't plan on pines growing here. And that's why we make adjustments for the Drift. We make 'em by pushing branches out of the way. We make 'em by going around the pines. Rook, you've got to see beyond trees is all, look for the star formed by the slope, and the ridge, and the gully. You've just got to not let the Drift throw you."

L.T. picked a metal detector from a pile of shovels and he went to work. Cranking up the volume, he checked the pointer and the tone indicator. And then holding the search coil steady a few inches over the ground, he swept for the sweet spot. Right, left, right and left, left and right, the sweeps were as slow as they were regular, and as hypnotizing as they were mesmerizing. As for us, we made no sound—didn't dare to. And still L.T. held up his hand, wanted us quieter still.

Each second a second over, each instant an instant closer, I raised my eyes just as Rook raised hers. Her eyes meeting mine,

mine hers, we gazed without blinking, floated over the spot as if suspended not only from it, but from all place, all time.

Piercing the quiet, suddenly a strong tone rose as if rising from right out the spot. It jerked my eyes downward, planted my feet in the ground.

Sweeping the coil with ever more and more precision, L.T. swept the metal detector till its discrimination settings locked fast, locked on. "Non-ferrous," he said. "The pointer shows it's non-ferrous."

"What does that mean?" Rookie asked.

"Means it's gold, maybe silver."

"It could just as easily only be copper or aluminum," I said. "Might even just be lead."

L.T. laid the metal detector on the ground, drew an X with his heel, picked a pickax from the pile of shovels. Then he swung. And then he swung again, and again, and again. He swung at the precise heart of the X, swung till the earth at his feet was soft, till the X before his eyes was no more. Then placing his foot on the heel of a shovel, he let his weight sink, let the shovel go inside the ground.

Scooping, tossing, scooping and tossing, L.T. threw aside mounds of brown dirt, scraps of gray rock. Shirt drenched with sweat, L.T. was picking up steam, if anything scooping faster and tossing faster. He was turning into a digging machine, turning from notion to obsession, turning before our very eyes.

"L.T." He didn't hear me.

"L.T.! L.T.!" I tapped him on the shoulder, hit him on the shoulder, hit him till at last his eyes darted my way, darted to me.

Taking his arm, Rook took him to the shade of a tree and there she sat him down. Dabbing at the sweat on his forehead, she talked to him, talked to him while I—I went to the shovel so as to pick it, so as to shovel with it.

The dirt was heavy and the digging hard, but soon enough

I made a dent, 'least one big enough and deep enough to pass for what could be considered a hole. Each scoop of dirt on my shovel darker, every glimpse of blue sky over my shoulder bluer, I couldn't somehow help but not feel I was separating myself, just separating myself not only from everything that mattered, but from everyone that mattered. And it got bad—it got real bad.

It got to being so bad that the aching of my muscles was nothing, really nothing, as compared to the aching of my heart. Digging deep, digging shallow, sorting or sifting or scuttling, dirt-naps were gonna be as much forever as they were gonna be inevitable. So that being the case, how precious, I thought, just how so very precious was life? And that being the case, why shouldn't life—if it couldn't be forever—at the very least be eternal? I mean there had to be some way of at least somehow making it eternal? I mean, like was that asking too much? Was it? I mean, I didn't think it was. Then again, it was only part my call. I knew that.

When Ollie finally stepped into the hole to take the shovel away from me, I gratefully stepped out. L.T., I saw him smiling now, smiling and nodding to things Rook whispered to his ear. And he was watching too, watching as first Ollie and then Richie took their shots at oblivion, their turns to dig to kingdom come.

"I mean we all heard the metal detector," Richie said, stepping on out of the hole. "We heard it beep. Maybe it's just deeper."

"Definitely deeper," L.T. said. "Has to be deeper." Tearing up a sheet of paper, he wrote down guard times on each piece. Then, finishing, he closed his eyes, reached his hand into his cap. "Alright! Alright, I got the twelve to two."

Rookie, she was up next, got the two-to-four. "I'll switch with you, L.T."

"No way. Two-to-four's a real graveyard shift. Besides,

Rook, this way I'll get to wake you. And if there's anything I like, it's waking people up."

Ollie, Ollie he pulled the ten-to-twelve, while me, I got the four-to-six—not bad, not great either. As for Richie, he lucked out, drew the eight-to-ten. "Know how I got it?" he asked. "Know how? Dead Reckoning! I reckoned my hand right to the right piece of paper."

"It was the last piece of paper in the cap," L.T. said, "the last one left. But who knows, Richie, maybe you really do have a talent for Dead Reckoning. But Michael, now take him for instance. Michael, he's the exact opposite, an anti-talent if ever there was one. Michael stinks at Dead Reckoning. He doesn't know how to use it. And it doesn't help any that he doesn't understand it. And it really, really doesn't help any that he doesn't believe in it—doesn't even in the least believe in it. Sure, Michael, he sees rocks. And sure he sees animals. And sure he sees trees, sees those too. But Michael, he just doesn't see what he should be seeing. Like, I mean, how is he ever going to find what he wants to find when he doesn't know where to look, doesn't even know how to look? See, Richie, Michael—and people like Michael—just can't see the forest for the trees."

I'd heard the expression before, heard it plenty of times. And I never did understand it, I think the word 'for' being the part in the expression always tripping me up. The other thing I didn't understand, or for that matter appreciate, was L.T. using me and my good name to compare and contrast the comings and goings, the highs and the lows, and the good and the bad of talent and anti-talent. It kind of all sounded to me like he was saying I smelled, was stupid, was Godless, and had no vision—had absolutely no vision whatsoever. Oh, and no strength of character, I had none of that either.

"Oh, yeah. Oh, yeah, L.T.," I said, winding myself up to zing him with an expression I knew everyone understood.

"Well at least I know shit when I see it, tell you that!"

Coming over to whisper in my ear, L.T. whispered some thanks or other for saying shit and not bullshit in front of the others, his thinking, I think, being that shit meant he'd only been talking crap, while bullshit, on the other hand, would've meant that not only had he been talking bullcrap, but slinging it. And that was a sure-fire no-no when it came to his highfalutin' standing with the others. It all, though, kind of left me somehow wishing that I'd actually said bullshit—bullshit, bullshit, bullshit—his highfalutin' standing be damned.

Soon enough we broke up, the breaking a pretty good thing too. Ollie broke to lollygagging himself and his knock-knees away; Richie broke to riding himself and his neon-like redness away; and L.T. broke—and for good riddance—to paddling himself and his good-for-nothin' bullshit talent away, his bullshit Dead Reckoning and Drift away too.

As for Rookie, as for her, she rode her red bike around, rode it around and around me, her circles so uneven we didn't get a good eyeful of each other—that not really a bad thing, 'least not when real talking needed to get done.

"L.T. scared me, Michael. He really scared me back there. He was in real meltdown to find this thing."

"You know him, you know how he gets. Don't worry about it."

"So what do you think? You think we're actually going to discover something?"

"Yeah, yeah I think we actually will. It's there, Rook. It really is out there. And you know what? It's not that far away."

Wheeling 'round her bike, Rookie wheeled it to a stop, a stop so as to see me, and me see her. "Funny, Michael, but I've got the same feeling. Except for the part about it being out there."

"What do you mean? If it's not out there, then where?"

Rook pushed off, zigzagged from one side of the path to the other, circled back around so that we got a good look of each other. "You know, Michael, even though L.T.'s not Portogeez like us, he gets it. He really does. He understands. He understands that good Portogeez see the forest, and not just the trees. And you know what else? Know what else he understands? He understands what all good Portogeez sailors understand: that you can't Dead Reckon your way to actual treasure. You can only use it to figure out where you are."

And with that Rook stopped her circling, pedaled away, pedaled straight away so that she was gone.

5

It wasn't fair—Mom and Dad even having to admit as much.

"Life isn't fair," Mom said. "And just for your information, Michael, it doesn't have to be."

"But it's not fair!" I said again, said for what must have been the umpteenth time, maybe the umpteenth and first. I was getting desperate, running out of ways to explain to them right from wrong, leastwise my take of right from wrong. I mean, how could they not get it? How could they not see that being even-handed, being sympathetic too, that that was right, that that was justice? I mean it certainly wasn't this, this I'm-bigger-than-you bullying sham of a court in which—without so much as even being offered up rights to defend myself—I'd apparently been judged, found wanting, sentenced, and what's more pretty harshly sentenced at that. Hell, like I didn't even know I even was on trial. I mean, since when are kids on trial? And, like, who made their parents judge, jury, prosecutor, and executioner, anyway?

"But it's not fair," I repeated for one last and really lame time.

"Look, Michael, it is what it is," Dad said. "There are

things you can't change. And the sooner you understand that the better."

"So nothing I say, no argument I make, can change your mind?"

"That's right, Michael. Nothing."

That settled, I went up to my room and put on a dirty shirt, the really dirty shirt that once was white but now was gray and had the big wrinkle running down the middle of it—that one. I also pulled on a pair of pants, the ones that were two inches too short and for which I had to suck in my stomach, and then followed that up with brown socks and black shoes, the shoes with heels worn down to nothing at all. I mean just 'cause Mom and Dad were winning didn't mean all was lost. Payback was a weapon, one I still had—and I was going to use it, damn it.

Mom gave me a look-over as we headed to the truck, shook her head. "I give up. I just give up."

"If he wants to make a jackass of himself," Dad said, "let him."

The ride to Fall River was quiet, nobody saying nothing. Dad wore a coat, a tie, and a scowl. Elbow resting on a rolled-down window, his fingers wrapped the steering wheel so tightly they were white. I could see his eyes in the rearview mirror, could see he was wicked pissed. As for Mom, she kept her eyes over to the river on her side of the truck, didn't look up, didn't look ahead. Alongside her pretty face, teardrop crystal earrings wriggled with each bump of the road.

It wasn't only my choice of clothing that had them so upset. 'The incident' had shaken them up but good, and I suspected it as much as anything was why I alone was being made to go with them to hear *fado* music. Patty, she got to hang with friends "because she's old enough." Billy, he got to stay home and watch television "because he's too young." But me,

I apparently was just right for the undertaking, was "at the age to go," whatever that meant.

Though only a short ride, day became dusk by the time we reached Fall River, dusky city kids already hanging with their skateboards on their street corners. Dark Cape Verdeans, tough Italians, newcomer Latinos—each to its own. But in a few weeks I would be at Taunton Regional, and while not all these city kids were going to be in my freshman class, other kids—new kids—would be. In a new place, each of us plunked on down, we'd each have to find new ways to survive. And that's all that would matter too—survival—'least for those first few days, and having friends would be crucial. Of course I already knew who I could count on: Ollie, Richie, Neal, Steve, Danny, Jeff—all the kids I'd grown up with since about the age of five. More than friends, these kids were family, like almost actual family. I mean we shared something—some bond or other I couldn't explain, couldn't even explain to myself. Raised together in much the same way, we understood we were the same—understood we were the same as to be one. We understood too that we were different—different from others. If push ever came to shove, if ever there was a threat, I knew my guys—I knew who they were.

L.T. though? L.T.? I don't know. I just don't know about him. Though as of right now my best friend, could I trust him? I mean—could I really trust him? Such a different background, such different stock; so different a history, so different a future—would he be there, be there for me?

It was dim to dark inside of Café Saudade, the little light that there was coming from glass-enclosed candles on tabletops. And with no hostess coming over to seat us—with no hostess really necessary to seat us—we went about seating ourselves. Walking among tables, we sought out familiar faces, the faces we passed looking us over—sizing us up, too. Packed

though the place was, most of the tables were pushed back—
pushed so far back as to be away. And that's where most of
the faces were too—at these pushed back and away tables,
the candlelight there flickering just enough to reveal the faces
indeed back there, not however flickering enough to allow the
seeing of the faces—the faces surely watching us.

Those faces back in the recesses and the shadows—I
decided they were strange faces—would just have to be. And
those people behind those strange faces—they were strange
people—would as well pretty much just have to be. Misfits,
misfits and losers, those strange misfit losers, they only wanted
to watch, watch without so much as ever letting themselves get
watched, lest, I guess, they be seen as human, seen as human
even if only of the misfit kind.

Mom and Dad slowed a little as they recognized friends
and acquaintances at the tables we passed—be those friends
Azoreans, Madeirans, or Cape Verdeans; be those acquaintances
from Best, Fall River or New Bedford. But as for actual
stopping, stopping and talking, Mom and Dad didn't, they only
went so far as to point out how so very good all those friends
and acquaintances looked, while they on the other hand only
went so far as to point out how so very tall I was now getting.

Suddenly a hand shot up at one table, Uncle Jiggy snapping
his fingers to direct us over to the group he sat with. Aunt
Lolly, of course, was there, the Pereiras and Oliveiras too,
Aunts Edna and Debbie offering up their cheeks for me to
kiss, Uncles Joe and Buzz offering their open hands for me to
shake.

It was just last year I learned that my aunts Edna and
Debbie, that my uncles Joe and Buzz, weren't my real aunts and
uncles, weren't in fact even at all related to me. At first it was
kind of weird to keep pretending that they were, but over time
it got easier, and with time I got better—pretending that is—it
dawning on me ... what did it matter? I mean pretend aunts,

stand-in uncles … so what? Grandpa always says anyways that the strength of the wolf is the pack, the more the wolves, the better the pack. That naturally and of course so long as the wolves work together, work as one.

So what that meant, I think, was all I really had to just do was keep up the relationships I always anyways had with them—those pretend aunts, and stand-in uncles, and phony and bogus cousins—maintain that oneness I anyways always had with them. And besides, they at times really were so all and frighteningly real—they really were just like my real Aunt Lolly, my real Uncle Jiggy, my real cousin Ollie—that real, that frightening.

Only Rook, only she, God bless, was there to remind me that though almost real was real enough—that's to say real enough to matter—and though mattering was all that really mattered, at the end of the day, when you came right down to it, almost still was only almost—almost by definition just not quite enough, almost by laws of nature just not enough, and almost by laws of God just never enough—never enough, never enough, never enough. Like, I mean, no phony and bogus almost cousin of mine could ever possibly be so almost as real as to be so perfectly unreal as her, that divinely unreal.

"So, have you ever been to fado, Mookie?"

"No, Uncle Joe, but I've heard the music. I've heard it lots of times."

"So a fado fan are you then?"

"I wouldn't say that exactly. It's okay, I guess. I don't understand the words. They're in Portuguese."

"You don't need to understand the words," Aunt Debbie said. "All you need know, Michael, is that the songs hit on all the big things taking place in the course of a life. You know, stuff like betrayal, despair, death, obviously always death."

"Can't they sing about happy things?"

"If they did it wouldn't be fado," Uncle Joe said with a

laugh, it coming with a smoker's cough. "Fado means fate, and fate, Mookie, is never happy. Look, I don't understand the Portuguese words either. But I know what the songs are about, know they always ask the same questions: 'Why did you leave? Where did you go? Why can't I find you? How can I go on without you?' See, you don't need to understand the words to understand the songs. A good fado singer sings from the heart anyway, Mookie, and those songs are always understood."

Mom put her menu down so as to watch me, her watch so strong and tender I blushed. "Fado is an expression of saudade, Michael, the fado songs a heartfelt expression of that which is lost. Understand that we have just a vague memory of the loss we suffered, and our minds simply are incapable of understanding such a loss anyway. So it's left to our hearts, that's where it's left. But hearts aren't very good at remembering, aren't for that matter very good at understanding much either. The only thing hearts are truly good for is hurting. Hearts are experts at it, that and breaking. And there is where our saudades live, Michael—in our hearts. Yours are there too. You feel them sometimes, I know you do."

I already felt miserable enough as it was; the last thing I about now needed was hearing grownups telling me just how to be sad. I mean, betrayal, despair, death—they at least had enough of that stuff in their lives to justify their sadness. But me, I had none of that stuff, 'least not yet. So if anything, whatever sadness I did have made me—me—the one with true and genuine saudade, real saudade. I mean like I remembered nothing, knew nothing, and understood nothing. I mean really, like what more could a good saudade ask for than to have that? And as for hurting and breaking, what more could a miserable kid with a good saudade want than to have that? A month shy of fourteen and already I—my heart too—pretty much had it all: a saudade like no other, the saudade to beat all saudades!

I looked off Mom—by now, had to—spotted Captain Jack

but a few tables away with some drinking buddies. He once and again and forever the legendary sailor of the Grand Banks there but for to regale them—like wow, was he ever pounding them back! I mean it was as if he didn't just want to numb his heartaches, he wanted to obliterate them! And by the looks of it, he was succeeding, at least some of the time, his face every now and then lighting up over something a buddy said, before, and just as suddenly, dissolving into just a blank stare, an empty look, just a blank and empty look into the bottom of his glass.

"We don't do that," Dad said, his eyes following mine.

"Do what?"

"Get drunk. It's okay to drink but it's not okay to get drunk, 'least it's not okay to get that pissed drunk."

"How come?"

"A drunk doesn't feel pain. And he doesn't much appreciate pain either, Michael, and pain is sometimes really not a bad thing. If pain hurts, it hurts. The thing is, pain lets you know something is wrong. It reminds you something is always wrong."

"And besides," Uncle Jiggy said, "a little pain ain't never hurt no one. Take, for instance, my knee, Mookie. Pain in my knee reminds me I played football. And since the pain is real, the memory is real. And since the memory is real, still I can think myself a football player. I can still be who I was, if just a little of who I was. And that really is as close as I—or you, or any of us—can still truly get."

I looked again at Captain Jack. Having for a moment nodded off, something—or nothing—now startled him. His eyes opened, and his mouth muttered.

"That's another thing," Uncle Jiggy went on. "When Cuss is drunk, his land legs get shot. He loses control; talks too much. And you know, 'Loose lips sink ships'."

"Huh?"

"Means when you say things you really should not be

saying, likelier than not, your adversary will use what you say against you."

Ships? Sink our ships? I mean, like what were our ships carrying—gold or something? Plutonium? Top-secret stuff about us being Martians, maybe even zombies? Okay, we were different. Okay, I got it. I mean that much I always felt anyway, somehow always knew too. And okay, being different was dangerous. I got that too. But really, what were we—combustible or something? Too flammable? Too damn burnable? Was that too much of a danger for others? Was that just too much damn danger for ourselves?

So I didn't ask, didn't dare, knew I shouldn't.

But asking about others, asking how others were different from us, was that okay? "Dad, when Captain Jack wakes up, you know and gets sober, he'll remember, won't he? I mean he'll remember his being here tonight, won't he?"

"He probably will. But each time he gets drunk, he forgets a little. Each time he gets drunk he's less who he is, and less who he was. Now, maybe that works for him, I don't know. I mean everyone knows him already anyway, can remind him he's a sailor. But what does anyone know of us, Michael? What does anyone really know of us? No one knows us. And we don't want anyone to know us. What that means is we have just ourselves. And having just ourselves—what that means is, we can't afford to forget anything about ourselves. After all there is just so little we still have."

A pretty waitress came over to our table for orders, and as usual, Uncle Joe went to work. In practically no time at all he wangled out her bio, took her credentials, shook her family tree. I mean like he found out who it was she went to the movies with last night—and he found out the movie!

Turned out Jenny, "pretty as a penny," studied European history, "cause of the mystery" over at U. Mass., Dartmouth. "So, Jenny," Uncle Joe asked, rhyme-time over, "so are you

Portuguese?"

"No, I'm afraid I'm just Spanish. But I do like fado. It says something to me, you know, something that I think I understand. Guess that's just the littlest bit scary, huh? Anyway, I'm Majorcan actually, going back hundreds of years."

"Well, that's almost Portuguese," Uncle Joe said. "We're island people too, from the Azores, also going back hundreds of years. We got there almost soon as they were discovered in the 1400s. But, who knows, Jenny, maybe you're Portuguese and just don't know it. Who knows, maybe we're even long lost cousins."

"Maybe," Jenny laughed. "Who knows? And how would you tell anyway? Now, back to your orders. There are two specials today. The first is Pork Alentejana, cubed pork sauce and clams over fried potatoes. And the second is also a pork dish, our Grilled Chouriço Saudade. Would you like a little time to think about it?"

Uncle Joe looked at us as if there actually was even a doubt. Of course, but of course we'd have what we always had when we went out. "Know what, Jenny? I think there's a consensus here. Seeing as we're big cod fans, we'll make it easy for you and go with the salty bacalhau, the Bacalhau Fest. And bring lots of fava beans and salads, okay?"

At times like this I always expect the waitress to raise an eyebrow, say how boring our order of cod is, say how boring we are. But Jenny didn't miss a beat, a sure sign she'd been waitressing here a while. "And what can I get you folks for drinks?" she asked.

We ordered beers, a bottle of Madeiran wine too. I, of course, I got stuck with a coke. And what with a full evening of fado still ahead of me, I excused myself to go to the bathroom, kill a little time—maybe even throw up.

"Why, Michael Costa!" boomed a voice, one I knew. Father Sousa pushed a wine glass away from his mouth, waved me over. "You here, you here for your indoctrination?" he asked.

I guess as surprised as Father Sousa was to see me here, I was much more surprised to see him here. Wearing a black turtleneck instead of a white collar, he was about as red as the wine in his glass. Bad enough to cross paths with him each and every Sunday, the last thing I needed this Saturday night was seeing him out for a good time.

"Huh," I said. "I mean I'm sorry Father, but I don't think I understand your question."

"Don't look so surprised, Michael, you're a smart boy. You think priests don't have a right to kick back every now and then? Relax, will yeh," he said, his gray eyes inspecting me from over his spectacles. "I'm not here tonight to watch the flock, I'm here to be with them. What I was asking—and all I was asking—was whether your parents brought you here for your indoctrination to fado. Mother of God, what kind of indoctrination did you think I meant?"

"I don't know. I guess they brought me for the fado. And to eat, they brought me to eat too," I said, a line that must have been funny judging by the way those at Father Sousa's table laughed, especially the way Mr. Alves laughed.

Mr. Alves, a Best Harbor selectman—we don't like him. We Spitters don't like him, know he's not one of us, know he always sides with Besterners. We also don't like that he's head of the parish council, not that we do much complaining in public about that either. I mean seeing as we Spitters are more than half the congregation at St. Peter's, and yet even aren't half as involved as Besterners in church matters, really we have no right to complain. Besides, and again, Mr. Alves—he's parish council head—and he's somebody we don't whatsoever want to go ticking off.

"I'm sure they also brought you to eat," Mr. Alves said, his mouth a smirk, smug and sickening. "Personally, myself, I recommend the chouriço. But you're bacalhau people, isn't that right? Bacalhau—isn't that right, Michael?"

Father Sousa made his hand go flat, moved it over the table in a cutting motion that I sensed was meant as much for me as Mr. Alves. Poking and probing, pushing and prodding, Mr. Alves knew what it was he was doing—knew exactly what he was doing. And so too did Father Sousa, and so too did I. I knew precisely what he was doing. And I didn't like it. I didn't like it at all.

Screw You!— is what I wanted to say. Punch him in the mouth!—is what I wanted to do. Tear the smile off his ugly face; tear his cold heart from his chest!—all that and more is what I wanted to do. But doing anything—doing much of anything at all—not only would be bad, it would be real bad. It would only create a scene I did not want, cause problems I was not in the least prepared to handle.

Fact was, I was small. Fact was, I was weak too. And in that way I was not that different from my family, my family over there at their table. They too must often have felt much the same as me, must also often have wanted to do what it was I now wanted to do. And yet, yet they swallowed it—somehow swallowed it—learned it was best to say nothing, best to do even less.

But young as I was, and stupid too, I couldn't. I just was not ready to let this go.

"Bacalhau people?" I said. "Bacalhau people?" I repeated, my voice trembling. "Actually we're peanut butter people. We eat it all the time, just like chouriço people eat it. Thing is we don't eat peanut butter, and we don't eat mallasadas, and we don't eat bacalhau, really don't eat anything at all in church. Now if you chouriço people want to eat there, fine, go eat. But us, we're not there for that."

I turned quickly, my steps turning over faster the further I got away, and by the time I finally reached the bathroom, by the time I looked in the mirror, I scared even myself. Staring back at me was a ghost—me as ghost—my blood having drained from outside to in, my blood having pooled from my face to my core, the draining and the pooling one last and all-out effort to protect the inside, save the core.

I managed somehow to avoid Mr. Alves and Father Sousa on my way back to our table, and when I reached it I was more scared than ever. Never before had I spoken like that to an adult, and I was sure I had screwed it up, screwed the whole thing up.

Seeing that somehow all was not right by me, Uncle Buzz pushed his mug of beer my way, moved his hand to his mouth in quick little gestures for me to sip. I naturally emptied it, pretty much drained half of it on my very first swig.

"Good. Good, Mookie. Now maybe you'll like the fado."

I didn't, of course. But much to my surprise I didn't totally hate it either. The fadista wore a black dress, wore way too much makeup too, sang with her arms down at her side, sang with her arms up in the air. Stretching out those arms every so often as to pull the audience in for a hug, she played with the shawl on her shoulders, played with her black dress too, played with the cleavage of her breasts, even played as her breasts made as if to rise from right out of the black dress. And oblivious to the two musicians behind her—one playing a Portuguese guitarra and the other playing a bass guitar—she wrapped herself in a world of sorrow.

"Is she any good, Uncle Buzz?"

"She ain't bad—but that's for the audience to decide. If they cry she's good, sings from her soul. And if they don't cry then she's not good, doesn't sing from her soul. And if that's the case, well, let's put it this way—the audience won't be happy. They might hiss, might boo, and may even create so much bedlam the performance can't continue. I've seen it before."

I looked around, hoped for the bedlam. As far as I was concerned, the audience could become a mob—that a far sight better than seeing any handkerchiefs rise up to blot away any tears. I wanted booing, wanted the hissing part too. And as for blood, while a little blood would be good, a lot of blood would be all so much the better. What I wanted was a saloon fight, a good old-fashioned saloon fight with bottles smashing and tables flying—a saloon fight is what I wanted. And our table, of course, would get its licks in, of that I was certain. After all, we had Uncle Jiggy, and he could toss a table as well as anyone. He'd flatten Mr. Alves, crunch anybody who so much dared look at us the wrong way, let alone dared speak to us in the wrong way.

But instead of bedlam—instead of the booing and the hissing and the blood—there only was disappointment, the crowd I guess just too mesmerized by the fadista—I guess by her soul too. I mean like from Jenny, to Captain Jack, to Mr. Alves, everybody but everybody turned weak on me, had the gall to actually lose themselves in a memory or other.

As for me, truth be told, I felt kind of weak too. I mean seeing Mom cry, seeing her cry darn near made me cry. And yet whenever she so much as peeked my way—peeked to see me watching her—I simply looked away, acted just as if I didn't feel a thing—nothing. And Dad? Seeing him close his eyes— seeing him close his eyes and hold his head in his hands—it just made me sadder than I ever again wanted to be. And yet whenever he so much as glanced my way—glanced my way so as to see me watching him—I simply looked away, just acted as if I didn't feel a thing—nothing. Of course I knew what they wanted, knew that what they wanted was for me to share in their emotions. They wanted to show me—show me who they were—let me have even the just the slightest of clues as to what mattered to them.

And really, really it would have been good to share more

with them, see more from them, get even just that slightest of clues. I mean I wanted that, really I did. But I couldn't do it. I just couldn't. I just couldn't let them see me. I just couldn't let them see me bring myself there, there to that edge, that edge that would have let them know I got it, at least got some of it. The problem—my problem—was that I didn't want them … didn't want them to share in my emotions. I simply didn't want them to get even an inkling of a hint of a clue as to what mattered to me. My saudade was my saudade. Like, did they really need to know how messed up I sometimes got? Did they really need to know how lost I sometimes felt? Did they really need to know just how much I wanted to remember? I mean, they already had enough heartache and loss—they for damn sure didn't need more coming from me.

When the fadista at last took a break, we at last stirred to life: Aunt Lolly calling out names; Mom seeking out eyes; Uncle Jiggy touching Dad's shoulder, touching mine too.

"How you doin', Mookie?"

"I'm fine," I said, not sure whether or not to ask. "And you, Uncle Jiggy, how you doin'?" I went ahead and asked.

"I'm alright," he said, prying Uncle Buzz's beer away from my hand. "Thanks for askin'."

Just then as whatever little lighting there was got juiced all the way up from dark to dim, just then as silverware began to again clank and glasses began to again come together in toast—just then Mrs. Haymaker walked in.

Wearing a strapless black dress—wearing a convoy too— the tall guy in the suit held on to her arm as if it were a prize. And her hair—her along-the-banks-of-the-river hair—it was now stepping-out-on-the-town hair, all blond and shiny and flowing over those smoothly tanned shoulders of hers.

Walking by—she and the tall guy—I could just see everyone's eyes turning to follow, could just see just what it was that they thought of her. But whatever it was they thought, and whatever it was they felt, they couldn't have been any more wrong. I mean Mrs. Haymaker, she made me sandwiches. Mrs. Haymaker, she made me cocoa. I mean she talked to me about things she was working on, listened to me about things I needed to work out. If they even for a moment felt they had any issues with her, Mrs. Haymaker, then they really should look at themselves. They should look there.

Me? I was fourteen, at least almost fourteen—already knew my issues. And I knew them to be mine, mine just as they should be mine. And I tried to keep them that way too. And if I couldn't always succeed, well, well then ... I was after all only fourteen, at least almost fourteen.

About to sit down at a table not far away, Mrs. Haymaker spotted me. "Hi, Michael," she said, coming over. "Look at you, all dressed up!"

"You look good too, Mrs. Haymaker."

She nodded to everyone at the table, the tall guy meanwhile gesturing to two empty chairs. "May we?"

"Of course," Mom said, her hesitation over.

"This is Hal Ricci, head of the anthropology department at Harvard. He's helping me with my work on Dighton Rock."

"How's that coming, Cindy?" Mom asked, lacing her fingers under her chin and using Mrs. Haymaker's first name as if they were actual friends.

"I'm learning new things all the time. There really are a lot of Wamponoag artifacts in the clay down by Grassy Isle, you know, things like arrowheads and fishhooks. Not much, though, when it comes to Miguel Cortereal, him or the Rock, at least not yet there isn't. But it's only a matter of time. Hal and I are turning over every rock there is there."

"So you came for the fado?" Uncle Joe asked, arms folded over his chest. "You like fado?"

"I'm not familiar with it enough to say. But as long as I'm

in Best Harbor, I want to experience everything. I want to learn whatever I can about this culture, that's to say, your culture."

"Our culture?"

"Your Portuguese-American culture, of course. What other culture is there?"

"Well, we Azoreans certainly have a rich history, to be sure. Some of us as you may know go back a hundred years, even over two hundred, back all the way to whaling days."

"I know. I know all about it. Ironic though when you get to thinking about it."

"How's that? What's ironic, Mrs. Haymaker?"

"That you, that's to say particular Azoreans like you, found your way here, that you made your home at the very same spot Cortereal made his."

"That's coincidence," Dad said. "That's just coincidence is all."

"True, I'm sure that's all it was, maybe even all it still is. But coincidence only goes so far. After a while you start to see patterns, patterns that make you wonder whether there wasn't something more at work here. I'm not denying that things happen by coincidence, even as a result of them. But when there are a whole series of patterns that are in and of themselves odd—and when strung together downright bizarre—the only plausible conclusion is there must be something that links them."

"God has his ways."

"People have their ways. And people are responsible for those ways even if and when—how can I put it—even if and when otherworldly motivations are behind them."

"So it's by people's hands that patterns get drawn?"

"I think so. But here's the thing. Despite my training as an anthropologist—even with years of using the scientific method to approach problems—even I have to concede there are times when the linking of one set of points to another set of points to yet another set of points is, well, 'funny' at best."

"'Funny'—that's quite the scientific term, Mrs. Haymaker. Why if I didn't know better I would say your term sounds—how can I put it—spiritual, spiritual if not all together religious. But 'funny', well, I don't know about that. Maybe it all only seems 'funny' to you, you who don't believe. For people with ways, though, nothing really is ever too 'funny'. And that's not because people with ways don't have a sense of humor—actually they have good ones. And that's not because people with ways already understand what there is to understand—trust me, they don't. But these patterns, Mrs. Haymaker, you're not a part of them. And for that matter, they're not a part of you either. See, you can look, and you can try to understand, but to you, patterns are just patterns, mysteries simply are mysteries—both, you think, just begging for solutions and resolutions.

"But you need to understand there are mysteries, and then again there are real mysteries. And real mysteries—real mysteries shouldn't be solved no matter how great the desire to solve them, no matter how pressing the need to solve them. And it's because they shouldn't be solved—precisely because they shouldn't be solved—they can't be solved, at least not truly solved. What's more, these mysteries, they especially should not be solved by those who are part of the patterns, those built into them. It's a matter, Mrs. Haymaker, it's just a matter of construction, and if a set-up like that doesn't take a sense of humor, I don't know what does."

"Sounds to me it's more a matter of self-preservation. And faith too, that, I suppose, that is also required."

"Mrs. Haymaker, Dighton Rock is one thing, a mystery that can or can't be solved. But a real mystery is something else, something altogether different. And you should know the difference, really you should."

"I'm not sure I should, Mr. Costa. For that matter, I'm not

sure I even can."

Standing to go back to her table, Mrs. Haymaker hesitated, sat herself back down, brought her hands down to her lap. "Thanks for driving L.T. home the other day. He told me what happened, admitted he was snooping and looking into your kitchen from the basement window. He also told me how nice you were to clean him up after the collision by the chicken shed. All that said, however, I have to tell you how disappointed he was that you didn't let him stay for dinner. He said you haven't actually had him over for much of anything at all. So frankly, I'm disappointed too."

"I have to apologize, Cindy. It simply wasn't a good time. Maybe another time—a better time—we can have L.T. over."

Suddenly the Café lights went dim, the fadista about ready to sing yet another round of song. Snorting, and then wiping his nose with his handkerchief, Dad wished Mrs. Haymaker well, and then wished the tall guy well. Meanwhile, the tabletop candles, they cast white streaks all about the room, all about the room and all about us too.

"Thanks," Hal, the tall guy, said. "Thanks for your good wishes concerning our work." Then looking at us—looking carefully at each and every one of us—Hal leaned over our table, seemed to lean right over us. "Funny thing is you never really do know how or when a discovery will be made. Back in 1920 Professor Delabarre, he made an accidental one, but a remarkable one nevertheless. Climbing up a ladder way above Dighton Rock, he happened to shine his flashlight on the Rock, shine it down at just the right angle. It was three o'clock in the morning and he needed the extra lighting for a 5 x 7 picture plate he was making. Anyway, without that light, without that light the plate wouldn't have shown anything. Professor Delabarre called this angled lighting Shadow Lighting, explained it as light glancing so close to the surface as to leave shadows, give just the right contrast. In daylight, without the Shadow Lighting, he never would have been able to see clues on the Rock, would never have been able to decipher the particular markings there, would probably never have even learned the Cortereal story. And that's the great thing about clues. You never know how or when you get them. But when you do get them they tell stories, and the more you collect the better your chances to hear a story. And, at least from my experience, the funny thing is that the tougher the unearthing of a clue, just all the better the secret, just so much better the story."

6

Just the thought of it sent a worry bug crawling, sent it to scuttling directly from my brain to my stomach. I mean like I already had dread as it was, so much I even could start my own dread manufacturing business. What I needed just now was this new dose of queasiness—needed it like someone already with runs needs a goodly dose of food poisoning.

Did I do my homework?

Here Dad was waking me—waking me up—and I had nothing.

I'd been floating on my stomach, dreaming something or other about last night, something or other about Mrs. Haymaker and her strapless black dress, and as yet I was not ready to let the dream go, 'least not for something like Dad's wake-up for school. Pulling my pillow out from under my face, I turned my head away from the side Dad was waking me.

Suddenly my eyes opened, I think the right one first, and then the left. Lying still—lying stupid, too—I stared at my pillow for a while, made a half-hearted try to stir myself out from under my horny stupor. Room in twilight, moonbeams dancing from my computer to my soccer ball to the pair of shorts I'd left on the floor, I mindlessly took them in, realized that basically I was an idiot—just an idiot!

Summer, idiot! No school, idiot! No homework, idiot!

So who the hell was it trying to wake me?

Wake up!—said the call once again. Wake up!—it said, from the window, definitely the window.

"Michael," it softly called. "Michael," it came sweet. "Wake up, Michael."

WAKE UP! WAKE UP! WAKE UP! This time I heard the call alright, heard it and good, the call, after all, mine—in my voice, sharp and hard and urgent, telling me to get up, truly but truly get up—GET THE FUCK UP!

I bolted straight up, rushed for the door, looked for an instant back in the direction of the window.

Rookie?

Stubbing my toe on any one of a number of books on the floor, I pulled a sheet from the bed, held it tight around my waist. "For crying out loud, Rook! Like I'm in my underwear here. Couldn't you have called up from the yard or something? You know, maybe thrown a rock?"

"I throw like a girl, Michael. And I did call up from the yard. But you didn't hear me over your snoring."

"I don't snore."

"You snore like you're sawing logs, Michael."

"Why didn't you just give up, you know, go on home? That's what Richie does, Ollie too. I mean isn't that better than climbing up to my window?"

"No, actually, it isn't better. I like watching you. I like watching you from the window."

"What time is it, anyway?"

"Ten past four. That's A.M., Michael, A.M.! God—I can't believe I'm doing this."

"Well, climb back down and try not believing it from down there, okay? I need five minutes, Rook."

I got dressed, threw on shorts from the floor, a t-shirt too—it also from the floor—then grabbed my flashlight and walkie-talkie two-way radio.

"L.T. woke you okay?" I asked, once I'd shimmied down the tree by the window.

"Yeah. He came to my windowsill to get me, and I do mean to my actual windowsill. I mean any more sill and he would've been waking me from by my bed. I'm not happy about this, Michael. I'm not happy."

"So now you know how I feel when you go sticking your face in my window. But the real problem here, Rook, is L.T., his watching you in your pajamas, or in your nightgown, or in whatever it is that you wear to bed. I mean for all I know you wear nothing—nothing at all! And now L.T. saw you—he saw you wearing even just that!"

"I sleep with clothes, Michael. Okay? I wear clothes. You know this whole thing could be avoided if we used alarm clocks, you know, the way normal people do."

"Shift changes have to be done person-to-person. Nobody, normal or not, gets up in the middle of the night to watch a hole if they don't have proof the person watching before them was sucker enough to have done it too."

"But in going to the house of the next watcher, you know, the replacement watcher, isn't the hole left unwatched anyway, at least for a little while? And when we're there standing watch by the hole, why just then would the hole-filler-upper just then go and fill it? And so long as I'm goin' good here, have you ever considered that the hole-filler-upper may be filling the holes in the daytime—you know, when nobody's there watching? I mean, like have you thought this through, Michael? Have you and L.T. really thought this thing through, 'cause frankly, I'm starting to think you haven't?"

Rookie obviously had had way too much time to think on her watch, so much in fact she was totally missing the whole point of the hole-watching—emphasis on the watching. Smart though Rook was—and she was—she just didn't get that we weren't so much guarding the hole as much as we were watching the hole. Of course we couldn't protect the hole, protecting holes being kind of a dumb idea to begin with. Mainly, we only wanted to learn about the hole, and while at it, learn a little something about holes in general.

And sure, while it'd be great knowing who the hole-filler-upper was and why he kept filling our holes, what we really wanted knowing was—why holes? Why did they get dug? Why did they get dug by diggers?

Me and L.T. thought—'least what I thought we thought—was that it was the diggers, and not so much the fillers, who mattered most. And a real-life honest-to-goodness hole-watch was the very best way of learning about them—the diggers. I mean, there certainly was time at a hole—opportunity too—to do some discovering there. And no matter whether if what we discovered was new and surprising, or old and mysterious, it'd all be great, pretty great if for no reason other than it being personal—this whole thing long ago having gone personal anyway.

I mean … *it was our holes.* It was our holes. And if anyone was going to do any filling it should be us, really it should. And even if, and even if all that turned up during a real-life honest-to-goodness hole watch was something about the hole-fillers, and not the hole-diggers, even just that bit of knowledge probably would be good enough. I mean, armed with just that, I think both me and L.T. felt pretty good we then could go figuring out the rest.

"Here," Rook said, once I'd walked her back to her farmhouse, "my thermos. It's coffee. And I took only a couple of sips of it so it's not like you're going to get my cooties or anything. Here, brownies too."

On an impulse I leaned in, gave her a kiss on the cheek, nice, quick, and light. "Well, good night," I said. "Sleep well."

"Good night, Michael. Guard well."

I walked back to the hole by way of the dirt road: my guard up; my flashlight off; my pecker up as if to go off; and Rook's thermos at my side and at the ready. What exactly it was ready for I didn't know, but I was squeezing the living daylights out of the thing, I'll say that much, and singing a bit too—I was doing that too. I sang 'Michael row the boat ashore'; sang of the river Jordan being 'deep and wide;' sang of its waters being 'chilly and cold;' and sang also of its other side, the one with all the 'milk and honey.' Honestly, I almost honestly didn't know what on earth it was I was singing about. I honestly almost did not know. And yet the spiritual helped, and the singing of it worked, both the spiritual and the singing reassuring me that just being scared shit didn't necessarily go and make me one.

Like … I hate being a shit, pretty much the only thing I hate more being a chicken-shit. A shit—he'll do the wrong thing, do it for a lousy reason, and do it for a selfish reason to boot. A chicken-shit, on the other hand—he'll do nothing, do nothing for no good reason, not even a selfish reason being reason good enough. A shit—he decides it's best to turn for home because he doesn't want to be buried alive, or buried dead, by some hole-filler-upper. A chicken-shit—he wanders home, simply wanders back home and to bed, simply wanders back because it's a bed, just wanders back home because there's a warm bed.

'Go home', is how the shit starts. 'Go home to live another day,' is how it tempts.

'Dream your dreams', is how the chicken-shit starts. 'Dream the sweet dreams of the dreamy', is how it tempts.

I hear them, the shit and the chicken-shit, hear them both alike. And what with the black of the night being so black and everything, and what with the open watching eyes of the night being so open and everything too, it's easy for them, the two shits, easy for them to have an explanation for every question, and an excuse for every weakness. That's not even to mention the hole of the hole, it being so empty and everything, being so open and everything too. I mean like the hole of the hole—the shits really don't have to even go raising that one.

I mean like poor Ollie, he had to be petrified, just had to be. I mean like I surely was. What if Ollie, what if he didn't want to be buried alive, or dead, wanted so badly not to be buried alive or dead that he went back to bed, back to his safe bed? And good-for-nothing Richie, what if he wandered back to bed, wandered back to his nice warm bed, wandered and snuck on back to his bed, kind of like I now wanted to?

Why, that shit! Why, that good-for-nothing chicken-shit! They'd been scamming me! They'd been scamming me, those shits, probably scamming me all along!

Well, just maybe I wanted to do some of that too, my bed right about now looking pretty safe, looking pretty nice and warm too.

But if I wanted to scam, and they already were, who then was watching the hole?

Nobody. Nobody, that's who. Nobody was watching. And nobody had been watching, nobody, that is, but me.

I hate being a sucker, it just about the only thing that I hate more than being a shit or chicken-shit. And now those two shits ... now those two shits had come up with reason enough to make me think that I'd been played for one.

I turned myself around. I turned myself right around for home and for bed. And as I turned I slipped ... on the white garbage bag, the one from Rook's recruitment picnic, the one left as a marker to show the break in the woods. And nudging it carefully with my foot—nudging it ever so carefully just to make sure it wasn't like a ghost or anything—I noticed another bag, a smaller bag, one that had a note attached.

'COOKIES, MICHAEL!'—it read.
'Love, Rook'—the note read.

ROOK! Rook, Rook, Rook—ROOK! She was killing me—just killing me! Not enough that she was in my thoughts and in my dreams, now she was leaving behind evidence that she actually was man enough to actually go and do her hole-watching duties. And if she did it, how in the world could I turn shit now? How could I turn chicken-shit? How could I now just let the shits go off, persuade me that it now was okay to be one?

I turned on my flashlight. Though its light made me a target, I realized that I needed it to find the next marker—the outcrop of rock. Another thing that I realized was how I now needed to take a leak—take one something awful. But could I just stop in my tracks? Did I dare? I mean if a search party ever was to find me with my fly down, and my pecker out, and lying in a puddle of my own piss—how could I live with that? And even dead—how could I live with that?

Night noises ... deep dark woodsy noises ... screeching and moaning and groaning noises ... were coming at me from all sides now, worse even than noises from earlier watches at other holes. My hand shook, the darting light of my flashlight turning trees into killers, turning killer trees into dancing killer trees, and turning them all into dancing and prancing and salivating killer trees, the trees just gone wild in expectation of a kill—*me as kill!*

Scary too was how with just a sweep of my hand, dark areas turned to light, and areas of light turned to dark. Just the slightest jiggle, only a jiggle, made all the difference. It all seemed so haphazard—one way light, the other way darkness; one way vision, the other way the abyss, the abyss so bottomless—vast too.

And that's where the hole-filler-upper lived—right there in the abyss. The hole-filler-upper didn't like light; didn't like it at all. He didn't like holes, and didn't like treasures, and didn't like discoveries, and for that matter, he probably didn't like me or L.T. none either. If the hole-filler-upper had his way the world would be just like his life … just an abyss. It would be a stupid world, a stupid world that never did learn, and never would, just what a little light could do.

Pathetic—that hole-filler-upper—just pathetic! He was just a pathetic nobody who only survived, and only could survive, by keeping himself out of my flashlight's beam. He was a pathetic nobody who had to survive, and could only survive, by every so often reaching into the beam, reaching on in so as to trouble all the good people of the world, those good people who only wanted to be in light, and away from dark.

He could, of course, always be watched, that pathetic nobody. And if watched—if really, really carefully watched— then maybe just maybe he could be caged in his abyss, actually caged in so well that his long slimy fingers couldn't reach us, and couldn't hurt us … us the good people of the world. And if watched carefully—if watched so well as to be for all intents and purposes guarded—then maybe just maybe he would just be who he was, a pathetic nobody, a nobody from whom there was nothing really to fear.

Frozen in the beam of my flashlight, the outcrop of rock now before me looked white, bright, somehow so actually bright it seemed to have an energy all its own. Kneeling on down to it, I brought my nose in close.

L.T. was right! He was right! It stunk! Stunk, stunk, stunk—I mean stunk to high heaven stunk! Like, what was this rock trying to do, call on everyone passing by to piss on it, take a leak, take a really good long leak?

I mean it called to me. It certainly did call to me. And what with my bladder by now all but dialing 9-1-1, sending an S.O.S., and posting an A.P.B., I figured the rock as good a place as any to leave my mark—hole-filler-upper be damned!

I mean a waterfall—a crashing and splashing and wild waterfall—pissing on this thing was like Niagara Friggin' Falls! Every wild animal … every crazed hole-filler-upper … every wild animal and crazed hole-filler-upper in the state was going to no doubt hear this thing! Torrential! I mean … *torrential!*

I shuffled back my feet, shuffled them as fast as I could, but by now it was a jailbreak—full-blown—a jailbreak pouring and gushing at me like a river gone all tsunami on me. In an instant, a flood—I was standing, just standing there like an idiot, just standing there in a flood of my own making, and the only thing to really do was laugh—first to myself, then out loud.

I searched out the tree cluster. One, I began, once I spotted the right one. Two, three, four, I paced, my eyes flipping from ground to cluster and back to the ground. Five, six, seven, eight, nine, ten, eleven, twelve, thirteen, I went on, taking a breath, stepping around the cluster and reaching the other side. Fourteen, fifteen, sixteen, seventeen, eighteen, nineteen, twenty, and—twenty-one!

Twenty-one? Hadn't L.T. reached the spot at eighteen? Didn't he say eighteen was a lucky number? If eighteen was a lucky number, what then was twenty-one, an unlucky number? I mean like was it a really unlucky number, like a really, really horrific one?

The mounds of dirt left behind caught my eye even before the hole did. I mean the mounds as a result of our digging were at least something. The hole, on the other hand, it was nothing—nothing, that is, but a black hole from which it would be near impossible, should I fall, to escape.

Making sure not to shine my flashlight directly in, I instead shined it where I stepped, close to the hole, but not too close.

As bad as it would be to see a hole-filling boogeyman inside the hole, it would be even worse to trip and fall and see him from the inside, on the outside, the boogeyman just standing there just over me.

I posted myself back by the cluster of trees, back about as close to the break in the woods as I could possibly get. Intentionally looking away from the hole and the mounds of dirt just by it, I found myself instead gazing up and upward … to a clearing of the tree branches … to a patch of open sky. Stars twinkling before me, I thought they were somehow twinkling at me, happy no doubt to see me.

Easy enough, I found the Little Dipper, located the North Star too by its position just up the outer cup rim of the Big Dipper. To my right east … to my left west … behind me south … all the directions in the world—and still I was lost. I mean for the life of me I didn't know where I was, more so what it was I was doing, more so still what it was I was doing here.

Celestial navigation, all well and good but—where was I? Maybe L.T. was right, maybe he was right about Dead Reckoning being the way to go, 'least when it came to finding treasure. And maybe Rook was right, maybe she was right about 'good Portogeez' using Dead Reckoning to figure their way, 'least to figure out where it was they the heck were. But me, and for star-gazers like me, Dead Reckoning might just as well have been dead, and treasure, it might just as soon have stayed in the ground. My answer, and maybe even my treasure, lay heavenward.

I'd read once in an astronomy book how it took light from the stars like a gazillion years to reach the earth. And what that means, I think, is that everybody coming before me would have seen the exact same stars—in the exact same way—that I now saw them. They would have seen the exact same Little

Dipper, seen exactly the same Big Dipper, and it wouldn't have made any difference just when it was, or just where it was, they lived. I mean, trees in the woods, boats in a river, faces in a crowd—like I know they aren't the same ones my great-great-great-great-great-grandparents saw. But for certain and for sure, I know I'm seeing the exact same skies, in the exact same way, that they saw them.

This, this was a start, a connection I maybe could use. Could the skies help? Could they help me find my way? Could they help me find out just what it was that needed to be found?

The stars above dazzled. And standing beneath them was overwhelming, so much so that my ancestors would no doubt have also felt much the same. Small as they were—and as big as the sky was—my ancestors would have felt helpless, absolutely helpless, and yet they'd have felt a whole lot inspired too. They would have tied their hopes to the beauty they saw, would have tied their wishes to the shooting stars they glimpsed, would have tied their dreams to the outer limits of their imaginations. They would have been optimists who put all their faith in the future still all right there before them. And they would have believed in God and would have trusted in Him too. All that being the case, my ancestors would surely have passed their hopes, and their wishes, and their dreams, on to their kids. And they would have wanted their kids to pass that same faith on to their kids, and their kids, and their kids.

So what was it, what was it my parents were passing on to me? Well, to believe in family, the Patriots, the Red Sox, Celtics, and Bruins too. And to believe in God. He was kind of a big deal. And to do right, do good, they were passing that on to me. But there was something else, something that could only be described as being different, and private, and hidden, I suppose … secret-like.

Traditions, customs, ways of doing this and ways of doing that, they passed from generation to generation to generation.

Thing was, when they reached me they landed just with a thud, pretty much just a hollow thud. I mean it was meaningless! All of it—meaningless! Meaningless, that is, so long as my parents weren't fulfilling their end of the bargain, teaching me what it was that made them them, and why it made them them. And if they weren't going to teach me what it was that made me me, and if they weren't going to teach me why it made me me, they simply weren't fulfilling their obligation, weren't fulfilling their end of the pact. I mean so long as they weren't going to teach me, how was I to know what it was that made us us, and why it made us us? My parents were holding back, hiding something—but what? And why?

I looked at the stars, couldn't connect the dots. Maybe it was Drift? And maybe L.T. was right? I mean was there really just so much Drift from one generation to the next to the next that whats and whys were now just too hard? And maybe Rook, maybe she was right? Maybe all good Portogeez really do eventually see the forest? But for me, at least for now, I just could not see the forest for the trees. And trees is what I saw. And for what it was worth, they were all I saw.

The stars. The hole. The stars. The hole. The stars. The hole. I looked back and forth, a watchman of both. As much as I wanted to, I couldn't touch the stars, couldn't get a handle on an empty hole. Looking out, looking in, even the best watchman in the world couldn't do it, and I was hardly the best. I didn't want to be. What's more I didn't want to be just that, just a watchman. I mean if the Michael in the song only watched the boat and didn't row it on account of his being just too damn tired, how was the boat ever going to get ashore? If the Michael in the song only hung around watching the river on account of it being just too damn deep, and just too damn wide, how could he ever even hope to reach the other side, the one with the milk and honey? I mean … what a shit! What a chicken-shit!

The hole! If only I could figure out the hole-filler-upper, maybe I could then figure out the hole-digger? Like the hole-filler-upper—I mean what type of person was it that didn't like treasure? Just what kind of person was it that didn't like discoveries?

Suspect Number One was the creep, the tall guy, Hal Ricci. A Harvard professor, sure he liked discoveries, but probably he only liked them when he was the one actually making them. Was he afraid that it would be me and L.T. finding out something new about Dighton Rock? Was he worried it would be me and L.T. finding out something new about Miguel Cortereal? Hadn't Hal Ricci brought up all that Shadow Lighting stuff, talked about some guy slinking around at three A.M. with a flashlight? Hal Ricci—hanging by Mrs. Haymaker like a dark cloud hanging to the sun—he was dangerous all right, just a tall creepy dangerous guy ... and a slinking-around guy to boot.

Suspect Number Two was the rich snickerer, Mr. Alves. Nosy, he liked poking through other people's stuff, probably didn't like other people digging through his stuff—his stuff being pretty much the whole damn town he thought he owned. Like a puppeteer behind the curtain, he had strings reaching out over Father Sousa and everybody else in town, and certainly didn't like any strings reaching out over him. Mr. Alves, he was dangerous all right, just a nosy snickering dangerous guy ... and a lawyer to boot.

Looking east toward the river, in the low sky I could see the first stripe of morning light like a silver sliver. There were, of course, other suspects—other hole-haters whose motivations I could pick apart—but the stripe of light grabbed hold of me. And the longer I gazed, the more it looked like a fire: rip-roaring, spellbinding, and alive. And that's how they are—fires—just spellbinding in how they move, mesmerizing in how they grow and change.

I'm a good soldier, Grandpa says, likes to say. As a soldier in the Big War, Grandpa had also been a good soldier, and he knows pretty much everything there is to know on the topic. And the trick, he says, the trick to good soldiering is simply to stick to your post, stick to it till morning relieves night, till light relieves dark. Now watching the stripe of light burn up the dark ... burn it and good ... burn it, *and how* ... I think what Grandpa is saying is I'm a good soldier not so much because I stick around, but because I like sticking around, because I like life, like the fire it comes with, and really appreciate it as something really worth sticking for.

I suddenly sensed something, something out there in the still low darkness of night. Dropping down onto my stomach— right on down to where the ground would catch me—I saw a fire hovering in the air, scorching the night, scorching it up as if feeding on it.

I knew what it was, that fire, or at least I thought I knew what it was. I just couldn't believe that it really was what I thought it was.

A torch?

A torch?

It was being held up in the air by somebody, though by whom I could not tell. How long had its holder been watching over me? How long had the torch ... how long had it been burning over me? Was it moving closer? Was it moving away? It was hard to tell. It was hard to tell just what the hell the torch was doing, other than just burning. Blackness behind it, blackness in front of it, there simply was no perspective. What with the distance between us, did the torch holder see me? What with the blackness around us, did the torch holder see me? Did he see me at all? Did he see the real me? At very best he only would have a sense of me, same as I had of him.

A torch?

Like what did the torch holder think it was—the Middle

Ages? Any normal person, any thoughtful person, any sane person, would be using a flashlight.

A torch?

The realization raced through me like the voltage of an electric chair. The torch holder didn't care whether he could or could not see. What he cared about, and all he cared about, was having his torch be seen, and having his face not be seen, there after all being no way better to warn, and no way better to scare.

The torch holder wanted it known that he was the executioner, the sick executioner who burned that poor animal by the other hole. He wanted it known he tortured it, tortured it and burned it to a crisp. And he as well wanted it known he was prepared to do so again.

Shoot it! Kill it! For the love of God, just kill it! Kill it before it kills you!

Springing to my feet, I took up a shooter's stance: left leg forward and bent at the knee, right leg back and planted in the ground; left arm up and straight to the air, right arm out and cocked at the elbow.

Shoot it? Shoot it with what? How could I attack an enemy camouflaged in darkness? How could I kill an enemy walled in by flame?

Suddenly the torch lurched—forward and closer—no doubting that now. And its flame raged, lapped up fresh mouthfuls of air, great huge bites of the stuff. On the move, did it mean to devour and burn me too, burn me till I too was nothing but crisp, pitiful ... unrecognizable?

I darted to the left, sent twigs snapping and rocks skittering with my every step. But the way left, it was the wrong way—the wrong way—was the way of the hole!

I skidded to a stop, about-faced and scrambled right. But the torch swiveled with me, matched my every move, swiveled left when I went right, swiveled right when I went left. Like a reflection in a mirror, there just was no shaking it, no shaking it but to run—run, run, run—just as fast as I could and just as far, run till my post was at my back good and abandoned, run till it was behind me good and gone.

And still the torch chased.

It chased me.

Looking back but running ahead, I tripped over a rock and got myself up. Looking back and running ahead, I collided with a tree but got myself up again. But with every trip, and every stumble, and each and every fall and fall and fall, my legs got heavier, my legs got weaker, and I got weaker ... I got weaker too.

All at once my legs flew out one way, my arms flew out another way, and my head, it just flew out in a way all its own. I'd slipped, landed hard ...landed really hard. A moment, then another, and another, I was face down, I realized, going cheek to cheek with a smooth white rock, a smooth and really smelly rock—Smelly Rock!

Lifting my head, I saw the torch was not giving up. It chased fast and it chased close, chased with purpose and chased with urgency, its chase so fast, so close, so purposeful, and so urgent as to be terrible—terrible! I laid low and hugged the Rock for all it was worth, hoped that staying still would keep me from being seen.

Just as the torch was at its most terrible, it slowed, 'least it seemed to. I could tell it had lost sight of me, was waiting for my next move. And I had to move—I just had to. I mean like— I had to do something! Doing nothing was being dead. Doing nothing ...doing nothing wasn't looking back and running ahead, wasn't looking ahead and running back. I mean it wasn't any looking, wasn't any running, wasn't any ahead, wasn't any back ... it just was ... it just was being ... it just was ... it just was nothing.

I scrambled up to my feet, sprinted for the dirt road,

sprinted with the stink of Smelly Rock still on my clothes and
still in my nostrils. But the torch, it sprinted too, so fast I just
could not gain on it. Then at once it stopped, I mean at once
and suddenly, its stopping point as best I could tell somewhere
back by Smelly Rock.

But why? Why did it stop? Why did it just up and stop?
Was Smelly Rock too white for it, like just too bright for it?
Was Smelly Rock too slippery for it, just too smelly for it? I
mean, was that it? Did it stop 'cause it hated the smell? Did it
stop 'cause it hated the smell of me too?

Though I could now no longer see the torch, still I sensed
it out there tracking me under cover of darkness, out there
somewhere tracking me under cover of flame. Had it switched,
I mean like just switched up? Had it decided to track me in a
different way, maybe by way of the river? Was that how it now
was doing it? I mean, like, that really was the way to go and do
it anyway. But what did it matter? Like, what really did it really
matter just how it went about tracking me? On foot, along the
river—even riding the stupid wind—it was in my mind now …
and doing its hunting there.

Me! The torch wanted me … my memories … my dreams
too.

"L.T.," I called over the walkie-talkie. "L.T.," I called again.
Checking my emergency channels, I saw they were still set, saw
they were still on. "L.T.?" I called out yet again. "L.T.? L.T.?
Damn it, L.T.!"

I was almost in town now, almost back at Rook's. If I could
just make it to her window, then I'd be safe. I'd hide in her
room, hide in her bed, hide in her arms, just her watching me,
and just me watching her. But suddenly I heard a cow make a
Moo that sounded like a Boo! And suddenly I heard a barn owl
make a Hoo that sounded like a Whooooo? And chickens, the
chickens over at Rook's barnyard of a house, they all together

altogether went cuckoo, so cuckoo I could just picture Uncle
Jiggy slashing 'em, slashing 'em at the throat, just slashing 'em
and then upside down hanging 'em till every last drop of blood
drained from out of their bodies and down to the hay below.
I mean for me the picture was kind of an all too real picture
anyway, real 'cause I'd actually before seen Uncle Jiggy actually
doing it. The horror of it, in fact, was so firmly pressed in
my mind that it'd likely take a therapist years and years to just
nudge the horror thing—nudge it, let alone dislodge it.

As for L.T.'s picture though, his no doubt would have the
Butcher of Best doing lots and lots of whacking, lots and lots
of hacking, lots of hacking and whacking and lots of whacking
and hacking, lots and lots so and until every last one of those
chickens was a pulp … a bloody pulp! Then, what with that
handiwork done, L.T.'s picture no doubt would have Uncle
Jiggy torching those chickens, just torching 'em in a big fire
until they were crisp … a blackened crisp!

Truth be told though, I worry sometimes that L.T.'s picture,
I worry his is kind of a little like mine, a little too much like
mine. But unlike me—and my anti-talent—L.T. has talent …
all that Dead Reckoning talent. I mean I see things, and then
don't see them, go so far as to even sometimes distrust those
things which my eyes see. I think things, and then don't think
them, go so far as to even sometimes un-think them, really un-
think them. I sense things, and then don't sense them, go so
far as to even sometimes deny them, just up and deny them.

L.T. though, he can't do that. He can't. He sees things he
shouldn't be seeing, thinks things he shouldn't be thinking,
knows things he shouldn't be knowing, and he doesn't distrust,
or un-think, or deny … just doesn't distrust, or un-think, or
deny any of it! He even has the nerve to use it, I mean actually
go and use it!

Owing now to the Moo, and the Hoo, and the cuckoo, I

changed plans on the fly, ran from Rook's bed and Uncle Jiggy's slaughter house, straight for town, arriving soon enough at the Village Green, its lone lamppost light flickering on and off, and on and off, flickering as if somehow unsure whether to just stay on, or stay off, or just die already.

Directly ahead, the big double doors of St. Peter's lay just before me, just yards away, the church's pathway lights lit like runway lights, signaling me to approach, land, taxi in close, and come on in.

Looking back, I saw the torch, it still right there behind me. Looking ahead, I saw the church doors, they there right before me. And on the lawn, all aglow and smiling, there on the lawn was the image of the Virgin Mary, and nearby it a statue of the Lady of Fatima, it too all aglow, it too all wondrous. I mean like … I mean like I saw them … I saw them alright … saw too the figure of Jesus on the Cross set back deep in the stony church wall … but …

Scary, scary, scary.

Images, statues, figures—just scary as heck in the half-dark of night, the half-light of day, scarier even than usual. In ways that I don't understand, for reasons that I don't understand, I can't get close to them—those images, those statues, those figures—can't get too near them, won't allow myself to get pulled in by them. I mean grand enough for some, I guess, but me, me they made feel low. Warm enough too for some, I guess, but me, me they made feel cold. And so far as seeing any light or beauty in them, the only rush that I had was a rush to be ready—hair-trigger ready—ready to go, ready to run.

I rounded a corner, saw that the light in my room was on, thought that I'd turned it off. Then again … it could be I left it on. But I thought I'd turned it off. Whatever. I was way too tired and frazzled to now be sure of anything. I mean like maybe Mom and Dad turned it on, my light? But like why would they be up? And if up, and if about, what were they up to?

Before going on inside, I took a look behind me, saw again the torch. It was maybe fifty yards back, keeping its distance, just there in the still remaining darkness of night. The torch … it knew where I lived now. Then again, maybe it had always known where I lived, showing up and everything as it did from seemingly out of nowhere. But now that for sure and for certain and positively the torch knew just where it was I lived, did it mean to burn not just me, but my home—burn that as well?

I stayed in place, shined my flashlight onto my home, why I did not know, other than to maybe show the torch I could, show it I would. And that—that was important. Somehow it seemed important to show the torch I was going inside my home, going inside walking, going inside walking and not running. And it was important too to show that the running that I did do, it wasn't from it, nor was it from the dark or the night. Rather, the running was a running for my home, my home always.

But stepping past the threshhold, tip-toeing up the stairs, entering my room and slipping myself into my bed and under my covers, I had to admit to myself that not only did I really not know the torch, really I did not know my home.

7

Kind of a shame is what it was.

In olden days—like before I even was born—they say that Sunday Mass was held in Latin, the Latinese oozing off a priest's tongue as spooky chants, mysterious incantations. Sounding somehow cut in mid-stream—with the cut part left to just trail off somewhere or other—the chants could well have been calling out pleas and prayers, teachings and warnings, thank yous and no thank yous, maybe even spells, hexes, or hocus-pocuses. They could have been calling out curse words, swear words, four-letter words, or maybe even super-squared four-letter words. I mean, who knew? Who knew what the hell was going on? Who knew what was oozing? Who the Hell even knew Latinese? Whatever it was going, or oozing, or Latinesing, it was better that way though, better that way for hearing that which there was to hear, believing in that which there was to believe, getting inspired by that which there was to get inspired by.

Callings? Inspiration? Beliefs? For the most part that stuff really is better anyway coming not so much from the outside, but from the inside, and if it has to come from the outside, better to have it come in unintelligible pulpit Latinese, and not intelligible, but nonsensical, English.

I mean take the little prayer of the little girl up there in front, or the new thank you of the new mother up there in front, or the old hex of the old witch alone there in her church pew—all of 'em go out better if at first having gone down better … down better in unintelligible Latinese.

Patty, ramrod straight to one side of me, like here she was wearing a color to match her mood—blue. And Billy, squirming himself into knots just to the other side of me, like here he was done up and buttoned down in white—like entirely white—looked just ridiculous, I mean ridiculous-ridiculous.

As for me, well, like here I was good and glowing, good and glowing in just the exact same color that I was feeling—red. I mean like we weren't brothers and sister as much as we were the Costa trio—a damn red, white, and blue flag. If L.T. were here to see this—which, of course, he wasn't … the whole church thing in every way against his religion—he'd dub us, 'the Costa Kids: All Americans in their Sunday Best', leastwise he'd dub us a dubbing something like that.

First off—I first off was pissed 'cause owing to last night's torch watch I got no sleep. Second off—I second off was pissed 'cause Rookie and Ollie weren't here, they probably having successfully done what I couldn't do, namely convince their parents just how tired they were without at the same time having to explain the reason for their tiredness. Third off—I third off was pissed 'cause I was in church, having yet and again utterly failed in my attempt to find a way out of Mass.

"Isn't Sunday School enough?" I asked Mom, asked just this morning. "I mean, really, isn't that enough?"

"No," Dad answered, his answer coming from behind his paper's sports pages.

"But Mom, really, it's like too much already. Too much! You and Dad don't go to Sunday Mass, 'least you normally don't go. And Grandma and Grandpa, like they never go."

"We always went when we were your age," Dad said. "So did Grandma and Grandpa."

"But Mom, what harm is there in skipping Mass just this once?"

"Look, Michael," Dad said, his paper now down on the breakfast table, "you're going. When you're Catholic you go to church. That's the deal."

Three times a loser and three times pissed, so naturally I then went doing what any good big brother would—punched Billy in the thigh, punched him for no good reason, pretty much just punched him just because. Billy, well, Billy, so he naturally then went doing what any stinky little brother would—kicked me, just up and kicked me, like that just kicked me. And Patty, well, Patty, so she naturally went doing what any rotten big sister would—elbowed me, hard she elbowed me, really hard to the ribs she elbowed me … the elbow a kill shot if ever there was one.

"Stop it!" she whispered without so much as even turning her head in my direction. "Stop it! You're embarrassing me, Michael. The whole church is looking at us like we're demented or something."

"Oh, yeah … it's you they're looking at. You look miserable, like you've just lost your best dog or something, or your best friend, or in your case the two just about the same anyway. Can't you at least try looking like you kind-a, sort-a, somewhat want to be here?"

"I don't even have to be here, Michael, 'least I no longer have to be here every Sunday. The only reason I'm here now is to keep an eye on you and Billy—mainly you."

"If you don't have to be here, how come me and Billy have to be here?"

"It's what we do when we're young. You're still too stupid to understand, so just trust me with this one, Michael. I mean like I'm older than you, and smarter than you, and know a whole lot more than you, and even I don't fully yet understand it."

"What we do? What we do? Do like getting baptized? Do like getting confirmed?"

"Yeah, do like that."

"But it's not do as in Communion, right? It's not do like that? It's not do like that at all, is it?"

"Don't even go there, Michael. And don't get smart. You know we don't do Communion. You know that's not a part of it."

"But going to church is, right?"

"Yeah. Right."

St. Peter's is small as compared to the churches of Fall River and New Bedford, but it's still big enough to have ceiling domes, sculptured angels, stained glass windows. And the colors of those glass windows today seemed to be especially amazing, the sun brilliantly lighting up story scenes both from the Old Testament, and the New. I, of course, focused on the story scenes from the Old, the ones always getting discussed in my Sunday school class of Spitters.

The window of Joseph and his coat of many colors was one of my favorites, the story one of my favorites too, just today's class topic even being: Joseph and his Brothers in Egypt. Seems after years of separation from his Hebrew brothers, Joseph had become an Egyptian, and a successful one at that. He in fact was so good at it that when his brothers again saw him they couldn't even recognize him. For that matter, Joseph probably couldn't even recognize himself, having changed as he had. Anyway, Joseph didn't reveal himself to his brothers, but seeing them again after so many years made him remember his father, Jacob, and his little brother, Benjamin, both still in Canaan. So Joseph went and had his brothers bring Benjamin to him, and only then, when all the brothers were at last reunited, did he reveal himself to them, explain just who it was he in fact was. Jacob, he too joined them in Egypt, but when he died he had himself taken home to Canaan according to his wishes, the burial taking place there. As for Joseph, he continued to live in Egypt as an Egyptian. And when he too finally died, he too was taken to Canaan. In his case, however, the taking for reburial taking four hundred years, to when the Children of Israel at last broke free of slavery and had their great exodus.

"Hey, Patty. So how old are Grandma and Grandpa anyway?"

"Over eighty. Grandpa I think is eighty-one, maybe eighty-five, maybe older than that. Even Grandma is eighty-two."

"Boy, that's old, too old, I guess, to be going to church. You think Mom and Dad will be going to church when they're that old?"

"No. Well, I suppose they might if they feel it necessary to go, you know, like if things change."

"I guess when you're really old you want to stay close to your home, or at least get close if you're not already there."

"Yeah, maybe, Michael. Maybe that's it."

"But by staying home, won't Mom and Dad, you know, like show that they don't want to be going to church? Won't they show too much of themselves, show too much of their thinking? I mean what are other people going to think? Won't they care? Won't Mom and Dad care?"

"Look around, Michael. Look at the people here."

So looking, I saw some people paying attention to Father Sousa up at the pulpit, saw others meanwhile just looking down into their laps. Mainly what I saw though were backs, that and a whole lot of heads. And then turning, and then twisting too, I saw Mr. Alves standing by the door, his hands squarely on his hips. He stared—at me, of course—but then again he pretty much stared at everybody.

"Well, Mr. Alves there, he looks mad."

"He's always mad. He's especially mad when it comes to us. What I mean though is, look at the people way up front. How old are they?"

"Some young, some old."

"Okay, now look at the people way back here. How old are they?"

I saw a couple of young fathers with little kids, saw too a couple of young mothers with even littler kids, but mainly what I saw were just kids, just Spit kids, just Spit kids here and by themselves.

"So what do you think, Michael? You think Mom and Dad when they get old will care what others think about their not going to church?"

"Guess not."

"Of course not."

"But Mom and Dad, why won't they care?"

"'Cause there's no future in it. Being old—like what future is there in that? I mean when you're old you don't much care about your now frail self, and you don't any more care about your once-younger self, all that kind of caring kind of pointless. All that matters is the young … what they think … what they do. That's the future. That's all the future there still is. Only they carry on what was. Only they carry everything important, everything dear. Old people don't matter, Michael, they just don't. And you know what, they know they don't."

A lady three rows up turned and placed a finger over her lips for us to shut up—Holy Communion now ready to start. So Patty nudged me, and I nudged Billy, and together we went to the aisle. And then, then as always, rather than walk up to the front of the church, we walked ourselves to the back. And we were hardly alone. A whole lot of people, Spit people, did the exact same.

Standing there, standing there in back, standing there in back and waiting in the cool dark hollow of the church, standing there in back and staying there like bad children in a corner—we watched as others made their way forward for the wafers that would be placed in their mouths. And we could have joined them. We could have joined them, I mean nobody keeping us back on the sidelines. But we didn't. We never did.

When I was just a little kid I thought we didn't step forward to accept wafers because we were shy. Then, when I got older, I thought the reason we didn't take Communion was because we felt ourselves somehow undeserving to receive the body of Christ. But now, now that I'm older still, I have a different take. I think we don't step forward because we don't want to step forward.

It's almost like we've drawn a line or something, a line that says something like, 'beyond this point we will not go.' The line separates us, separates us from those who do go. But the line— why did it get drawn? I mean it seems to me a line doesn't get drawn unless there's a need to draw it. And we wouldn't have had a need to draw it unless we somehow already had been pushed, pushed off from where we were, pulled already away from where we were.

A drawn line is a line of separation, our separation from others. It's a statement: We're different. And if we're different, then I'm different. And I don't think ... I don't think I like being different. I mean being different, yeah, that may be good for L.T.—he likes being different. And if people don't realize that he is he'll show them, just up and show them, will even go so far as to tell them. The thing is though ... the thing is ... he isn't different, 'least not really different, other that is than that difference in his head, the one making him want to be different.

But Spitters, we really are different—really different—and yet we can't show anyone we are, let alone can't tell anyone we are. In the end what we do, and all we do, is make ourselves even more different ... ever so different. I mean we make ourselves crazy. We make ourselves paranoid. And that sucks—it just sucks! I mean it makes me uncomfortable, makes me self-conscious, makes me think too much, and makes me worry too much. And I hate it—I just hate it!

I could still see Mr. Alves there by the door and just looking at me, just looking down on me, just looking like he looked the night of the fado music. For him the line I was taking was mutiny on the high seas, and my hanging back at the back of St. Peter's wasn't the only thing now bothering him. What really got him was my hanging back at the back of St. Peter's looking pissed—pissed and pissed off. What he wanted was for me to give up, and my being pissed was a sign I wasn't giving up. What he wanted was for me to give in, and my being pissed off was a sign I wasn't giving in. What he wanted—what he really wanted, that Mr. Alves—was for me to let myself get pushed, let myself get pulled, let myself get pushed and pulled all the way across that line.

And this … I could see this was going to be a problem. He, that Mr. Alves … he wanted it all. And I … I didn't want to give, didn't want to give anything.

I turned his way, and he saw me turn. Then I saw him squint, and then he saw me glare. And now truly face-to-face, now truly and actually eye-to-eye too, the distance between us became no distance, and the difference separating us, well—that became all the difference.

Working myself up onto my toes—working myself out and away from the crowd too—I stood up and stood out, looked tough and looked cool, did lots of good standing, did lots of good looking, stood and looked even while all the while I wondered just how it was, and just why it was, I let myself get into this predicament. Too late—too late I realized I just was too old to win a staring contest. Too late—too late too I realized I still was too young as well to go and make myself an enemy, an enemy such as Mr. Alves.

I was making this much too personal, and in the end not only would Mr. Alves dislike me even more than he already obviously did, he would hate me. And idiot me, I was giving him all the reason in the world to do just that. I felt myself wilting ... wilting ... wilting here right before his eyes, and though I badly wanted to get away, I couldn't.

Somebody—anybody—needed to walk between us. Somebody—anybody—needed to tap him on the shoulder, or punch me in the mouth, do both—do something! But somebody didn't show. And anybody, anybody for all intents and purposes being nobody—nobody did nothin'. For what it was worth, me and Alves were alone in the church, not a soul having even a clue as to what was happening here. This was a grudge match, an insanely personal grudge match, us just killing each other—*I mean just killing each other*—and what with my not yet being in his league, it was by far he doing the better killing.

A blink ... a flinch ... a deep breath ... and over ...match stopped, mercifully stopped, me doing the caving to stop it.

"I'm out of here," I said to Patty.

"Out to where?"

"Out to get lost."

Walking from St. Peter's, I was in an all-out run by the time I hit the Village Green, running first this way and then that way—and then back this way, and then back that way—my every way a circle, just me in an orbit around myself. Angry ... stupid ... ashamed too—I was lost all right—my problem being I simply could not ... just could not ... lose myself from myself.

Wandering on over to Captain Jack's, I spun myself around and around and around on a counter stool, and when I at last came to a stop, there was Ol' Cuss fixin' me with his steely eye.

"You look like hell."

"Thanks."

"You just walk the plank?"

"Pretty much. And sharks, Captain Jack, I think the sharks are circling. I think they're even laughing."

"Laughin', you say?"

"Yeah, laughin'. Seems I have a knack of spilling just enough of my own blood to drive them into a frenzy."

"Frenzy?"

"Yeah, frenzy. I think I'm kind of in a frenzy myself."

"Then swim, boy. You know how to swim, don't ya?"

"Yeah, and that's kind of what I'm doing. But swimming, Captain Jack, my swimming just ain't cuttin' it. It's screwed up. I mean I know I should just swim with the tide and everything, but that kind of swimming just ain't my nature."

"Nature?"

"Yeah, my nature. I'm thirteen, you know, fourteen in just a couple of weeks."

"You're that old?"

"Yeah, I am that old."

"How did this happen to you, Michael?"

"I don't know. One minute everything's going pretty good and then, without even knowing how or when, things got complicated."

Ol' Cuss poured brandy into a cup, added black coffee and set it in front of me. Pouring in some sugar, about a cup's worth, I then topped it off with cream, about a white-out's worth.

"That's quite the combustible combination," Ol' Cuss said, wincing. "It reminds me of you and that gangstah friend of yours, the one you call L.T."

"How's that?"

"Well, he's a strange bird, your friend, a curious bird. He's got you thinkin', Michael. He's got you thinkin' and doin' all kinds of stuff."

"Stuff like what?"

"Stuff like diggin' holes. Damn it, Michael! Holes—you damn well know what kinds of stuff! Frenzy? Sure sharks are in a frenzy 'bout stuff like that."

I swallowed some coffee, it burning my tongue a little, the brandy blowing my mind a little, and the cream and sugar screwing with my stomach a lot. "How do sharks know stuff like that?"

"Never you mind, Michael. But this is a small town, a pretty one at that, and the townspeople, they don't like holes in their landscape. If you go diggin' holes, if you go messin' with their view, the townspeople will have nowhere else to look but themselves. And believe me, they don't want to do that."

"Captain Jack, do you know who's playing with our holes?"

"Playin'?"

"Yeah, playin', not that it's fun any more or nothin'. I mean burning animals—that hole-filler-upper's crazy! I think he's crazy. Captain Jack, I think he's evil."

"Hold on. Burnin'? Burnin'?"

"Yeah, burnin'. Didn't you know?"

"Hell no, I didn't know! Just 'cause I keep my ear to the ground doesn't mean I bend it to hear every little thing or big thing you got cookin' in that thirteen, almost fourteen, year-old kitchen-brain of yours. Now Michael, listen up. Seein' as you're not half as good at keepin' secrets as you are diggin' for 'em, you need to know: there are secrets, and then there are secrets. Some can be; some can't be. More important, some should be, and some shouldn't be. Listen to me, if they're goin' 'round fillin' your holes then they don't like your holes, and for that matter, they don't like you. But if they're goin' 'round burnin', if they're goin' 'round burnin' God's creations, then not only don't they like you, they don't like themselves. And that, Michael, that's dangerous. You know there's an old expression, goes somethin' like: if ever you find yourself in a hole, stop your diggin'. If you do, Michael, if you do stop diggin', then their problem with your diggin' goes away, and your problem—it goes away too."

"I don't think the problem does go away, Captain Jack. See, I don't see our digging as the problem, 'least as not the real problem. The real problem is the holes, the holes themselves. Whether we dig them or don't dig them, they're still there. Thing is you can't get at them, can't even get to them, without first digging."

"Michael. Michael, Michael, Michael …you're makin' my head hurt, Michael."

"Captain Jack, I'm digging. Okay, one way or another, I'm digging. And you know what? I kind of even know why I'm digging. What I don't know is what I'm digging for. But the solution's there, there in the holes. And if people don't like the holes 'cause they ruin the view, or if they don't like the holes 'cause it forces them to look at themselves, then they don't like themselves. They don't like the holes there—there in themselves."

Ol' Cuss rubbed the back of his head. "Do you like the holes, Michael?"

"No. I'm like everybody else. I don't like them either."

"You know, I'm thinkin' I might just know what's botherin' you."

Taking a swig of brandy, thinking a while, Ol' Cuss took another swig, went to thinking a while longer. He was stalling, and needed a push.

"You're old, aren't you Captain Jack?"

"That I am."

"My grandparents are old too. So tell me, when you're old, do you care? I mean, you know, do you care about the same stuff as you did when you were young? Do you care about it in the same way?"

"Hell, I'm still the same person, ain't I? Sure I still care about the same things. But it's different now. When I was young what I cared about was how things affect me. Now I couldn't give two shits about how they affect me. The things though, mind you, the things still are there, and nowadays what I care about is how they affect young people like yourself. Michael, you already know what I care about. The sea, the sea and everything that is sea, is what I care about. And it's just no good to anyone if all I do is wind up goin' down to Davey Jones' locker of a grave with all its mysteries in tow."

"So tell me, Captain Jack. Tell me a good mystery. Tell me the best you got."

Ol' Cuss rested his elbows on the counter, and I could see his eyes look and search, search then twinkle. I practically could see his thoughts drift and then anchor.

"We was in the Grand Banks," he began. "Lloyd, Harry, Gus, Willie, Vic, Black Jack, Tinker and me, each of us in our own little dory. Hector, he was there too, he in his. We'd been at sea three weeks, and the saudades was bad, real bad. Each and every one of us was withdrawn and lost in saudades all our own. We rowed slow, moved about even slower, and our eyes, they was like those of the old men, milky dull as if full of cataracts. We talked little, slight nods passin' for a greetin', mumbles in a pinch just fine for conversation.

"We'd all have given our eyeteeth to be home, home all safe and warm, I mean the cod on our hooks anyways more like paupers than kings. Our muscles ached from all the rowin', and our hearts, they ached even more. To make matters worse, our dories just lay still on the waters, and for sailors that ain't natural. It just ain't normal.

"Then the fog, the fog it rolled in. Well, it didn't so much roll on in on us as it did drop on in upon us. In no time at all not a single one of us could see the other, and this, mind you, this bein' the daytime. At first it wasn't all that bad, the fog, us kind of sick and tired of lookin' at each other anyways. But after a while it spooked us. And that's just what it does you know—isolation—it spooks. For us it all just got to bein' so bad that each man in his little dory thought himself all alone in the big ocean."

"So what did you do?"

"What could we do? We called out to each other, called out to make sure each man in his dory was okay. But there was one problem."

"What was that, Captain Jack?"

"Hector, he didn't answer. 'Hector, Hector, Hector' we all called, but nothing came back. What's worse, the fog was playin' tricks on us. One moment Lloyd's call to Hector sounded like it was somewhere out in front, then it sounded like it was somewhere out in back. One moment I heard Tinker to my right, and then when he called again, I could have sworn he was to my left. We was disoriented. And soon enough, what with the mix of worry for Hector and the loss of our senses, we started losin' our minds. There was only one thing to do."

"What's that?"

"Sit tight. Sit tight, shut up, and ride the thing out. Gettin' frenzied, that's no help. Frenzied minds don't work. So alone in my dory as I was, and alone in the silence too, I laid myself down, laid myself low."

"Huh?"

"I prayed."

"You? You prayed?"

"Understand, even somebody like me, when faced with silence or madness, even somebody like me thinks things they never in a thousand years would think to think, does things they never in a thousand years would think to do. Anyway, the silence, it went on, and on, and on some more. And though I hated it, I was afraid of it goin' away. See, silence in my book, silence is a far cry better than madness, and I certainly didn't want that comin' back round. But then, just as things got to bein' their most silent, I at once heard someone singin', the singin' so sweet, and calm, and inspiring I swear it the most beautiful thing I ever did hear. Do you know, Michael, do you know who it was doin' the singin'?"

"Hector?"

"Yes, Hector. None of us knew he could sing like that. I mean Hector, he never sang, barely even opened his mouth. Well, I suppose the silence got to him, got him to singin' a song deep inside, the song probably his way of settlin' himself down. Funny thing was, the song Hector sang, even though it was in a language I didn't understand, somehow or other I seemed to know the melody.

"Now, Michael, I'm goin' to tell you somethin'. I'm goin' to tell you a secret."

"You're going to tell me a secret? You're going to tell me a secret after my spilling the beans about what's been going on at the holes? Captain Jack, you don't have to. Really you don't. I mean, like, what makes you so sure you can trust me?"

"I can trust you, Michael, I can trust you because I know you. I can trust you because my secret, it's your secret too. Ready and swear to keep it?"

"Swear," I said, my breaths turning over so shallow I couldn't breathe. Whether I wanted it, or whether I didn't want it, I was being drawn in, both fear and anticipation growing so damn wildly as to be suffocating.

"The song Hector sang was a song of the *Nação*, the Nation. I recognized it because I could. I recognized it because I have some Nation in me too."

Taking a swig of brandy, Ol' Cuss used his hand to wipe his mouth dry. "The song long ago has been forgotten, Michael, so I can't sing it any more. But still I can hum the melody, hum it if only for a little while. And though I no longer am part of the Nação, still it is a part of me, a proud part of me."

Ol' Cuss stared at the counter, his shoulders drooping, his head drooping even more. He looked like he might fall, the fall falling for a good long while, if not forever.

"Captain Jack, the story. What happened next? What did you do?"

"Well, Hector's singin' was so clear I was able to row my dory over to help him, the others doin' the same. But it actually was Hector doin' the helpin'. His song calmed everyone, and together we waited till such time as we could rejoin the mother ship. As for Hector, nobody ever did ask him about the song because, truth is, whether we dory men were Nação or weren't Nação, what did it matter? What does it matter? What does it matter now to anyone? These days it doesn't. It's late, Michael. It's too late."

"It still matters to some," I said, thinking about the hole, thinking too about the hole-filler-upper.

A bell rang over the diner door, and I spun myself around.

"It's your little friend, Michael, your little strange friend."

L.T. was practically skipping, his shit grin wide, his beady eyes just as beady as ever. "He ain't really strange, Captain Jack."

"I know. I know he isn't."

L.T. placed his hands on a stool, vaulted, and stuck the landing. "Judges?"

"A seven," I said, "on technical, a ten on artistic. I'm giving you points for doing it with that idiot smile on your face."

Ol' Cuss grunted. "The usual?"

"The usual," L.T. said.

I stared into my brandy coffee, tried ignoring L.T., his good cheer threatening to ruin what pleasure there was in sharing saudades with Ol' Cuss.

"So what did Captain Jack have to say?"

"He said 'Aaargh'. Like so where the hell were you last night? I called you on the walkie-talkie and you didn't answer."

"What time?"

"About 5:00."

"Mom and me were at the movies. Hal tagged along. Mom's been seeing a lot of him, you know."

"No, A.M., you idiot! I called you at 5:00 A.M.!"

"Guess I was sleeping. I mean that is what normal people do, Michael, at 5:00 A.M. Why, where were you?"

I spun myself around on the stool, gave it another spin, and another, was a whirlwind by the time I lit into L.T. "Where was I? Where was I? I was watching that stupid hole, the one you got us all watching! While you were sweet dreaming, while you were concocting all kinds of sick things for us to do, I was running for my life from a guy with a torch! A torch! He and the torch, they chased me, chased me all the way through the woods!"

"Really?" L.T. said. "Wow, really? A torch? A real life torch?" He launched himself off his stool, practically knocked me off mine. "The torch, was the Butcher of Best under it?"

"I didn't really get a good look, you know, running for my life and everything as I was. I guess it could have been just about anybody, but no way was it Uncle Jiggy. He likes me too much, L.T., 'least he used to. It's just you he wants to kill."

"Oh, yeah, that's right. I almost forgot. Anyway, Michael, I went by the hole just this morning and guess what?"

"The hole got filled?"

"Yeah, of course it got filled. But it's better even than that."

"Gee, what in the world could be better even than that?"

"If you stop begging for a second, I'll tell you. Next to our filled-in hole, there's now a new hole, a brand new one. It's six feet long, and three feet wide, and maybe four feet deep. You know what it is, don't ya? It's a burial hole, Michael, a grave, a stinkin' rotten grave! I mean like what did they think … that they could scare us? Did they think they could make us give up? Don't they understand? Don't they understand anything? Like who do they think they are? Who do they think we are?"

puzzle of the rock, the hole, and the river. "So, Michael, that makes you one mixed-up kid."

We were walking in the woods of Dighton Rock State Park, L.T. picking up a dried-out stick and throwing it before then shading his eyes to see just where it wound up. Vacation now as good as over, and with still plenty of insanity and criminality surely yet to come, I changed up my metaphor— that whole hanging one. L.T. hanging wasn't a vacation with the criminally-insane, but a life sentence with the L.T. brand of criminally-insane, a life sentence no doubt going on forever, and affecting me forever, the only relief in sight a rope to the neck and a trap door underfoot—I mean … just a rendezvous with a rope … just an appointment with a trap door.

"Me? I'm mixed up? Look who's talking. If you were me right now and looking at you, you'd be throwing up all over the place—that's how sickening and mixed-up you are."

L.T.'s mother and the tall guy, Hal, were strolling on up ahead, Hal's golden retriever, Fetch, nipping at their heels. Letting his arm slip from Mrs. Haymaker's neck down to her shoulder and waist, Hal kissed her on the lips, she leaning into him and resting her head on his, Fetch meanwhile just running into the backs of both of their knees till they nearly buckled. And what with the afternoon sun just splashing them and everything in shimmering light, all in all, it—the whole thing— it pretty much was the most sickening sight I ever did see.

"You like him?" I asked L.T.

"Hal? Yeah, he's cool. He's got Fetch and he's got a Harley. My Mom took me to see him in Cambridge and I sat in on a class where he showed slides from his work at Machu Picchu— that's Peru, Michael—you know, South America."

"I know South America! What, you think I don't know South America?"

"Simmer, Michael. I'm sure you're big on South America,

absolutely and positively could find it on a map, you know, like if your life depended on it."

"Of course I could find South America if my life like depended on it. Just the same though, thanks for pointing out the continent that that country's in."

Hanging with Mrs. Haymaker, that too is a lot like hanging with L.T., only better ... much better. Her puzzles, her mysteries, her challenges are about Dighton Rock—not about me. She's cool; I chill.

As for my family though, they're not cool; I never chill. I mean like whenever we sit down for supper there's tension coming from the TV that's reporting the news; tension from my mother over whether supper's good or not good or even enough; tension over real problems and imagined problems; tension over the knock that may come at the door, or the ring that may ring on the phone, tension for tension sake—tension all the time!

It's normal though, the tension, just a part of who we are. And it comes natural too, the tension, just passing from generation to generation to generation. We Costas are born worriers, our guard never down—never. I mean like poor Patty's got an eating disorder over how she sees herself in the mirror; poor Billy's got issues that are issue enough to have him go see a therapist; and poor me, my blood pressure's so high my doctor's always threatening to go and put me on pills.

Mrs. Haymaker and Hal sat on a tree stump and waited for me and L.T. to catch up to them, he there massaging the back of her neck, she there taking in breaths of river air. Lacing her fingers and stretching her arms over her head, sun rays flickered between cedars and pines to speckle and warm her, the speckling and warming a little like a magnifying glass concentrating light upon a leaf, golden and gold.

L.T. meanwhile, he just sprawled himself on his side to

rest, put his head in his hand and chewed on a blade of grass. I, meanwhile, sat myself down on the ground away from the three of them, my back to a walnut tree, my knees up to my chin. I rolled rotted walnut shells around in my hand; heard the flapping of blackbird wings as they flew on by. Otherwise it was quiet, maybe too much so, the calm of the woods and moment both somehow warming me and chilling me.

"This is an interesting town, Michael," Mrs. Haymaker at last said, "and its people are unusually peculiar," she went on, her chosen words for my liking a little too much like those L.T. had used. In the way trial balloons go up and up and up in the air, just who knew where they might end up, just what they might bump up into? I for sure didn't know, 'least not exactly. However what I did for sure know was that the words rat-a-tat-tating from out of her mouth rat-a-tat-tated with a purpose, and that the trial balloons released into the air, that they were released with a purpose.

I rolled the shells out of my hand, lay myself down. Sky of blue, clouds of white, sun so very strong—they were what they were—beautiful, and strong, and sure … surer now than even the ground under my very back.

"Michael," Mrs. Haymaker said, "as an anthropologist I look at people. I look at their culture. A bracelet tells me the Wampanoags cared about their looks. An arrowhead tells me that they hunted, and that there was need to protect themselves. A clay jar, it shows me they worried about food, stored it for the winter. And these things, these practices, they're understandable; they make sense. You follow?"

"Yes," I said, the ground cold under my back.

"But here in Best Harbor, and certainly in Spit, I see practices that aren't understandable. They don't make sense, are just strange. Here cousins marry cousins, marry them at rates far higher than those in the general population, even small-town populations. Here kitchens are in basements without windows, and if the kitchens have windows, they're blocked in with shrubbery. Here people slaughter chickens in backyard sheds, slaughter them even when there's a perfectly good market close by. Seeing these things, Michael, seeing them doesn't really require any special digging. The only real digging required is finding out why these things are done."

I lifted my head, turned it, saw L.T. looking at me … then saw him looking away from me. For a moment somehow he looked different, as if I somehow didn't know him, at least know him like I thought I knew him. And after another moment, and yet another, not only didn't I for sure know if I really knew him, I didn't think I liked him.

"Michael, L.T. tells me that when you were in the woods with Rookie for an initiation circle of some sort, you asked her some tough questions. And I understand that, I totally do; it's what clubs do when taking on a new member. But, Michael, here people ask questions all the time, especially ask them of newcomers. I mean it happened with us, the questions at first seemingly all straightforward enough, and our answers for sure all straightforward enough too. However, clearly the questions weren't so straightforward after all, and obviously our answers, they were too straightforward, straightforward and incorrect, because, Michael … because never were we accepted here. Never.

"So what is this club? And what's with this club? Newcomers like us never even knew there was one, and not knowing, we never had a chance, certainly not with questions that obviously were much tougher than they first appeared. It's as if there's a secret society here and you have to know the correct codes to enter it. Rookie seems to have known them, she after all making the cut. But we didn't make it. Why, Michael? How come we didn't make it? Is it that we're not part of this thing you call … the Nation? Did we not make it because we didn't know the codes … know to answer that we live on the right road ... live by the flow of a river?"

"Stop it, Mom!" L.T. screamed, springing up to his feet. "Stop it! Leave him alone. What do you want from him? Can't you see he doesn't know the answers? Don't you understand he can't answer? Don't you understand that a secret's a secret 'cause that's what a secret is."

"Oh yeah, sure, like you understand them, L.T.! I ain't no secret! And you know what? Obviously you don't even know the very first thing about them—*keeping them*!"

"I'm sorry, Michael. I didn't tell to tell. I told 'cause I wanted to talk, to know. I wanted to understand."

Mrs. Haymaker rushed over to me, held me by my shoulders, looked me in the eye. "Michael, the absolute last thing I wanted was to make this uncomfortable for you. And I'm afraid I didn't do a very good job, did I?"

I felt horrible, was way too sensitive, was much too weak, and worse still, I let it show. They were saying I was different. They were saying my family was strange. They were saying that we Spitters were up to something, and I showed them all right—showed them that they were exactly right. Seeing through me they saw a fugitive. Seeing straight into me they saw a suspect—that after all being what I was—what I myself even saw when I looked at myself.

It wasn't fair! What did I do wrong? Why did I look guilty? Why did I have to run?

The whole thing when looked at from really close-up or afar was ridiculous, but I was in no state of mind to really do any real up-close looking, was in no position to do any real from afar looking either. I mean, here I was with my best friend, talking with nice people, and smart people too, talking with them on a beautiful summer's day ... and it was all I could do to not break down and just cry my heart out.

"Let's get a move on," Hal said. "Things go down better walking."

We walked quietly, in single file, L.T. behind me I think to keep an eye on me. The dirt path we were on after a while turned to a paved one, moss and grass poking through asphalt cracks here, cracks themselves going this way and that there … and the path itself leading us straight for Dighton Rock Museum.

Hal said hello to a ranger at the info center, and we sat ourselves down at a picnic table just by the river. Nearby, the chalky white of the museum stuck out against the non-white summer colors all around it, and the eight-sided museum's octagon, it fitted in none better. By comparison, though, the homes on the far side of the river, the Spit homes, they blended with their landscape so well not even an artist could've done any better.

However, just like the whitey-white of the museum, and just like its octopus-armed octagonal too, there of course was nothing natural to the Spit homes … nothing normal with the people inside them either. Just like a 'What's Wrong With This Picture' puzzle in a kids' magazine, you just had to know how to look. You had to know how to look for the not normal, the not natural. You had to know how to look beyond the illusion, past those tricks that made the eye see what it wanted to see.

"Have you been inside the museum before?" Mrs. Haymaker asked, handing me a tuna fish sandwich, pouring me a cup of ice-cold tea.

"Yeah, once, when I was ten or eleven. Back then I didn't think the Rock was that interesting. But now, like with L.T. telling me all the time about your research, now it's real interesting."

"Let's go inside then," Hal said. "I'll give you the insider's tour, the insider special."

We went past a chain link fence gate and went in, nobody there but us. At the center of the octagon was the Rock enclosed under glass, the scribbles on it hard to see and even more impossible to read, only the blown-up photos of them on the nearby paneled walls letting us see them better. On each panel was an explanation, another theory as to how the scribbles came to be.

In the 17th century it was thought American Indians made them, while in the 18th the honor went to the Phoenicians, in the 19th to the Vikings. Only in the 20th century did Miguel Cortereal get his due.

"You guys ever hear of Cotton Mather?" Hal asked, his voice echoing all around the octagon's walls.

"I've heard the name. Was he one of the Pilgrims?"

"No, Michael, he was a famous Puritan religious leader of the 1600s who helped prosecute witches at the Salem witch trials. Anyway, Cotton Mather, he was so fascinated by Dighton Rock that he sent sketches of its inscriptions to the Royal Society in London for decoding. But alas, the Society was stumped too, and not only couldn't they decode the sketches, they couldn't even bring themselves to come up with a response. So fascinatingly strange were the inscriptions that they thought them a hoax, thought the great Cotton Mather at long last had lost his marbles. But now we have the answer, and the funny thing is all along it wasn't really so much a question of decoding—it just simply was seeing the scribbles on the Rock for what they were." Hal hit a light switch, turned on a flashlight.

"Shadow Lighting," I said to L.T., remembering that he wasn't with us at Café Saudade for fado, probably had never heard the term. "Hal can explain it to you better than I can."

"Just imagine, guys, that it's 1920. And imagine if you will that it's three o'clock in the morning, pitch black. The Taunton River is at low tide, and a man named Edmund Delabarre climbs up a ladder above Dighton Rock and shines his flashlight down onto it. With the light glancing ever so close to the Rock's surface, deep shadows emerge, the shadows revealing markings that never before had properly been seen. Unable at the time to read them well enough, Delabarre instructs his assistant to capture the markings on a glass photography plate. Then, in the morning, he reads the plate, and lo and behold ... these words appear: 'Miguel Cortereal, by will of God, here chief of the Indians.' In addition, Delabarre makes out the date 1511."

Hal raised his own flashlight above his head, shined it so that light glanced down over his face. Sudden shadows appeared below his nose, and below his lips, even the milk-white of his eyes seeming as if to float in the hollow dark of their sockets. Laughing—laughing the villainous laugh of a good cartoon villain—he shined the flashlight from the right side of his face, and from the left of his face, and shined it up from below his chin too.

"Stop it!" L.T. screamed. "You're freakin' us out!" He ran for the light switch, turned it on, the tiny museum again appearing as it did before—Hal even almost appearing as he did before.

Pointing to a photo panel, Hal showed a V-shaped Portuguese coat of arms, explained how somebody named Joseph Fragoso in 1951 deciphered the three Portuguese Crosses of the Order of Christ that we now saw.

"So was Cortereal Catholic?" L.T. asked. "You know, 'cause of the Crosses on the Rock."

"That's an interesting question. What do you think, Michael?"

"I don't know. I suppose Cortereal was Catholic. I mean after all he was Portuguese."

"Actually," Hal said, "we don't know if Cortereal was Catholic. He probably was; we may never know for sure. At the very least he would have appeared Catholic. But the Rock itself having Crosses doesn't necessarily mean he was. The Crosses of the Order of Christ that appear here are exactly like those made by other Portuguese explorers, be they in Africa, Asia, anywhere. The extremities of the Crosses are all shaped at forty-five degree angles. The Coat of Arms, the styling of numerals, they're just like those found everywhere. What I'm saying is that the symbols were just how Portuguese navigators claimed discoveries they made, no matter where they sailed, no matter where they explored. All Portuguese navigators of the time were taught to claim discoveries this way, all of them receiving the exact same training at the Nautical School of Prince Henry the Navigator in Sagres, Portugal."

I was thinking quickly … quickly and recklessly. Hal noticed me grimace, noticed that the look in my eyes was as wild as those in my thoughts.

"Something the matter?" he asked.

"I don't understand. What did you mean when you said Cortereal would have appeared Catholic?"

"Well, Michael, at the time Cortereal lived terrible things were going on in Portugal, Spain too. In Spain the Inquisition was already on."

"L.T.," Mrs. Haymaker called from the museum doorway. "Come over here. I need a hand with all this picnic trash."

"Now?"

"Yes, now!"

L.T. dragged himself out with a promise he'd be right back.

Alone now in the museum, me and Hal stared at Dighton Rock, he thinking his thoughts, me thinking mine, the silence awkward for the both of us, more so, I think, for me.

"Guess he really didn't plan for the return trip," I said.

"L.T.?"

"No, Miguel Cortereal. Like his brother, Gaspar, I don't think he wanted to go back to Portugal."

"Coming from you, Michael, that theory has some credibility."

"From me?"

"Yes, from you. You see, I think you may be in a unique position to offer special insight on the matter. I think you may even view things the same way Miguel Cortereal did."

I hesitated. "And what way is that?"

"Well, let's have a look."

Hal once again turned off the museum light switch, turned on his flashlight. Swinging one way and then the other, the beam of his light went after my position, went after it in ever shortened sweeps, more accurate sweeps. And with his footsteps slap-slapping all about the eight-sided museum—all about me too—one instant behind me, and the next to the right of me, and the next to left of me, Hal's slap-slapping steps ultimately stopped in front of me ... right in front and very close by.

"You know, Michael, as the Salem witch trials went on, there was a famous quote attributed to Cotton Mather: 'an Army of Devils is horribly broke in upon the place which is our center.' Now what do you suppose that means? What, Michael, could it mean?"

Hal's flashlight in my face, it shined into my eyes, the shine hurting ... burning ... betraying.

At the last he said, "Ah, ha! Now I see it, Michael. Ah, ha! Shadow Lighting—revealing markings the likes of which have not been seen in a long time ... a very long time."

9

I dangled my legs off the boatyard dock, thrashed my bare feet all through the morning air. Like a centipede making his way, even a hundred legs wouldn't have really helped me any. My toes just did skim the river water below, and that only on every third, or fourth, or fifth swing.

"You're scaring the fish," Uncle Jiggy said. "Good fishermen don't ripple the water. They don't even breathe. Look!" He took in a big breath, held it, his puffed-out chest, swollen stomach, and rounded cheeks turning him into a blowfish, a pretty bulgy-eyed and red-faced one at that.

Dad poked me in the ribs, pointed at Uncle Jiggy. "You know how Besterners say all Spitters are at least half-crazy, well, one look at your Uncle here and they'll know beyond any doubt that at least half of us are all crazy."

Smothering my laugh—or at least trying to—I heard air explode out of Uncle Jiggy's mouth, saw his bulgy eyes unbulge and his red face un-red. He leaned on Ollie's shoulder, pretty much had to.

We'd been fishing about an hour, since 5:30 in the morning. There wasn't any hole watching last night anyways, and what with me and L.T. having told Ollie, Richie, and Rook how someone with a torch chased me, nobody really wanted any hole watching. Besides, as they more or less kind of all correctly pointed out, what sense was there watching our hole when it no longer was a hole.

What they didn't know however—didn't know 'cause we didn't tell them—was that there now was a new hole, the burial hole ... the grave.

Fishing's a big deal in our family. Spring's when we do our serious fishing—fish run permits permitting—when striped bass are good and juicy as they head on upriver to spawn. In summer though, most of the fish we catch are non-keepers, just small two-to four-pound schoolie bass and blue fish. We keep some of the ones bigger than that, but actual fishing—fishing for fish eating sake—that's not why we now were here. We were here to talk. We were here to talk and go after a different fish, a different kind of keeper ... a wholly different kind of keeper altogether.

"Doesn't look like we'll be getting our Hero today," Grandpa said. He grabbed a small eel from a bucket, stuck it onto his hook and cast the bait out over the water.

"Grandpa," Ollie said, "how are we gonna know the Hero when we see him?"

"The Hero, Ollie, is a beauty of a fish, a fish without fault. I think we'll know him when we see him, but more importantly, he'll know us when he sees us. He's here to help us, Ollie. Why, he'll probably jump clear out of the river just to be with us."

"But he'll die out of water, Grandpa."

"The Hero doesn't die."

I'd heard stories about the Hero since I was little, and for the most part the stories were easy to believe, the Hero easy to believe in. The stories told of how the Hero's arrival would make us happy, make us safe. No ordinary fish, the Hero was magical and his arrival would signal a magical time. Grownups hoped for him too, believed his arrival to be some day … God-willing some day soon.

Santa Claus? Santa Claus? Him I stopped believing in a long time ago, not that I was sure I ever really did. He was for kids, little kids, and even when I was one of those I'm not sure 'belief' was the best way to describe the relationship me and him had. I mean for whatever ideas I may have had about Santa Claus, there was nothing he had about me … someone like me. It was always Mom and Dad anyway that were my primary suspects when it came to presents. And the funny thing was they seemed to even go out of their way to make sure that I suspected them. They seemed to even go out of their way to make sure that not only I not believe in Santa Claus, but that I not believe in Christmas. Like, I mean, they were the ones asking me what presents I wanted. They were the ones telling me if a present was too expensive, or not practical, or wasn't what I really wanted.

Santa Claus? I mean what … he wouldn't know what I wanted? He would worry about expense? He would care what was practical?

Give me a break!

Santa Claus? Mom and Dad all but told me he was just some fat guy in red, just some fat guy tied up with the whole present-giving thing. And as for Christmas, well, as for that, as they made sure to tell me each and every year the tree got put by the fireplace, as they made sure to explain to me each and every year it got placed near the big picture window for all to see: 'Christmas, Michael, Christmas is just a time for presents. The tree, Michael, is just the place we put them.'

My relationship with the Hero, though, now that was different. The feel of it, the thought of it, everything with it—different. The Hero had nothing to do with presents, his purpose nothing to do with presents I may have wanted.

The Hero's purpose, however, did have everything to do

with helping, bringing help, help for me, help for my family, help for us Spitters, help for us and everyone like us. The catch was that the help, it wasn't now. It was tomorrow, always for tomorrow, and if not tomorrow then for next month, or next year, or such time as we needed help—but I mean really needed help. The help was for such time as we found ourselves up a creek, a shitty creek … a really, really shitty creek. It was for such time we found ourselves without solution … without even a shitty solution. It was for such time we found ourselves without direction … without even a shitty direction.

That's when the Hero would arrive. That's when he would arrive with a plan. That's when he would arrive with a plan and a way.

I guess I really didn't have any doubts about the Hero, about me and him. I only had questions. And now that I at long last was ready to ask them, I only hoped that the grownups were ready at long last for me to ask them.

"Grandpa, so when's the Hero going to get here already?"

"Good question. I don't know, Michael. I suppose he's waiting for just the exact right moment."

"So it's not bad enough now?"

"It's not great now, but things could be worse. Believe me, they could be much worse. God knows they've been far worse before."

"So it's got to be absolutely, positively horrible?"

"Well, I don't know if it's got to be absolutely, positively horrible, but it's got to be bad, okay, real bad. But don't worry, the Hero knows when it's time. See, a lot goes into it. Until then, we believe. So long as we do, he'll come. And the stronger our belief, the sooner he gets here. Have you boys ever heard of the term *esperança?*"

Me and Ollie shook our heads that we hadn't.

"It's a Portuguese word, means hope, though its true meaning goes beyond just the actual meaning of the word.

Esperança is a trait, one found in Portuguese people. It's intense, esperança, more so even in us Spitters. See, we don't just hope, we expect."

I'd always wondered why the Hero would be a fish. I mean if I were a hero I'd be a lion, maybe an eagle. Better yet, Superman.

"Grandpa, why a fish? Why is he a fish?"

"He isn't, 'least he isn't really a fish. It's a disguise, Michael."

"A disguise?" Why would a hero, I wondered, need a disguise?

All at once hearing a whistle I quickly turned … Grandpa, Dad, Uncle Jiggy, and Ollie doing the same. On our dock and walking towards us was Mr. Alves. Fancy tackle box in his hand, he had a wide shit-smile on his face.

We shut up.

"Are they biting?"

"They're not interested," Dad said.

"I'm not surprised, not with that bait and rigging you got going. For Christ's sake, you're only skimming the surface. You've got to get in there, get in there deep. That's where the hooking is. You know, this really is just like you, pretty much like everything you do: always half-assed, always half-way."

I looked away, tried focusing on the end of my line, another stare-down with Mr. Alves just about the last thing I needed, or wanted. And not that I genuinely thought it would happen, but it sure would have been great for the Hero to decide that just now was the exact right time to make his magical big leap out of the water, bring some happiness, bring some peace too. And so long as he was at it, that Hero, maybe he also could just sort of land on top of Mr. Alves, land on him and squash him like a bug. I mean like, what harm was there in a thing like that?

"Say, Mookie," Mr. Alves said, "so nice to see you at church yesterday, even if you were just kind of hiding there out in back. But you, Ollie, I didn't see you. Were you there? You know, just because your folks don't God-forbid care to go to church, doesn't mean you shouldn't be there."

"If he wasn't there," Uncle Jiggy said, "then he wasn't there. Lolly and me decide that. It ain't your business." He handed his fishing rod to Dad, stood up.

"Sit down," Grandpa said. "Sit down, I said."

Taking his rod back, Uncle Jiggy reeled in his line, did not sit. Instead, he kept his eyes on Mr. Alves, kept himself up on his toes.

"I'm going to try upriver," Mr. Alves said. "You know, if the fishing here doesn't work for you, you can always try Café Saudade. Tonight they're having their Chouriço Fest, but you, of course, still can have your fish. There's always bacalhau on hand. There's always plenty of bacalhau on hand for people like you ... and bacalhau-loving people just like you."

My head snapped 'round and I saw Mr. Alves, saw him wink my way ... I alone seeing it. He was at it again, at it just like he was at Café Saudade when he suggested I try the chouriço pork, only to then of course remember that we were 'bacalhau people', ate salted cod.

"Asshole," I mumbled, once he left us.

Ollie's jaw dropped—surprised, I guess, that I would say the A-word what with grownups around. For their part though, Grandpa, Dad and Uncle Jiggy just went back to their fishing, or at least the motions of their fishing, their silence an indication they very well just might have been thinking over what exactly happened.

And just what did exactly happen? Something, I knew, though exactly what I wasn't sure.

"Like what was that?" Ollie asked. "I mean, what's this guy's problem?"

"We're his problem," Uncle Jiggy said.

"Don't worry about Alves," Grandpa said, scooting over

to help Ollie with his line. "His kind have been with us since forever, and though he might know us, we know him too, know him and people like him only all too well. And what we know is he won't change, and we won't change. Alves knows that too. He knows how it works. Deep down, he may actually even realize that the more he dislikes us, the stronger our resolve to not change.

"The thing we have to really watch out for are people who haven't lived around us, people who don't know us. These people don't know how it works. These people are curious. They think they have a right to know us, think also they have a right to change us. No, Ollie, what's really dangerous are these people. They're capable of hurting us not only because they think they should change us, but because they truly believe they truly can."

"They only can hurt us if they don't first get hurt themselves," Uncle Jiggy said.

That sounded like a threat, 'least to my ears it did, Uncle Jiggy sounding much as he did the time he caught me and L.T. snooping round the house.

Though L.T. didn't, and though L.T. couldn't, know how it works, like what exactly was my excuse? I mean even if I didn't understand why it worked as it worked, shouldn't I by now have known how it worked? Shouldn't I by now have known how important it was I be careful, how important it was for all of us that I be careful? Shouldn't I by now have known that our way required constant caution, constant vigilance? Shouldn't I by now have known that our way was unforgiving—no mistakes, carelessness, or weakness allowed? Shouldn't I by now have known that we lived on the edge—our God-forsaken lives on some God-forsaken ledge? I mean that stuff … that stuff … I knew that stuff since the day I was born.

But how exactly was it I should have known? I mean was that stuff inherited somehow? Was it natural? Instinctual?

I mean, I could like see how tiny alewife herring swim upriver each and every April, swim from the salt of the coast to the fresh water of rivers and streams, swim despite fish-eating gulls, terns, and fishing nets at the ready to nab them all along the way. Like they're programmed to spawn, programmed to create new life, programmed to carry on the life they have, despite the risks they face. Sure, some don't make it. But some do, 'least enough so that each April new fish wash themselves up all exhausted along the same little streams that their ancestors washed up along.

But they're fish! They're fish! I ain't no fish!

Then again, I suppose, if alewife herring are so much the same from one generation to the next as they swim about in murky and threatening waters, why would it be any different for me? Why should it be? I mean, why should I be any different from my great-great-grandparents who, despite hardships and dangers, went about preserving the way of life they knew? I mean like even if I'm not actually swimming around in any murky waters or anything, didn't I too not walk below the same magnificent stars my great-greats walked below, the exact same?

Until now whatever learning I'd learned just was picked up, maybe that why my handle of why things worked as they worked a far cry worse even than my handle of how they worked as they worked. Sure ... caution, fear, worry ... I mean sure those semi-learned, instinctual, natural, or whatever things would keep me alive, for now they a good part of whatever it was making me me. But deep down I knew that I never would, and never could, truly be myself until such time I was taught, taught to learn, and taught to use whatever it was I should be learning.

"Say, look who's here," Uncle Jiggy said. "Why, if it ain't the little troublemaker himself."

Stopping every so often on the dock parking lot, L.T. stopped to look around, his each stop and look just his way of taking his good sweet time to decide whether or not to join our little fishing expedition. Of course after a while he did join, at least sort of anyway, his wandering join landing him kind of close … kind of away too.

"I wish you wouldn't hang around him so much," Dad said, his voice good and low. "He ain't like us, Michael. You know that, don't you?"

For my part, I would have argued that though L.T. wasn't one of us, he wasn't all that different. But what with L.T. already now within earshot—and what with his ears being half-rabbit, half-bat, and half-Mickey Mouse—I said nothing, and signaled nothing.

"So I'm the Butcher of Best, am I?" Uncle Jiggy said, his voice good and loud.

"Sorry, L.T." Ollie said. "I told him 'cause I thought the name was funny."

"L.T.!" Grandpa blurted. "L.T.!" he blurted and bellowed. "What kind of name is that for a boy anyway?"

"It stands for Lost Tribe, Grandpa," Ollie said. "Show him, L.T. Tell him."

Turning his cap around just long enough for Grandpa to read the words, L.T. put it back as it first was, backwards and slightly off-kilter.

"There are ten Lost Tribes," L.T. began, taking a breath, letting loose: "Reuben, Simon, Issachar, Zebulun, Menasseh, Ephraim, Dan, Naphtali, Gad, and Asher. Those are the tribes of the Northern Kingdom of Israel, the tribes that were never heard from again after they were sent into exile by the Assyrians in the eighth century B.C."

"Wow," Ollie said, his 'wow' more whistle than a word.

"Like wow," I said, admiring yet one more talent I never before knew L.T. had. "Wow."

As if finding out that somebody you thought you knew was in point of fact a Picasso, as if finding out that your best friend in reality was a Mozart, as if finding out that your screwball of a best friend whom you thought you knew was not only an Einstein, but was Einstein, I mean even as if finding out that that best friend of yours in all actuality was a trained C.I.A. killer, the only thing really to say was—'wow'.

Dad reached for a dirty cup, pinched out a sandworm. "Who's been teaching you this stuff?"

"Mostly I teach myself. You know, the Internet. But Hal, my mother's friend, he's really got me learning. He's a Mormon, says Mormons believe they descended from the House of Israel, from those tribes that were scattered. He says the tribes are a blessing to the Gentiles with whom they live."

"And this is what you believe?" Dad asked.

"No. I'm not Mormon."

"He's Jewish," I said. "He says he is, anyway."

"So I've heard," Dad said. He studied the sandworm, gave it a good squeeze. "Go on, tell me more about these tribes."

"Well, the two southern tribes, Judah and Benjamin, that's where most of the now-a-day Jews come from."

"Not you, though?"

"No. I'm from one of the lost ones."

"Now why ever would you go thinking a thing like that?" Grandpa asked.

"Just because. You wouldn't know it just by looking at me, but actually ... actually ... actually I'm actually just the littlest bit screwy. My mother says I'm eccentric, says I march to the beat of some drummer, says to Hal I'm an individualist, and he says to her I'm a rugged individualist. Then they laugh. But both agree: since I wasn't born Jewish, I must be a Lost Tribe kind of Jew. They don't really mean it, at least I think they don't really mean it, but it doesn't matter. I think it. I believe it."

"You're the same age as Michael and Ollie," Grandpa said.

"At this age you're supposed to be screwy. You're supposed to be lost. It's got nothing to do with being Jewish."

"Nah, I'm Lost Tribe Jewish and that's that. The Talmud, that's a Jewish book, it says the Lost Tribes live beyond this river called the Sambatyon. It says they live on the far side of what are the now-a-day Jews, you know, the real-life Jews. Now I know the Taunton may not exactly be the Sambatyon, but it is a river. And me, I'm on the wrong side of it."

"You know," Dad said, "you really are screwy. Like what are you thinking? Like why ever would you go around believing any of these thoughts that you're thinking? That's not the way it works, 'least that's not how it's supposed to work."

"Look, I don't fit, okay. I don't fit here. I mean here I am by a river, a real-life river, and not only don't I know if it's coming or going, I sometimes really don't know if I'm coming or going. Upstream goes down, downstream goes up, and in the end this tidal river it goes nowhere. But for you, for you there is no up, no down. This river just is as it is, and you just are as you are, and somehow it works because to you this river isn't just a river, it's your mainstream. Your lifeline. All you really have to just do is make sure you stay on the right side of it—your side of it."

"Maybe if you went across it," I said, "maybe if you, you know, went across the river, L.T., maybe then it would make sense to you too. Maybe then you wouldn't feel so beyond it."

"I can't do that. I can't do that, Michael. The Sambatyon's impassable six days a week. And then on the seventh day, the Sabbath day, on the day when it finally quiets down, Jews can't cross it. They aren't allowed to; it breaks the Sabbath."

"So there's the catch," Dad laughed, his laugh more bitter than funny. "You're up a creek, son. You're up a creek without a paddle."

"Not that a paddle would really do me much good anyway. Hal's got this book about this explorer named Prester John, and a few hundred years ago he actually went to the Sambatyon. He wrote that the river was powerful, so powerful it carried not only small rocks to the sea but great big ones. Like I'd need more than a paddle to cross something like that."

"In that case," Uncle Jiggy said, "why not just admit you've been hitching your wagon to the wrong horse, announce you're now going to switch horses. Then you'd be on the right side of the river, wouldn't need to cross. It'd be easier for you that way. You'd fit that way."

"I don't know. I don't see it. Truth is I kind of like being L.T. And while I don't like being lost, I've gotten to thinking I kind of like the idea of being lost. It's part of who I am now, and I'm not sure I really could think different, am not sure I could be different. So long as who I am is important—important in ways that are important—why wouldn't I just hang in … hang on … hang just for as long as I could, in any way I could?"

The tip of my fishing rod suddenly buckled, my line becoming so taut that I thought it would snap. But I held tight, held and leaned back.

Jumping to his feet, Dad peered over my shoulder at the bubbles and ripples in the water. "She's a beauty, Michael. Let her struggle a while and then give a good yank to set the hook."

"Right," Grandpa said. "Get to know her and then go get her. When she's yours, reel her in."

My fish thrashed violently, flung itself out of the water, back into the water, and then back out again. It thoroughly splashed me, completely soaked me.

It was a striper, and a big one too, going maybe about five pounds, maybe ten, maybe fifteen. Putting a net under it, Dad grabbed it by the lips, released the hook. "Put up one hell of a fight. One hell of a fight."

The fish safely up on dock, it heaved huge breaths, the black horizontal lines all along its silvery side rising and falling, rising and then falling. Eye sharp, to me its eye was sharp with what looked to be sheer terror.

Grandpa shook his head. "Throw her back. Throw her on back."

Hitting the water, the fish did not move. Then—and like that—she was gone.

We gathered our gear, nobody saying nothing 'bout nothing. The sun already hot ... already the air hazy ... it was another day ... one like the last ... and still—nothing.

"Hey," Ollie said. "Hey, L.T. So let me get this straight. The Lost Tribes want to join the other tribes, right?"

"Right."

"But they can't?"

"They can't, you know 'cause of the Sambatyon river thing. Most days the water's too rough; they don't know how to cross. Then, on Sabbath days, when the water's calm, they can't cross. There are too many problems, too many rules, simply too many ideas about what is and what isn't the right thing to do. They're afraid, Ollie."

We stopped at the lot at the end of the dock, the heat off the pavement rising at us like fire. "Are you afraid?" Ollie asked L.T.

"Me? Nah, not really. I'm not stuck on the Sabbath days. I'm in with the days of not knowing how to go, you know, the days of not knowing how to cross an impassable river. But I'm trying to figure it out. Till then, and till I do, for me what it says right there in Chronicles is on mark: 'The Lost Tribes still exist to this very day'."

"So what about the other days, the Sabbath days? What about those people stuck on those days?"

"I don't know, Ollie. Maybe they're gonna just always be stuck. Maybe they're just always gonna be Lost Tribes."

Grandpa spit, his loogie sailing in a majestic arc to the

ground. "It may take a while, maybe till the end of days, but they'll get there. They'll get there too. They'll stop being afraid. They'll cross the river, reach their good safe place. As it says in Isaiah, 'God will recover the remnant of his people.' That, that there, that's on mark."

We split on up, us going one way and L.T. going the other. And turning my head, turning it so as to carefully look back at L.T., I just did not know who he was, just why he was as he was, or just what he was even capable of.

Then I looked away, walked away.

10

Rookie sat on the far side of the bench I sat on, her arms folded across her chest, her right leg crossed over her left, her right foot twitching back and forth like a whacked-out metronome. The wind blew her hair over her face and she swept it out of the way, a gesture that probably pretty much reflected just what she wanted to do with me. She looked straight ahead, but I could still see the whites of her eyes visible behind the cheap sunglasses I'd given her to wear.

"For the one hundredth time, Rook, I'm sorry. Okay, maybe I did lie, but it was the only way I could get you to come here. I mean would you have come with me if I told you the truth?"

We sat on a park bench beneath an elm tree, the bench a perfect spot to view the comings and goings at Café Saudade. I adjusted my own sunglasses—also cheap—and carefully raised the digital camera on my lap from out under some newspapers. Then I fired from the hip, no doubt most shots off the mark.

"This is so humiliating, Michael. You said we were going to check out the Holy Ghost float route. You said we were going to check out the angles, see which ones were best for my photo shoot. But look at me, Michael. Look at me! In a few days I'll be queen of a float and here I am in cheap sunglasses, with my cheap sunglass-wearing cousin, and he's groping through his newspaper-covered lap like some cheap sunglass-wearing pervert. Like who do you think you are? James Bond? Austin Powers? If all you wanted to do was spy, why didn't you just get L.T.? From what I've heard you're both already pretty good when it comes to that."

"This ain't spying, Rook, it's surveillance. Besides, L.T. doesn't know what to look for. But you're a Spitter, you know what to look for and you know how to do it."

"It'll be dark soon, Michael. Let's go home. By the way, how are we getting home?"

Rook, a Holy Ghost float queen? My ass a Holy Ghost float queen! A royal pain in the ass, she was, just a holier-than-thou self-righteous royal pain in the ass. And now that 'her royal highness' had caught on that I had no plans for the return trip, she'd be pretty much impossible. "Okay, the moment we finish what we came for we'll go."

"You mean what you came for."

"Whatever. Anyway, are you noticing anything strange about the people going in?"

"Well, none are Spitters. But that's not strange."

"You don't think so?"

"No. Why would we go to a chouriço pig-out? We don't eat pig."

It was with Patty's help I realized most kids at Mass were Spitters, that they sat at the back of church. Now that Rookie had pointed out just one more peculiar and particular difference between Spitters and non-Spitters, between us and them, I got mad that it wasn't me who realized it. It wasn't that Rook and Patty were any smarter than me. They just saw more because they knew more, knew more because they already had been taught more.

"What are you going to do with the pictures anyway, Michael? They're not porn shots, you know. You can't bribe anybody with them or anything."

"They're evidence, Rook, though about just what I'm not real sure. But evidence can be used, though just how is something else I'm not real sure about."

"Evidence? Evidence against who, for who?"

"Remember how you said good Portuguese eventually see the forest and not just the trees? Remember how you said a good Portuguese sailor uses Dead Reckoning to figure out just where he is?"

"Yeah, at the hole. I remember saying that."

"Well, Rook, I want to see the forest; I want to see it already. I mean like here I am Dead Reckoning like crazy, just Dead Reckoning my guts out—my head and heart out too—and you know what? I'm sick of it. I'm just sick of it, just sick of the whole damn thing. I want to know what's going on. I want to know what's going on with me. And I want to know it now."

I was standing, I realized, suddenly standing, and the strange thing was I didn't remember standing. For that matter I'd probably been screaming too, it curiously quiet the moment I shut myself up.

Taking my hand in hers, Rook pulled me close, hugged me a little and rocked me a little, her cheek warm by mine. Then, ever so carefully, I felt my heart give a little, and felt my mind slow a little, my feet feeling the ground, in the ground.

I opened my eyes. "Okay, let's go. Let's go in."

Café Saudade was loud, the conversation of customers and the music of a band throwing a blanket of noise over pretty much everything. Unlike the night of fado when customers sat still and listened to a singer sing, people now seemed to only care about balancing plates of food and glasses of wine, balancing them even as they made their way past other people balancing plates of food and glasses of wine.

"Michael," Rook said, pointing to a sign, "there's a ten dollar cover. Let's get out of here."

"Ten bucks ain't bad; I mean it ain't bad considering it's all you can eat."

"Well, I'm not eating any chouriço, I'll tell you that right now. And the price doesn't even cover booze so what good is any of this anyway?"

I paid my ten; Rook giving me a 'look' before reluctantly pulling ten dollars from out her jeans pocket. Then she gave me another look, and then one more, and then one more just for good measure.

Straight away we went over to a long table of salads, beans, and Portuguese sweet bread. Then I stopped by a platter of red chouriço sausage.

"Don't," Rookie whispered. "Don't, Michael."

"Why not? Give me just one good reason I shouldn't."

"For one," she said hanging onto my arm and pretending to gag, "how about pigs being ugly and disgusting."

"That's not good enough," I said, spooning some chouriço into an empty area of my plate. "You know, this stuff actually doesn't smell as bad as I thought it would."

We found a bar table in a corner, sat ourselves on high swivel stools. Turning myself around, I watched the crowd, picked at my food. Faces, they seemed recognizable enough, though none recognizable enough to know. Smiling, laughing too, the faces were strange, and as for the people behind the faces, they were strangers.

Then, squinting, I spotted Ol' Cuss back at a back table. He was back in a not-well-lit area, back in a hollow area where others really did not care go. He was looking gray, I thought, kind of strangely gray, looking old too, and the man he was talking to, that man listened to Ol' Cuss, leaned in and listened. As for the listener's face, it wasn't so much strange as it was creepy. And as for that man behind the face, Mr. Alves, I knew him.

I raised the camera, got my picture.

"Jenny!" I said, seeing at last a friendly face, a familiar face.

Putting down a basket of bread, she came to our corner. "Hey there. It's Michael, right?"

"Yeah, right. This is my cousin, Rookie. She's not a girlfriend or anything."

"Nice to meet you, Rookie. I'm Jenny. I met your cousin here a few nights ago. He was here for fado music."

"Jenny's not Portuguese, Rook; she's Spanish. But Uncle Joe—you know what he's like—well, he thought we might still be related anyway on account of her family also being island people, island people going back hundreds of years."

"Impressive," Jenny said, nodding her head. "Surprising too that you'd make a point of remembering something like that. Don't get me wrong, I'm flattered you consider me a missing link in your family tree, it's just surprising is all. Now, Michael, let's see how good your memory really is. Do you remember what island my ancestors are from?"

"I'm not sure. I remember it sounds like Madeira."

"It's Majorca, a Spanish island."

"Majorca," I repeated, not telling Jenny that it was Uncle Joe's stupid rhyming—'Jenny, pretty as a penny, studies history 'cause of the mystery'—that helped me remember. In part, the rhyme had been part of a quiz, one she passed. We liked her. And me, I liked her.

"You study history, right?"

"Right. I'm working on my Master's."

"Let me ask you something then," I said, "seeing as you're wicked smart and everything. What's the Inquisition?"

"The Inquisition? You're not really much for small talk, are you, Michael? Well, seeing as I'm of Spanish ancestry the Inquisition is something I do know a little something about. The Inquisition, Michael, was how the Church controlled people. Using scare tactics, they got information out of people, got information out about other people. And armed with that they then could accuse anybody of anything. Heretics, is what they called the people they accused. The heretics, they said, were dangerous to the Church, and it really didn't matter if they truly were or weren't. For that matter it really didn't matter if the information they got out of people with scare tactics was true or not true. When scared, people will say just about anything, do just about anything."

"This was in Spain?"

"Yup, it was in Spain, but Inquisitions were all over the place, in Portugal too. The Spanish had one of the worst ones, the worst of theirs taking place in the fifteenth and sixteenth centuries."

"Is that when your ancestors left Spain for Majorca?"

"They left when Torquemada was around. Ever hear of him?"

Me and Rookie shook our heads that we hadn't.

"Torquemada was the Inquisitor General of Spain. Inquisition means interrogation, and Torquemada had the power to interrogate anybody he wanted, in any way he wanted. Torture was used to extract confessions, and trials were conducted in absolute secrecy. The sentences, however, were announced at public hearings called *auto-da-fés*. At these *auto-da-fés* heretics by the thousands were burned at the stake."

"What was so dangerous about the heretics?"

"Nothing really. The Church just hated people who didn't believe in what the Church wanted them to believe in. Funny, but in a way the Church, even with all its power, was afraid of these people."

"So did the heretics run?" Rook asked. "Did they run away?"

"Well, some did. I don't know if my ancestors were considered heretics but I'm sure there must have been some heretics on the same boats as them to Majorca."

"Well, if some ran then that means some didn't. Right?"

"Right. Actually a lot didn't. Most of those who didn't run were later expelled, you know, kicked out."

"What about the ones who didn't run and weren't kicked out? What happened to them?"

"Well, there's all kinds of running, Michael. Those who stayed behind agreed to conversion, in truth most of those forced into doing so. They became Catholics. That was the only way they were allowed to stay."

"We need water," a lady from a nearby table complained. "This pitcher's empty."

"Got to go. To be continued," Jenny said.

"Let's get out of here," Rookie said once Jenny left. "I don't like this, Michael. I'm scared."

"Just up and run, huh? Look, we bought our chouriço just like everybody else. We'll go soon enough, Rook. But I want to talk to Jenny again. I still have questions."

"What, Michael, like she's a friend now? You think she's 'a friend?'"

"Yeah, I think she is 'a friend.'"

"Okay then, let's find out. Here she comes."

Jenny put a plate of hot chouriço down in front of me. "Yours looked cold, Michael."

The steam from the sausage came up at me like steam from a vaporizer. Whirling into my nose and my eyes, it made my head light, my legs heavy. Through it all still I could make out Rook's fork stab at a piece of sausage, the meat just dangling and the red juices just dripping. Holding it up to the air, Rook stuck it right under Jenny's nose. "Are you allowed to eat on the job?"

Jenny blew on the chouriço, closed her eyes and took a bite. "Hot," she said, reaching for a glass of water.

"So Jenny, so long as we're like waiting for my chouriço to cool, let me ask you something else about these heretics. If they converted then everything was cool with the Inquisition, right? I mean in the end it all worked out, right?"

"No, actually it didn't work out. Ever hear of a book called Don Quixote? No? Well, there's a character in there named Sancho Panza and he says, 'I am an Old Christian, and to become an Earl that is sufficient'. See, Michael, only Old Christians, only they really could get ahead. New Christians were hated. Eventually they were even deprived of just about all their rights."

"How come? I mean they converted, didn't they?"

"They did, but Old Christians thought the New Christians weren't sincere about their conversions, thought they maybe were even faking it. In time the Old Christians thought the conversions made no difference anyway. Purity of Blood laws, the *Estatutos de Limpieza de Sangre*, got enacted. If who you are is determined by what's in your blood, then what good are the conversions anyway? In the end the Inquisition treated New Christians far worse than it treated even those who never converted in the first place. They called the New Christians *Marranos*. In Spanish that means pigs."

Jenny turned, walked away, and walked back. "Why this interest in the Inquisition anyway? Where did you hear about it?"

"My friend's mother's boyfriend mentioned it. Something to do with a Portuguese explorer in the 1500s."

"Why didn't you ask him to explain the Inquisition to you?"

"Because he's not a friend. You are."

Jenny smiled, disappeared then into the crowd.

"You know what," Rook said, "you know what, Michael? You talk too much. You ask too many questions, don't know how to shut up."

"What did I do? I only wanted to learn. Besides, Jenny's cool."

"How do you know? Like I mean how do you really know?

How do you really know Jenny's 'a friend'. You saw her eat the chouriço, didn't you?"

"Yeah, but she had her eyes closed. She probably would have held her nose too if she could have. You shouldn't have gone sticking your fork right under her nose in the first place, Rook."

"We don't know anything at all about her, Michael, really we don't. Even if Jenny once was like us, she's not like us now. I mean she went eating the chouriço, didn't she? Maybe it really is just what L.T. says it is. Maybe there has been Drift, in her family—maybe just too much Drift. Maybe with time stuff just happened, and now she doesn't keep all the customs, maybe doesn't even have the slightest idea why she keeps some and doesn't keep others. But it doesn't matter. It doesn't matter, Michael. Even if Jenny once was us, she isn't us anymore. And you know what you've now done? You've made her suspicious. You've made her suspicious, Michael. So from now on, do me a favor, okay? From now on ask your parents your questions. Get your answers from them. Now, please, can we please get the heck on out of here?"

I picked up my camera, handed it to Rookie. "Know what, Rook? You're right. When you're right you're right. I do need to get the answers from my parents." I scooped up some chouriço, struck a pose. "Now go ahead, click. Click away."

"You're crazy, Michael. You're asking for trouble, you know that don't you?" She put the camera on the table, pushed it away.

Stupid, wrong, what did it matter? Really, what did any of it matter? "Screw it," I said. "Screw all of it." I blew on the chouriço, closed my eyes.

Suddenly a strong hand clamped onto my wrist, squeezed it so hard it hurt, and my fork, it fell from my hand to my plate. Opening my eyes, I looked over my shoulder.

"Just what do you think you're doing, Michael?"

Hoisting me off my stool and steering me through the crowd, Father Sousa's one hand pinned my wrist to my back, his other hand square to my shoulder. Eyes welling in pain, mind numb with shock, I said nothing, could say nothing, had nothing I could say anyway. And before I even knew it we were near the door, at the door, and out the door.

"This is not your place," Father Sousa said, once we reached a back alley. Turning me hard so that I faced him, I could see veins bulge from out of his forehead, could see beads of sweat run down his face. He didn't let me go, wasn't about to.

"I told him we should leave. Please ... please don't hurt him, Father," Rook begged, her hands up in the air as if to plead, maybe to fight.

Slowly letting go of my wrist, Father Sousa straightened his collar, hovered over me still. "I'm sorry. I'm sorry, Michael. I didn't mean to hurt you."

Using his coat sleeve to dab sweat off his forehead, he looked at Rook, looked at me, but really, he really looked at me. "Oh, my God, you're afraid! Oh, my God ... you're afraid of me! Me—it's me that you're afraid of, isn't it? Even now ... even now we're still that scary? Even now? Are we really still so dangerous?"

Father Sousa shook his head, shook it and shook it. "I think it's best you go home. The two of you, you need to go home."

"Yeah, okay, but how?" Rook asked, another of her looks boring into me.

"My car," Father Sousa said. "I'll take you."

We filed on into his boxy white SUV, nobody saying nothing. But even in the twilight, even in the dark with my arm hurting and my head hurting, even with that and despite that, still I could not help but notice Father Sousa taking the long way, and the slow way, back to Best.

From the back seat I could see Father Sousa's eyes in the rear view mirror, could see them glancing to us, to the road, then back to us. "Rachel, you're going to be queen of a float at this year's Holy Ghost Festa, am I right?"

"Yes, Father."

"And Michael, I'm assuming you're going to soon be old enough to be welcomed into the Brotherhood. These are big steps, you know. They signify you're growing up. They mean that from now on you'll be responsible for your actions."

I sat up straight, just riveted to the eyes in the mirror.

"As you know there are many stories about the origin of the Festa. You probably heard about how Queen Saint Isabel defied her husband, King Diniz, how she dressed like a peasant to smuggle out food to the poor at the palace gates, of how, when forced to by the King, flowery roses and not food tumbled out of her basket.

"But what you may not know is that among the poor that the Queen helped were twelve of the poorest men. She placed her crown on their heads, and on their children's heads, used her influence to protect these twelve families. What you also may not know is how the Festa almost totally died out on the Portuguese mainland, this at the time of the Inquisition, or how it continues now mainly just among Azoreans.

"Let me ask you something, see how observant you are. Ever notice how Christian symbols aren't involved in the Holy Spirit parades? Ever notice how the *Imperio* chapels, the chapels in which you make a *promessa* promise to God while the Brotherhood is laying a crown on your head, ever notice how the chapels don't have crosses, have only crowns, have only scepters? Ever wonder about these things?

"Have you ever wondered how in certain places in the Azores beef that's distributed during the Festa comes only from cows whose blood is drained? Have you ever wondered about how in some places on the islands candles are still lit on

Friday nights? Have you ever wondered how candles still are lit in Imperio chapels on the Friday night before the climactic final week of the Holy Spirit?

"I suspect you have wondered a little bit about these things—a little but not much—not much though because more or less like the vast majority of Azoreans, whether on the islands or here in the States, you simply don't know … don't know enough. But you're different from the vast majority— are for sure different from the Portuguese wherever they be— different in that you only as yet don't know. See, they, other Portuguese, they don't know because they simply don't care to know. They don't take note of certain customs because they simply don't care to take note. They don't ask how and why because they simply don't care to ask how and why. But you, you people—you Spitters—you're different from those others. You care. And you, you two—you two and Spitter kids just like you—you're different still. You wonder. You still wonder."

Father Sousa took a breath, a big one. He'd been rambling, talking fast, talking as if he had a lot to say and not a lot of time to say it.

"Michael, Rachel, take time to notice these things. Take time to wonder. In that way when you learn more about them and about yourselves, it'll mean all the more. Understand that these things … these things are precious. Understand that you, you people … understand you are unique. Understand that you, you two … understand you are special. I never again want to catch you eating chouriço. I never again want to catch you taking part in anything that shames the Nation."

Me and Rookie didn't even need to ask Father Sousa to drop us a little distance away from our homes, that he understood too. In fact, Father Sousa seemed to understand so much, so well, I was only left wishing that it were my parents who could understand as well, understand me as well … only understand just how much I only wanted to understand.

If Rook had only snapped the picture of me about to eat the chouriço, maybe then I could force my parents to understand. But now, now that Father Sousa warned me to not do anything to shame the Nation, even that option seemed good as gone.

"You got the camera?" I asked Rook.

"Me? No, I don't have it. Don't you have it?"

"No, I don't have it either. Oh no … what did you do, Rook … leave the camera in the car?"

"Maybe it's back in Café Saudade. Father Sousa bull-rushed you out of there so fast it might have been left there."

"First off, he didn't bull-rush me; I rushed myself. Second off, if the camera is there, then the pictures are there. And third off, if the pictures are there, then shit's there too."

I stood awhile, around awhile, watched Rook go to her home and into it, and then unsure whether to go home or just where to go, I stood some more.

L.T. solved the problem. Appearing seemingly out of nowhere, he was running straight towards me and, uncertain if he was readying to tackle the snot out of me or just sideswipe me with another new and nutty plan, I braced myself. Not that it really much mattered; either way I had a strong feeling I was about to get myself bowled over.

"You won't believe it!" he said, trying to catch his breath.

"Won't believe what?"

"Come on. Let's go. You'll see."

We ran from Spit in the direction of Chippascutt Point, my mind racing a hundred miles an hour, and whatever surprise L.T. had in his mind racing a hundred miles an hour right at me. Sights, sounds, thoughts and feelings—everything around me and close to me—it just got plowed under by the anticipation of the coming collision. Streets like takeoff runways—was there any earnestness in the world to match our earnestness? But then again the ever-blackening night, so long the launching point for all coming our way—was there any inevitability in the universe to match that inevitability ... that one?

L.T. was a step ahead, his excitement infectious and spurring on mine. Clearly he had something, some breakthrough or other that he wanted to just scream about, just yell his lungs out about. But all he could do was smile, smile and grimace. And when we at last reached the dirt road, and when he at last put his hands on his knees for just a breath, just then he whirled away, his eyes all afire to whirl me right there along with him.

Faster ... further, faster ... further, faster and further.

Just beyond the river, over to my right I could still make out the very top tip of a setting sun. Looking as if suspended from above, it dissolved even as we ran, the top orange tip replaced with a silvery moon looking as if propped up from below. I was racing, racing time ... racing time itself—and time waiting for no one—the only real question was whether I could run faster, could run any further.

Dirt road becoming dirt path, breaks in the woods becoming more breaks in the woods—we popped into them and out of them and didn't miss a one. Heart pounding, my chest heaving, what was it L.T. wanted to show me? What?

Was it the filled-in hole? Was it the burial hole? I mean surely something or other must have happened to them? They had to be gone, transformed somehow into God only knew what? Was Captain Kidd's treasure there? Was Miguel Cortereal's treasure there? Or was some other treasure there, somebody else's?

L.T. made a hard landing onto Smelly Rock, two-footed and emphatic, and he turned to watch me do the same. He was laughing, laughing—laughing as giddy as giddy got—and me, I was laughing too.

We were almost there; I was almost there.

We ran around the cluster of pines with L.T. yelling out the paces. "Fifteen, sixteen ... and seventeen makes eighteen!"

The original hole was still there and still filled, and the burial hole, it was still there still awaiting. But next to them there was now another hole, a new hole round and deep. I looked in and what I saw ... well, it looked more odd-like than it did treasure-like.

L.T. jumped down inside of it, handed up to me the three items inside.

I watch a lot of TV, more than I maybe should, so I was pretty sure I knew what the inside items were: a seven branched candle holder (bronze), a skullcap (satin), and a Star of David (brass, six-pointedly sharp, and somehow shield-like too).

"The Lost Tribes are here, Michael. They're here! Do you realize that? I mean like maybe they're not all here, but at least one of them is."

"It ain't exactly treasure, L.T."

"Maybe, maybe not, that all kind of depends though, doesn't it? Thing is, even if it isn't actual proof of the Lost Tribes, still it's evidence. And you know what my Mom and Hal do whenever they come across something like this? They expand the search. They dig deeper."

I turned the three items over in my hands. They were brand new as yesterday, and yet felt old. They weren't really valuable, and yet had value. And they were just what I'd been looking for ... were just the evidence I needed.

By tomorrow morning my life never again would be quite the same. I knew that. By tomorrow morning I would know so much more than I now knew, maybe actually would even understand more. Changes were coming, adjustments too, the Drift of generations past coming at last home to roost. I was shaking, really shaking, the shivers of night just before dawn climbing up my back, climbing right back down it too.

Walking through the woods, me and L.T. walked down the dirt path, the dirt road, neither one of us saying nothing. A new moon, full and bright, showed the way.

"Where have you been?" Mom called from the den.

"Out."

"I know you were out, Michael. Where out?"

"Out nowhere."

"Doing what?"

"Doing nothing."

"Well, dinner's downstairs in the kitchen. Go eat."

I ate slowly, washed my plates when I finished. Then, carefully, I then carefully placed the three items from the hole on the kitchen table.

And that done, I kissed my mother good night, said good night to my father, took myself up to my room, took myself to bed. And the last thing, the very last thing I think I thought before sleep took me over and dreams took me away, was just how well I was going to sleep.

Sleep … sleep … sleep …I was going to sleep, and in the morning the day it would be different … I'd be different.

11

I didn't want to open my eyes.

Bed sheets spun around me from head to toe, from my cocoon I listened for the sounds of life. From off somewhere I heard little feet step lightly, heard big feet step loudly, floorboards underfoot groaning a little, groaning a lot too. And over at the screen front door, opening with a creak— shutting with a slap—that I heard too, could even through my window make out Billy's whimper, the sleepy one, his confused one. A car door slamming, an engine revving, and just like that both car and Billy were gone.

For a moment I let myself wish that I were Billy's age again, that it was me in that car. But I wasn't his age. And I wasn't in that car. I was where I was, knew exactly where I was. I was in my room, and I was alone, my old-young self gone with Billy in that car ... my old-young self gone away.

That's sometimes just how it goes.

"Michael. Michael," Patty said, shaking me by the shoulder. "I'm sorry, Michael. You have to wake up. You have to wake up now."

"Now?"

"Yeah, right now. Get dressed and come down to the kitchen. Oh, and put on your good clothes."

"Is everything okay?"

"It will be. You'll see."

When Patty left I remembered last night, remembered what I'd left on the kitchen table. So I got out of bed, got on a clean shirt and an unwrinkled pair of pants, got on my lucky shoes too. And then washing my face, and then brushing my teeth, I felt last night's supper just up and make a break for it, the break sudden and like that, like that and without me.

I guess just every shit for itself; every shit to itself.

Head in my hands, my eyes floating all over blurry octagonal floor patterns that shifted 'round like so many shifty little kaleidoscope pieces, I took a crap, a good one, ran through a checklist of what other body parts wanted to go make a break for it, go and be a shit. But seeing as all I pretty much just had left was my mind, and that just barely, and that just due to my hands vise-like holding my head in place, I finished up the inventory, and went downstairs.

The door leading to the kitchen was open, the stairway lights on. To me it felt a little bit like I was about to walk in on my own surprise party, except of course for the surprise part … and the party part.

About halfway down the stairs, I heard the door behind me close. And crouching low to see, I could see scores of candles flickering there in the fireplace. With the basement kitchen window curtains drawn, I knew they were drawn good and tight.

I paused on the bottom step, looked around. And though the scene before me was almost like I always pictured it would be, still it left me breathless. Mysterious, secretive, scary … the scene was all that and more. And another thing, it was also real.

Dad sat in a wooden chair, his feet on the floor and his back to the candles in the fireplace. He stared straight ahead, the lights of the candles behind him dancing wildly. Grandpa, he sat in a chair to Dad's right, Uncle Jiggy sitting in one to his left, the chairs in a circle of chairs. Uncles Joe and Buzz, Uncles Jack and Ike, Uncles Bob and Jeff, they and all of my so-called uncles, they all were there. They looked to me—did not look at me.

Were they nervous? Were they afraid? I couldn't tell.

Grandma and Aunt Lolly brought a chair to the middle of the circle and there sat me down. Tears in Aunt Lolly's eyes like a dammed-up lake, worry lines in Grandma's forehead like some damn checkerboard, they took hold of my hands, rubbed them warm.

And then, appearing from the fireplace light behind Dad, came Mom. She rested her hands on his shoulders, her soft eyes watching over me ... her baby.

"It was our intention," Dad said, "to wait another year. Even though thirteen is the customary age, your mother and I felt you weren't ready. It's risky, of course, to wait. At fourteen, almost fifteen, some boys just don't adjust well to a different way. They're too accustomed to the way they know. Sometimes they view their parents harshly. Sometimes they perceive their parents as being hypocritical, and being the teenagers they are, they rebel. Waiting another year certainly would have been cutting it close, but we were willing to take the chance, because your recent behavior showed us you simply were not as yet careful enough, not as yet discreet enough. And that, of course, is just the problem with telling a boy too early. Too early and a boy could be careless, even reckless, with a secret.

"But, Michael, you've left us with no choice, not now, not after finding what we found on the table. We simply can't wait. We simply can't wait any longer. That would be dangerous for us, might even be dangerous for you. See, Michael, you're curious—you're too curious—and we already know that as it is there's more than enough suspicion out there. Curiosity and suspicion are trouble. They're trouble, Michael. So what we will do is deal with the curiosity now, deal with the suspicion later.

We will teach you. We will teach you who we are, so you know just who it is you are.

"Michael, what's a secret? Tell me, what does a secret mean to you?"

"Means you don't tell," I said, with a shrug. "You don't ever tell."

"So as long as you don't tell, then everything's okay?"

"I think so."

"But aside from telling, actual telling, in what other ways might somebody learn a secret?"

"I guess they could see you doing something, doing something specific that gives it away."

"Okay. What about other ways?"

"I don't know. I can't think of any."

"What if people were to see the way a home gets cleaned, when it gets cleaned? What if people were to see the way food is prepared, when certain meals get cooked? What if people were to see which foods are eaten, which foods are not eaten? Might behavior reveal secrets? Might patterns of behavior reveal secrets? Might there be patterns in the questions that are asked of strangers? Might there be patterns as to who visits someone's house, when they visit that someone's house? Could secrets also be learned from patterns like these?"

"Maybe. Those are clues. But I guess if enough of them are strung together stuff gets given away."

"So what does that mean, Michael? What does that mean about how to keep a secret?"

"Means you've got to be careful. Means you've got to be careful all the time."

"Exactly. It means the secret always has to be with you. It means the secret always has to be first and foremost. It means you've got to live the secret in all you do, in all you think, with all your heart. The secret, in large part, has to be who you are."

I knew the moves as they came, realized I was getting boxed

in, understood that checkmate was only a move or two away. Short, however, of upsetting the board, there was nothing to do to stop it.

"Michael, do you promise to keep faith with the secret, live it, believe it, and believe in it?"

I looked at the circle on my left, looked at the circle on my right, saw it lean ever so slightly forward and towards me, it living, it breathing—a real-life life-force not so much waiting on my answer as counting on it. I mean the circle just prayed for it … prayed for it! My answer meant everything to them, was what kept them alive. And my answer meant everything for me too, it, after all, what would be my life, for the rest of my life.

"Yes," I said. "I promise. I promise to keep the secret. I promise to keep our secret."

I heard a sigh, saw hands clasp together, saw them rise in gratitude. Nudging me up from the chair, Grandma and Aunt Lolly moved it between the chairs of Dad and Grandpa … circle whole … circle complete.

"Michael," Grandpa said, "we are the *Nação*, a people of the Nation. The Nation is bigger than just us of course, and we are but a small part of it, a small and forgotten part of it. But though we may be forgotten, we haven't forgotten.

"Michael, if ever you hear the term 'People of the Nação' mentioned by Portuguese, know that in all likelihood it is us who they are talking about, not the larger Nation.

"At one time, Michael, our ancestors lived in Spain, in the cities of Seville and Toledo, Cordoba too. Their lives were horrendous, first legalized discrimination taking away their rights, and then, whipped into a frenzy by local authorities, howling mobs taking to the streets to attack them. All sorts of organized inhuman torture followed, the tortures the kind of stuff you thought existed only in legend. Our ancestors were put to the *potro*, the stretching rack, and torn limb from limb.

They were put to the *toca*, the water torture, and had water poured down their throats to the point of drowning. In the *garrucha* a pulley hung them by the wrist, and with their wrists bound behind their backs, dropped them. Worst of all, our ancestors were burned alive, burned at the stake.

"Now this was over five hundred years ago, Michael, and the world was larger then, scarier too. Sailing away, of course, was an option, but sailing meant weeks of uncertainty and hardship at sea. Besides, few places wanted our ancestors, and fewer still were willing to take them in. So your ancestors, Michael, came up with a solution. They figured if only they converted, if only they moved just enough away to outwardly look like those around them, their problems would then stop. Eventually things would change, times would get better, and they then could revert to being as they were. Until such time, they decided they would simply do the best that they could to preserve that which they believed. That meant passing down their beliefs to their children."

I was about to ask whether all this stuff was Inquisition stuff, thought better of it. Any mention of the word and the circle could then figure out I'd been talking, first to Hal, and then to Jenny. If they knew that, then how could they ever again trust me? If they knew that—that by my carelessness I'd nearly betrayed them—why then should they?

"Times never did get better for our ancestors, did they?" I asked.

"No," Grandpa said. "Spain hated our ancestors even more than the larger Nation that did not convert. In the end our ancestors became more secretive, went further underground. See, there were spies about, Michael, informers who were all too willing to go expose them. Then, in 1492, at a time when Columbus sailed the ocean blue, there was the Great Expulsion from Spain. Hundreds of thousands of the Nation fled to Turkey and North Africa, were scattered about to Holland,

Italy, Greece and other places.

"Our Nação ancestors took advantage of all the turmoil, decided they better escape while they still could, and took the short route to neighboring Portugal. And they weren't alone, thousands just like them went there too. In fact, so many went that for over two hundred years anywhere in the world, whenever the term 'Portuguese' got used in business dealings or even in gossip, it was understood the term referred to us, the Nação."

"What happened when they got to Portugal? Things went bad for them there too?"

"Just four years later, Michael, in 1496, they did, and those of the Nation who previously hadn't converted now were forced to do so. And just like in Spain, it was but a matter of time until secret investigations started all over again. Terrible vengeance was done both against these brand-new converts and those who had previously splintered, those like our ancestors who converted and yet still clung to the old beliefs.

"That's when our ancestors had enough. They decided to flee, sail hundreds of miles west, straight to the middle of the Atlantic and the newly-discovered Portuguese islands of the Azores. Our particular ancestors settled on the island of Terceira, the island that even now has more Imperio chapels than any other place in the world."

I remembered Father Sousa's mention of Imperio chapels, how promises to God were made there, how they had no crosses, just crowns. I again said nothing, there no reason for the circle to know I also had talked with him, what the circumstances of the talk were. "So this island in the Azores, it being like so far away and everything, even there our ancestors couldn't unsplinter, couldn't unconvert? Even there they couldn't change back to who they were?"

"They couldn't and they didn't. They continued with their secret lives and were wise in doing so. Neither Portugal nor

Spain gave up, such was their hatred. They chased our ancestors to the far corners of the world, even to the New World, to places like Brazil, Peru, and New Spain, Mexico."

The key questions, I knew, still had not been asked, the key problems still had not been answered. Not that I thought they could be answered, 'least not answered well.

The thought of the Nação splintering, the thought of it splintering away reminded me of a splinter I once had. It'd lodged its way under my skin, went so deep I couldn't find it. It irritated when touched, hurt when pressed. Eventually it just went in so deep I almost forgot about it, 'least almost forgot about it till it went and got infected.

So I asked an easier question, one the circle had an answer for. "What were our ancestors converting from?"

"Michael," Grandpa said, "*somos Judios. Somos Judios*—these words the same from generation to generation, said to you in the same way that they are for every boy and girl of the Nação."

"Michael," Dad said, "we are Jews. We are Jews. But you already suspected that, didn't you?"

"Sort of," I heard myself say.

I felt funny, kind of like on an amusement park ride where the spin's so fast I think I'm going to fly off. I don't, of course, the centrifugal force of the spin pinning me in place, forcing me to stare ahead, stare and focus even as everything all around me is just a blur. From my left I heard the words 'legacy, customs, belief.' From my right I heard something about 'Laws of Moses, Messiah, and One, One, One.'

I felt dizzy, everything a whirl. And I had to make it stop. "So, we're Jews."

"In a way," Dad said, his words trailing away, becoming a sigh, a pause before the continuation I sensed was coming.

I missed something, had missed something, didn't understand something or other that he and Grandpa were telling me. "In a way? What way? What kind of Jews are we?"

"*Secret*," Grandpa said. "Michael, 'Somos Judios', but we are *secret* Jews."

The extra word, the one Grandpa emphasized, that was the important one. What kind of Jews were we?

Secret Jews.

But Jews nevertheless, right?

In a way.

What way?

The secret way.

The circle was quiet and I had time enough to think. Of course we weren't Jews! Of course we weren't real Jews! I mean, how could we be Jews if we were only Jews in our homes? How could we be Jews if we only were Jews in our hearts? How could we be something that we didn't also live, really live? It didn't make sense! Why would we do that to ourselves? Why would we do that to ourselves … now? Why would we to that to ourselves … here?

"I know it's confusing for you, Michael," Dad said. "It was for all of us at your age. But we'll help you. We'll teach you, and ultimately you'll reach an understanding you'll live with. It'll be okay, you'll see."

Dad stood up, kissed me on the forehead, the circle breaking up, kisses and hugs all around. Then, his hands on his knees, Dad leaned in close so that we were face to face.

"So, Michael, now you know. Now you know who we are. So tell me," he whispered, his mouth to my ear, "how did you get hold of the things you left on the table? Tell me," he whispered, "tell me who's been helping you? Who's been helping you learn you're a Jew? Or is that a secret too?"

A crazy thought crossed my mind.

I was being tested!

But what was I being tested for? Was I being tested to see how loyal I was to the Nação? Or was I being tested to see how well I could keep a secret? Either way there would be a right answer, and a wrong answer. I mean, wouldn't I be unfaithful to the Nação if I kept the secret? And if I divulged the secret, wouldn't I be unfaithful to secrets, just plain insensitive to the purpose and meaning of a secret? I mean, did Dad want me to tell him, or did he not want me to tell him? If he wanted me to tell him then it must be important for the circle to know from whom there was danger. And if he didn't want me to tell him then it must be important to the circle that I prove I kept secrets.

There anyway was so little I knew, anyway so little I could figure out about the holes, just who it was filling them, digging them, putting things beside them, or in this case, putting things inside of them. I mean what was it that I really could tell Dad anyway? I knew next to nothing. I mean was I like somehow sworn to secrecy about all of the hole-related stuff? Was I sworn somehow to secrecy about all those who might have been involved in all the hole-related stuff?

For that matter how important was any of this anyway? What difference really could it make? How dangerous could it be? Really, like how dangerous could it now be? I mean— Hello!—the last time I checked this was the 21st century! Hello!—the last time I checked this was America! Hello!—I mean for crying out loud this still was 21st century America!

Would I keep secrets?

Should I keep secrets?

I cupped my hands over Dad's ear and whispered, and he nodded, thought about what I was saying, and then nodded again. And then with a tussle of my hair, he went to join the others, join them even as I instantaneously worried over what I'd said, wondered about what I'd done.

12

Ollie lobbed up yet another dirt bomb at L.T., the dirt exploding into an atomic mushroom cloud of dust as it smashed onto the dirt road.

"Hey, cut it out," L.T. hollered. He was up ahead of us and kept right on walking, did not look back. "I know it's you, Ollie. Don't make me go back there."

Just what it was Ollie was up to I didn't know, maybe something, maybe nothing. I mean with Ollie, who knew? If he was trying to get under L.T.'s skin it seemed to be working, 'least a little, but not enough though to draw L.T. out, see what was there. However, if Ollie's goal was to rattle L.T., make him squirm, make him hide, he might just as well have been lobbing dirt bombs straight up to the air.

"Cut it, already," L.T. yelled again, other dirt bombs smashing into smithereens all around him, to the front, to the back, to the right, and to the left. The explosives encircled him ... encircled him as if to isolate him.

I hung to the back of the straggler line—it more straggly by the minute and more out of line too—and waited to see if whatever it was Ollie was up to would bring on an escalation of hostilities. If it did I'd stay out of it. Not that I was neutral; I mean I wanted Ollie to beat the crap out of L.T. as much as anybody, though I somehow doubted that he could. No, I'd stay out of it simply because whatever had gotten into Ollie I suspected had also gotten a little into me, and not yet exactly knowing what whatever was, just beating the crap out of L.T. alone was not yet cause enough to go and make me want to fight—though it was close, real close, awful close. I mean, really, why go and fight if I did not yet know what my fight in this fight was?

Rookie swatted a clump of dirt out of her brother's hand, blocked him from rearming by standing between him and the better dirt stocks. "And empty the one in your pocket too," she said.

"Damn it," Richie said. "Leave it to a girl to stop a good fight just when it starts getting good."

Up in front, L.T. was marching through the break in the woods as if he was a General—just a little William Tecumseh Sherman trampling through the South—the little General L.T. just tramp-trampling his way through shrubs, wild flowers ... pretty much everything just happening to be in his path.

We, meanwhile, we his growingly unfaithful but as always ever-stupid foot soldiers, we still followed in line behind him as if he were like the damn pied piper himself. The difference was, this time it was getting hard not to notice how we lagged just a little bit further behind, how we questioned him and his sense of direction just a little bit more, be it with grumbles, or be it with dirt bombs.

"Hey, L.T." Ollie screamed, "just 'cause you found Jewish stuff in a hole, that don't make you Jewish, you know. And it don't make you found either. You're lost, you're gonna stay lost, and you ain't crossing no Sambatyon river."

I cringed. Mutiny in the air—all-out stupidity too—I should have realized that once the circle of elders felt it had no choice but to tell me who we were, they also had little choice but to go tell Ollie as well. What, or how much, they told him

I didn't know, but at the very least they obviously told him that me and L.T. found the stuff in the hole. They must also have somehow or other given Ollie the notion that L.T. was now dirt bomb eligible and that unlike us, L.T. was screwed, mixed-up, really mixed-up, hopeless, not really Jewish, and that that was how he was going to stay for eternity—for eternity, if not longer. And the funny thing was, for the life of me I just didn't really see how we were all that different.

I waited for a reaction from L.T., but he just kept right on going, his head up and on the lookout, and his nose down and on the smell-out for Smelly Rock. Striding as if on a damn quest or other, he looked now to be more great explorer than little General, no amount of criticism or skepticism—especially from the likes of us—about to knock him off-course.

"What's the Sambatyon River?" Rookie asked.

"Yeah," Richie said, "what's this about crossing it?"

"L.T.'s mixed up," I said, remembering Rookie and Richie weren't at the fishing dock the day L.T. told us about the Tribes. "He thinks he's one of the Ten Lost Tribes of Israel, the ones separated from the two remaining tribes of Israel by the Sambatyon River. On most days the Lost Tribes can't cross the river on account of the currents being too rough. And on days the water is calm, on the Sabbath days, then they don't allow themselves to cross."

"How come they don't allow themselves?"

"I think it's against their religion."

"But if they want to go across, why not just do it?"

"I don't know, Richie. People do and don't do all kinds of things, no matter whether it makes sense or not."

"Maybe they don't really want to go across."

"Sure they do."

"Maybe they just wish they'd go across. Wishing and wanting aren't the same thing, you know."

"It all just seems a little sad," Rookie said, her eyes soft as she watched L.T. jump onto Smelly Rock, the lost puppy happy to once and again be home.

"Don't feel too bad for him," I said. "L.T.'s gonna be fine. His tribe, at least, both wishes and wants."

L.T. was kneeling on the Rock by the time we caught up with him, several twigs in his hand. Working the twigs like blades of straw, he held them to the air, worked on figuring just which way the wind blew. Then he grinned, his toothy one, the Cheshire cat one.

"Oh no!" Richie said. "Oh no, L.T., don't tell me you're Dead Reckoning again."

"Over the past few minutes there've been lots of snapped twigs a little off to the side of where we walked. See? They're broken."

"Maybe we made them, I mean it's not like we haven't been by here before."

"Yeah, but we've always reached the Rock by the woods' natural break, went by way of the normal path, the same one we took just now. We didn't do this, Richie, couldn't have. These twigs were broken by somebody who didn't follow the break, didn't know the path, didn't care about it either."

Scooting crab-like from off the Rock, L.T. rose to his feet, zig-zagged himself a ways away, us a ways away right there with him. Then swiping at the ground, he cleared away some pinecones, pointed to an imprint of a boot in dirt.

"Maybe Captain Kidd was here," Ollie laughed. "Maybe Blackbeard himself," he laughed some more, this one more a hoot than an actual laugh. "Maybe they came for their booty."

Ollie and Richie hadn't brought up anything about pirate treasure for a long while, I realized, they having probably long ago lost all hope of finding any.

"Hey, Ollie," Richie said. "Don't be a such a jerk. It was good that we dug for Captain Kidd's treasure. If we hadn't dug holes, who knows just how long it could've taken to discover the Jewish stuff."

I blinked, Richie's remark yet another straw, this one floating in the air, coming back around my way.

Even once Ollie said that Jewish stuff was discovered in the hole, Richie's only follow-up question had been about the Sambatyon. I mean it wasn't about the Jewish stuff ... wasn't about that because that he already knew. And of course he already knew because he too had met with the circle, met 'cause ... he too was Nation.

I'd always known that Richie was like me, but just how that was, that I didn't know. But now that I knew just how that was, I also knew just why that was. And now knowing the why ...why, but of course Richie wanted to learn, wanted to learn maybe almost as much as me, maybe even almost as fast. I mean, really, why would he—he or any Spit kid—ever be any different from me?

One common history, one common religion; the same customs, the same beliefs—it almost all made sense. And yet, it didn't make sense. Nothing about it made any real sense, not our history, not our religion, not our customs, not our beliefs, not our situation, not even our thoughts and our feelings— nothing.

Ollie took out a dirt bomb from under his cap, chucked it like a grenade out and over the cluster of pines. Disappearing, it made no sound, surely landed somewhere by the holes.

"Kaboom!" he yelled. "Kaboom! Kaboom! Kaboom!" Pushing Richie and Rook to the ground, Ollie jumped on top of me, his chunkiness smothering, absolutely positively.

"Get off of me! Get off me, you idiot!" I tried rolling myself away, noticed L.T. alone, he alone still standing.

"I wonder what we'll find this time," Richie said, getting himself to his feet, dusting dirt from off his shirt. "Like it's always something with these holes. You should've brought your camera, Mookie, you know, as proof of what's like going on here."

"Someone lost my camera, lost it at Café Saudade," I said, looking to Rookie. "Anyway, Ollie, I don't think proof is something people here really want."

L.T. pulled down the brim of his cap, used his hand to shield his eyes from the sunshine filtering through the trees. And following his lead, I squinted too, just to see whatever it was that he now saw. Maybe fifty yards or so away, I spotted a tree limb bounce, saw its leaves quiver, both the bounce and the quiver seemingly caused as if by nothing at all.

"Did you see that?"

"I saw it," I whispered. "Is someone watching us?"

"I don't know, maybe, maybe not. It doesn't matter, though. I mean it ain't like the be-all or end-all or anything."

"It doesn't matter?" I said, turning to see if Ollie, Richie or Rook had noticed the bounce, seen the quiver. "What do you mean it doesn't matter? Whoever or whatever is out there is the footprint, L.T.! It's the one messing with our holes! It's the one chasing me off my watch!"

"What I mean is it's not the only one thing that matters. You're making a pretty big assumption about all this, Michael. Who's to say … who's to say your 'one' is one and the same?"

"What are you talking about?"

"Look, so far there have been filled-up holes, burned animals by the holes, newly-dug grave-like holes, and Jewish stuff in the holes. Does that seem to you like the work of one person?"

"I guess not."

"Of course not, not unless your person or your monster has a multiple personality disorder."

I looked back again at the tree limb, its leaves sunning themselves now, just dancing here and there in the wind. "But even so, L.T., like even if there really is more than just one nut out there, why doesn't it matter? Why does it still not matter? I mean why wouldn't it matter that someone or someones are watching us?"

"'Cause of Drift, Michael. Drift is why it doesn't matter. I know that you hate the word, think that it's funny, but Drift is real. Like someone watching, or no one watching, so what? We're sailors, Michael, sailors at sea, just sailors adrift on an open sea. I mean what's watching—a ripple? A ripple in a sea—you think that's gonna make one bit of difference in a sea? Drift isn't any one thing—it's everything. It's an everything everywhere that changes the course. You think in the big picture watching means squat when it comes to wanting to Dead Reckon your way back, Reckon your way back to what you want … what we want?"

"You mean like, to treasure?"

"Yeah, like to treasure."

I peeked over my shoulder, saw Ollie, Richie and Rook looking too to where we looked. "Know what, L.T., you know what Rookie says? She says every good Portogeez knows that he can't Dead Reckon his way to treasure, that he only can use it to figure out where he is."

L.T. turned his cap around. "Oh yeah? Oh yeah, Michael? Well, Rook's wrong. Who's to say that finding treasure and figuring out where you are aren't one and the same, can't be the same? Who's to say that if you figure out where you are, not only will you not be lost, you'll be home?"

I looked back again at the branch, noticed a ripple run through its leaves, noticed it disappear in with the woods. Jumping off his feet, I saw Ollie reach into his shorts and fire a dirt bomb its way.

"It was a dog," Richie said. "Just a rabid dog."

"No way," Ollie said. "A dog up a tree? It was L.T.'s mom's boyfriend, maybe even L.T.'s mom. Whatever it was though, it looked a whole lot like L.T."

I wasn't sure just what it was I saw, but to me it seemed big, inflated big, a big monster that in wanting to be everywhere, was nowhere.

"It was the Butcher of Best," L.T. said. "It was your old man, Ollie, just as fat and ugly and crazy as you. Good thing you took all the fat, ugly, crazy genes, that none were left for Rook."

"Thanks," Rookie said, "but I don't think any of you have it really right. Let's think normally for a change, okay? Let's think motive. Who would want to cover our holes, dig new holes?"

"Somebody who's sick," Richie said.

"Somebody who's a troublemaker," Ollie added.

I looked at L.T., looked away too before the others could see me looking. Wasn't L.T. a troublemaker? Wasn't he more or less sick? What if he was the one with the multiple personality disorder? I mean hadn't it been his idea to dig for treasure in the first place? And wouldn't it be just like him too to cover the holes just for the fun of it, dig a burial hole just to have even more fun with it? Just why was it he didn't answer my walkie-talkie call the night I got chased off my watch? Couldn't he have planted the Jewish stuff in the hole, done the planting after telling Hal of our kitchen customs, Hal then telling him our customs were the customs of 'in a way' Jews?

"There's only one explanation," Rookie said. "Only one logical and sane answer: Miguel Cortereal."

Richie locked his hands over his head, brought them down onto his head. "That's your logical answer? This is your sane answer? Just one problem, Rook. Cortereal's been dead only for say about a few hundred years already."

"No, no, I don't actually mean Miguel Cortereal. I mean the Ghost of Miguel Cortereal. Don't laugh! I mean weren't you guys after his treasure? Didn't you want to find what it was he was hiding?"

"This is a little weird, Rook."

"Okay, then answer this: Who else but the Ghost of Miguel Cortereal would have the kind of motive to cover our holes, cover them so that we don't come up with his treasure? Who else but the Ghost would have the motive to chase Michael away from his treasure? Who else but the Ghost would have the kind of motive to dig a grave hole, scare us from digging any more? And it's not just motive either, it's opportunity. Who else but the Ghost could do this stuff right under our noses? Who else but the Ghost knows these woods the way he does, knows them 'cause he's always haunting them?"

"But why would the Ghost of Miguel Cortereal put Jewish stuff in a hole?"

"Maybe he thought that if he threw us a bone it would be enough to keep us away. Maybe he thought that would be enough to keep us from digging any more."

"If the Ghost thought that," L.T. said, "then the Ghost is an idiot."

"The Ghost isn't an idiot. I don't think a Ghost can be a Ghost and an idiot at the same time. And just think about it, since he's invisible he can spy on us, know everything we're up to. I mean wasn't he smart enough to get a hold of the Jewish stuff?"

The obvious question, the one none of us was asking, was how the Ghost knew? Like how did he know to put Jewish stuff in a hole? I mean like, how could he have known who we were before we sort of even knew who we were? How could he have known just what we were up to before we even knew what we were up to? How could he have known that we were just four mixed-up secretly Jewish kids, and one kid so mixed-up that he not only thought himself to be Jewish, but Lost Tribe Jewish?

Even if the Ghost's invisibility let him watch everything we were up to, when it came to stuff in our minds, weren't we invisible too? When it came to stuff in our hearts, weren't we also invisible? I mean, like what was this Ghost, some sort of mind reader or something, some sort of soul reader?

Like just who was he, this Ghost? Just who, for that matter, was Miguel Cortereal? Though I had my ideas, and L.T. had his, they were really just stabs in the dark, just stabs at pinning a shadow to a place. And all the while, I just couldn't help but wonder if in trying to make Miguel Cortereal into more than just a person, into more than just a mere mortal, I'd somehow or other made him a Ghost.

Rook's theory was really crazy, really pretty out there, but just the same I was glad that it too was in the mix. So long as Ollie and Richie were fixated on all this Ghost mumbo-jumbo, then maybe they wouldn't be suspicious of L.T., 'least as suspicious of L.T. as I was. Besides, in its own crazy and unbelievable way, Rook's Ghost theory made about as much sense as anything, not that sense was all that much of a requirement to begin with.

"Ten, eleven, twelve," L.T. said, his paces bringing us to the cluster of pine trees, "thirteen, fourteen, fifteen, sixteen, seventeen—"

Stopping dead, stopping so dead I bumped into him, I heard L.T.'s breath escape like the rush of air out of a dying balloon.

There, one step ahead, one step so close we practically could already feel the spot's earth in our hands, and feel its air in our lungs, was our hole ... the Jewish hole ... covered now with so much dirt that it spilled up and over the rim. What's more, planted at the very spot where the dirt was piled so high as to form a peak, there now was a cross, small and made of stone, big and built for the bringing, the bringing down to earth.

"A grave!" Ollie cried. "A goddamn graveyard?"

Kneeling on down, Richie took up dirt, watched it sift through his fingers. "Chippascutt Point Pines! Is this all this is? Just a graveyard where holes get buried? Just a graveyard where holes get a stone all their own? I mean really, what else did we expect? I mean really, what else can you really do with 'em anyway, these holes? Look, we started this, and we should have known too that this is what comes of this. For what it's worth—we, us—we as good as did this."

L.T. turned away, and he turned quickly. Pushing his hands to the air, I saw his back heave fits and starts, the fits powerful and the starts terrible. "They're the ones making a cemetery," he sobbed. "Like what did we do? What did we do but dig holes? Is something wrong with that? Is there something the matter with that? We didn't do this, and we shouldn't be liable for it, not any of it. Making life doesn't make you liable for the death."

He went to a tree and sat under it, his back to us still. It bothered me—but I mean really upset me—to see L.T. like this. The only other time that I'd seen him lose it like this was that time his metal detector picked up a treasure blip, the time he wound up digging himself halfway to China in a try to reach it.

It wasn't L.T.!

I realized that it couldn't be him. L.T. would never have wanted this to finish, and he certainly would never have wanted it to finish like this. As a Lost Tribe, what he wanted was to join up with the other Lost Tribes, be with them the day they ultimately were found. That's what he believed, Drift just his way to explain how he got lost, Dead Reckoning just his way to becoming un-lost.

For him, Jewish, Jewish was his religion, his even if he didn't think of it in those kinds of terms. And it was his faith too, his though he might not have thought of it quite like that either. For him, being Jewish was a way, just his way to live and just his way out. Being Jewish took him from himself, let him think and ask questions, let him dream and wonder. But even he, even he being the Jew that he thought himself to be, even a Jew like that must have surely seen the significance of a cross being placed over a hole of Jewish stuff, must have surely seen it even if the significance that he saw in it was different from the truly religious significance that I saw in it. I mean for him, first and foremost, the meaning of the cross was about Lost Tribes, other Lost Tribes who even if close by were now beyond his reach, and he beyond theirs.

Me? As for me, I work in circles. I mean I dream in circles, and wonder in circles, and even walk in circles. And walking that way now, with my head down and my eyes to the ground, more than anything else I just found myself just really getting good and mad.

Maybe Ollie he did see a graveyard. And maybe Richie he did see some natural consequence to all of our digging. And maybe L.T. he did see some sort of hope killing field. But me, what I saw was a cross, just a cross on top of some dirt, the dirt back now in the ground from which it earlier had been taken from, taken from to reveal a hole, the hole a hole of Jewish stuff, the Jewish stuff inside ... well ... inside stuff.

But was it simple as just that? I mean it couldn't be, could it?

I got madder, walked in ever-tightening circles, kept my head down and my eyes down even more to the ground. Something was wrong ... something was wrong?

The dirt!

It was brown, dull brown, the dirt to re-fill the hole from the exact same mound of dirt left to dry when first the hole got dug. But there also were streaks, rich brown dirt streaks sprinkled on in with the dull dirt. New dirt was brought in to re-fill the hole, just had to be. Dirt from the mound wasn't alone enough to do the job. Somehow, in the whole process of hole-digging and hole-filling, dirt had to have been lost.

But where did it go?

I couldn't figure it out. With each step of the process dirt was lost, new dirt brought in to make up the difference, and what should have been enough wasn't. Sure enough, from out the corner of my eye, just feet away, I saw scrapings in the ground, the scrapings revealing where the new dirt had been taken from.

"Hey, L.T.!" I hollered. "Come here!"

"What?" he said, standing to the far side of the cross, his cheeks still streak-red.

"See the dark dirt over the hole? It's been brought in, brought in from over there."

"So?"

"So it ain't original to the hole. It had to be brought in to re-fill the hole."

"Why would dirt need to be brought in? Why would dirt need to be brought in when there's a perfectly good mound just right by?"

"'Cause the hole, L.T., the hole doesn't want to be a hole. I think what the hole does is find ways of continuously losing 'least some of the dirt. That way when the hole is filled next time, there ain't enough mound dirt on hand to completely cover it. The hole-filler-upper has to always keep bringing in fresh dirt, has to keep bringing it just to try and keep the hole covered in the way he wants it covered. But the dirt he brings in, it ain't the same, and not only that, each time he brings in dirt still it ain't enough. It's a losing proposition for him. Eventually he gives up, just has to."

"I don't get it," Richie said. "Just how is the hole losing dirt?"

"Over time everything with the hole changes and dirt always kind of just drifts away. I don't know how that happens, or where it goes, but it happens, it goes. And the fresh dirt, the dirt that's brought in to cover the hole, that's all part of this thing, just part of the process that makes the hole look different from the way it used to. But when you think about it, the new dirt, it's nothing, just a ripple, an insignificant ripple just mainly there for the show. And the same goes for the cross. It's only there to make the hole look different than it used to. It's only there to keep things covered, make this place look like a cemetery, make us give up.

"You were right, L.T.! You were right all along; we really are close. All we have to do is make adjustments. All we have to do is just make adjustments for all this Drift. And then, that done, go Dead Reckon our way back to how things once were, to who we once were."

"I agree," Rook chimed in. "You're absolutely positively right," she said, nodding enthusiastically, looking to L.T., holding him by the arm. "But how do we do that, Michael? What's the best way we make the adjustments?"

"Ol' Cuss once told me how he and his buddies this one time were off the Grand Banks, how they got so disoriented in fog that all they could do was wait the thing out. But this one dory man, he starts to sing a song in a language they don't understand and yet still somehow or other know. So what these dory men do is use the man's voice and the man's song as a beacon to bring their dories together. And that's just what we should now do. We should sit tight and listen, anything else we first doing just keeping us lost."

"I don't know," L.T. said. "Just sit and listen?"

"Sometimes the best thing to do is listen. I mean you can't listen, let alone think, if you're running around at a hundred miles an hour. Look, the Lost Tribes want to be found, right? Well, who says they have to wade across the river? Maybe if they only just listened they'd hear others out there just like them, others who could help them figure out where the heck it is they are. Then, that way, the Tribes wanting to be found will be found. And those Tribes not wanting to be found, well, they won't be found, not ever."

"I don't get it," Ollie said. "What is it that we're listening for?"

"We're listening," Richie said, with a point to the woods, "for what's out there, the Ghosts that are out there."

"No," Rookie said, with a nod to the holes, "that's not what we're listening for. What we're listening for are the ones in there, the Ghosts in there."

13

There is no road that leads to the Imperio chapel of Spit. It has no address. It has no name. And for what it's worth, it has no place in this world. Sitting somewhere between a drying cornfield and a cracking pumpkin patch, the chapel is not really here, but then again, neither really is it not here. And it's not really there either, but neither really is it not there. All of which is to say, it's not here and it's not there, but really—it is here. It is there.

The Imperio chapel is a squat barn of a building, kind of blue with white shutter windows, those same white shutter windows also trimmed by yet one other kind of blue. I really don't know how, but somehow Spit homes manage to always be near the chapel, always around it, the chapel in back of the homes, always in the back, always behind. Most of the time closed, 'the Gathering Hall,' as some call it, or 'the Empire,' as people wanting to be funny call it, is not in use, a heavy chain and a big lock on the door enough to convince even the most curious of passers-by not to trespass. Usually quiet, usually empty, the Empire—'cause I want to be funny too—is like an old barn, one whose barnyard smells somehow continue living on despite the cows being gone, despite the horses even being long gone.

Lengthening my stride to try keeping up with those of my father, each right leg step of his made the lantern at his side jiggle, sway light my way. And off to both sides of us, other lanterns jiggled too, other lights swaying in the dark as other fathers made their way to the chapel with their sons, their daughters.

Disappearing with each swing behind a leg, only to then reemerge with each swing before a leg, the spectacle of lights made me think of fireflies sparkling, resting, and sparkling all over again.

Nearing the chapel, I glanced at my watch and saw that it was almost midnight, saw too older and bigger Saturday night kids standing guard by the door, their coffee cups in hand, their cigarettes too.

"Mookie," Richie's big brother whispered in my ear. "You're in the first class, the first grouping. Richie, he's in this one too."

The hall was already pretty full when we entered it, just bunches of kids on folding chairs around folding tables, bunches too of candles under glass to light them up. I knew most of the kids, they within a year of me either way in school.

Sitting down in the last chair at one table, I noticed a plate of cookies and pitcher of milk in the middle of it, couldn't help as well but not notice Dad gone now to the darkness away from the tables. In his place, though, there was Mr. Fernandes, the principal of my grammar school. He seemed to show up right from out of nowhere.

"All of you already know there is one God," he said, tucking his chair in. "Just as importantly though, we believe God is One. Michael, what does that mean? What does that mean to you?"

"I don't know, Mr. Fernandes. I don't know what that means."

"Think about it. I'm not grading you on your answer. From now on your High School principal will have the pleasure to make your life miserable."

The candlelight on Mr. Fernandes' face made his eyes like crazy mirrors, and I could see myself in those mirror-crazed eyes, just me at the table, just a stupid look on my face, just everyone at the ready to snicker at pretty much anything I would say.

"Maybe it means God is One," I said. "I mean, he's God, right, so he can be Himself, be who He is."

"So God, God the all-powerful, because He is who He is, can be Himself, can and does at all times speak with one voice. Is that right, Michael? Do I have that right?"

"Yes. You have that right."

"Good. Good, Michael. God is One. We don't believe in the Trinity."

I thought about the idea of God being One, realized I was okay with it. Even though the symbols of the Trinity always had been around me, it never was with me. I mean nobody close to me believed it nor ever told me to believe it. God the One was the one talked about, not Jesus, nor the Holy Ghost either.

Sure, Father Sousa in church sermons spoke about the Trinity, but in our Sunday school discussion groups of Spitters, the idea of Trinity didn't come up. For that matter neither did the word. Like Jesus himself didn't come up, and I don't mean just ever, but never. There wasn't a figure of him in my church classroom, and there most certainly wasn't one of him on any cross. And just as well too, what with the whole creepiness factor and everything. It was why I never did look his way for very long, that and of course the danger I sensed whenever I did. And those few times that I did allow myself to look, I felt like a fish out of water, felt myself wriggle, felt myself gasp for a breath to breathe. And while those instincts may have been understandable for an alewife herring … to me … for me … in me—they were absolutely petrifying.

"We believe," Mr. Fernandes continued, grabbing my attention with a grab of my arm, "that the Messiah has yet to come. Of course we hope that he will come, and come soon, but we understand that he won't show until such time that he absolutely must. But when at long last he does show, the world will be a good place, a safe place, a place where everyone who ever lived righteously will return to live among the living. Then God will gather in the remnants of His people, the remnants willingly coming together because they no longer will be afraid. When the Messiah arrives, their days will be anew, and all of our days will again be as they once were."

"Are we a remnant?" Abbie asked. Her fingers playing with a curl of her blondish hair, her blue eyes looking crossed, probably just bewildered. Living outside of Spit in Best, Abbie hadn't gone to the same grammar school as me, and the little I knew of her came mostly from back-row church observations. Usually sitting with her mother, she, like us, did not take Communion. But when she sat with her father, she sat way up in front and did take Communion.

"Do you know what a remnant is?" Mr. Fernandes asked her.

"People that remember?"

"Actually, it means 'the remains.' But in a way your answer is closer to the real meaning. You see, Abbie, remains are what are left behind, while remnants are those that don't keep up. The reason we are a remnant of sorts is that we didn't keep up with our Jewish family. And since we didn't keep up, it only was natural for the family to let us go, leave us by the wayside and eventually just forget about us. But the important thing is: we haven't forgotten. Jewishness can't be forgotten. And though we no longer know all the ways of the family, we remember we are in the family."

"Am I also a remnant?"

"Yes, Abbie, you're one of us. Your mother thinks it's

important you remember. And that makes you important. You're a link in the chain of all those who over time have struggled to remember, and in so doing have suffered. So long as you remember, there is always hope that the Messiah will arrive soon, peace be with him."

"Is the Messiah One?" I asked.

"No, Michael. Only God is One."

"That's kind of what I figured. The Messiah sounds like the Hero fish my grandfather is always hoping to catch. Since the Messiah isn't one, I guess he can be both a fish and a Hero."

"The Hero fish is folklore, Michael, many in the Nação holding to the idea the Messiah's arrival will be in the form of a fish. In that way he can fool those who wish to harm him. In that way he lessens the risk of being burned at the stake."

"You mean it's so dangerous that even a Messiah isn't safe?"

"He's not God, Michael. His role is to usher in an age of peace. That's why God sends him. God is all-powerful, the Messiah isn't. Do you understand the difference?"

I thought I did, but there wasn't much time to think about it, Mr. Fernandes switching from talking about beliefs to talking about customs.

Unlike other Jews, he said, who fast on a day called Yom Kippur, the Day of Atonement, we fasted on *Dia Puro*, the Pure Day, the eleventh day after the new moon, a day different than Yom Kippur. By doing so, he said, what we do is trick others into thinking that we aren't Jews.

Another trick, he said, was the baking of bread on the first two days of Passover, days that other Jews don't even think about baking bread, let alone eating it. It only was on the last six days of Passover that we didn't eat bread. During that time we go to the river, go in small groups, and strike at the river water with branches; it a reminder to ourselves how Moses parted the Red Sea during the exodus out from Egypt.

The flicker of candlelight and the late hour, the whir of questions and answers and answers and questions, it all went to making my head spin. It felt like that time I walked into an Indian casino with my parents and felt kind of drunk, felt kind of out of control, felt kind of a little too good. Then, as now, I had a feeling that I was up to something, up to something with friends and adults alike, the up to something somehow daring, even almost outlawed.

L.T. would have loved something like this if only he were here. But he couldn't be here. His only being like us—that wasn't actually being us. And of that we not only would make ourselves sure, if need be we would make him sure.

When Mr. Fernandes got up to go over to another table, Lieutenant Roza came over from another table to ours. Best Harbor's Police Chief, Lieutenant Roza was a skinny lady whose face was like drying fish hung too long in the sun. Slapping her gun down onto the table with one hand, and slapping her badge down on the table with her other hand, she certainly got my attention—got everyone's attention!

"Most of you already know me as a police officer. But as hard as it is to believe, I'm also a grandmother. And as a grandmother, while I don't enforce the same laws I do as an officer, I still deal in them. The laws of a grandmother are rules, rules for the family, and I make sure my family knows them and tries to observe them. These rules, they're to be observed inconspicuously, even secretly."

Pork, she said, was *entrefeda*, not pure, and should not be eaten. Cows and chickens, they had to be slaughtered at the neck in one fell swoop, hung so that all blood drained out from them. Candles were to be lit on Friday evenings, lit to welcome the Sabbath Queen of Peace. And to get ready for the Sabbath a house was to be clean, clothes were to be clean, and we were to be clean. In preparing for the Sabbath, pieces of dough used in the baking of special loaves were to be tossed to a fire, tossed as a reminder of those who sacrificed their lives to preserve our faith.

Of course I'd been around these practices my whole life. But I considered them to be quirks, not really customs, and certainly not rules. But if they were rules then as rules they made some sense. I mean, rules could have reasons, reasons to carry out something, carry out something no matter whether the carrying out was in shadow, in a backyard shed, in a basement kitchen fireplace, or even in the middle of a night pumpkin patch Imperio chapel. As Father Sousa himself had pointed out when he drove me and Rook home, even an Imperio Chapel had rules, rules about not having religious symbols inside or out, these particular rules at long last at least having some reason behind them.

When Lieutenant Roza finished laying down the law, she got up and went to another table, Father Gomes appearing at ours, and any understanding I thought I had about any of this, it pretty much went abracadabra, oogie pallokie, shazam—as poof and as gone as a rabbit from a magician's hat.

Unlike most Best Harbor families who traced their ancestry back to the days when New Bedford whaling ships took on crew in the Azores, Father Gomes' ancestors came from the Cape Verde islands, and they came State-side just a generation or two ago. As Father Sousa's second in command at St. Peter's, Father Gomes' Cape Verdean features were much darker than our Azorean ones, almost black. And his customs, they seemed darker too, seemed more different.

Father Gomes' hiring three years ago had been controversial, most Besterners against the hire claiming that his 'credentials' weren't proper Azorean-like ones; most Spitters, on the other hand, while ideally wanting an Azorean, liking Father Gomes' 'references'. In the end, and against the wishes of certain Besterners like Mr. Alves, Father Sousa wound up choosing Father Gomes to help teach our Sunday school class of Spitters.

"The thing about sides," Father Gomes said, "is everybody has them. We have a good side and a bad side. We have a loving side and a hateful side. We have a believing side and a doubting side. And some of us," he said, twisting in his chair, "have more of a backside than a front side, or more of a front side than a backside.

"What we also have is an outer side and an inner side. Take you for example, Michael. Inside maybe you're laughing on account of my joke, but outside you try to stay polite and not laugh. After all, what kind of person laughs at another person's expense? On the other hand, what kind of person doesn't laugh, never laughs? Who would you be then, Michael? What kind of person would you be?"

"I probably wouldn't be me. I probably wouldn't be human."

"Exactly. Your two sides go into making you what you are, who you are. Both sides are essential. They work on each other and they work with each other. Ultimately, your outer side reflects your inner side. And your inner side, that'll be affected by your outer.

"Take for instance the case of Joseph. You all know that when his brothers met him in Egypt they didn't recognize him. Joseph had played his role in Pharaoh's court for so long they thought he actually was Egyptian. And truth be told, he was Egyptian. But he also was still a Hebrew. In the end he used both his powers as an Egyptian, and his values as a Hebrew, to do right by God and right by his family.

"We do right by practicing circumcision, circumcision a covenant between God and Abraham. But to do right by our families we perform circumcisions secretly, perform them at home. We also do right by our families by baptizing children like you in church, only once at home quickly scrubbing off the chrism to also do right by God. To do what's right for our families, we have marriages in church, only later at home conducting a private Jewish ceremony. Even in death, even in death we do what's right for family. We bury our deceased under the cross, bury them there for the sake of the living. Then our living, they mourn according to Jewish law, mourn in secret, mourn for the sake of the dead."

"Is it an even split?" I asked. "I mean is our outer side even with our inner side? Is our Catholic side even with our Jewish side? I mean it can't be even, can it? That's not how it works, is it?"

"There's an individual element to this, Michael. And every person has to find what works best for him.

"In my own case, when I was your age and I first learned about my Jewish heritage, I determined never to forget just how important my Catholic side was to me. It, after all, had held me in good stead for the first thirteen years of my life, and I desperately wanted it to continue. Understand, I was comfortable in church. I loved the church. So I decided to become a priest. In that way I could do what I love, namely uniquely serve our family's outer side while at the same time uniquely also serve our family's inner side, that's to say teach kids like you to develop their inner sides."

But you're a priest, Father Gomes! You're a Catholic priest!

How does this work for you? Christ, how can this possibly work for you?

How does this work for us? By God, how ever can it work for us?

"So you became a priest," Abbie said, "so that we would love our Catholic side, maintain our Catholic side, while at the same time love our Jewish side, all the while develop our Jewish side?" She curled her hair into knots, clearly about as confused as I was.

"I became a priest so that kids like you know how important both your sides are. If something isn't important, or doesn't seem important, you wind up forgetting it. You wind up losing it. Over the centuries there have been many among us who have lost sight of how important their inner sides were. The result? The overwhelming majority of Portuguese who were once Nação now are Catholic—have that, and only that, as their inner side. Fact is most of these Portuguese don't have even any idea that their ancestors once were Jews. And even if they continue to keep certain customs like lighting candles on Friday nights, still they have no idea why they do so, other than it just being a custom. These people, they no longer are the same as us. They no longer have the same insides as us, the same soul as us. They aren't part of our Nation."

"But couldn't you teach about our Jewish sides without, you know, becoming a priest? Why a priest?"

"I became a priest, Michael, so that when kids like you do learn about your Jewish sides you still will remember your outer sides, know how important your Catholic sides are. Just as some over the centuries lost sight of their inner sides, there also have been actually been some among us who lost sight of their outer sides. Finding themselves among Jews, in countries such as Holland that tolerated Jews, they felt free to go back and practice only their inner religion. The result? They abandoned their Catholic ways. These people, they too are no longer the same as us. Without a Catholic outer side they no longer have the same makeup as us, the same definition as us, the same unique spirit as us. They too aren't part of our Nation. They can't be."

I buried my chin into my hands, turned my mind over, and my heart over, and then my mind once again. Was Father Gomes saying what I thought he was saying? Was he saying we were better off remaining as we were rather than becoming only Jewish? Was he saying we should thank our lucky stars

for being Catholics on the outside, Jewish on the inside? Was
he saying it was better to believe something that we faked?
Was he saying it was better to be afraid of revealing that which
we believed? Was he saying it was better to feel lousy, feel
paranoid? Was he saying it was better to feel ashamed? I mean,
was he saying this outside/inside thing, this soul/spirit thing—
this precarious unique thing—that it was a good thing?

Who were we fooling?

When Dad's circle told me we were secret Jews it sort of
made sense, well, at least some sense. I understood why we
pretended to outwardly be Catholic. And when Mr. Fernandes
and Lieutenant Roza told me about fooling people, I more or
less kind of got that too.

There was an Inquisition going on!

But Father Gomes, what he was saying was something
different, something altogether different. He was saying we did
what we did because we wanted to do it in the way that we
did it. He was saying we did what we did because we chose
to. He was saying we did what we did in the way that we did
it because, somehow, it made us balanced, made us complete,
made us better.

The realization of just what it was Father Gomes was
saying hit me hard, hit me right where a thirteen-year old, soon
to be fourteen-year old, was most vulnerable. We weren't a
more balanced people for being as we were. We weren't a more
complete people for being as we were. We weren't a better kind
of people for being as we were.

We were just a more hypocritical people!

I mean, what if real Catholics found out we didn't? What
if real Jews found out we couldn't? What if they found out
that for us there was no one belief as strong as our belief
in trickery? What if they found out that for us there was no
practice as strong as our practice of deception? Worse still,
what if I—even if only accidentally—what if I were the one to

give it away? What if I were to give away that we were frauds, give away that we were deceivers?

I told myself to calm down, told myself it would all be okay. Eventually wrongs would be righted, mistakes surely would be corrected. It was just temporary, this sham. It was a necessity, what with the whole world being as dangerous and everything as it was.

Father Gomes was wrong, just had to be. We only were as we were, and only would be as we were, until such day as the Hero's arrival, his bringing with him the promise of a safe world, a better one. I mean, we didn't choose this. I mean, it couldn't be that it was us who wanted this, could it? Why would we do this to ourselves?

And the Sambatyon River, Father Gomes was wrong about that too. It existed, just had to. Why else would we be in the situation we were in? I mean, after all, we wanted to go home, didn't we? We wanted to reunite with family, didn't we? We wanted to join up again with our real family, didn't we?

"Joseph's remnants," I said out loud, interrupting something or other Father Gomes was saying, "Joseph's remnants eventually were brought back from Egypt, weren't they? He got to be buried in the Land of Israel, didn't he? He got to be buried as a Hebrew, didn't he? In the end he got to live his death in the way he'd wanted to live his life, didn't he?"

I must have been screaming or something, everyone in the Imperio hall suddenly looking my way, their eyes wide, sad somehow too. Rushing on over, Dad wrapped his arm around my shoulder, hurried me out.

"It's not fair! Joseph got to go home! He got to be with family! He got to be with his people! He got to be … he got to be with his real Nation!"

14

What with my little meltdown at the Imperio hall, I knew it probably wouldn't be long until Mom and Dad suggested I see Dr. Carvahal, the same therapist Billy sees.

Dr. Carvahal's office is in his house, a big house with a big porch, sits on a hill overlooking the river. Sometimes as poor Billy is lying there, just lying there on Dr. Carvahal's couch with his head split and open like a melon, I wait for him on the big house's big porch, and there see what seems to be pretty much be half of Spit just filing in and out of Dr. Carvahal's waiting room. Anxieties, fears, phobias; guilt, shame, depression; worries, bad dreams and nightmares—a suitcase full of troubles is what Spitters leave at Dr. Carvahal's door, or at least try to.

Of course we Spitters, we wouldn't just be opening up to any old somebody if that somebody weren't one of us. And happenstance being as we wanted it, Dr. Carvahal was one of us, and that if anything made him even more screwed-up than us, I mean what with all that listening he was doing. Unfortunately for poor old Dr. Carvahal, it all just went into making him a bobblehead, his head nodding and shaking and bobbing, the wonder being just how it didn't just up and bobble from right off of his shoulders.

From my vantage point on the Haymaker's deck, I squinted into my binoculars, could see Dr. Carvahal's big house on the hill just before me as my hand before my face, its big porch a merry-go-round onto which Spitters jumped on, jumped off, and got absolutely nowhere. As far as I was concerned, that merry-go-round could just go on forever, could circle and circle and circle—I wasn't jumping! And Dr. Carvahal, he could listen till forever too, wouldn't hear squat coming from the likes of me.

Like it was L.T. who first noticed just how really mixed-up Best was. It was Mrs. Haymaker who pointed out just how different we were, how strange we were. It was Hal who 'Aha'd, 'Aha'd that time his flashlight shadow lighted my face. Outsiders, outsiders all, they were the ones who saw us for what we were; it wasn't Dr. Carvahal. I mean outsiders, outside anthropologists and outside wannabe anthropologists, they were the ones who could pick and poke and pry, see past our cobwebs.

"What are you looking at, Michael?"

"I don't know, Mrs. Haymaker. I guess I'm just looking at this place. I'm looking at my place."

Mrs. Haymaker crossed her legs and sat down on the floor without so much as using her arms. Putting a watering pitcher down by a plant, she looked at me, reached to touch my chin and lift it.

"You know what, Mrs. Haymaker? Sometimes I'm jealous of L.T."

"Really? That's funny, because sometimes L.T.'s jealous of you. He wishes sometimes he could be you."

"He does?"

"He does."

"Like when? When does he wish that?"

"Well, like that time he told us about how he and you watched your mother's kitchen, watched it through the window. He thought it just about the most interesting thing he ever saw. He had a thousand questions about it. 'Why is their kitchen in the basement? Why do they slaughter their chickens in the backyard, hang them by hooks so that their blood drains? Why do they light candles in the fireplace? Why, why, why?'

"Michael, L.T. he thinks your family is cool. Then again, though, he pretty much thinks most Spitters are cool. Deep down he thinks that you, and Ollie, and Richie, Rookie too—he thinks you're agents, like agents on a secret mission. I mean he's still trying to crack that code of yours, the one you spoke of the time you took Rookie into your club."

"That code?"

"Yeah, the code words you used. You know, 'the nation, the right road, living by the flow of the river.'"

"Oh, that. That code. So just how close … how close is L.T. to cracking it?"

"Pretty close, I think, but still not quite there. Sometimes the hardest puzzles to solve are those that you're in. Hal and I don't have that problem though, the one L.T. has. See, unlike him, we're not members of any Lost Tribe. We can put two and two together. We can combine that which we see with that which L.T. told us he saw from the perspective of being with you, and still usually come up with four."

Like L.T., I too had a thousand questions that I wanted to ask Mrs. Haymaker. But I didn't know how to ask them, didn't for that matter, dare ask them. So I instead asked them of myself.

Would they have learned the secret if not for me, my carelessness? And now that they knew the secret, would it be safe with them? And most important of all, just what was it that real people like her thought of me, somebody like me, a faker, a chicken-shit faker who faked stuff because there wasn't any one thing I was capable of believing in, at least believing in enough?

"Michael," Mrs. Haymaker said, "so why is it you're jealous of L.T.?"

"Have you ever heard L.T.'s ideas about Dead Reckoning?"

Mrs. Haymaker shook her head that she hadn't.

"L.T. uses Dead Reckoning to figure out where he is. Once he pretty much knows that he corrects his position and heads in the direction he wants to go. But me, I can't do that. I only can use Dead Reckoning to figure out where I about am. And even though there's all this Drift around me—around me as much as there is for anybody—there's just no real point in my correcting my position. I mean why go correct my position if I don't know my direction? And even then, even if I was to know it, how would I do it? Besides which, and it's a big besides which, my direction, I think that's all but already set."

"Michael," Mrs. Haymaker said, lifting my chin again, "maybe your direction isn't as bad a thing as you think it is. You can't imagine just how much L.T. wishes our family were like yours. I mean you eat together. You fish together. You stick together. For L.T. there's just him and me, sometime soon maybe Hal as well. But us, we have no customs, at least no customs to speak of, and we have no rituals either. Don't ever underestimate how important those things are. They transcend time, Michael. They transcend space."

The screen door squealed, Hal and L.T. out on deck to join us. Fetch bounded out too, barked a Hello and then went to sticking his wet nose inside a cardboard box of sniffed-out pottery pieces.

"We found these Wampanoag Indian shards just last week," Hal said. "Some of them may date all the way back even to when Cortereal lived among them."

"Miguel Cortereal," L.T. said, turning his cap around, "Miguel Cortereal, King of the Lost Tribes!"

"King of the Indians," I corrected him. "That's what it says on the Rock."

"I know that's what it says, but Indians are one of the Lost Tribes. Hal told me so."

"Hold on there, L.T.," said Hal, "I said no such thing. What I said was that at the time of Cortereal many thought that the Indians of the Americas were the Lost Tribes. In the early 16th century there even was an explorer, Bartholeme de Las Casas, who theorized that Indians originated in Ancient Israel. Then about a century later, a Portuguese traveler named Montezinos, claimed he actually saw Indians carrying out Jewish rituals, reciting a Jewish prayer called the *Shema*."

Jewish Indians? I couldn't believe it, thought again about Miguel Cortereal and his brother Gaspar, and why they didn't go back to Portugal. "So Indians are Jewish? They're Jews?"

"No, Michael. I see your hearing about Indians being Jewish is as selective and wrong as L.T.'s is over their being a Lost Tribe. Indians weren't Jewish and they aren't Jewish. But what is true is that in those days the Christian world very much wanted to believe that they were one of the Ten Lost Tribes of Israel. Christian tradition of the time maintained that messianic redemption—the Second Coming—could only take place once the Ten Lost Tribes were found, and reunited in the Holy Land, and then converted over to Christianity. That's why everyone from the Indians, to the Aborigines in Australia, to the Kenyans in Africa, at one time or another were thought to be the Lost Tribes. Even others such as the Irish and English have at various times claimed themselves to be the Lost Tribes. See, Michael, everyone wants to think they're special. Everyone wants to think they're special enough to bring about the Messiah."

"Oh," I said, making a lunge for L.T.'s cap. "Now I see, L.T. Now I see why you've been thinking all this time you're a Lost Tribe. You think you're special, huh? You think you're special enough to bring the Messiah, don't ya? Don't ya, L.T.?"

"No way. No way do I think that. Those people, those who claimed they were a Lost Tribe, they weren't Jewish, and what's more, they thought they could be a Lost Tribe of Israel without being Jewish, without ever even first wanting to be Jewish. Like how does that make sense? I mean it doesn't, not if to bring the Messiah you have to go get yourself converted away from Jewishness, first go get yourself converted away from the very most important thing it takes to bring him.

"The way I see it, I can't be Lost Tribe without first being Jewish, but I can be Jewish and not be Lost Tribe. And since being lost isn't a forever thing, and doesn't have to be a forever thing, and shouldn't be a forever thing, when I'm no longer lost what then will I be but Jewish, still Jewish. And when no longer am I L.T., who then will I be, but Jewish? Still Jewish, always Jewish. And that, if there's anything at all special about me, Michael, is all that's special about me."

My hand went tingly, so numb I no longer could feel L.T.'s cap in my hand. I barely even could sense it slip away from my fingers and fall, the fall not unlike an autumn leaf from its old, and heavy, and bent tree.

It wasn't fair! It wasn't right!

Why was it that L.T. could decide how long he was going to be a Lost Tribe? Where was my say as to whether or not to be lost? Why did L.T. get to be kind of Jewish, get to be kind of Jewish even when he wasn't, while I, I didn't get to be Jewish even when I kind of was?

"Are you okay, Michael?"

"I'm fine," I lied. "I was just wondering, Mrs. Haymaker. So let me ask you something. Do you think Miguel Cortereal wanted to find Lost Tribes? And if he was trying to find them, what kind of Lost Tribes did he want to find?"

"That's hard to say," Hal went butting in. Pushing the box of pottery shards away, he held Fetch's head, inspected his eyes. "Who knows his true motivation for sailing—other, that is, than his supposed going to find his brother? Who knows, for that matter, his true motivation for staying in the New World, or Gaspar's motivation for staying? But it seems to me if Miguel believed he actually found Lost Tribes he would have wanted to go back to Portugal, and Lord knows as best we can figure he had ships worthy to make the sailing. By finding the Lost Tribes he would have been a hero. All that would have been left is unifying them, and converting them, and presto— at long last redemption."

Mrs. Haymaker leaned back into the deck railing, tilted her head to better catch the sunlight on her face. "You would think that even if Cortereal didn't believe he found Lost Tribes he still would have wanted to go back to Portugal. The fact that he didn't indicates he may have found something important here, something important enough to make him want to stay in this, the New World."

"Well," L.T. said, "I think Cortereal thought he did find Lost Tribes." He rolled a ball toward Fetch, sat down on the floor to play with him. "I mean, it says right on the Rock that he was King. As a King he could unite the Tribes, then together they could wait for the Messiah. Maybe he thought that's what it took, all that it took. Maybe he thought the rest of the world didn't need to know about the Lost Tribes. Maybe he thought the rest of the world didn't need to know because there was no need for them to go converting the Tribes."

"So you think, L.T., that Cortereal didn't go back to Portugal because his ideas about converting the Lost Tribes were different from those of the Christian world?"

"I guess that's what I think. I mean maybe Cortereal was like that Montezuma guy, the one you said came a century later."

"Montezinos," Hal corrected him.

"Montezinos. Maybe he thought that he not only found

lost tribes, but found the Jewish Lost Tribes. Maybe he thought that they even, you know, were kind of maybe like me, Jews like me, Jews who would stay Jewish even when they were no longer Lost Tribes. Maybe Cortereal thought that converting them wasn't necessary. Maybe he thought that it wasn't even right."

I thought about what I'd learned in the Imperio hall, thought about how God would gather in the remnants of his people. I thought about how when he did gather them the world would be a good place, a safe place. Could it be Cortereal didn't want to go back to Portugal because it wasn't a safe place? Could it be he didn't want to go back to Portugal because it wasn't a good place, 'least not a good place for a remnant?

"So what if Cortereal himself was a member of a Lost Tribe?"

"Cortereal? What do you mean, Michael?"

"Well, Cortereal must have known what the Portuguese would do with any Lost Tribes that were found. Maybe he thought that if the Portuguese found out he too was a Lost Tribe he too would have had to go through conversion. What if he didn't want that? What if he felt safer staying with the Indians in America? What if he preferred being lost to being found?"

"Hmmm," Mrs. Haymaker said. She stretched her arms over her head, twisted them one way, and twisted herself the other way. "You might be onto something, Michael. I can look into it. Maybe there were actually even other Lost Tribe explorers, other Lost Tribe explorers who sailed the world so as to remain lost. But enough already with all this lost and found stuff. Who wants to go for a walk? We can take Fetch and walk along the river."

"I'll go," L.T. said.

"You coming, Michael?"

"I don't think so. Go ahead. I'll stay and watch the game

on TV," I lied, truth being I wanted Spitters watching me hang along the river with Hal and the Haymakers about as much as someone wanting to get themselves spied on collaborating with the enemy.

Over the past several days sides had been drawn, drawn especially carefully, and I knew how I'd been drawn. I'd been drawn to be on the side of the Nation. I'd been drawn to be on the side that was different, on the side that feared everyone, feared everyone precisely because of that drawing, the one with us to one side of a line and everyone else to the other.

Problem was, while I did sort of fear those who were drawn in on the other side, I didn't fear Mrs. Haymaker. And Hal—him I only feared a little. I mean at most all I felt when around them was a little funny, and all that I really concerned myself with was, well, being seen with them. I mean like what if the circle were actually to see me, and them, see me and them, and wonder just whose side I really was on?

Grandpa, Grandpa he always says that nobody circles wagons like we Costas. That said, if the Fernandeses and the Rozas were to see me running with others outside of the side I was drawn in on, would they believe that I still was in their circle? Could they believe I still was in their circle? Or would they instead believe I'd broken their circle, and in so doing broken our circle, broken it wide open, broken it as wide open as a canyon, as wide open as the canyon of the freakin' Grand Canyon? I mean what would they believe? Really, what could they believe, other than that I'd gone and broken our circle by being careless and reckless with my wagon?

I sprung into action.

The house empty now, I started my search, started it for anything and everything that might implicate me, might implicate them. I mean, what were they up to, Hal and Mrs. Haymaker? I mean were they just curious? Or were they dangerous? Were they friends? Or were they actual enemies?

Pouring through dresser drawers, poking into kitchen cabinets, just plowing up closets and hampers and files, I thought about what Grandpa said the time we went fishing about there really being nothing to worry about from people like Mr. Alves, those people who'd lived among us for a long time. Instead, what we instead needed to worry about were those people who hadn't lived among us, those people who didn't know the rules. They could hurt us, Grandpa said. Or they even could get hurt themselves.

Thing was, I didn't want anybody getting hurt, certainly not us, certainly not Mrs. Haymaker, maybe not even Hal, not even if they actually and really were more than just the littlest bit curious.

Was there something, was there anything, here in the house that could implicate, that could hurt?

When I'd gone through all of the dresser drawers and kitchen cabinets, gone through all of the closets and hampers and files, I went through all of them all over again, and yet and still nothing, no written eyewitness accounts with which to testify, no super-secret binoculars with which to peep, no super-secret audio recorders with which to eavesdrop—nothing.

I slumped down into an overstuffed chair, stared at a big old TV, the TV not on, but off. With its curved glass screen pulling everything in, I could practically see every object in the room, could see them as they got distorted, tugged, stretched, their shapes dissolving to nothing but shadows of gray, speckles of light.

Everything behind me in the TV reflection small, everything got small. Everything before me in the TV reflection big, everything got big. Compared to my body, my face looked insignificant, ugly, sad. And compared to my outstretched legs, my body looked puny, weak, tired. And legs, my skinny weak legs, compared with my humongous feet, they were popsicle sticks. And just there, at the very endings of what before had looked to be humongous feet, there were my ten toes, little but mighty as to be huge, the ten toes rocking themselves back and forth like warriors preparing for battle, a battle that might be fought, or might never be fought.

At my signal my ten could spring into action, spring into battle. But would the signal be given? Would it ever be given? And if given, if the great torch were lit and the great horn were blown, how far would my ten warriors spring? How hard would they fight? Just how bad did they, my usually hidden and usually secret weapons, want it—but really want it?

I placed my feet square on the floor, then looking at the ten, and then to them too, I saw it.

There in the reflection of the TV, I saw reflected a cardboard box right by my feet, right under the chair. I reached on down, pulled it out.

Its flaps folded closed, the words, HANDLE WITH CARE, were written right on top. Carefully I unfolded the flaps, pushed aside Styrofoam chips.

The book was about the size of my hand, leather-bound, its gold-leafed page edges as shiny as bars of pirate gold. Opening to a page, I saw mysterious looking words, the letters of the words strange, the lines just running up and running down, running sideways and running diagonal. On the opposite facing page there also were words, these in English, an obvious deciphering of the mysterious ones.

Turning the book over for the cover title, I saw that there was none, the title instead on the opposite cover side, almost as if the book were meant to be opened from that side, opened from right to left. The title page also was on the inside of the cover, the letter of the word farthest to the right capitalized and big as if the words too were meant to be read from right to left.

And opposite the title page, on the facing page, there were words as well. These were written in English, written in pen, written by hand.

> Dear Michael,
> It is with great joy we present you this book.
> We hope it empowers even as it enlightens.
> We present the book with the full knowledge that it likely will raise some questions even as it answers others.
> However, as a Bar Mitzvah, we believe you are now mature enough to understand that even as one hole is filled, a new one is created, must be created.
> And so, Michael, please—

A sudden and loud crash shattered the moment, shattered the living room window. Diving to the floor, I saw that a brick had come to rest near me among the pieces of broken glass. A note was taped to the side of the brick.

> STOP!
> YOU DON'T BELONG HERE!
> FOR YOUR SAKE –
> LEAVE!

Crawling out of the room, I saw my knees bleeding, saw my hands bleeding worse still. And at last reaching the kitchen, I leaped from fours to my feet, leaped from my feet to the back deck, leaped from the deck over the railing, me falling, the book falling, just sailing from out my hand upon impact with the ground.

Landing in dead leaves, the book disappeared, and for a moment I was sure I'd lost it. But I searched for it, from my knees I searched for it, just sent armful after armful of leaves flying up to the air, they by their lonesomes falling down onto ground. And while searching, I could just hear, and could not shake, threatening voices moving all around me, closer to me.

Leave, the voices seemed to say.

Leave, I heard myself say.

So I stood, caught a breath. Legs trembling, legs wobbly; head frantic, head hurting … surely I'd pass out. I felt sick, breakfast suddenly erupting from out my stomach, gushing from out my mouth … what to do, what to do, what to do?

And that's when I saw it. With its gold leaf edged pages shimmering like a mirage, the book came into focus, went out of focus, and came back in focus. Lying there at my feet with its pages open, the pages seemed open as if open for me.

And picking it up, I could just feel blood instantaneously rush to my head, my legs, my heart … the warmth of the rush waking me, making me move … move … move …

MOVE!

And I did. And as I did, there just was this one question I just could not shake, could not answer.

Was the warning meant for the Haymakers … or was it meant for me?

15

First light broke over me like a floodlight over an escaping
P.O.W., the still lingering darkness at first just creeping
a bit at the edges, then scooting from view, then finally
making an all out every-man-for-himself break for it.

Abandoned to the light, I knew that my location, even my
every move, now could be seen by just about everybody. I was
staggering, going 'round in circles, looking drunk and feeling
drunk, looking lost and feeling lost, the feeling just so strange
considering how well I knew these woods.

I was tracing what amounted to two circles of a crazy figure
eight, and though the intersection of the two circles had me at
the crossing point twice as often as any one stretch of track,
when I reached that point I just didn't know, just did not know.

Was I coming? Was I going? I mean the intersection was
like the intersection of nothing to nowhere. And the other
stretches of track, no matter which circle I actually was on,
while they seemed familiar enough, familiar too to the counter
stretch of the counter circle, it was opposite, felt opposite, felt
not at all familiar.

Stranger still was the hole—no, not that hole—but the one
in the pit of my stomach, the one that was there when it really
should not have been there. I mean like the crazy figure eight

track I was on, honestly, was it really any more unnatural as night turning to day turning to night? The crazy figure eight, was it really any more inevitable as the old day that gives way to the new, that in turn gives way to one newer still? I mean like what did I expect? What could I expect?

I mean like, it's a track, not some sudden great transformation.

Dew on pine, mist on holly, the woods smelled as sweet as a scented candle. And butterflies, yellow and white, they danced just ahead of me, just beyond me. Butterflies so light, butterflies so beautiful, butterflies so free—boy, did I ever hate them!

I mean, I'm trudging here. 'HEY!'—like I'm trudging here! For crying out loud, I'm trudging like a pig, like a pig I'm trudging, some poor pig not just and only stinking himself up, but just stinking everything up! I mean, even the flies they swarmed me, they just flew in a frenzy to me—me, their freshly warmed over dump of shit!

A stinker!

That's what I was, a stinker. A weasel. I betrayed the Nation. I dug where I shouldn't have dug, all but led L.T. to spy on us in our basement. I talked too much, talked much too much, talked much, too much—to Ol' Cuss, to Jenny, to Father Sousa, and to Mrs. Haymaker. I antagonized Mr. Alves, gave him even more reason than even he needed to look at us closely. Worst of all, I let Hal look into my eyes.

I got myself watched, got myself followed, got myself questioned. I mean, was it any wonder I was under suspicion? From getting rushed out of the Imperio hall, to getting caught up in L.T.'s schemes, to way too readily getting help from outsiders, I mean if I was them—them Spitters—I'd suspect me.

But I am them, I reminded myself.

And yet and still, was I really them, was I really enough

them to be one with them? I mean, was I enough them so as to not be an informer, even if accidentally? Was I enough them so as to not go behind their backs to the Inquisition, even if unintentionally? Was I enough them so as for Dad to trust me, but totally trust me? I mean I did whisper to him what he wanted to know as to who it was I thought was helping me get hold of the Jewish stuff, didn't I?

Then again, though, in so doing, did I not at the same time prove to him that I could not be trusted? In so doing, did I not prove to him that I in fact did not understand secrets, did not understand the hows, or the whys—simply did not understand that a secret was a secret?

It was my fault, that brick through the window. And I could only hope that it wasn't intended for the Haymakers. I mean I, I at least deserved it.

The sun was climbing quickly now, just a ghost of a moon still stubborn in the low sky. Day was here, night was gone, and with it, at least for now, went my tracking crazy figure eights. But if only I put one foot in front of the other, if only I went in the usual way along the usual path, I knew soon I could be at the break in the woods, and Smelly Rock, and the holes.

Not that there was anything at all usual about them, the holes. If anything my relationship with them only got stranger and stranger. And though it scared me to never know just what I'd find there, somehow I couldn't stay away from them. I mean everything I saw there, everything I heard there, everything I sensed there, hinted questions.

I stopped, kicked at the ground, used my heel for a pick ax and my toe for a shovel. Then, from down on my knees, I peered on in on my little creation, and thought about what Father Gomes said in the Imperio hall.

Did holes also have sides? Did they too have an inner one, an outer one?

The little hole that I looked in on certainly had inner sides, gentle here, steep there. But as for an outer side, I didn't see it. So I pushed its dirt back in, patted it down, saw a flat side of ground, the outer side. But now, now there was no inner side. For that matter, there wasn't even a hole. It was gone.

I waved my hand over the ground, waved it back and forth like a spectator suspicious of a magician's trick. Surely there was hocus-pocus here, just had to be. So I closed my eyes, could just about picture it, could just about see it, how deep the hole's sides once had been, the way they slanted. But how could I keep my eyes closed forever—like I mean I couldn't even keep them closed any longer! So I opened them. And closed them. I opened them, and closed them, opened, closed, opened, closed—each closing taking me further away from the picture, each opening not changing the fact … the hole was gone.

The hole, this hole, it was gone.

By feeding the hole to give it an outer side, all I did was eliminate it, kill it. If I'd only dug more, if only I'd dug deeper, there would have been more sides, more inner sides. But as for any outer side, that only existed when the hole no longer did.

Funny thing, I thought, to miss a hole. Funny too, to have saudades over a hole.

Glancing back for one and last time at what had been the hole, my little hole. I left it. Then head down, eyes down, I slid towards the break in the woods, into it. Like a pinball to its slot is how I slid, to it and into it, and while to some it may have seemed random, while to some who believed in luck it may all have just seemed like blind luck, for me it was normal, very normal, the whole damn thing so normal as to be natural, the whole damn thing so damn natural as to be not normal, not in the least natural. The one and only difference between me and the pinball, while it at least had a puncher's chance, while it at least had an element of luck, be it blind, dumb, one-in-a-million, or otherwise ... I had none.

I was the alewife herring. I was the alewife herring, just thrashing through life without so much as a choice. Except that while the alewife at least had sense to know it could go against the flow, and sense to know it was going against the flow, I didn't know if I could, and didn't know if I should. I mean against the flow, with the flow, either way was hard, and each was hard in its own and particular way.

Such, I guess, is just how life comes on a tidal river. So too, I suppose, is just how it goes.

Smelly Rock was just up ahead, and taking a running start, I long-jumped for it. But unlike a track star floating gracefully to a landing in the pit, my float was a cry for help, my landing just an utter train wreck, me as train, the Rock as Grand Central. My arms going one way, my legs going every other way, my head all but flying off in ways all its own, the Rock's slippery outcrop took me out, the back of my head hitting the Rock, hitting it hard.

Stars, lots of them, pulsated before my eyes, and my hand under my head, it felt the warm sticky oozing of blood. For all I knew, or could care, I was lying in it, just lying there in my very own self-made blood bath.

I closed my eyes.

Drifting, drifting, drifting, I was on a ship, a caravel, its timbers creaking from its ups and squealing from its downs. Above me I could see the caravel's masts, could see the eagle's nest against a blue sky, could see the sea gulls hang motionless in the air, then at once dive away.

I was hallucinating, I knew, but unlike other dreams where I was on board a ship full of anxious women and crying children, this was different. This time I was a sailor among sailors, and we were navigating our way in Atlantic seas.

The ship's captain, a tall man with a coat as long as he, and with hair nearly half as long as that, leaned out over the forward bow rail and then slowly turned my way. Though a graduate of the Prince Henry School of Navigation and highly accomplished, he needed help, needed my help.

Was the bay we were about to enter indeed the Narragansett? Was the bay up ahead indeed Mt. Hope?

I nodded yes, nodded that indeed they were.

With a flick of his cutlass, the captain signaled his men to trim the ship's huge white sails so as to better catch the wind. And the two smaller ships of our flotilla, they did the exact same.

From way off behind I could see storm clouds chasing us. Big and dark, they had chased us long and chased us far, and now were angrier than I'd ever before seen them. Though the bays up ahead would provide at least some protection from the coming storm's turbulent seas, I knew they would not be enough, storm clouds, after all, having a long reach, shocking with thunder and striking with lightning.

Our flotilla needed to move—and move now—but move to where? We were just about at the end ... there were no more seas to sail.

Squinting through my spyglass, suddenly I saw blue herons, great and free, flying over groves of beech.

That way, I nodded to the captain.

There, there I pointed, there is where we should go.

The captain swung his great cutlass forward. In a mighty arc he swung, his sailors instantaneously heeding his call, scrambling to lower the sails and prepare the smaller rowing boats we would need.

Our oars took us to the herons, propelled us to the beech trees. And when we at last reached the river, we saw it to be flat water, saw it to be tidal, and saw that if only we would have one caravel follow another and then the other, the river would be just wide enough for the ships of our flotilla.

But the true beauty of the river, the true miracle of it all, was that while the river was just wide enough for us, it wasn't wide enough for our chasers, not wide enough by far.

"Thank you," said the captain. "Thank you, sailor, my friend."

And so we waited, and stayed alert, and at precisely the right moment, *just when the tide turned and the waters rose, I again nodded to the captain.*

"Now! Now is our chance! By God, now!"

The river's banks were lined with rocks, and we were careful to stay in the waters' deep middle. And the woods, thick with white pine and ripe with red maple, they made us feel we would not easily be seen.

Back in Portugal we'd all heard stories, fantastic stories, about New World explorers who encountered strange natives—strange natives with even stranger customs. But afraid of them as we were, in time we hoped to meet them, and learn from them, learn from them those things we did not know, learn too just what it was we had in common. Surely, there was much we had in common.

Just as surely, and most definitely too, we wanted to leave behind the Old World—leave it—leave it and all those Old World thinkers and non-thinkers who, as we knew only all too well, did not look for similarities, only for differences.

"I don't know about this," the captain whispered to me. "Here? When I no longer can see the gaivotas, the sea gulls, I become worried, my friend."

"So long as we still can smell the salt in the air we will be fine," I said. "Your brother, Gaspar, would not have gone so far as to not smell the ocean, but this far, my Captain, this far he would have gone."

"So, you think my brother is here?"

"I don't know, my Captain. But a place like this, a place like this by a river, it's exactly the type of place our brothers will make for themselves a home. It's exactly the type of place all brothers yet to come will make for themselves a home."

Up ahead I could see a rock, a dory-shaped rock jutting out from the waters as if wanting to leap right from out it. The rock was etched with strange inscriptions, ones unfortunately we could not decipher. Natives were indeed here, and clearly what they wanted was for others to know that they were here. They wanted others to know a little something about who they were, to know that they were different, different but the same ... but different. And that was good. And this was good, so natural and so human, so much in keeping with our nature, and our humanity, so much as well unlike anything that we ever could allow for ourselves back in the Old World. Yes, truly this thing, this natural and human thing, it was good. Yes, this good thing, this good thing—freedom—it was good. It was very, very good.

We anchored our ships along the river in the very best harbor we found. Tucked away, the harbor was a cove of cobbled stone, and pulverized gravel, and it was perfect.

Suddenly my eyes popped open. The stars that I had been seeing now were gone, replaced instead by a wicked, shooting jolt in the back of my head. Everything around me spinning, I held onto Smelly Rock, held on as if it were a rock face, sheer, and steep, and sharp. I had to find the way off. I just had to.

Four, five, six, stepped my feet.
Seven, eight, nine, beat my heart.
Ten, eleven, twelve, raced my mind.

I was behind the cluster of pines, heard what I thought was the drifting of voices coming from the direction of the holes. Familiar yet strange, giggling yet tender, the voices rose up, rose up so as to get right in my face. Through the branches I could see L.T., could see Rookie, could see Rookie and L.T. digging up the hole that had the cross, the one once also having the Jewish stuff inside.

Resting his arm on a shovel, and resting his other arm on her shoulder, L.T. smiled.

And working her hand on his neck, and working her other hand so as to tickle his ear, Rook smiled.

They had no right—no right to up and dig, let alone no right to just up and dig with each other, he with her and her with him. Rook was family, a Spitter like me. L.T. wasn't of our Nation, and never would be.

I mean, really, they weren't even digging for the same thing. L.T. wanted to dig for lost tribes, dig for them so that they could be found and brought together. And Rook, me and Rook, what we dug for was Cortereal, all the ways that he hid, all the ways he stayed lost, all the ways he stayed apart.

Rook's destiny was my destiny—it wasn't L.T.'s! His destiny wasn't even of the same place as ours. His came from a place called Esperança, and to Esperança he headed. While me and Rook, ours came from a place called Saudade, and it was to Saudade we headed—it, after all, our place, our only place.

I hated L.T., hated him for what he was, for what he could do, for all he could be.

And so without so much as really one more thought, I charged him. I charged him to kill him.

I could see L.T.'s eyes widen, could see his mouth open. I could see Rookie scream, scream something my way. But I couldn't hear, couldn't hear anything. I was out of my mind. And no words, or thoughts, or reasoning of any kind would stop me.

From somewhere off to my right I glimpsed Ollie and Richie running, running like crazy to the fight, seemingly appearing from out of thin air. L.T. spun his head their way, then he spun it back around at me.

My first punch caught L.T. on his temple. My next punch drilled him in the chest. He tripped backwards, and over Rookie, and in an instant we were on the ground and fighting.

"Michael!" I suddenly heard Rookie scream. "Stop!" she screamed again, her voice shattering the silence that had surrounded me. "Stop it, Michael!"

I was hearing again, and thinking again, that really not at all a good thing when in a fight. And with the surprise of my attack now over, L.T. was fighting back. He kicked me in the stomach, kneed me in the balls, he now out of his mind. And for an instant I thought I would lose, knew in fact I would.

Ollie and Richie jumped us, and flattened us, tore L.T. from me, and me from L.T., hitting the both of us as they did. The strange thing was, they were hitting me … hitting me harder even than they hit L.T.

It didn't make sense. I mean I was a Spitter, same as them. I was Nation, same as them. And L.T., he wasn't, wasn't any of those.

Ollie whirled me to the ground, the effort throwing him off his feet. Nearby, L.T. collapsed to his knees, Richie doing likewise, his collapse looking as if he'd just been shot. And Rook, she just covered her face with her hands, just shook her head from side to side.

"Asshole!" L.T. yelled, whipping a hand of dirt my way.

"You're the asshole," I said, chucking dirt right back.

"You're both assholes," Ollie said. He scraped up some dirt, threw it at both of us.

"Me? It's your sister L.T. was digging with. It's your sister he was messing with. Ollie, you moron, don't you realize that he's not us?"

"And you, Mookie? Who are you? I mean—who are you? You go and show him who we are, and then it's to them you run when you have a problem with it. Me and Richie, we saw you running from their house with the book."

"You're following me? You've been following me?"

"Well, a little. 'least we've been following you since the time you freaked out in the Imperio."

"You threw that brick at me? It was you?"

"No, it wasn't us. I swear it wasn't. But just so you know, the brick wasn't for you. They didn't know you were in the house."

"It was for us," L.T. said. "The brick was a warning to us. It wasn't for you, Michael. My mother and Hal knew that much as soon as we got back from the walk with Fetch. The thing I want to know is, what's this book? What's with this book you took?"

"It was just a book, a book is all. It wasn't yours, L.T. It was mine."

L.T. knew better than to ask anything more about the book, just as I knew better than to ask anything more about who threw the brick. Some things more or less we knew anyway, and that which we didn't know, sometimes it was better to figure those things out, and figure them alone. And that was no more so than when things concerned home, and could hit home.

"So what were you and Rook doing anyway digging at the hole? Like what were you going to do, claim that the hole-filler-upper struck again, only this time as a hole-digger-upper? Maybe, L.T., it's been you all along behind all the shit with the holes. Maybe you're in deep with it."

"You know that's not true, Michael."

"It was my idea," Rookie said. "It was my idea to dig up the hole. I just couldn't stand the thought of the hole that had had the Jewish stuff getting covered with dirt, topped with a cross."

"And I didn't like the cross just sitting there," L.T. said, "you know, just sitting there like that somehow was the ultimate destination of the Tribes."

"Aren't you sick of it?" Rookie asked. She sat herself down to the ground, wrapped her arms tight around her knees. "Aren't you just sick of it?" she asked again, her cheeks red where she pressed her hands to her face, her cheeks streaked where she wiped her tears.

"Sick of what?"

"This place. Our place. Where we are. We've Dead Reckoned our way to figuring it out, but so what? We've listened to family and friends teach us where we are, and we've heard our enemies and non-friends tell us where we are, and you know what? You know what? We're nowhere. We're still lost. We're still as good as lost. And in the end all that's really going to happen is the same old thing. This hole, the hole L.T. and me just re-dug, it's just going to get re-buried all over again."

I looked at the ground, didn't know what to say.

"I hate this," Rookie said. "I really, really hate this. Why does where we are … why does it have to also be who we are?"

I nudged a rock with my toe, nudged it back and forth over the dirt, the stirrings of a plan coming together in my mind. We'd been on the right track with the holes, made no mistakes in the digging up of the dirt. Rather, our mistakes were in what we didn't do with the dirt.

"L.T., how'd you get here? Walk or kayak?"

"Kayak. And Rookie, she came with hers."

"Then let's bring 'em. Let's bring 'em here from the river." I kicked at the ground till there was a small hole, pointed to it.

"You want to dig some more?"

"Yeah, I do, Richie, only this time we're gonna do something different with the dirt."

With the shovel that L.T. and Rookie had been using, and with the kayak paddles double-dutying as shovels, we scooped up all the dirt we could, all the dirt that had covered the holes. And I do mean all of the holes: the original hole, the grave-like hole, and the hole with the Jewish stuff. Then, pouring all that dirt into the kayak cockpits, we made sure that no dirt spilled back out to the ground, and I do mean none.

"You know," Ollie said, "if hole filler-uppers want to still fill these holes back up, they always can."

"Good," I said. "Good for them. But if they want to fill them they'll just have to dig new holes, dig new holes for all of the dirt that they'll need to do it with. Either way, Ollie, make no mistake, there are going to be holes here."

The first load was a bitch, me and Richie holding the bow by the end grab, his legs colliding into mine every third step; while back at stern, Ollie's legs banged with L.T.'s every two steps. And every six steps or so, we just dropped the kayak, dropped it to yell at each other.

And Rook? Rook meanwhile, she supervised, yelled at all of us.

The second load went even worse. Bruised and tired, I got stuck with Ollie at the stern, while L.T., he paired with Richie up front.

And Rook? Well, we fired her. We fired her ass. Of course she tagged along anyway, her bossy yelling now just outright snippy put-downs, just a long listing of our many shortcomings, be they our intelligence shortcomings, our character shortcomings, or our manhood shortcomings.

By the time we finally set the second kayak down by the river, I was pretty sure my back was broke. I dropped in a heap, L.T., Ollie, and Richie, doing much the same.

And leaning onto the kayak as we did, like capsized men clinging to a lifeboat, the river before us might just as well have been the ocean, the far side might just as soon have been Portugal, and if not Portugal, then the past.

We said nothing—didn't need to. I think all of us pretty much at the same time realized that the dirt in the kayaks was but a grain of sand, a mere grain in a river that was ocean. And all that dirt, it wasn't just a poorly-imagined land bridge, it was no bridge.

On the brink, there was nothing else really to do now but go ahead and dump it, the dirt, go dump it into the river. And there was nothing else really to do then but watch it, the dirt, watch it sink and disappear.

16

This time I didn't put up a fight over going to hear fado music in Café Saudade. I mean, what difference would it make anyway? There was no standing to Mom's philosophy, the one that had life being unfair, and not having to be fair. There was no standing in the face of Dad's truth that life pretty much just sucked—sucked, sucked, sucked—just was what it was, and was just as it was.

I mean their arguments, they were powerful, and I wasn't. Their stories, they were stories of generations and generations past—like real evidence—and I had my thirteen years, my thirteen nearly fourteen.

I sat in the back seat of Dad's truck, looked out the window to the river, saw how it disappeared where the road wandered away from it, and saw too how it came back into view where the road ran close to it. But the river, I mean it had bends to it too, not big bends but bends nevertheless, and for just an instant I thought I saw one spot where the road and the river … where the road and the river even met, damn near kissed.

"Michael," Mom said. "Don't be mad."

"I'm not mad."

Turning, leaning back from her seat, Mom's fingertips touched my cheek, touched and lingered, and though she didn't want to let go, she did.

"This book," she said, holding it up. "We found it in your top dresser drawer."

"I wasn't like hiding it or anything. Believe me, if I wanted to hide it I would've found a better place to hide it than that. And you sure as heck know that, I mean you know everything else there is to know about hiding."

"If you weren't hiding it, Michael, then why didn't you tell us about it?"

"The book was for me. Do I have to tell you everything?"

"When it comes to things like this, yes Michael, you do have to tell us. They know. Do you understand, they know. Do you understand what that means? If they know it's like everybody knows. If they know not only do they know you, they know all of us."

"What's more," Dad said, "not only do they know, they think they can just go and interfere. The inscription, the one in the book, it supports the hunch you whispered to me about who you thought it helping you learn that you're a Jew. It proves they were the ones planting the things you found in the hole. But don't you see, Michael … don't you see that they're just leading you? Don't you see that they've just been leading you all along?"

"They're just trying to help."

"Help? Who are they to help? We're your parents, Michael. We're your parents and we know what's best for you. We're your parents and we do what's best for you too. To them you're an excavation, just one of many. To them you're an experiment, only one of many. Let 'em go experiment on their own kid. Lord knows, they've screwed him up already anyway. And we won't let them do that to you. We won't let them do to you what they've already done to your friend."

"You mean you won't let them experiment with teaching me to be Jewish?"

"You're already Jewish, Michael, 'least Jewish enough for a secret Jew. It was so for your grandparents and so too for their grandparents before them. Michael, *in secret*, do you understand, *in secret* is how they lived their lives. And it's how we live our lives. This, Michael, this is legacy. This here is legacy. Do you understand? This is our legacy and your legacy. We are who we are by the way we live our lives."

We are who we are by the way we live our lives? But if we weren't living as Jews, what kind of life were we living? And if we weren't living our lives as Jews, what kind of Jews could we be?

"Jewish secrets," I mumbled.

"What was that, Michael?"

"Jewish secrets. That's what we are; that's how we live our lives. And that, that there, that's our legacy."

Dad pulled the truck over to the side of the road, reached back and smacked me across the mouth. And as he was about to do so again, Mom grabbed hold of his hand.

"It's sick," I said, doing as best I could to keep from crying. "The whole thing—sick. We are who we are by how we live our lives? Why can't we live our lives by who we hope to be? Why can't we live our lives in the way we want to live them?"

Dad put his arm over his seat, nearly rose to his knees to better face me. "Let me tell you something, Michael, okay, something you should know. Only children believe such nonsense. Only stupid people think such things possible. So seeing as you're already so consumed by them, Michael, secrets, here's one more for you, okay, one more secret for your collection.

"Those people, those people who think such things and believe such things, they're hated. They're despised. People don't like the kind of people who try to understand what they themselves won't. People don't like the kind of people whose purpose on earth seems to be to meddle with what's wrong, tinker with what's not quite right. Fixing takes effort, and effort is hard. Tinkering takes understanding, and understanding is hard. Sure, for the most part the meddlers and the tinkerers are tolerated well enough, but when the winds change, when the meddlers and the tinkerers happen to find themselves in the wrong place at the wrong time, not only do they wind up getting hurt, they wind up getting everyone they love hurt.

"Even here in Best, Michael, don't you notice the way others look at you? Don't you see their faces? Can't you just guess their thoughts? And don't fool yourself, Michael, don't fool yourself that it's any different here than it is elsewhere. Believe me, if it's like that here, just imagine what it's like out there, there in the big bad world, there where the meddlers and the tinkerers get burned at the stake."

I shut up, bit my lip and felt it throb. I was pretty sure Dad was wrong, pretty sure he had to be. Not being liked was one thing, not being tolerated almost another, I mean who really likes anybody who seems to always stick his nose into everything, seems to always have a new way, a better way? But an Inquisition, burnings at the stake, that was just impossible stuff, un-understandable stuff. Not that it didn't happen, I had no doubts it did, but for the life of me I couldn't see that stuff happening on account of just a change in the wind. For the impossible to happen conditions had to be perfect, everybody doing their part. I mean somebody's got to go fanning the flames, don't they? Somebody's got to go providing the combustible material, and a lot of it, don't they? Obviously the Inquisitor burners were at fault; of course the burnings wouldn't have happened without them. But could it be, could it just be that the meddlers and the tinkerers too, in part—could it just be they too, they the victims, were at least the littlest bit at fault?

I mean our ancestors must have been doing something wrong to have the flames fanning the way they did? They must have been doing something wrong to guarantee that there was enough combustible material? If others watched us, and examined us, and fixated on us, then there must have been some reason, some reason more than just our meddling, more than just our tinkering.

Didn't Jenny say that the New Christians who stayed in Spain and Portugal, stayed behind to be Christians on the outside and Jews on the inside, didn't she say they had it far worse than Jews who fled the Inquisition? Didn't she say those who stayed behind to be secret Jews, didn't she say that they suffered much worse than Jews who kept on living as Jews, kept on living completely as Jews?

Could it be that the reason for the burnings wasn't so much in our being Jews, but in our being secret Jews, our being Jewish secrets? If that was the case, 'least as I saw it, while Jews may have run way back then for being real Jews, it actually was us, us and our secret, that have been running ever since.

Back again on the road, Mom turned the radio to a music station, Dad rolled down his window, and I asked questions. "So are the people who decided to not convert way back when, you know in Portugal, are they better off than us?"

"Who do you mean?" Dad asked. "Jews? You mean Jews?"

"Yeah, Jews," I said, intentionally leaving out the word "real" from the word Jew.

"I don't know, Michael. I don't know if they're better off. We haven't exactly talked recently, actually for about the past five hundred years. I suppose in some ways it's been better for them. But it certainly hasn't been easier for them. It wasn't all that long ago, you know, that they got burned in the ovens of Europe during the Holocaust."

I'd forgotten about that, not that I really forgot. I think I pretty much just made myself not see those grainy black and white pictures that one time I caught them on TV. That's not, of course, to say I didn't actually see them, the pictures—I mean I saw them all right. I just didn't let them form into anything more than flashes, grow into anything more than images.

And in that way the stick-like bodies and the bony faces and the big hollow eyes, they remain just flashes, right? Only flashes floating off to some far corner of mind, right?

And in that way the stick-like bodies and the bony faces and the big hollow eyes, they remain just images, right? Only images tossed to some God-forsaken wayside of mind, right?

And in that way pictures don't form, and images don't grow, and neither are real, right?

And in that way nothing is more than just the out-of-the-blue bad feeling, the once-in-a-while bad moment, the now-and-then bad nightmare, right?

And all, all of it … all is just that … and only that … that and nothing more, right? Right? Isn't that right too?

And it worked. It worked! For the most part my plan of action—and inaction—worked! For the most part the images and the pictures, they remained only a feeling, only a moment, and only a nightmare, only that, only that and not much more. And that's how they would have stayed too, 'least stayed maybe for a little while longer.

But then Dad had to go sticking the images and the pictures practically up to my face, go make me think, go make me realize just how wrong I was.

Burnings, they weren't just for the secret Jew, they were for every Jew.

"So how come Jews are always going and getting themselves burned?"

"I don't know, Michael, I suppose 'cause they're Jews, you know, always insisting there's a better way. And they don't stop, those Jews, they don't stop. They just keep insisting, keep right on insisting that that's how they're going to live their lives."

"As meddlers and tinkerers?"

"As Jews. But really, Michael, what does it matter? It's all one and the same. And people hate that. And people hate them for being that."

"They don't hate us for being that?"

"They don't know we're that, leastwise they shouldn't."

But do we hate ourselves for being that? For that matter, are we the Nation still that? Are we Spitters still that? I mean as far as I could tell the only problems we meddled in or tinkered with were our problems. And the only way we pretty much did that was just by wondering and worrying over stuff like who was going to sit on a Holy Ghost float.

"So how are Jews better off, you know, better off than us?"

"I don't think about that, Michael, really I don't. Understand that what's done is done. What happened happened. They have their way and we have ours. And I don't think our paths will ever again cross."

"That's your father talking," Mom said. "I have hope that our paths will someday cross. I still have hope that we once again will be together. You know, Michael, some Portuguese have saudades because they miss the sea. Others have it because they miss their homes. Most probably don't even have any idea why they have them. But me, I know what's missing, and I know what I miss. And frankly, Michael, I'm tired of saudades."

I could see Dad's eyes in the rearview mirror, could see them there on the road ahead, there but not there. He wasn't angry. Nor was he daydreaming. He was just thinking. His elbow on his rolled down window, his head in his hand, he just was thinking.

As usual it was dim to dark inside of Café Saudade, candlelight on the tops of tables like stars in the darkness, each star a constellation, each constellation a universe all its own. Eyes and mouths, ears and noses, they orbited in flickers of candlelight, reaches of shadow.

We sat ourselves at a couple of corner tables where others already sat, sat just as the fado singer began her wail. Of course the room was filled to bursting with all of the usual stuff: an air of betrayal here, a pang of despair there, and thoughts even of death everywhere. As usual too, I again did not understand the Portuguese words. But now I found I really did not need to. The songs were all the same anyway, and I now knew the questions, if not the answers.

Why did you leave? Where did you go? Do you know why you have saudades?

Mom joined Aunt Lolly and Aunts Debbie and Edna at a women's table, while Dad and me pulled up chairs at the men's. We picked at some bacalhau cod, picked at some fava beans, Dad tossing back a beer, me getting the chance even to sip some of it. We weren't, I knew, getting ourselves drunk. We only were getting ourselves ready.

"We've just got to be more careful," Uncle Joe said. "This is what happens when windows aren't covered. This is what happens when doors aren't locked." He brought his hands to his mouth, tapped his fingers to his teeth and looked as if he was about to bite them to the bone.

"Maybe we need to go deeper," Uncle Buzz said. "Maybe we need to blend more."

"Blend?"

"Yeah, blend."

"Become more Catholic?"

"No, not become more Catholic. Look more Catholic."

"For Christ's sake, Buzz, we're already doing everything we can. We've got Lady of Fatima statues on our front lawns. We wear crosses. We go to church."

"But we don't take Communion. We don't take Communion, do we, Joe? I mean even in a place like this we're not doing everything we can. Look around, while others eat chouriço, we eat bacalhau."

"So what are you saying?"

"I'm saying times change and situations change. Those before us made hard decisions. They made them when they had to. And we have to make them too, whether they be about Communion, or chouriço, or anything."

Uncle Jiggy brought his beer down to the table, pulled up just before it slammed. "No way. Forget it. Maybe not eating pork does set us apart. Maybe not taking Communion is a red flag. But straying any more will only lead to forgetting more. And that's something we cannot afford."

I saw Ollie lean in from a second row of chairs, his face a moonbeam, his hand on his father's shoulder. "Besides it's one thing to just go wear a belief. But to swallow it, that really is something else. That's something different. Pork? Communion? Swallow that?" He put a finger down his throat and half gagged.

Ollie!

Ollie, Ollie, Ollie! He was funny all right, as funny as a burning building with me outside the building and a flamethrower in my hands. Swallow pork? Swallow Communion? Funny stuff maybe, and the gagging funny stuff surely, but neither would ever have been brought up, not even jokingly, if not for my screwing up, if not for my throwing the Nation into crisis.

Though nobody at the tables looked my way, nobody really had to. Every Spitter in town, I was sure, by now already knew about the Jewish book, the one Mrs. Haymaker and Hal were gonna give me.

I slouched in my chair, pretty much got down lower than low. And as I turned my face to the shadows, as my mind redirected me to the darkness—to the darkest deep of shadow there was— I spotted Jenny. She was working another area, one maybe almost as murky as ours.

Easing my chair backwards, I stayed low. Easing myself

further back, I crept away.

"Jenny," I whispered, waving her over.

"Hi, Michael. Why are we whispering?"

"I don't want to be heard. I don't want to be seen."

"You mean you don't want to be seen talking to me?"

"No, not you. I don't want to be seen talking to anybody."

"I don't know what's going on, Michael, but your huddle there looks intense. I mean even your uncle didn't 'Hi' me."

"No 'pretty as a penny?'"

"Not even a 'studying history 'cause of the mystery.'"

"Jenny, do you know if anybody found a camera here? I lost one a few days ago."

"Yeah, me, I found it. I gave it to some guy who said he knew who the rightful owner was. Said he'd give it back to him."

"What some guy did you give it to?"

"I'm not sure of his name, but I've seen him here before. He wears nice clothes, sits sometimes with that priest who comes here."

"You mean Father Sousa."

"Yeah, him. He sits with him. I think the guy I gave the camera to is called Ales, or Aves, or something like that."

"It's Alves, Mr. Alves. But I call him Mr. Asshole."

"Yeah, that's the guy. That's the guy I gave it to. He gave it back to you, didn't he?"

"No, actually he didn't."

"Michael, the tables are going to miss me if I don't get back to work. Can we take this up later? Can we?"

"Just one thing, Jenny. There's something I have to ask you. The Inquisition, does it exist? I mean does it still exist? Do interrogations still exist?"

"The Inquisition doesn't exist," she said, smiling, straightening my cap. "You know that it doesn't. But as for interrogations, well, that's just something that we do of ourselves. It's something we do to ourselves."

Jenny left, and just then I saw Mrs. Haymaker and Hal come in.

Leaping from a crouch, I practically ran to them, my mouth mouthing for them to stay low and stay away, my hands gesturing them to stay away and stay low. Guiding them to a bathroom door, I took one quick look around, gave them a push. And crouching once again, I made sure that nobody was in the bathroom stalls.

"Michael!" Mrs. Haymaker said. "Michael!" she said again, looking me over as she would a very deranged, and very paranoid, pervert.

"Sorry."

"Sorry?"

Hal held her by the shoulders to check she was okay, then whirled to me as if to drop me right on the spot.

"Sorry. I'm really sorry."

"What gives, Michael?"

"I didn't want them to see you. I didn't want them to see you and me talking."

"Do we embarrass you?"

"No, no, it's not that."

"Then what? And them who? Michael, are you in trouble? Are you in some kind of trouble?"

"I don't think so, 'least I don't think I'm in any real trouble."

"Are we in trouble? Are the people who threw the brick through our window in here?"

I shrugged, realized I not only had no plan, I had no idea what even to say.

"Okay," Mrs. Haymaker said. "We'll leave, Michael. We'll leave, God forbid you be seen with us and dragged any further into this. But before we go, you should know I looked into your hypothesis, you know, the one about Miguel Cortereal possibly being a Lost Tribe explorer. And I'm sorry to tell you there simply is no evidence he was one."

"Oh," I said, seeing my reflection in the bathroom mirror, it showing me stooped and pale, somehow sort of blurry. "It doesn't matter. It was just a crazy idea anyway."

"Not quite so crazy. Four names for you, Michael: Luis de Torres, interpreter, Maestro Bernal, physician, Alphonse de la Calle, second mate, Rodrigo de Triana, first to sight land."

"Who are they?"

"They, Michael, are four documented Lost Tribe explorers who sailed with Columbus. All four, as well as three others, converted one day before his first sailing, converted so as to be allowed to sail. And you know what? All chose to remain in the New World. All decided it was better to be lost in a strange New World rather than go back to what they knew awaited them in the Old."

"Does any of this really make any difference to you?" Hal asked. "Does it really matter?"

"No," I said. "Yeah," I said, thinking it over. "I guess it does. It's nice to think there's a link, you know, a special link with them and me. It's nice just to think that somehow someway there's something for me in this, something to me in this."

"Links are important, but they shouldn't be chains." Hal walked to the bathroom mirror and positioned himself so that I could no longer see myself. "Maybe Cortereal really did do what he did because of the times he lived in. But if Cortereal, or for that matter any Lost Tribe explorer, were alive today, I think their being found would be just fine by them. If Cortereal were alive today maybe he would stay here, maybe he would go back to his family home on the island of Terceira, I really don't know. But one thing I can tell you, he would have found his way to doing whatever it was he wanted to do. This, Michael, is the 21st century. This is America."

Hal was right, I knew. And in theory what he said made

sense. Problem was it wasn't about making sense. It never was. And it never would be. Making sense? Since when do we do what we do because of that? Making sense? Sense was for others. Sense was what others have, or what others make, make if only they were in our position, in our world. Sense was what others have and others make if only they were you.

I walked away, caught an image of myself by the bathroom door, the image still stooped and pale, still blurry too, but not quite so stooped, not quite so pale, and not quite so blurry. "Thanks. Thanks for finding that stuff about Lost Tribe explorers. Thanks too for finding out and letting me know that Miguel Cortereal was from the same island as my ancestors. And thanks too, you know, for that book you were gonna give me, the one I took."

I headed back to the tables, to our tables, slipped back in and slipped in close. And camouflaged as I was in shadow and in dark, really, it wasn't all that hard to do. Now though there was something different, something odd, going on with the tables.

The people gathered around them, they were pushed in tight, packed as if squished. Like a constellation, one all its very own, they were pulled in and pulled together, all of them in, all of them together, all in and all together as if in a spiral, a spiral to a core, a black core.

Though I could not see the actual core, still I heard it. It spoke with one voice, one I could almost place, and almost identify. But however familiar the voice was, still it was strange, strange in that it simultaneously argued a plea, pleaded an argument. And while the plea was weak, it also was powerful. And while the argument was ludicrous, it also was serious. And while neither made sense, both made sense.

As I listened, and the more I listened, the more I understood just how both the plea and the argument made sense, made all the sense in the world, made all the sense in the world to people squished by shadow, caught in flickering light.

"We have to dig better. We have to dig in better. Every man finding himself in tough times needs to ask of himself: 'What is it I should do? What should I do?' Now the answers he comes back with, they don't need to be popular, and they don't need to be liked, but they do have to be right. And for our sake, our answers need now to be right.

"In olden days when a sick man who was one with us would question his life, it wasn't so important his answers come back as true, or even that they come back as honest. All that mattered is that his answers not come back as delirious hallucinations. All that mattered is that they not come back as dangerous accusations, delirious and public accusations that could do his people harm. And should they come back as that, as harmful incriminations that the Inquisitors could use, his people knew just what to do. They knew to do what they had to do, knew to do what was right—dig the sick man's hole … dig it fast … and dig it deep.

"And when others who weren't us, and weren't one with us, would come back with answers that could harm us, then too our people knew what to do. And sometimes, sometimes they even would actually do that which needed to be done.

"You know the beauty of the hole? The beauty of the hole, 'least a good hole, isn't the way it's covered up. The beauty of the hole is how from it one can go out to do that which needs to be done, and then, that done, go on back inside."

17

"I got laid," Ollie screamed into my ear.

"Hey, me too," Richie screamed, his hands cupping my other ear, blowing out that eardrum.

Our hands clapping to the beat of a marching band from the Azorean island of San Miguel, we followed them and the Fall River Holy Ghost Festa as they turned from Columbia to South Main. Red vested *Folias* followed too, their singing of Portuguese folk songs just loud enough and just off-key enough to destroy whatever little hearing we still had left.

"We all got laid, Richie."

"What? Can't hear."

"We all got laid," I screamed. "I mean we're thirteen. Like what else did you expect?"

"I'm fourteen," Richie screamed back. "And Ollie, he's fourteen too. And San Miguel, Michael, did you know that's St. Michael? Did you know that?"

The laying of crowns had to be just the all-time perfect opening for the joke that year-in and year-out made the rounds with Spitter kids our age.

It was Dad who last night in the Imperio hall laid the crown on my head, put the scepter in my hand. "There is one God," he whispered to me. "We call him King. We call him Creator. We call him Redeemer. But we don't call him by his name, one we don't say, one that we don't even know how to pronounce. However, Michael, your name, the Hebrew name that you've been carrying with you since the day you were circumcised— it's Mordechai, after my grandfather, your great-grandfather. The name itself originates from the Persian Mordechai, the Mordechai that in ancient times made sure that his niece, Esther, hid her faith. Only by hiding her true faith were she and Mordechai ultimately able to save their people.

"Michael, when I first told you that we were secret Jews you made a promise to keep the secret. That promise is one that you made with the Nation. But now you are being called upon to do something different, the promessa that you are about to make is a promise you will make with God. It's a pact, a covenant between you, Mordechai, and God. Do you understand?"

Mordechai? I didn't feel like no Mordechai.

Mordechai? Like I didn't know no Mordechai.

Yet there it was. And there was no getting around it either. The stranger who for so long was ignored, though not quite ignored; the voice who for so long was unheard, though not quite unheard; the inner side that for so long was squelched, though not quite squelched—it now had a name. And now that I knew his name, and he knew that he had one, would there be any stopping him? Would there be any stopping him, this soul, this spirit, this Mordechai? For that matter, why would I want to?

"Do you see her yet?" Ollie asked, teeter-tottering under the weight of my riding on his shoulders.

"No, not yet," I said.

I peered out over the heads of the thousands of tourists

who'd come for the *Bodo de Leite* parade of floats, saw some
funny floats, saw too some really funny floats—one showing
how Azorean women stomped on grapes to make wine,
another showing how they hung underwear to a clothesline
full already with clothes—all good, but I knew the best of all
yet was to come.

Then, looking up the street, I saw her.

Waving to the crowd from her throne on high, her help at
her feet to attend to her every wish, the junior empress queen's
gown was white, and her silky white cape whiter still. And the
smile on her face, it was more brilliant than the brilliance of
any jeweled crown.

A roar rose up, Queen Rookie at last here, the masses clearly
as much in love with her as I was. Bending to place crowns on
the heads of the little children gathered around her, she held
up a loaf of sweet bread, quickly brought it behind her back,
swung out a handful of red roses for one and all to see. Again
the crowd roared, her reenactment of the way good Queen
Isabel set her crown on the heads of children and twelve of
the poorest men in her kingdom absolutely perfect. And as
for the playful depiction of the way Queen Isabel smuggled
baskets of food to the poor only to have them miraculously
turn into flowers as evil King Dinis searched them, that was
more perfect still.

"I want to see," Ollie said, spilling me from off his
shoulders.

"Hold on. Let me first at least pick myself up off the
ground, okay?"

Ollie dug a knee into my back, pushed down at my head.
And as for what he was doing with my eyes and my nostrils, I
didn't even want to think about what was going on with that.
Then, just as I was about to try and stand with Ollie up on my
shoulders, just then I saw him.

Watching me, watching me, watching me—he stood at

my back, stood with hands on hips, stood to watch every little move I made, and hear every little word I said, and feel the every little beat of my heart, not just for Rookie, but for every little goodness Good Queen Isabel showed the Nation.

Looking down where I knelt, he knew me, and did not like what he knew. His face to mine, and mine to his, it was just like that time he watched me not go up front for Communion. And just like that time, I again found myself in a stare down, one I knew I would lose.

I tumbled backwards, dropped Ollie on his head, saw the watcher's mouth turn to smirk, saw his eye turn and wink.

"Michael, where you runnin'?" Ollie and Richie yelled after me. "Where you runnin' to, man?"

I didn't know. I just knew to run.

Flying up Main, I ran down Hope, the street full of people making their way to the parade even as I was making mine from it. Then turning, then stumbling, I glimpsed the watcher behind me, he ripping down Hope too.

"Stop! Hey! I'm onto you! I'll get you!"

I paused at Broadway and Water, looked this way and that, saw the 'FALL RIVER—THE MYSTERY, THE HISTORY AND THE SEA' banner hanging from a lamppost just over my head.

Where to go, where to go, where to go—

Off to my right was Battleship Cove, the destroyer *Joseph P. Kennedy* berthed with Big Mamie, the *U.S.S. Massachusetts*. Maybe just maybe I could lose the watcher there in the Cove, lose the watcher turned chaser there among the ships and their maze of passageways. But having back in the day seen the *H.M.S. Bounty* berthed there, I doubted somehow I could.

I mean, the *Bounty* was the *Bounty* of the Mutiny, wasn't it? The *Bounty* was the ship used in the filming of *Treasure Island*, the island and all its pirates, wasn't it? The *Bounty* was rebellion, and trouble, recklessness and betrayal, all that and murder, all that and more, wasn't it?

I ran to the left.

Kennedy Park was just three blocks away now, and already I could see volunteers from various Holy Ghost Organizations cutting up loaves of sweet bread and preparing cups of milk for all the people going there following the *Bodo de Leite*. Richie's mom, she was there, by a *sopa* soup table, and Richie's bike, it was there too, there just leaning against a table.

"Mrs. Ferreira, I'm stealing Richie's bike, stealin' it."

I rode north, hop-scotched from one Fall River street whose name I didn't know to the next Fall River street whose name I didn't know. Down alleys having no name, and into holes-in-the-wall having no address, I rode 'em all, but as I rode, and all the while I rode, I prayed for there just to be a way into the next alley, the next hole-in-the-wall. And I prayed just as hard for there to just be a way out of all of 'em too.

The chaser? He'd be the cat, not following me in, but waiting instead for my out. Then, being the cat that he was, he'd trail me, trail me till the trail's end.

Fall River at long last behind me, I now could stick to gravel paths away from the busier river roads. Though slower, they gave me time to think, the roundabout route giving me ways to think.

I knew the chaser by name, but how well did I really know him? I mean until now he'd just been the watcher, just the boogeyman under the bed, the boogeyman in the fold of a curtain, always watching, but only watching. He kept himself low; I kept him away. That was the deal. And I was used to him being low, used to him being a little away, used to him being the watcher.

But him as the chaser, that was new for him, and new for me. I mean what did I know about him as the chaser? What, for that matter, did I know about myself as an honest-to-goodness chasee? Like would he now be at the door, come in, and chase me in my home? Would he now just pop up in the quiet of the day, explode in, explode on in to chase me then? Would he now chase me in nightmares too? Would he now not just watch every move I made, but tap into my every move, tap into my mind, my soul ... chase me there?

I had to get to know this guy, this chaser. I mean unless I knew him how good a chasee could I be? Unless I knew him how could I keep him from turning my world even more upside-down than it already was? Unless I knew him how was I ever going to run from him? Unless I knew him how was I ever going to hide from him? Unless I knew him how was I ever going to fool him?

Run, hide, fool. Run, hide, fool. Run, hide, fool.

I mean that was the strategy, wasn't it? That was our strategy, wasn't it? That really was our strategy for living, wasn't it?

But just how to run, and hide, and fool? Running home? That was out, what with Mom being a *mordoma* this year, a Festa hostess. She no doubt would be home right now, home with Patty and Grandma cleaning up after last night's food-fest, and cooking for the one tonight. Running home? That was too risky to everyone, much too dangerous.

Empire hall? Now, the Imperio, that was a possible hiding place. Already I could see it there in the distance, all tucked away in a cornfield, its shuttered windows shut, just a stubborn mule stubbornly standing there after pulling a cart of flowers with which to decorate the hall. A swarm of flies were there too, just hovering by the mule's mouth, the mule's eyes. But other than that—the hall, the mule, and the flies—there was nothing, certainly nothing to be mistaken, or even taken, to be a sign of life, 'least any real life.

But yet as a place to hide, the hall just had way too many problems. First off, the front inside room of the hall would be bare, only silver crowns and silver scepters on a table. Second off, the scepters' pointed fingers, they always pointed at me, or at least seemed to. Hell, being fingered hiding out among a bunch of silver crowns—one of which that may as well have been sitting all off-kilter 'top my stupid head—I about needed that like a hole in the head.

And as for the hall's kitchen, the one out in back, sure it had hiding places among its large cabinets of pots and dishes. But just yesterday I really did see slabs of cow meat there, the meat just hanging from stainless steel hooks in the ceiling, hanging till every last drop of blood drained from right out of them.

And as for hiding anywhere else in the hall, say among the cabinets of big books that year in and year out recorded every promessa ever made to God, wasn't that trespassing? I mean someone's promessa to donate food to the Festa with hopes a sick kid gets better, or a missing loved one is reunited with family, or a lonely soul find a soulmate—wouldn't hiding there among those kinds of promessas be too personal, too wrong, just too much of a violation of something or other?

And then of course, there was the biggest problem of all to hiding in the hall: being found there, actually being found there, my founding being just one more way I went and betrayed the Nation.

I pushed on, cranked away at the pedals of the bike, leaned full bore into gusts at my face.

Passing Captain Jack's, I saw it empty, dark too, no doubt Ol' Cuss off having just a pissin' good Festa time with drinking buddies. Just as well. After seeing him in Café Saudade with the man who just now happened to be chasing me, truth was I wasn't sure I wanted Ol' Cuss' help anyway. A better talker than he was a listener, a better talker than he was a helper, more and more I was seeing him just that way—as a talker—be it of how Hector sang his songs in the fog of the Grand Banks, or of how his singing the familiar songs helped calm the dory men down, or of how his singing the sweet songs tugged at their hearts.

But did Ol' Cuss himself ever sing? Did he ever sing the songs of the Nation? I mean even if he didn't know the words to the songs, did he ever at least hum the melodies? And if he couldn't sing, and if he couldn't hum, did his heart at the very least ever beat to the rhythms of the Nation, beat for the Nation? I mean maybe Ol' Cuss truly once was one of us, and maybe he truly was proud to have once been us, but was once enough? Was once better than never? Did his once make him a 'now is'?

When I reached Best's Main Street it was deserted just as I knew it would be, just a lone girl working the ice cream parlor, just one lone man inside, half-asleep and half-passed out.

I circled 'round the Village Green, circled 'round again, and then yet again. There just had to be reasons why I shouldn't just go ahead and do it? There just had to be reasons why I shouldn't just go and do that which I'd pretty much done my entire life? But for the life of me, I just couldn't come up with any, 'least any good ones. Instead all I could come up with were reasons why I should go ahead, should go and do that which I'd pretty much done my entire life.

Wasn't St. Peter's a second home? Wasn't I baptized there? Wasn't I confirmed there? Wasn't it the place I prayed with family? Wasn't it the place I played with friends? Wasn't it the place I studied the Bible? Wasn't it the place I thought things through? Wasn't it the place I asked God for forgiveness, and asked God for help? Wasn't it a sanctuary? Just because I knew more now, and just because I knew different now, so what? I mean really, what was I expected to do, only be Catholic on the outside? I mean really, what was I supposed to do, only be Catholic when others just happened to be around? I mean really, what else really was it that I should do when I circled and circled and circled and still there was no other place to go? I mean, really, wasn't it by now just a little too late to go anywhere else?

I leaned back, and hoisting the bike's front wheel off the ground—gunned it. My back wheel hitting the Green's curb to launch me, I sailed through the air for what seemed like forever, my landing like a skier off a mogul. Then tearing ass, more off the bike than actually on it, before I knew it I was there, right at the doors of St. Peter's.

Once inside, I realized my mistake immediately.

I moved like a stranger, my every move careful. I moved like an uninvited guest, as clumsily as that. I moved haltingly, as haltingly as the invited guest who never really wanted an invite in the first place. Nothingness in the air above me, emptiness beside me in my pew, there was no floor under my feet. Except for stained glass windows, except for the brilliance of their reds and greens and blues, whatever lighting there was seemed dim, and distant. Did the church architect intentionally design the interior to be like this, a place nearly void of perceptions of sense? Did he design it to be like this, as empty as this … a vacuum?

Of course not, of course he didn't.

It wasn't built for me! It wasn't built for someone like me! Rather it was designed for believers, built to be a serene place in which believers could grow their faith, grow it away from the bothers of the outside world. In that way, for that way, it was a cocoon. And in the end, when all believers believed, and all growing was grown, there would be a wonderful butterfly, light, and carefree, and beautiful.

Whatever! Really, whatever it was that the architect had in mind—it worked—it also worked just fine for someone like me, a moth like me.

In building the cocoon what the architect did was build a veil, a veil so intricate as to block out all light, any revealing light. What he did, that architect, was create a sanctum so private and safe it worked for certain select worshippers, even as—knowingly or not— he at the same time also created a sanctum just private enough and safe enough for certain other worshippers, those worshippers worshiping one way on the outside even while, and all the while, worshiping quite a different way from the inside.

"Michael!" a voice boomed. "Michael!" it said, my name reverberating in the vaulted domes of the church as if trapped there. "Is that you I saw sneak in here?"

I raised my head, realized I was on the floor and under a bench, Father Sousa standing at the end of my pew and leaning back so as to better see me. "Yes," I said, "yes, Father, it's me."

"Well, don't just lie there on your belly like some snake. Get up. Get up, boy."

I gripped the pew's railing, rose up on wobbly legs.

"Come over here. What's the matter, Michael? You're not scared of me, are you?"

"No," I lied. "I'm not scared of you."

"So why the thief in the night?"

Suddenly I heard the roar of a motorcycle, heard it throttle up from somewhere beyond the door, heard it purr on down too. Jumping over the pew railing, I ran to a window, Father Sousa step-for-step at my side.

"Oh," he said. "Oh, is that it, Michael?"

I spun around, and for a moment I couldn't see, couldn't see even with my eyes as open as they were open. Wanting to run, wanting to just get the Hell away, Father Sousa held me in place. Then, his eyes mirroring mine, I saw Father Sousa's pupils dilate wildly, quiver uncontrollably.

"Help me!" I screamed, my scream soft as a whisper.

Father Sousa grabbed me by the hand, ran me to the altar.

Falling to his knees, he tore at a small rug glued to the floor, threw it aside, dug his fingers into the tight wood crevices of a floorboard. "I'm sorry, Michael," he said, lifting the board. "Never thought I'd see the day this tunnel would actually get used."

I lowered myself in and squatted down, saw the tunnel's rotting wooden beams stretching across the ceiling this way, stretching along its sides the other way.

"Stay put. Don't wander. The tunnel's old, Michael, going back a century and a half to when the Brotherhood had their architect build it. God knows where it leads."

Father Sousa pushed the floorboard back in place above me, a sliver of light still on my face through a crevice no wider than a fingernail. Then, as he laid the rug back over the floorboard, everything went black.

I counted Father Sousa's every creaky step, tried as best I could to gauge just how far he was from me, how far I was from him. It was hard to tell. Darkness pressed in on me; the stale air seeped into my lungs. Up, down, left, right, inner, outer—it didn't matter—not here, not in this netherworld. Life, be it as it was, be it as it might be, that only was at the exits, be it the one at one end of the tunnel, be it at the one at the other end.

"Where is he?"

"Who?"

"You know who, Leo, the Costa boy. His bike's right outside."

"Oh, Michael. He was here. He's gone now."

"Gone? Where to?"

"Not sure. You know kids, Thomas. Always on the move, never even knowing just where it is they're going to."

Unable to stand, and unwilling to sit myself down onto God only knew what was crawling under my ass, I felt my thighs burn, felt myself sweat. Wrapping my arms around my knees, pointing my face up to where the sliver of light had been, I tried to breathe quietly, sensed I was breathing too quickly.

What, I wondered, what if I pass out? What if Father Sousa was to have a heart attack, have a heart attack and die, just die right here and now? Who'd find me? I'd die here. I'd die here as a secret. I'd just die here as a secret, a secret in a secret tunnel, a secret tunnel in a secret church in a secret town.

Don't die! Don't! Don't die in this hole! Don't die in this shit hole of a tunnel! Don't let Thomas win! Don't let Mr. Thomas Alves win!

"Do you know what he's been doing, the little fuck? He's been spying, Leo, spying on us. I found his camera in Café Saudade the night of the Chouriço Fest. I developed the pictures and look here. The damn pictures show me, and you, show all of us good Christians, all of us real Christians, going in to have our chouriço. The little bastard!"

Mainly I'd only wanted Rook to take a picture of me about to eat the pork, force Mom and Dad to finally explain things to me. Fact was though, I really did take pictures, and took a lot of them. Fact was, I really did spy, spy on them, the chouriço-eating people, those chouriço-eating people who weren't like me, weren't like us.

"Well, Leo, I've been using the camera to take pictures of my own. And I got pictures of those Spitter boys by those holes of theirs, got some too of some others by those holes. I also got pictures of Spitters going to that cornfield chapel of theirs to do whatever heathen stuff they do in there. I got pictures of the Costa boy at the Haymaker house, got some also of his running away from there with a book in his stealing little hands. I even got some pictures of the Spitters who threw the brick through the Haymakers' window."

"Give me the camera, Thomas, the pictures too. And so long as you're at it, hand over the fish-gutting knife I happened to see you taking from your motorcycle tackle box. Good God, Thomas! Good God! If I didn't know better I'd swear you're making like you're going to harm the boy. He's just a kid and you're scaring him half to death."

"He's a kid on the fast track to becoming one of them, as rotten as them. For Christ's sake, Leo, you're a priest! Act like one! Act like one for a change! Save his soul, damn it! Save it!"

"All right, Thomas, enough. Just give me the camera, the knife too."

"I didn't want it to come to this, Leo, really I didn't. I thought filling up those holes would spook them, discourage them. See, I don't like holes. And I don't like those digging them. But they, those boys, they just kept right on digging—right on insisting that it's their right to dig. So I dug a hole of my own; I dug a grave. I figured finally at last that'd put the fear of God in them. But that didn't work. And I chased them with a torch. But that didn't work either. Nothing worked.

"And it's not just them, you know. There are others, others too who are digging, others too who are filling, others too who are tampering. I mean, aren't you just tired of it, Leo? Aren't you sick of the way they infiltrate us? Aren't you sick of the way they pretend to be us? Why, even here in church they spit on us."

"Thomas!"

"The pictures I took caught them all. And you won't believe all the people in town who are one with them, one of them. Father Gomes, he's one of them. Did you know that? Father Gomes! I got him in the cornfield on the way to the Imperio chapel. Did you know he's one of them, Leo, because, you know what, I think that maybe you did? Damnation, isn't it bad enough that you don't make them take Communion? Isn't it bad enough that you don't teach them any New Testament? But this—this hiring of a fake priest—it far and away crosses the line. I can get you defrocked for this. I can get your ass over this."

"It's over, Thomas. The hatred, the fear, it's over."

"Over? They're mocking us, Leo. They're deceiving us, spitting on us, plain hating on us. My ass, it's over!"

"It is over. And you know why it's over? Because we won. We've poked and pried, torn and squeezed, burned and flayed till at the last they said uncle. And they said that, said that a long, long time ago. Don't you see they've joined us? Don't you see that they can't even live without us? Don't you see they can't live the life they have without us? This life that they have, it's all they have. It's all they know."

"They only pretend to have joined us. If they can't live without us, leeches that they are, then that's their problem. But until they really do join us, then it's our problem. Until they join us, heart and soul join us, how can we trust them? How can we ever stop watching them? How can we ever stop going after them? Don't you understand, Leo? Don't you understand? Won? Won? They shouldn't be here! No way in Heaven should they still even be here!"

I heard the steps of Mr. Alves, quick and hard, leave the church. I heard too the steps of Father Sousa, quick and soft, leave with him, maybe even go after him. And alone now in the dark, in the dark of a tunnel dug especially for me, and people just like me, I felt stillness all around, stillness that might as well just have been the stillness of death itself.

There was nothing here. The exit at the end of the tunnel—if it at all existed—was as far away as China. The exit above my head—if it at all was an exit—was as far away as a reach for a star. There was no map here, and no light to show the way. This tunnel, it was a hole, just a hole in which to die.

I straightened my legs, reached for the trap door. Finding it, I pushed it away, hoisted myself up till at last I was at the level of the church floor. Then, looking down into the tunnel I'd just come out from—and some day again would likely be back in—I placed the floorboard back over it, and placed the rug back over that.

This … it wasn't great. This … it wasn't admirable. The dirt on my hands, the filth on my shirt—this, here, now—it for sure wasn't easy. But it was a life, of sorts. I mean it worked. For a Nation that did not want to be lost, and yet did not want to be found, the opening that I just crawled through … it worked just fine.

Run, hide, fool! Run, hide, fool! Run, hide, fool!

I now knew how to do it.

There was just one last thing to do, one last thing for me to do because, after all, Mr. Alves, or anybody at all, might yet still be watching.

I kneeled at the altar—at the feet of Jesus on the Cross himself—the Cross directly in front of me, above me. Eyes up, head down, my hand went to my forehead.

My God is in my thoughts, I silently said, making sure, just like I'd been taught, to not mouth the words.

My God is on my lips, I said, my hand passing by my lips on its way down.

My God is in my heart, I said, my hand passing over my heart.

I worship neither stone nor wood, but the one all-powerful God, blessed be his name—forever.

18

A big mug of Captain Jack's coffee virtually blotted out L.T.'s face from about the nose on down; and a Go Tribal cap shielded it from about the forehead on up; and I only could see L.T.'s eyes, misty from the hot coffee in his mug, and distant from the head games in his head, and sad too, from what exactly I did not know.

But I kind of knew. I knew. Leastwise, I knew enough to kind of know.

"What's up?" I said, settling into the booth across from him. "So, what you got?"

"Got news."

"Oh, yeah?"

"Yeah."

"Okay then. Go."

"You ready?"

"No," I said, pushing down his mug to better see his face. "Not really. But so long as you've got something to say and I'm here, news me."

"Sure you're ready?"

"For crying out loud, L.T., I just said that I wasn't. You're not listening. Just say it. Say it, and be done with it."

"We're outta here."

"We?"

"We."

"Outta here?"

"Outta here. We, Mom and me—not you—we're going to go live with Hal in Cambridge."

"When?" I said, popping back the last of a muffin, feeling it stick in back of my throat.

"Soon. Before the start of school."

"Why?"

"My mother's found out whatever it is to find here. Besides, I think she's going to marry Hal."

"Geez, L.T.! You're moving? You're moving? Just like that?"

"Well, there's more to it than just that."

"Like what?"

"Like another brick through our window. Like the spray painting of our garage, the message for us to pretty much just get the hell on out."

"Shit, L.T. I'm sorry."

"What have you got to be sorry about? You weren't the one throwing. You weren't the one spraying."

"You saw who did it?"

"Yeah, we saw the throwers as they were running away. You know who they are. What I don't get is Mom and Hal. They're not going to the police, they're not telling the throwers to stop, they're not doing much of anything really, other than running, just like the throwers want."

"That's what being afraid does to people, L.T.—turns some to throwing, some to running. You runners are small, just don't have the numbers. And as for throwers, though bigger, they're so afraid of losing whatever little they still have, that they're capable of just about anything. You bet your mother and Hal are afraid."

"I'm not afraid."

"I know you're not."

"How do you know that?"

"You don't lose. You've got nothing to lose. You only gain, L.T."

Pulling down the brim of his Go Tribal cap, L.T. pulled at it again till it was as off-kilter as ever I'd seen. Hunched, head down, eyes floating down the barrel of his mug, I saw his hand rock coffee up to a lip, and roll it down over to the opposite lip, up to the lip … over it. Sighing, he got up.

"Where you going?"

"The bathroom. To think. And I can't think with you watching me like this."

Ol' Cuss came over and, setting down a plate of grilled cheese sandwiches, sidled on in to L.T.'s spot. "On the House, kid. You're lookin' like Hell, kid, like you're losin' a best friend or somethin'."

"I am. And what's more, I'm pretty sure I've lost another."

"Another?"

I looked at Ol' Cuss, said nothing.

"Me?"

"You. You, Captain Jack. Know how you're sayin' you've got some Nation in you? And you know how you're sayin' you're proud of it too? But I mean even if you really do got some, so what? Even if you really do get something out of it, so what? What does the Nation get from you? What does it ever get? Talk? Talk? Like your talk only goes into hurting the Nation. Just 'cause you heard everything doesn't mean you can just go passing it on. And for damn sure it doesn't mean you should.

"Captain Jack, don't you know others hate us? Don't you understand they'll hurt us? I mean having Nation should've made you know that, should've made you understand that, really it should've. Having Nation should've made you careful, should've made you smart. You know, just having Nation doesn't automatically make you one of us. And for sure it doesn't automatically make you one with us either. That takes something else, something more."

"And what's that, Michael?"

"Takes awareness, you know, some understanding or other that everything you do affects your friend. And it takes some sense too, sense to sense that sooner or later, and one way or another, everything with your friend affects you too."

"Look, Michael, I have big ears, okay, and sometimes those ears just can't help themselves. I also, unfortunately, have a big mouth, and that I should've kept shut. But believe me, I only told Alves to protect you. I figured his fillin' your holes would discourage you, keep you from diggin' any more. All I ever wanted to do was to keep you out of trouble, Michael, 'cause that's what diggin' is, you know, trouble. And holes? Hell— holes? They're only there for the fillin', be it with dirt, or be it with you."

"Did you know he dug a grave? Did you know he stuck a cross there, stuck it there as a headstone? Did you know he chased me through the woods? Did you know he hunted me all the way from Fall River to Best?"

"I'm sorry, Michael, really I am. Just tell me how I can make it up to you and I will."

"Can we just drop it, okay? Can we do that?"

"Tell me, Michael, tell me and Ol' Captain Jack he'll do it, by George he will. Want he should hit Alves over the head? Clock him but good with his fryin' pan? Want he should lash him to the main mast, let him bake in the midday sun? Want he should hang him by the highest yardarm, hang him till the gulls pick out his eyes and the terns pick off his balls? 'Cause, Michael, for you, by George for you he'll do it. For you Ol' Captain Jack will do anythin'."

"No," I laughed, though I didn't want to. "I don't think Ol' Captain Jack has to go doin' any of that stuff just yet."

"Well, if he doesn't have as yet to go doin' any of that stuff, what is it then that you, you Michael, has now to do?"

"What I have to do is keep Alves close for watching, and, if need be, for reaching. But really, like you're the one I just don't know what to do with. I mean, Captain Jack, Ol' Cuss—I thought I knew them, turned out though that it really was you who I didn't know. So you, you I think I'll keep close too, close for watching, and reaching. All I'm saying is you're just going to have to be a better friend, okay, and me, I'm just going to have to be a better friend too."

"So in the end, Michael, in the end did you find what you wanted in the holes?"

"I found what I needed to find."

"Then you're done?"

"I'm done with holes. I don't think I'm done digging."

"You can't have one without the other."

"I know."

"And your friend, Haymaker? Did he find what he needed to find?"

"What he needs to find ain't in no hole, 'least not one in the ground."

"Then why's he diggin'?"

"I'm not sure. Probably he isn't even sure. I sometimes think though that the diggin' he's doin', he's doin' it for me."

"Trust me, Michael, nobody digs holes in the middle of the night for somebody else."

"A friend does."

"Well, maybe, but still there had to be somethin' for him in all this. What is it that he wants to find, but I mean really find?"

"Everything."

"Everythin'?"

"Everythin'."

"Well, I can tell you right now, everythin' he won't find. But I suppose if it's everythin' he wants to find, then he'll probably find some things 'cause his holes, Michael, are big as the ocean. He'll never truly be satisfied though, not if it's everythin' that he wants. So let me ask this different. Assumin' he won't find everythin' he wants, what is it that he truly needs?"

"That's the problem. Not that he's crazy or anything, Captain Jack, but L.T. thinks he's on the far side of some river, thinks he's stuck there. And he can't cross this river on account of most days it being just too choppy. Don't laugh—that really is what he thinks."

"And on other days, on the calm days?"

"On the calm days when there isn't any wind and there isn't any water rushing all over the place, on those Sabbath days the only thing really moving is his mind. He thinks. And then, though he really doesn't show it, he gets sad. That's what he does, gets sad. That's all he's allowed. That's all he allows himself."

"He thinks about what?"

"He thinks about everything that's in holes, and everything that could be in holes."

"What does this have to do with what he needs to find, Michael?"

"Well, he's by himself on the far side of this river, by himself and just thinking. What he needs to find more than anything are people like himself. If he could just do that he could join up with them and not be so lonely. He could join with them and maybe not be so damn lost."

"Is that how you two came to be friends?"

"I'm not lonely. But I suppose maybe what he saw in me was somebody a little like himself, somebody not sure of his way. And maybe that's what I saw in him too. But now that's over. And I don't mean on account of his moving. With his help I now know where I am."

"Which is where?"

"A place I can't change. A place maybe I can't ever change.

Not that I know if I even would if I could. I'm not sure. I don't know. But with L.T. it's different. He's part of nothing. And what that means is he can change anything, can pretty much change everything. Thing is he just doesn't know what to do. I mean he just doesn't know how to go do it, you know, 'cause of the whole water, wind, and Sabbath thing. And you know what? Know what? It sucks. The whole thing—it sucks!"

"We're river people, Michael, you, me, really all of us here are. But as a young man I thought different, thought I could be different. So I took to the sea, took to the sea to see and do just about everythin' that there was to see and do. But you know what? I wasn't cut for the sea. I just wasn't cut out for it."

"Sure you were, Captain Jack. You sailed the Grand Banks."

"True, but the whole time I was there I missed this place, this bay, this Mt. Hope Bay. And what I especially missed was this river."

"What did you miss about it?"

"What didn't I miss? The shoreline, for sure, the river banks too. See, the thing is, Michael, I needed landmarks. I needed trees. I needed trees and hills to let me know where I was. But this ocean—it's just too big—so big it just drives you crazy. It's got big horizons, too many of them. It's got big horizons, horizons too big to ever reach. And your friend, that's where he is, 'least where he is up in the head. He's on an ocean."

"No, Captain Jack. He's on the far side of a river. He told me so himself."

"Your friend, Michael, your friend is mistaken. He may not even be right in the noggin', I really don't know. But understand this: your friend is not like you and me. And he isn't where we're at. Livin' by the river as we do, what matters is where we are—where we are. And we look for markers to help clue us in about where we are. But we don't look for 'em to help us reach a destination, and we don't reach for 'em to help us reach some pie-in-the-sky horizon, 'cause, Michael, that not only already is set, it's how we want it.

"But your friend, with him it's destination and not location. Not that he knows how to get to his destination, mind you. But so long as it's unknown anythin' is possible. Everywhere is reachable. Your friend can't cross the river 'cause he shouldn't be by the river. I mean for cryin' out loud he's a fish out of water here. I mean this river, this town, they're poison to somebody like him. And you can't very well expect somebody to go crossin' a river of poison, can you?"

"I guess not."

"Of course not. Why, your poor friend probably just wallows away his days thinkin' about nothin' but the high seas he really ought be sailin'. And that's just not right. Trust me, leavin' Best is the best thing for him."

"And when he gets to the high seas, then what? Like you said, Captain Jack, it's big. There's nothing but horizons. There's nothing but lots of big horizons that all look the same. There's Drift everywhere and he'll be adrift. I mean no amount of Dead Reckoning will help him through something like that. He'll be as lost as ever."

"Not so lost as his stayin' here. Besides, I think you can help him, Michael."

"Me? How? How do I do that?"

"You know, the ancient mariners, after weeks on end sailin' the high seas, they'd naturally get to thinkin' that not only would they not reach their destination, but that they'd never reach any destination. Over each horizon there was another over the horizon. Why, even modern-day sailors with all their GPS gadgets get the dumps when at sea too long. It's cruel, when you think about it, cruel that the very thing to take sailors to sea in the first place, and sustain them there, should ultimately be the very thing to abandon them. You know what that thing is?"

"No."

"It's said to be a quality of the Nation."

"Hope?"

"Yes, Michael—esperança. For the ancient mariners a sighting of a dove or a seagull would be justification for the hope that they clung to. It meant that a destination, maybe even their destination, would soon be at hand. Now if there's one thing I know about the Nation, if there's one thing I know they have plenty of, it's hope. You're Haymaker's good friend, right?"

"Yeah."

"Then give him hope."

"I don't know. I don't know if I can, Captain Jack. I'm kind of in the dumps myself. I'm on the river, remember, a one-way river to God only knows where."

"For crying out loud, Michael, you don't have to row him all the way to shore! Just row him far enough to where he can see the seagulls. Know what your problem is, Michael? You think like a Spitter. Do you really think you have to just go with the flow just 'cause that's what others for so long have done? Do you really think things just are the way they are and that they just can't be no different? Michael, if you really want to go to the end of the river, you can. If you really want to see where the river leads to, you can. You know the difference between you and Haymaker? He's on a voyage, while you, you're in a passage. But even a passage has an exit, has one, that is, if you dare take it. You've got to be hopeful. You've always got to be hopeful. So long as you are, you'll be more like your friend than you think.

"You know, Michael, Miguel Cortereal didn't come here for the scenery. And Best Harbor's founders didn't settle here for the weather. They came here and they settled here 'cause they had foresight. They had vision. They knew this river was tidal. They knew that seawaters sometimes flow all the way back to the river. They also knew that like all rivers, this river's waters flow to the sea. If only you go with it, go with it even for just a little ways, you'll have the chance of seein' the sea, seein' it as it tries reachin' back to the river, and to you. Rememberin' is important, Michael. Hope is important too. But nothin' happens without the tryin'. Add it, and all is possible."

Patty!

I suddenly saw her at the door waving, calling my name. Her face white … her face was white. Her eyes red … they were red. And she shook … just shook something terrible.

I jumped from the booth, L.T. intercepting me as he came out the bathroom. "What's wrong?"

"Don't know."

"It's Grandpa," Patty said. "They asked for you, Michael."

"Better hurry, boy."

I whirled 'round, saw the eyes that went with the voice.

Watching me, watching me, watching me—the watcher was in a large booth, deep inside it. With a squeeze of the camera in his hands, and his dark eyes as much over it as over me, the watcher just played with it, my camera, and he played with me too. Having fun, he was having the fun of a big man with a tiny toy.

"Better hurry," Alves said. "Probably no time to lose. Probably not even time enough to call for the priest. But then again, somehow or other you Spitters always seem to call for the priest too late anyway."

"Let's go," Patty said, grabbing my hand, giving a strong pull.

"Here's a thought though, just a suggestion. But why not stop by the church on your way home? It's not like it's much of a detour or anything. And who knows, maybe you'll even find a priest there, you know, an actual honest-to-goodness priest. What do you think? Think you can do that?"

All at once I saw L.T. right there at Alves' booth, towering there right over him. "This isn't yours," he said, taking the camera from right out his hands. "It belongs to Michael. It's his. And he can do with it what he wants, whatever he goddamn wants."

Outside Café Saudade, we walked fast, L.T. and me trying as best we could to keep our pace even with Patty's. But we did walk, and only walk. And somehow or other, somehow that didn't seem quite right. I mean why walk when we just as easily could run? We were, after all, in a rush, weren't we? We were needed, weren't we? But yet we walked, and still we walked, and as we walked I figured out why.

Walking was just quick enough to get us to where we had to go, and just slow enough too to not get us there too soon.

Rook and Ollie arrived just before us, were waiting in the front hall with Aunt Edna. Seeing L.T., she gave him a look, then gave us a look, sighed, then just waved us in. "Hurry, your grandfather's slipping. He's leaving. I'll stay here in case Billy shows."

Outside Grandpa's room, Uncles Joe and Buzz were standing with other Spitters, and upon seeing us, they parted, kept on with their psalms and their prayers.

"O Guardian of Israel, protect the remnant of Israel; let not Israel be destroyed, those who proclaim, 'Hear O Israel.'"

We poked our heads in.

"O Guardian of the unique nation, protect the remnant of the unique people; let not the unique nation be destroyed, those who proclaim…."

"I'll stay here," L.T. said, "I'll stay outside."

"O Guardian of the holy nation, protect the remnant of the holy people; let not the holy nation be destroyed, those who proclaim…."

We went in carefully. And carefully we went near, both to the new, and the difficult.

Grandpa was in bed, his face to the wall, his breaths quick and shallow. Right by him was Grandma, stroking his hair, cradling his head, whispering into his ear. And there too was Doctor Nunes, massaging Grandma's neck, watching her face. And right by all of them were Mom and Dad, Aunt Lolly and Uncle Jiggy too, holding on to each other, holding so as to not crumble.

Carefully they drew us near. And carefully we drew ourselves near, near to their arms, and their hands that sought our cheeks. And though we too wanted to help, we were learning ... and just as yet did not know how.

And then, then they nudged us out.

> "Upon thy walls, O Jerusalem, I will appoint watchmen, all the day and all the night...."

We gathered up L.T.

> "Upon they walls, watchmen, all the day, all the night...."

We took up positions.

And then, with our positions taken, we took ourselves to Billy's room: Me in the top bunk, the one I had before getting my own room; Rook and Ollie in the lower bunk, sprawled on it as they fell on it; and L.T. by the window, alone and looking out.

My eyes searched for old ceiling spots, the ones that always looked like distant galaxies, and my hand reached for Billy's ratty teddy bear, the one I knew he always stashed there. And for a second, or two, or sixty—I don't know how long—I fell myself to sleep, asleep to the Psalms rolling in from the hallway, the lullabies rocking me in the cradle.

"Where do you think they'll bury him?" Ollie asked, his voice waking me.

"In the cemetery," I said. "Gethsemane. Where else would they bury him?"

"You know, you'd think that once a person dies he could at least get himself buried where he wants. You'd think that at last he could get himself buried in the way he wants. You'd think that finally it would be okay for him to get himself buried according to who he was, according to the person he at least thought himself to be—that's to say, according to the type of person he wanted himself at last to be."

"You'd think so," Rookie said, "but that's not how it works, not for us it doesn't. We don't live as we are. We don't die as we are."

"But why?" asked Ollie. "Why not? I mean … the person's already dead."

"A good secret deserves a good burial," I said. "A good secret deserves a secret burial. That's how the living can go on living according to who they aren't."

"If that's how it is then I don't want to go," Ollie said, slamming his hand onto the side of his bunk.

"Go where?" I asked.

"To the cemetery, to Grandpa's funeral," Ollie continued. "I mean, why should I go? Just to see how yet another secret Jew gets buried in some hole? Just to see how I'm going to some day wind up? If I can't even die according to who I am, then I'm nothing. I mean, like why should I even try and think myself Jewish? What's the point? Who am I fooling? It's not the *Jewish* that matter. It's only the *secret* that matters. Only it and its keeping matter to us."

I tensed, turned onto my side to look at L.T. Never before had he heard anything so clear and specific about our being secret Jews. I wanted to see his face. I had to see his reaction.

Did he know? Had he always known? Or did I just want to believe he knew?

Did he care? Did it matter? Or did I just want to believe it would?

If L.T. looked surprised, would that mean he wasn't one of us, wasn't actually enough us to be one with us?

And if he didn't look surprised, would that mean L.T. was one with us, was more us than he really should be?

It was taking too long, taking L.T. too damn long!

Doubts just too uncertain, expectations just too dangerous, I felt like a plucked guitar string, ready to twitch, or ready to twinge.

I had to know. I had to know if L.T. really was one with us.

I had to believe he wouldn't always be one with us, as half-assed as us, as hypocritical as us, as shut-down as us, as shut-closed as us.

"Ollie," L.T. said, "if you aren't who you want, if you can't be who you want, you at least can think yourself who you want. Just do it. Do it, believe it, and it can happen. If you don't do it, don't believe it, it'll never happen."

I leaned out over the bunk bed, looked down at Rook and Ollie as they looked to L.T. … her eyes wide and open … his tight and narrow.

"Easy for you to say," Ollie said. "You're not one of us, L.T. And you just went and proved you're not. I mean you can think yourself, and you can make yourself, into anything. But here in Best, Spitters like us really can't think that way. We can't think that way 'cause we can't let ourselves think that way. We can't let ourselves think that way 'cause we can't let ourselves act that way. We just are, L.T. Do you understand? We just are. We just are as we are 'cause that's not only how we are, it really is who we are."

I lay back down, the ceiling spots dissolving before my eyes, the distant galaxies too. A sad ripple, a slack wind, they huffed at me, and puffed at me, huffed and puffed and carried me … absolutely nowhere.

"It's not easy," L.T. said. "It's not easy at all," his voice sounding as if a million miles away, as if from a place I did not know. "You said it was easy for me, but it isn't."

I saw L.T. in the middle of the room, sort of turning and spinning, spinning and turning. "Ollie, just 'cause I try to think myself who I want doesn't necessarily mean I get there. 'There'—I don't know what that is. 'There'—I mean where's that? How can something be something and have no end? How can some place be some place and have no beginning? 'There'—it's hard, Ollie, a life that's hard. And you know what's hardest of all about it? You know what the worst thing is about it?

"I'm in it by myself. I mean like where are the other Lost Tribes? Here? In Best? I used to think they were here. I wanted them to be here. But you know what? They aren't here. And you know why they aren't here? They aren't here 'cause you guys don't try. Not that I blame you. Not that I should blame you. After all you guys aren't actually lost. I mean how can you be lost if being lost doesn't matter, 'cause trust me that it does. How can you be lost if you're in a place you don't want to be in, but also don't want to be out of?

"Shit, Ollie, you know what this is? Know what it really is? It's Limbo! This is Limbo! Not that you know it by that name, I mean not being real Catholics and everything, but then again you're really not being real Jews either, it's the only place you really do know. It's the only place you care to know. It's your place. And guess what—you're there. You're already there! And guess what too—it's here!

"Ollie, you, me, we aren't all that different. We both think ourselves who we aren't. And we both think ourselves who we're not. So here really is the only real difference: I try; you don't. I really try and you really don't. And that difference is why you Spitters will always stay right here. You don't understand, just don't understand the difference between wanting and believing, wanting and trying."

Rookie went over to L.T. and held him still, her hands on his and her eyes on his. But as she looked for him, she instead found me. "Hey, Michael, maybe, you know, L.T. shouldn't be here. Maybe he even should get away from here. You too, maybe you too should get away, with him, at least for a little while, 'least for a little ways. Then, that done, you, you should come back."

I climbed off the bed, tapped L.T., and holding him by his shoulders, we worked our way through the hall outside Grandpa's room, the hall now wall-to-wall with people.

I sat L.T. down in my room; I watched for a clearing. Then, with the slightest of head turns and the slightest of flinches, he looked for me. "What are you doing here, Michael?"

"This is my room."

"Then what am I doing here?"

"That's a better question, L.T. I don't know what you're doing here. But maybe it's time you got going. There's nothing for you here. There's nothing that should matter to you here."

"Are you sure?"

"I'm sure."

"Do you want to get going with me?"

I shrugged, could feel my eyes sliding over the floor, slip-sliding all over it. "I don't know. I'm not sure. But it doesn't matter. I can't. I'm sorry, L.T."

"Hey, I almost forgot to give you this. Your camera," he said, reaching for his pocket

"Thanks."

"You've got a good eye. You see things, Michael. You see them as they are. Sometimes you even see them as they aren't. So keep taking pictures. I mean, without a photo album, won't secrets eventually disappear? Won't they get to being as if they almost never at all existed? So like just do me a favor, okay? Promise me, promise you'll keep taking pictures."

"Don't do that, L.T. Don't. Don't go holding me to any promises, 'cause promises ... promises ... they just ain't fair. They're just secrets, little secret agreements between you and me, or them and me, or others and me, and somehow I'm always the one winding up getting sworn to them. Promises? I have no room. Promises? I have no patience. They go too deep. They stay too long. I've seen what they do, how they turn you. Why before you even know it you've turned from making a promise to making a secret. Before you even know it you've turned from promising a secret to secreting a promise.

"Now I'm going to go back on in there, L.T. I'm going back in not just 'cause I love my grandfather and parents, which of course I do. And I'm going back in not just 'cause I think it important that a museum have pictures preserving the secret legacy of vanishing people, 'cause actually, I think that is important. No, I'm going back in just so to always have what to watch, what to learn. See, my pictures aren't only for an album, or a museum, or a history book. They're for me, for my book. They're for my living book, my living and breathing book."

"I never meant that they should be for anything else, Michael. Just don't go let your pictures become you. And if you can't promise that, then don't. It's not really between you and me anyway. And it's not between you and them, or you and others either. It's between you and you. Okay?"

I nodded it was.

"Okay then, Michael. So seeing as you're gonna go on in there and everything, I'm gonna get going too, to out there, you know, if I'm ever going to find what's out there and everything."

"Wait," I yelled, L.T. at the door. Opening my top dresser drawer, I reached in. "Take this."

Taking hold, L.T. looked at the leather-covered book, its

strange letters running seemingly in every direction. Then reading the inscription inside, he stretched it back to me. "This is yours. My mother and Hal gave this to you."

"Well, I'm giving it to you. Turns out I won't be using it any time soon. But you can use it. See, it says so right here: 'As one hole is filled, a new one is created.' And the best thing, L.T., the best thing about this book is it's Drift-proof. You can't go wrong, 'least not with something like this you can't. So take it. Take it, L.T., and before you know it you'll be right there Reckoning with the Lost Tribes, Reckoning with all of them."

L.T. spun his GO TRIBAL cap once and again backwards, my way. Then he left my room. Then he left my house.

From my window I watched him go, watched as cornfields and pumpkin patches stretched out in every direction almost as if to dwarf him.

And a worry bug stirred in me, crawled from my head to my heart even as another crept from my stomach to my heart. The cornfields, the pumpkin patches—they were too big! They were too big for him!

Yet I watched, and the more I watched, the more I saw. And what I saw surprised me.

Much too wonderful to be illusion, much too unreal to not be real, the further along L.T. went the more I saw that it in fact was he who was big—too big for the cornfields, too big for the pumpkin patches, and just too big by far for a place such as Best.

And I wondered: If I could see such a thing happen with L.T., could such a thing happen also with me?

I just had to remember—remember is all—just remember what Ol' Cuss said, what it was he said that made all things possible.

But just then a strong river wind blew into my room from the window at my back, the opposite one I watched from. And taking a step back, and then taking another—and taking a breath too—I took another, and then another. And whatever it was Ol' Cuss said, whatever it was he said made all things possible, it just went ... poof.

A spot opened for me in the hallway just outside Grandpa's room, opened just as the vigil there closed with a recitation of Psalms.

Goodbye, I said. Goodbye, I said. Goodbye, I said, the crush of lives, and time, pressing me ... hurting me.

"You will go to the Valley of Jehosophat," said a voice from inside Grandpa's room, "and should Satan ask you, 'What is your faith?' this is how you will answer: 'All my life I have been a Hebrew, and if I have not always done what should have been done in the way it should have been done, it wasn't due to any lack of will, but rather due to ignorance. I did not know what to do.'"

EPILOGUE

I went back tonight.

Snow, heavy and white, clung to evergreens, shimmered below a full moon, a thousand brilliant stars.

The tracks of a snowmobile made the path easy to follow, and when I at last reached the break in the woods it was as open as a flung-open gate. Humming a song and crunching ice-capped snow under my feet, only my song and my feet could be heard. And the woods, woods tucked in and woods tucked down beneath blankets of white—I thought them sleeping.

I went back tonight because of a dream. Not that I could remember it but it woke me just the same, its wake-up-call something like a potro stretching rack and a toca water torture, with just a bit of good stake-burning thrown in. Like who doesn't love that, 'least only every now, 'least only every then?

Anyway, the dream, it made my heart inside-out, turned it inside-out, heart skin all ripping clear and clean of heart guts, heart guts all yanked clear and clean of heart skin, the skin just tossed by the wayside, the guts just stripped to their core. And exposed now as it was to the light, and now bared as it also was to the air, I worried about my core, wondered about it, prayed it not already be rotten, prayed it never again would be shamed.

Treating the dream pretty much like I treated all my nightmares, I shut my eyes, shut 'em and slammed a pillow over my head. When of course that didn't help none, I rolled onto my back, stared into darkness, stared on in on myself, punched my pillow to the floor, kicked my sheets and blankets to the floor, I mean everything hitting the floor, even me hitting the floor.

Mad, and angry too, I just wound up sitting—on the floor, of course—having to then think, having to then conclude: something had to get done. So I got myself up off the floor, put on my coat, put on my boots, put on my hat, and went to check in on the holes.

Snow tracks of what probably was a fox were laid down before me, and following them a ways, I noticed the imprints spaced ever further apart, ever deeper and deeper in the deep snow. That fox, he'd been running—eager no doubt to reach his home by the daybreak. His nose down and his head up, his eyes fixed and his eyes looking out, I could just picture him, that fox, so determined and hopeful, so very focused and curious.

And I thought—me, I would like to be the fox.

But was that possible? Was such a thing possible? Was it, for that matter, even at all doable? I mean, for me to be those things, all those fox-like determined and curious things, how was I at the same time to also be careful, always so very careful?

Sure, a fox, sure he could pull it off. But me? Was I that clever? Was I that sneaky? Could I also be so determined? I mean I wasn't even clever enough to make any real case for the sneakiness that I did have. And as for determined, I wasn't near sneaky enough to make any real case for not having any.

Suddenly my eyes darted this way, then that. And stopping myself dead as I stood, I jump-turned myself this way, and then that way.

Smelly Rock—where was it? Smelly Rock—like what the hell—where the hell was it?

Buried under layers of snow, I no longer could see it, no longer could even smell it. And unable to stand on it, and unable even to touch it, was it, I asked, was it even here? For that matter, I wondered, was it ever here?

I fell to my knees, threw armfuls after armfuls of snow to the air, and tried—with all my might I tried—but it just was too hard, just too deep.

So sitting right down in the snow, I put elbow to knee, put head to crook of elbow, put it right in there.

Ol' Cuss was right; I did need landmarks. Without seeing, without smelling, without touching, how was I to know what others coming before me saw, or smelled, or touched? Without landmarks how was I to think as Spitters thought, remember as Spitters remembered, or believe as Spitters believed? How was I to know just who it was I was? How was I to know just where in the hell it was I was?

I mean I never was any good at Dead Reckoning. And as for Drift, I wasn't that hot at that either, that or making adjustments for it.

So what was left me—holes, the nothing holes? I mean what kind of landmarks were they? Holes? Holes? They were emptiness. Holes? They were darkness. Holes? They were just nothingness, just so much nothingness, just as real as a memory, one about which there just really is not any real memory.

I looked up, just had to. Looking anywhere else was useless, was just too painful. Skyfuls of stars spreading out over me, I saw the North Star, and the Big Dipper, the Little Dipper too. And I remembered to ask of myself: were they not the same stars those coming before me saw, the exact same? Were they not the exact same no matter when they lived, or where? And seeing them, would they not too have wondered just how magnificent they were, and how small they themselves were?

And seeing them, would they not too have asked just who it was they were, just where it was they were, and just what their place was in a universe so great?

And all that being the case, if my sight lines were like their sight lines, and my questions were like their questions, then why couldn't my answers be like their answers? Why wouldn't they be? For that matter, why couldn't they be even better?

Ol' Cuss was right; I had to stop being such a Spitter. Spitters not only lived by memories there really were no memories of, they lived for them. Sure, all along the way there were little memories of having once been Jews, and even littler memories of having once been real Jews, but all that really filtered down were memories to remember, memories and reminders to be cautious, careful, and oh so afraid.

No, if ever I truly wanted to be the fox—so determined and hopeful, so focused and curious—I'd just have to stop being such a Spitter, that sort of Spitter who relies only on memory solely for memory, solely for memory's sake.

No, if ever I truly wanted to be the fox, I'd just have to stop being just such a Spitter—that sort of Spitter whose memories are only made of glass.

No, if ever I truly wanted to the fox, I'd just have to just stop being just such a Spitter—that Spitter who leans himself on a cane of glass, and stands himself on a floor of glass, and thinks and thinks himself into becoming glass, and yet, and all the while, has the nerve, the sheer gall, to wonder just how it is that his world is breakable and broken, obstructible and obstructed, dangerous and endangered.

Oh, another and just one more thing. It really would be of real help if I, the Spitter, actually really did wonder—but really wonder—and not just remember, and not mistake the two for the same.

No, if ever I truly wanted things to again be as they once were, if ever I truly wanted to be as my Great-Greats, or

even better than my Great-Greats, I would have to believe—
but really believe—believe more just than more or less sort
of remember. I would have to remember to ask questions, I
would have to wonder about answers, and I would have to have
faith in them both.

Four, five, six, I counted, my counting the same as L.T.'s
when he used to approach the cluster of pines. Seven, eight,
nine, ten.

L.T.! L.T.! He called me the other night, said that things
were good, that Cambridge was good, that his mom and Hal
and Fetch were good, that they were good too. We talked a
lot, talked a lot, that is, about a lot of nothing. We'd get
together soon, some time soon, he saying I should visit him in
Cambridge, I saying he should visit me in Best.

"Best you come here," he said, "to me."

"No, L.T. You come here. It'd be like the old days, you
know, the good old days."

"But Michael—I don't go back."

"You don't?"

"No, I don't. You know that. You'll just have to come here.
So like when are you coming?"

"Geez, L.T. Like how do I know?"

"How 'bout Christmas, vacation week?"

"We'll see."

"See?"

"Yeah, see. You know, we'll see. I can't like just up and go."

"Why? Why not?"

"'Cause it's complicated."

"Complicated? Why's it complicated?"

"'Cause it just is, L.T. Okay? It just is. I mean, for crying
out loud, you lived here once. I mean just 'cause you can't
come back, does that also have to mean you can't remember?
Does that also have to mean you can't remember just what it's

like here?"

"Hey," L.T. said, after a moment. "Hey, Michael?"

"Yeah."

"You know what?"

"What?"

"Around here I'm not L.T."

"You're not?"

"I'm not."

"Then what are you then?"

"Well, I'm still what I am, you idiot. What I mean is people here don't call me L.T. You know what they call me?"

Whacko immediately came to mind, Whack-Job too. "Dutch?"

"Dutch! Like where the hell did you come up with Dutch? No, here I'm Larry."

"Larry? Why do they call you that?"

"'Cause that's my name."

Sixteen, seventeen, eighteen, the cluster of pines seemed thinner than I remembered them, weaker too, the trees tired, maybe just sick.

As for the holes though, they of course were there, there just as I knew them to be there, there just as I knew them to be. Maybe a bit starker than I remembered, maybe sadder too—actually the holes looked pretty pathetic, empty, dark, neglected. And owing to our having dumped their dirt into the river that one time, there just was no real way for the holes to ever go away. I mean retrieving their dirt was impossible, and digging new holes for the dirt needed to cover them with, that was pointless. That'd only create new holes.

Hopeless. Hopeless, Hopeless, Hopeless.

I didn't want to live like this. I didn't want to live without hope. I wanted stars. I mean I wanted them. But stars, stars so far, and stars so twinkling, they really were so far out of reach as to be un-understandable, just so all twinkling as to be unimaginable.

And if I couldn't reach them, the stars, be it with understanding or be it with imagination, then screw it. Fuck it! I'd just go reaching for what was left me. 'Cause reaching, that was natural as the air, as natural as the water. And holding, having what to hold, it was normal, as normal and necessary as the breathing of air, the drinking of water.

I mean, was it really so bad to reach for what was left me? Was it really so bad to reach for what once was mine, reach for it even if and even though I couldn't actually remember it as being mine? I mean who knew, maybe if I actually reached back far enough, and reached back deep enough, in the end maybe just maybe I'd have my stars, have them after all.

All at once my mind went blank, as blank as the whiteness of snow, as blank as the white of snow falling into holes from the sky on high.

The river! The river! Wasn't it nearby?

The river—I remembered it, it flowing close by—so close I practically could just spit the distance from where I stood to where it was. And I could hear it—could even hear it. Why, in my mind's eye, I practically could see it. And with my heart I could just about feel it—the river waters splashing my face, washing over me, and carrying me … Far.

So there, to the river and its stubborn tidal waters, there is where I went.

And near? I needed near too—needed it just as much as I wanted far—'cause, after all, I was fourteen, almost fifteen, but still fourteen—fourteen not that removed from thirteen.

So of course, there toward home is where I went—home, after all, a river of stubborn waters too.

Home and the river, each in its own way good.

"He who achieved miracles for our forefathers and redeemed them from slavery to freedom — may He redeem us soon and gather in our dispersed from the four corners of the earth, all Israel becoming comrades. Now let us respond: Amen."
    — *Blessing of the New Month*

The Blessing of the new month is a prayer to set in motion a course toward deliverance. A major aspect of this deliverance involves the ingathering of exiles. Only then, when all Israel rallies as one, can there be a final redemption. "He who achieved miracles for our forefathers and redeemed them from slavery to freedom — may He redeem us soon and gather in our dispersed from the four corners of the earth, all Israel becoming comrades. Now let us respond: Amen."

HISTORICAL NOTE

The Spanish and Portuguese Inquisitions devastated the lives of the Jews that lived there; the Edicts of Expulsion from Spain and Portugal all but ended Jewish life on the Iberian Peninsula. Moreover, the combination of Inquisition and Expulsion absolutely traumatized the souls of virtually all the Jews of this region. Even to this day, these events still haunt to some degree the souls of their descendents, at least those descendents having at least some vague memory.

How is it possible that such memories persist for more than five hundred years and twenty generations? Think about it. Just one slip, and the chain is broken—one grandmother not telling a granddaughter, or one grandfather not telling a grandson; just one mother and father not telling daughters for fear of upsetting them, or just one mother and father not telling sons out of fear of burdening them and putting their futures in jeopardy—and the chain is broken, memory forgotten, identity lost, an entire way of life lost. And far more often than not, it was indeed lost. Everything considered, it only was natural that it should be lost. Five hundred years is a long time, and devastations are the kind of painful memories we prefer to forget. They're frightful as well, having ways of driving their targets underground. And as for trauma, that too has its ways, its way to follow, no matter how far, no matter how long.

So just how did Jews get to the Azores? How could Secret

Jews eventually have gotten to southeastern Massachusetts, the fictional setting of my novel? For that matter, how did Secret Jews get much of anywhere? And just where is *where* anyway? Like—where are they? How did they get to where they are? And where might they be going? A little historical background about the Jews of the Iberian Peninsula could be of help, and so could a little background on the travails of their descendents. First, a few definitions:

Converso: A person in any way forced to convert to Catholicism in Spain or Portugal, and all of their descendents too. Note that while they could certainly have been forced at the point of a sword, they could also have been forced by any kind of threat, perceived or real.

Crypto-Jew: A *Converso* who secretly and knowingly practices Judaism, even while outwardly conforming to Christian practice.

Secret Jew: The same as a Crypto-Jew.

Marrano: The Spanish word for "pig." The term was used by Jews who did not convert, to describe fellow Jews who did. That is, those Jews who, in their opinion, took the easy way out. The term was sometimes also used by non-Jews in describing *Conversos*.

New Christian: A term often used by Christians for *Conversos*, with the implication that newer converts— whether by choice or by force—were not true Christians, and could not therefore be fully accepted or trusted. Often it took several generations for the designation to be dropped.

Sephardi: In Hebrew, a Jew of Spanish ancestry.

Anusim: In Hebrew, the "forced ones." It's the term modern-day *Conversos* and Crypto-Jews often prefer to be called because it connotes their ancestors' forced conversion.

Though it was not until the Alhambra Decree of 1492 that Jews were forced to choose between baptism or expulsion from Spain, Jews had in fact been leaving or converting in substantial numbers ever since the anti-Jewish riots of 1391, and then leaving or converting in ever larger numbers with the enforcement of the Spanish Inquisition in 1481. And while some conversions were certainly sincere, most were not, most of the converts hoping for better times ahead in which they could again be Jewish—that is to say, fully Jewish, in every way.

Among all the Jews leaving Spain in 1492, an estimated 120,000 went to Portugal, where there already was a sizeable Jewish population. Large numbers also went to Turkey, Morocco, and Holland, though some went on to reach every corner of the Mediterranean rim. Of special note: in just the very first years after 1492, an estimated 5,000 Jews and *Conversos* also set sail for the Americas.

When Portugal's King Manuel asked for the hand of the daughter of Spain's King Ferdinand and Queen Isabella in 1496, he agreed to an understanding that in exchange he would give his country's Jews a choice either to convert or leave. And though technically, he was to give them forty years to decide, it didn't stop him from immediately gathering as many Jews as possible in a Lisbon square, sprinkling baptismal waters on them, and declaring them Catholic. And whether or not they wanted to, many Jews did convert. Many also left, many of them heading to the Portuguese colony of Brazil. In fact, so many went there that in a 1624 census, two of every three Europeans in the city of Recife were recorded as being New Christians, which is roughly the same proportion as the estimates of New Christians among the 50,000 Europeans in Brazil at the time. In 1630, a Jewish renaissance of sorts took place with the capture of Brazil by the more tolerant Dutch, and many of the *Conversos* took steps to fully and openly return to Judaism.

Religious freedom, however, was short-lived. Portugal again seized the colony in 1654, and many Jews and *Conversos* decided to head for Holland, the island of Curaçao, or the city

of New Amsterdam—today's New York. Those opting to stay
in Brazil ultimately fell victim to what in many ways was an
Inquisition more harsh than even that of Spain. Even as late as
1703, identified Crypto-Jews were rounded up, sent to public
auto-da-fé (literally translated "Acts of Faith," but actually more a
"Trial by Fire") in Lisbon, where the condemned heretics were
burned alive at the stake. The estimates today are that many
millions in Brazil have Jewish Sephardi ancestry, and studies
of paternal Y-chromosome and maternal mitochondrial DNA
reveal that up to twenty percent of people in both Portugal
and Spain have that same Jewish ancestry.

Overwhelmingly, however, today in all three of these
countries, few *Conversos* have any inkling of their Jewish heritage.
And even if they still have a family custom of a Jewish nature,
and pass it on, they really do not know why they do so. Even
if they still have a family heirloom of Jewish significance, and
pass it down, they rarely know what it is. And in the event that
they do happen to know the meaning of the family custom
or heirloom, they are understandably hard-put to appreciate
its true religious significance. After all, by now they are Old
Christians, true Christians.

Because both the Spanish and Portuguese Inquisitions
made it a point to chase down Crypto-Jews everywhere in the
New World, *auto-da-fé*s took place in Peru in 1639 and repeatedly
in Mexico during the decade of the 1640s. The situation for
Mexico's Crypto-Jews actually became so precarious that many
fled for 'New Spain Mexico', today's American Southwest. It
now is becoming increasingly apparent that a large proportion
of long-established Spanish-speaking residents of the American
Southwest have Jewish ancestry—are *Conversos*. Of these, it is
estimated that five percent have no knowledge of their Jewish
ancestry, even in cases where family traditions resemble Jewish
traditions, like for instance the lighting of candles on Friday
night, or the covering of mirrors in family homes of the

deceased, or abstention from eating pork. It also is estimated that another five percent knowingly practice two religions, that is, they secretly engage in Jewish traditions while at the same time engaging publicly in Catholic practice. These people are today's Crypto-Jews, observing their Jewish traditions not only because they are family traditions, but because they are Jewish traditions.

In the American Southwest, increasing numbers of *Conversos* are for the first time discovering their Jewish heritage, and many of the *Conversos* who know of their Jewish heritage are, for the first time, exploring that heritage. They want to know the reasons behind their traditions. They may even want to tell family members and others what they have learned.

But "many" does not necessarily mean "most." As with the *Conversos* of Brazil, Portugal and Spain, most *Conversos* of the Southwest are by and large content with who they are. And not wanting to potentially risk upsetting themselves—and for sure not wanting to risk upsetting, or scaring, or alienating family members—most *Conversos* do not explore their roots, and even if they explore, they do not tell what they have learned. They appreciate that their secrets have been secrets for a long time. They understand that in part, their secrets have been secrets *because* they have been secrets. And they know that their secrets affect their families—are the very identity of their families—and are therefore private. They know that secrets in some way are inherently shameful, and by their very nature scary as well.

While there are numerous individual Crypto-Jews in the American Southwest and elsewhere, it is exceedingly rare to find intact and active Crypto-Jewish communities such as the one described in my novel. But they do exist. In 1917, a community was discovered in the remote Portuguese town of Belmonte, Portugal. From out of a town population of 3600, some 300 were Crypto-Jews. Townspeople report that they have long known about their Jewish neighbors, yet still

Left: A table of crowns in an Imperio chapel in Terceira;
Right: A Jewish Torah scroll with its traditional decorative crown.

liked them anyway. When in the 1970s a Jewish organization opened a synagogue in the town, nearly half of the Crypto-Jews underwent formal Jewish conversion, with the other half remaining in essence Crypto-Jews out of both fear and a desire to remain as they were -- that is, as their ancestors were.

The Chuetas of the island of Majorca are yet another example of a Crypto-Jewish community. There are some 18,000 people with surnames like those most typically chosen by Crypto-Jews, and the DNA evidence supports that number. Despite a long and sordid history of prejudice towards the Crypto-Jewish community—including an *auto-da-fe* in 1509 and sentences of life imprisonment for several hundred people upon the discovery of a secret synagogue in 1679—the community clearly exists even with the full knowledge of others on the island.

Obviously, an organized secret Jewish community cannot exist without other people in a town knowing about it, and in my novel the townspeople of Best Harbor also knew about the Spitters among whom they lived. This, however, is quite a different scenario from that which exists for individual Crypto-Jews. With them, in the absence of a community, no one outside the family would know, or should know.

So just how and why did it come to be that a place like Spit could exist, and how and why is it that a people like Spitters could exist—exist even if only in a novel's setting? Well, the easy answer is that *The Nation by the River* is a work of fiction, and in fiction, all is possible. But I also have tried not only to make the existence of a place such as Spit and a people such as Spitters not merely possible, but plausible. After all, Jews and *Conversos* naturally would have wanted to sail away to the Azorean islands once they were discovered by Portuguese explorers in 1432. By and large remote from anti-semitism, and saved from the brunt of a later Inquisition, *Conversos* would at the very least have wanted a place to practice their Judaism safely, even if it also meant secretly. And in fact many Jews and *Conversos* did go to the Azores. Even today many Azoreans hold such Jewish customs as the baking of unleavened bread at the time of year which correlates with Passover.

The Cult of the Holy Spirit that is described in the novel is uniquely Azorean, and it has also accompanied Azoreans wherever they have gone. Born within Christianity in the 11th and 12th centuries by Brotherhoods contesting the Divinity of Christ, this Cult was all but wiped out by the Roman Catholic Church everywhere but in the Azores. After the 1583 Battle of Punta Delgada where Phillip II of Spain hanged Azoreans from the yardarms, Azoreans developed a special hatred not just for the Spanish, but for the Spanish Inquisition too. And when later the Portuguese retook the islands, they themselves were reluctant to impose another Inquisition out of fear of riling the island people.

Though the Cult of the Holy Spirit was not Jewish tradition, it proved a means by which *Conversos* and Crypto-Jews could exist within a larger Azorean culture. In essence, they used and

The Great Feast of the Holy Ghost, Fall River, Massachusetts.
Photo copyright Omar Bradley, the Fall River *Herald News*, August 2009.
Reprinted with permission of the *Herald News*.

developed the Cult. The Cult not only was independent of the Church, but embraced the belief that no intermediaries should come between devotees and the Divine. For the most part tenets of the Cult did not conflict with tenets of Judaism. Buildings associated with the Cult, *Imperio* chapels and earlier *Teatros* where confirmation-type ceremonies similar to Bar and Bat Mitzvas were held, did not have Crosses inside or out, and did not have Christian figures or icons either. The *Teatros* were even reminiscent of the booths used in the Jewish holiday of *Sukkot*. The crowns and scepters so prevalent in *Imperio* chapels—and so integral too in the practice of the Cult— were like the crowns and scepters which adorn Torah scrolls. From hooks in chapel backrooms for the draining of blood from hung meat, to *Promessa* logs recording vows made to the Divine, to the seven weeks from Easter to Pentecost which corresponded to the counting of days between Passover and the holiday of *Shavuot*, there was much in the Cult to remind

An Imperio Chapel in the Azores. Photo taken by the author.

Conversos of their Jewish heritage. There was much they could work with.

The real life explorer Miguel Cortereal mentioned in *The Nation by the River* was himself from the Azores. And as for how Azoreans—and with them *Conversos*—wound up in southeastern Massachusetts and Rhode Island, read what Herman Melville writes about them in *Moby Dick*: "No small number of these whaling seamen belong to the Azores where outward bound Nantucket whalers frequently touch to augment crews from the hardy peasants on the Rocky Shores."

Referred to worldwide in business dealings of the Middle Ages as "People of the *Nação*," just how is it, and why is it, that "the Nation" still exists?

Well, in the case of Crypto-Jews, newer generations were either told or they asked. Then they were taught or self-taught to cherish their heritage and to find value in preserving their legacy. However, when it comes to *Conversos*, the mystery grows. After all, why still carry on with customs that are not understood? Why pass down heirlooms that are not understood? Why— as in a growing number of instances, even in the absence of customs or heirlooms—do *Conversos* have strange feelings that

Dighton Rock, showing a number of petroglyphs, among which the rock inscription Miguel Cortereal, and the date 1511.
Photo courtesy of Dighton Rock State Park.

something is not quite right, that something is missing, that somehow or other they are not quite whole, and won't be whole till they explore just who their ancestors were?

The new field of epigenetics—which studies the biological ways generations pass on survival skills and unconscious senses of identity—holds great promise in this area. How do birds know that birds migrate? How do they know when and where they themselves should migrate? And just how—as described in the novel—do alewife herring know that they themselves as herring should swim upstream? And as Michael himself wonders, why shouldn't he too know or at least have a natural sense of just who he is and what he must do?

There also is a concept developed by Anne Ancelin Schutzenberger called the "Ancestor Syndrome," in which generations are psychologically and unconsciously affected by the traumas of previous generations. Worry, dread, loss, foreboding, misgivings, anxiety, and fear—all can be, and often are, passed down. It is said Jews in particular seem to have these trauma-associated characteristics, and justifiably so. Children of Holocaust survivor parents, like myself, seem in particular to sometimes have these feelings even more acutely.

Street marker at Miguel Corte-Real Square on the island of Terceira in the Azores. The home base of the Corte-Real family was the Azores. Photo taken by the author.

And all this being the case, just why on earth wouldn't today's *Anusim* and children of *Anusim* not have those exact same characteristics? Considering all the Inquisitions and Expulsions that their ancestors went through, how could they not worry whether their neighbor was spying on them, might even turn them in to the authorities? How could they not but dread the knock on the door? How could they not but fear that at any moment they could be dispersed, lose everything from their way of life to their very lives?

And all that being the case, just who is to say which secret Jews—and Jewish secrets—live among us? And for that matter, just who is to say that they also do not live in Best Harbor, Massachusetts?

*For more on *Conversos* and Crypto-Jews you might want to read such books as David Gitlitz's *Secrecy and Deceit*, Stanley Hordes' *To the End of the Earth*, and James Reston Jr.'s *Dogs of God*.

*To learn more about modern-day Jewish "Lost Tribes," you may want to go to such websites as Amishav, Shavei Israel, and Kulanu.

READING GROUP GUIDE

1) What were your impressions of Michael Costa at the beginning of the book, and at its end?

What impressions did you have of L.T. Haymaker at the start of the book, at the end of the book?

2) In what ways are Michael and L.T. alike? In what ways are they different?

3) What plays the greater role in preserving a secret society community: unsubstantiated—but very real—fears about the outside world; or a tradition of secrecy, a legacy of secrecy?

4) Consider the working dynamic of Besterners and Spitters. Though Besterners know about the Crypto-Jewish Spitters among whom they live, why do some like Father Sousa work with the dynamic, while others such as Mr. Alves work to destroy it? Why do some see similiarities among people, while others see only differences?

5) Was it wrong of Mrs. Haymaker and Hal to teach Michael about his Jewish heritage?

6) Describe the way Father Gomes comes to terms with being both Catholic and Jewish? Is his way rational? Logical? Expected? What of the individual element in how people come

to terms when faced with a similiar situation?

7) Is Ol' Cuss a good example of how a Converso may know about Jewish ancestry—may even be proud of that ancestry—and yet do no further investigation of it? Is Ol' Cuss like certain Jews who, while identifying themselves as Jews, or referring to themselves as being culturally Jewish, proceed no further with their investigation?

8) The Sambatyon River: how is it an obstacle when it comes to joining up with other Lost Tribes? Just what is the problem? Why do some like Michael's mother hope to someday be reunited with other lost tribes, while others like Michael's father hold no such hope? Knowing Michael, knowing the community of Spit, what do you think will become of Michael?

9) What are Christian ideas about soul? Jewish ideas?

10) Who are Spitters fooling: others, or themselves?

11) The field of epigenetics studies the biological ways generations pass on both survival skills and unconscious senses of identity. Birds know migration patterns. Certain fish—as Michael knows—somehow know to swim upstream. Are humans any different, or are new generations somehow psychologically affected by the transferred trauma of generations past? (Doreen Carvajal discusses epigenetics and ancestor syndrome in referring to her book, *The Forgetting River.*)

12) Why does L.T. not agree with the notion that Lost Tribe Jews must first be gathered, and then converted to Christianity, before there can be a 'Second Coming'? Is his argument a Jewish expression of what it will take for the coming of Messiah?

ABOUT THE AUTHOR

Gabe Galambos was born in Debrecen, Hungary. His parents, Holocaust survivors, escaped with Gabe and his brother during the 1956 Hungarian Uprising. After two years in various Austrian refugee camps, the family was allowed to immigrate to the U.S.A. Once there, they settled in Brookline, Massachusetts where Gabe currently lives. Gabe earned a degree from Brandeis University.

Upon graduation Gabe moved to Israel—made Aliyah—and joined the Israel Defense Forces. He did stints in an elite unit and in Armored Infantry. Gabe was pursuing a Masters Degree at Jerusalem's Hebrew University, when, in 1983, the American Association for Ethiopian Jewry (AAEJ) sent him to Sudan to assist in the clandestine rescue of Jews fleeing Ethiopia. In southern Sudan, Gabe and a fellow AAEJ worker were captured and interned in the notoriously wretched Juba city prison.

They later managed to escape through the bush to Zaire before being detained and turned back over to Sudanese custody. After several more weeks in the Juba prison and a Khartoum jail, they were released when several members of the Congressional Foreign Affairs Committee were able to intercede on their behalf.

Gabe's travels in Hungary, England, Spain, the former Soviet Union, and several African countries provided source material for his first novel, *Stealing Pike's Peak*, a globe-hopping political thriller. Further travel, particularly to the Azorean islands, was of great benefit in his researching "the people of the Nação," those mysterious people appearing in *The Nation by the River*.

When not writing and traveling, Gabe's other big interest is following the Boston sports teams. In particular he is an avid fan of the New England Patriots.

Visit Gabe on the internet at http://gabegalambos.com

Also by Gabe Galambos:

Stealing Pike's Peak

At the peak of his professional football career, quarterback Zach Pike is kidnapped right in Rockefeller Center. Terrorists spirit him away and announce their success in a grisly video delivered to CNN. Why has he been taken? Is it only for publicity for some radical cause? Or is it because of his friendship with an Israeli spy? Friends rally to find and extricate Zach, chasing worldwide through Israel and the Sudan, playing cat-and-mouse with the abductors. The story climaxes in a high-stakes international crisis that is also a test of the individual courage of three friends.

"***Stealing Pike's Peak*** is in the finest tradition of political suspense stories; it never lets up."
—*Bill Phillips, screenplay writer of "The Beans of Egypt, Maine" and "In a Child's Name"*

"***Stealing Pike's Peak*** is an exciting tale of espionage and intrigue, authentic and believable."
—*Hermann Eilts, former United States Ambassador to Egypt and Saudi Arabia*